BURNT TREE JUNCTION

THE ACCLAIMED HISTORICAL FICTION SERIES

- VOLUME 4 ANTHOLOGY -

EAT & GET GAS

THE HONEY TREE

JOANN KLUSMEYER

Published by Innovo Publishing, LLC
www.innovopublishing.com
1-888-546-2111

Providing Full-Service Publishing Services for Christian Authors, Artists & Ministries:
Hardbacks, Paperbacks, eBooks, Audiobooks, Music, Screenplays & Curricula

BURNT TREE JUNCTION: HISTORICAL FICTION SERIES

VOLUME 4 (ANTHOLOGY)

EAT & GET GAS
—
THE HONEY TREE

ISBN: 978-1-61314-680-4

Cover Design & Interior Layout: Innovo Publishing, LLC

Printed in the United States of America
U.S. Printing History
First Edition: 2022

—

Has God called you to create a Christian book, ebook, audiobook, music album,
screenplay, film, or curricula? If so, visit the ChristianPublishingPortal.com to learn
how to accomplish your calling with excellence. Learn to do everything yourself, or
hire trusted Christian Experts from our Marketplace to help.

CONTENTS

> She knew that everyone who asked the question actually meant well. At least that was what she told herself, as she gazed into the interworkings of a motorized delivery wagon owned by the United States Postal Service. On a good day, the breakdown would occur close to her place of business...otherwise, it must be hauled in behind a pair of patient mules. She hoped today was a good day.

> Cows can be kept in a pasture and hogs kept in a pen, but the bee is a free spirit...a child of the wind. A whole family of them can just pack up and be gone in an hour. To the human presuming to control them, they're a barrel full of exasperation and a lifetime of effort. Add that frustration to the loss of the person who held her heart in his hands, and the devastation was overwhelming. Victoria Spencer could have written a book about the next years, and she might just do that yet.

PART I

EAT & GET GAS

THE CHANGE IN THE TIMES

The mountains roads of Northern Arkansas had long belonged to the horseback rider, the buggy or the wagon, but now, in 1910, other vehicles appeared often…sometimes twice a month, giving the sturdy mountain residents a glimpse of the future. Everyone was free to make a comment, and they went rather like this:

"I wouldn't have one of those things if they paid me to take it!"

"They couldn't possibly be safe! Why, how could a person even breathe while he is zippin' along at 20 miles an hour?"

"Why'd'a a body need one of those? If they needed to get there quicker, then get started earlier!"

"Why'd a body risk life and limb just for a bit of excitement?"

"Seems those tin-lizzies break down faster'n droppin' Grandma's china cup!"

"When they stop runnin', how does a body know why? There ain't no sayin', 'Git on up there, Dumbhead!', and make the auto snort, wheeze and strain harder to pull up the hill. I'd say 'gimme as horse' any day."

"And mudholes! Ain't many puddles that'a good pullin' animal couldn't walk out of, but rollin' on them little slick rubber wheels? What else could they do but get stuck?"

Then, with a chuckle, one person confided, "I wouldn't never take one of them things out'a my yard, less'n I was haulin' along a pair'a strong mules to drag it back."

Kathleen had heard all of these things, and even said a few, but the automobile had imprinted an early and profound effect onto her life. Her twin brother, Keith, had a few remarks as well, but he tolerantly agreed that they were a thing of the future, and the future seemed to be piling in on them already. Breathin' down their necks, so to speak.

There would have been many more of them if the price had not been so high. Why, some of the fancy tin-lizzies ran as high as $500.00, and what kind of a person would have that much money to throw away? But then Kathleen owned one.

Kathleen's own Ford flat-bed truck had been almost forced upon her, free, in a round-about way, and to keep the vehicle running, it took a searching in the repair manual that came with each automobile.

Miss Kathleen, mostly called "Leena," was one to climb every mountain as it came toward her, and the care and repair of the blue truck was one of her first tall mountains. After a moment's thought, she squared her shoulders and began to climb.

There were many farms and cottages on Ridge Road that ran east and west along Arkansas's northern border. With much winding and twisting, the road attempted to follow the tops of the ridges, as valleys were so hard to climb up out of, and could really tire out a saddle horse or team in time at all.

On the top of one ridge was a small settlement referred to as Burnt Tree Junction, though it had been called Hilltop for a long time. There was the incident of an innocent man being hung from a limb on the massive oak, and a natural revenge had brought it down.

Some said it was a revenge of nature come down from the sky, and maybe it was, as a storm with a lot of lightning had just passed over, issuing fire bolts from the clouds with no rain. The tree's green leaves caught fire and the tree burned down from the top to about six feet from the ground, leaving a burnt stump with a ragged top. The location had every reason to get the name "Hangin' Tree Hill" from one end of Ridge Road to the other, but it was saved from this name by the lightning.

Some sharp resident attached a sign reading "BURNT TREE JUNCTION" to the burned out stump, and it's there to this day. No one along the ridge would have the nerve to remove it, and why would they? Besides, Hilltop meant nothing as a name or location, when the road had about a hundred hills along its many miles and about twice as many "tops"

Anyway, among the farms and cottage businesses that were being located up along Ridge Road was the sizeable building that displayed a bold sign proclaiming that one could, "EAT AND GET GAS" here. Brief and to the point, it was, but the building did not start out that way. In its infantile beginning, it was just a large farm house built for a big family.

Mr. and Mrs. Conner Sullivan, the owners, were killed when a spooked horse reared and overturned their buggy, and the two passengers passed on leaving their fourteen-year-old twins in the roomy house with forty acres attached. From one end of the road to the other it was discussed. What was to be done with the children? It would be community responsibility, of course, and they couldn't just be ignored, but who would want to take on a fourteen-year-old? Let alone two of them!

The community tossed the dilemma back and forth over back fences and at social gatherings, but they came up with nothing. A fourteen-year-old was obviously too old for a "home" and too young to be on his and her own. The thing that happened was the twins put their clever heads together and decided they would not be moved, nor would decisions be made for them. After all, two times fourteen was twenty-eight, and a person of that age could do whatever they pleased.

There was a small family savings in the buried jar by the garden gate, and there were vegetable gardens and a number of food animals and it was clearly time for the twenty-eight-year-old to get thoughts in line about the future.

But the thing was, the future had already come to meet them, butting them in the head with a most unusual opportunity. The first option was given to Keith, but while he demurred and hesitated, it was passed on to his sister, where it should have gone in the beginning.

Old Mr. Phillip Stanhope, who had an acreage directly behind the Sullivan place, had invested in the purchase of a top-of-the-line Ford truck, model year 1901. His driveway, and his only access to Ridge Road, trailed along the Sullivans' fence, usurping a ten-foot strip of easement land. In this way, the Sullivans were well acquainted with the blue truck by its regular trips in and out.

After decades of marriage, Old Man Phillip lost his mate, and eventually his sight became too dim to allow him to drive, but he still had occasional trips to make. His still-agile mind dreamed up a possible answer. If one of those clever twins would agree to drive him where he needed to go, he was in position to make it highly worth their while.

A generous offer was made to Keith, who would be the obvious recipient of the offer. When old Phil was turned down by Keith, he passed it over to Kathleen. Young Leena was game for anything. While he could still see, the old man would teach her to drive, which was actually a very simple thing. Possibly easier than a horse, truth be told. His wonderful truck didn't even need a crank under the radiator to get it started like a lot of the current automobiles. His truck had been the expensive, prestigious, top-of-the-line model, and it had the new choke and key starting mechanism.

Miss Leena jumped at the offer but made a counter requirement. If she offered her services at his disposal at all times, then she could have the right to use the truck when it was idle. He counter-countered the offer with the stipulation that she would have to learn to keep it in running order to get that privilege, and he would land over to her the repair manual. It was further agreed that the vehicle would eventually be hers.

There was a smile and handshake agreement until it could be made legal in writing and witnessed by the lawman who lived about a mile up the street.

It was in this way that Leena became a friendly observer to the underside of a gas combustion vehicle and a master at spotting its ailments. She'd always like the challenge of puzzles, and as she watched as other horseless carriages had pass by, sometimes two or three a month, her agile brain formed an idea. Attached to this idea was the sight of unfortunate vehicles being pulled along by a pair of mules. Repair facilities would be miles down the road in the town of Wishbone Hollow.

Such indecencies to inflict on the innocent creation of metal and paint! Such a sight of the auto being pulled by a pair of mules was enough to make a person cringe.

Her thoughts chased each other through her creative, inquisitive mind. "Hmmm, what could be causing the breakdown?" And the thought was followed by, "Do they not have repair manuals?"

And the next thought, "I sure do wish I could see under them. I might be able to see what's wrong." After all, how could they be very different from her truck, and the manual always told you what to check and what to do about it. What it didn't tell was what to do until a pair of mules was located, or how long it took to be pulled into a town.

These thoughts traveled around in her head until they began to wear a track through her brain. She could do something about the part of the auto's dilemma that happened on her road. A few well-placed words and a bit of gossip helped

The news got around about Leena's blue truck that she took care of by herself, and about that time that someone told someone else that, if they were having so much trouble and having to drag their vehicle all the way to the town of Wishbone, why not ask Leena Sullivan to take a look. She seemed to be able to keep that Ford flat-bed running. It only made sense. One thing added to another, and gave birth to a plan.

The next new thing to invade the homes on Ridge Road was those fancy machines called lawn mowers that could be pushed through the yard grass and cut it down, when a pair of sheep could do it with no human effort or expense. In addition, the sheep turned the grass into mutton. The lawn mowers also broke down.

Or, if the problem with the auto was already known, perhaps Miss Leena knew where to get the repair parts. Could be she had parts that she could sell. Parts left over from repairing her flat-bed truck.

So it was not so much that Leena chose what her life's interest would be, but that the interest kept hitting her in the head to be considered. Could there be that much difference in the lawn mowers and the horde of new automobiles that were now for sale?

So that took care of Leena, but what about Keith?

Keith, the fastidious, was a picky eater, and had insisted on cooking the food the twins ate. That was fine with Leena, who was willing to eat most anything that did not eat her first. And while she was flaked out under a greasy motor, someone had to keep the house in order. Share and share alike, and these two had been sharing ever since their time in their ma' belly.

The truck brought in the things they needed from the nearby town of Wishbone. And could even sit in for a pair of mules to bring in a disabled auto, simply by the use of a chain, and a heavy foot on the gas pedal.

During this time, Keith's love of cooking became known. Sure enough, men ran their own diners and eateries in the cities, so why not on Ridge Road?

So, little by little, in the course of natural progression, the large dwelling where the twins lived acquired an edifice along the front with two doors and the signs for two businesses. One said "TIN-LIZZIES FIXED" and the other said "SOUP BOWL DINER." Now, how could anything have come out more even?

But the road needed an inclusive sign, and that gave birth to the one that read, "EAT AND GET GAS." If someone didn't like the way that sounded, then they needn't stop over, no matter how delicious was the aroma that floated out onto Ridge Road, or how far is was for the mules to pull the Stutz Bearcat to the shop in Wishbone.

SOUP BOWL

The SOUP BOWL DINER was an example of efficient neatness, sporting a counter with four stools (two more could be squeezed in).

And a tiny French café table with wire legs and a trio of delicate-looking chairs. The diner had a simple menu.

Bean Soup or vegetable soup. Coffee or soda pop, biscuits or store-bought crackers. Pie or cake. Pudding or fruit bowl. Sausage or cheese biscuit sandwich. Bacon and eggs served any time. So anyone could see there was a wealth of choices if a body was hungry enough.

Prices, 5 cents per item. The prices were quite high, but if a person was hungry, it was a long way to Berryville in one direction or Wishbone and Eureka Springs the other way.

It took a while, but Keith became known, mostly by the choice of the words on the building front sign: "EAT AND GET GAS." It was a ready-made target for jokes of every sort…and it was the best advertisement that the twins could have ever thought of.

If one had something to do with the tin-lizzies, than one would also need the petrol to run them. Gas and oil companies were picky.

No oil company would put in a pump. Too far from nowhere, they said, and it would not be economically feasible. No matter, Leena could make a trip to Wishbone in the Ford flat-bed and bring back five gallon cans of gasoline at ten cans per trip. She would sell the gas for twice what she paid, and if the gas must be carried by the driver to a stalled car, there was a twenty-five cent deposit on the gas can.

Interestingly, there was a growing market for the gasoline by residents not even owning vehicles. Gas was regularly used for cleaning wool garments that could not be washed because of shrinkage, and used for a number of other little household chores, such as spraying on a wasp's nest if one got too close to a residence.

Considering that the twins started with a paid-for, free and clear building, and a small amount of capital in the savings jar, the two occupations could take their time in becoming profitable.

Then something happened that would change more lives than their own. It seemed to have descended from nowhere and who would have thought of it happening to them.

It happened six years after the death of the parents, and the twins were going on twenty when a young woman wandered wearily into the diner tugging on the tiny hand of a lad of about two. The tot struggled to keep up, but was mostly dragged along, sniffling loudly, his reddened face wet with tears. The young woman, girl, actually, carried a shoulder bag stuffed to overflowing.

She faced Keith with a tear-stained face and begged for food for the little boy. They hadn't eaten all day, she wailed, and were hungry but she had no money.

Well, that was not the first time that a bum wanted a free meal and he had been turned away, but this time it seemed different. There was a little kid. And Keith had bean soup bubbling at its tastiest, with shreds of ham scuttling around among the beans and chopped onions.

He sat the girl (mother of the kid?) at the tiny dinette table and placed a bowl of beans before her. He buttered a pair of biscuits, and furnished a glass of water. What else could he do? Oh, yes, would the little fellow like milk?

"Yes, he would, thank you!" And the girl began to eat like there was no tomorrow. She offered a bite to the boy, and he took it greedily, and drank all of the milk in the small glass without coming up for air. They were, indeed, very hungry.

While he was studying the situation, the girl leaned forward and fainted, spilling the remainder of her beans onto the table and into her lap. The frightened little boy screamed with terror and bawled at the top of his young lungs.

Keith stared, wide-eyed. What to do now? There was only one thing open to him and he went for it. At the door leading into the other side of the house, he yelled, "Leena, come quick! Emergency!"

She came. She surveyed the mess and picked up the little boy. "You tend to her, I'll clean him up."

It ended up that Leena cleaned them both up, and the girl was put to bed in one of the bedrooms, while she tried to pacify the little fellow who had been thrust into the reluctant arms of strangers. The little fellow was a stranger to Keith and Leena, and neither of them had experience with young children.

Sometime in the night the girl came to and yelled, "Where is my baby? Where am I?"

Leena, who had been trying in vain to rock the little fellow to sleep, happily put him into his mother's arms. The mother was not entirely lucid at this moment, but said her name was Margie and that she had been beaten and thrown out of the place where she was living. The little boy was Jackie.

She exhibited the bruises on her arms and a spot of dried blood from a head wound. The person who beat her had been in the habit of regularly doing so, but had never thrown her out before, and her with a little boy! Shameful! He was not the little boy's father, so the man didn't care. Likely he wouldn't have cared even if he had been the father.

Margie was not well enough to be sent away, especially with the little boy, for where would she go? It was not like there were city facilities to handle these emergencies. Residents on Ridge Road there were just ordinary people who tried to take care of each other, and Keith and Leena were people, so what was next?

The answer was clear. Margie would stay a while and they might figure a way for her to be safe, or they might even take her down to Wishbone or Eureka Springs where there was help. Anyway, she was at least in her own mind now, and little Jackie clung to her like he was drowning and she was a life raft. So, let's all get a little sleep, and talk about it tomorrow.

Neither Keith nor Leena got any sleep. What had fallen into their laps was something that did not happen to most twenty-year-olds. It took thinking in a vein that was totally foreign to them, that a grown man would throw out a woman who had been living with him, and her with a small boy to see after? It just didn't make sense. Most folks that they knew didn't do things like that.

The immediate answer would have to be thought up by Keith, as Leena had a job to do as soon as she had breakfast. A dinky, little Ford horseless carriage was currently setting in her shed. It seems it had taken to sputtering or something, and the woman who left it had accepted the loan of a horse and buggy to get to an appointment in Berryville.

The tiny vehicle of an auto was well named, as it appeared to be made to look exactly like a "ladies buggy" such as would be drawn by a small pony. Its roof was held up by slender rods. It had absolutely no windshield. Such foolishness. It was a car, for goodness sake, so why make it look like a buggy?

Anyway, if the horse and buggy the woman took didn't return, then the stupid little carriage would be hers, and she could sell it for more than the horse was worth. Some people will buy anything, no matter how ridiculous.

Leena insisted on doing business that way. She'd bet this woman, Miss Lillian Landrum was her name, would be back, for certain, and ready to pay a sizeable bill. The woman should have kept the little car for in-town driving, and purchased a decent car for the road. Or maybe a reliable horse.

New gasoline car manufacturers were popping up like fleas on a dog's back, with every imaginable name. Miss Lillian should have stuck with a Ford...or maybe a Chevrolet. The French-made model, Chevrolet, had a lot of potential, Leena thought. She'd need to keep an eye on it...maybe even to ordering a manual of their most popular model. She was sure to see one in her shop sooner or later.

She crawled into the green coveralls and bundled her mop of red-gold curls into a wad and poked it all under a knitted hat. The hat kept it from getting so dirty under the cars. This tiny car was so light, she had no trouble at all pulling it up onto the low platform where she worked.

She rolled her wheeled tool-carrier out from the door under the sign saying "TIN-LIZZIES FIXED." That was her side of the new addition, with gas, oil and accessories kept there. The SOUP BOWL DINER belonged to Keith, but got frequent visits from Leena. Food was always there, cooked, hot and ready for her at any time. As long as she was not particular what she had. Most of the time she wasn't. To Leena, food was something you ate so you could keep on doing something you wanted to do. Or needed to do.

The person who said her name was Margie arose later in the day having slept most of the time, her little Jackie awake and lying beside her. She found a comb and used it, greatly improving her looks. Washing her face highlighted a few bruises around her neck and ears, and she had apparently been able to grab up another dress and a few of Jackie's clothes before being run out of the house…if that was what actually happened.

It seemed it might be the truth. Jackie was certainly afraid and would not leave the bed and his mother even to eat, so Keith gave him a buttered biscuit. Now the bed would be full of crumbs… oh, well.

Keith was getting ready for the three or four hungry workmen who would pass by on the way home and the two or three persons who need a beef sandwich in their lunch. These were regulars. Others often stopped by picking up a sandwich to go.

Then there were the three old fellows who'd seemingly remembered each other from grade school. When the weather was right, they showed up around 3:00 PM and captured the French table with three chairs that had twisted wire legs. Chile and cornbread was usually what they wanted, and then they wanted the bowls cleared away so they could play a game of dominos, taking up the whole of the table top.

Jolly fellows these were, laughing and joking and thoroughly enjoying themselves. They used up the chairs for a long time, but mid-afternoon was usually quiet for the table trade. Most of them preferred the counter and a high stool.

A glass cake holder held a double layer chocolate cake that Keith had cooked earlier, and another, shorter holder held the cherry pie. The one other thing on the end of the counter was the immense glass cookie jar. He would give the cake and pie another day in their individual platters, and then what was left unsold would be stirred together with eggs and oatmeal and rolled into cookies. These were for sale at two cents each but free for children.

He was smart enough to know that children often influenced the decision to stop…or not. There were things to learn when starting a business, and for Keith a lot of them were learned at his ages seventeen, eighteen and nineteen. He was showing a regular profit now, and a reputation for being consistent and serving tasty, well-spiced food. Very satisfying.

Leena made more money in random lump sums, while his income was regular. Folks got hungry every day and needed food, while the tin-lizzies only broke down occasionally, and even then they might not often be close by the fixit shop. But the pair got a lot of community interest, and there were a few bets as to how the arrangement would work out.

GRADY THE GRADER

Leena mulled over the situation with their "guest." As she remembered it, it went like this. As Keith had explained, what else could he do than he had done?

Margie had appeared in the diner with Jackie by her side. Keith relieved her of the humiliation of having to ask for food. "Would you like a beef sandwich and some beans? Maybe something for Jackie? Like milk?"

"Yes, thank you. He would like milk. He can help me eat the beans."

Keith thought for a minute. "How about a small saucer of beans to mash up for him? Along with the milk."

He had set her up at the end of the counter where no one usually sat because it was almost into the small kitchen. "Where are you from?" he ventured. She shrugged and replied, "Most everywhere. He'd done moved us most everywhere to find folks that don't know him. He's mean."

Keith processed the answer to his question. "Uh…why would you stay with him if he was mean?"

"He made me stay, and I didn't have no other place to go."

"So where are you going now?"

"Don't know. Me and Jackie, we got no folks and no money. I'll be lookin' around for a place for us. We don't want to be no trouble to you folks. Maybe for another day…could you?"

What could he have said with small Jackie eyeing him with huge black eyes? With his fingers, he was picking up chunks of the mashed beans and poking them into his mouth. Never learned to use a spoon?

So she had stayed for a week…and then another one, and then how could he send her away? Actually she was rather good company and became something of a fixture in the kitchen.

Leena wondered about her, and shrugged her shoulders within the large work coverall. What Keith did was his business.

What the girl ate could hardly affect the joint funds…and she was rather pathetic. Leena had located a couple of her dresses and handed them to her. No loss. She had plenty. She'd offered to take her to…Wishbone…Eureka? Margie had not taken up the offer. Oh, well…she was Keith's problem.

If she had to go to Wishbone for something, maybe Margie would like to go along in the truck, and maybe she could help her find someone to help her in town. But no, it didn't seem to suit her. So she stayed another week. Did she think Keith was going to marry her…or something?

It happened six weeks later that she was gone in the night and so were a pair of Leena's shoes and some underclothes. Also a quantity of prepared food from the diner. It would have been good riddance, but she left alone. Jackie was left behind crying and calling for "Mama! Mama!" but it was clear there was no mama to hear him.

Keith carried him to the diner and gave him milk and a biscuit. Then he gave him a scrambled egg. The skinny little fellow did well by the food, and when Keith attempted to take him to the back room, he clung to Keith like a coat of paint. Holding onto the giver of food. Smart kid. If he had no mama, then take what he can get and don't let go. Somehow, Keith saw something smart in the kid, or maybe it was just his plain old sympathetic nature. One had to admire the survival traits in the boy.

He had options, and he could have taken Jackie to the "Boys Home" over in Berryville. He could have…but he didn't. Just didn't have time, he'd told himself, and that is how Jackie became part of the family. Not a bad deal, really. Smart little kid…must have gotten that from his father, whoever that was.

His ma had left a note. She said,

I'm sorry to do this to you, but I'm going to do it anyway. Please forgive me. I would tell you who Jackie's father is if I knew, but I don't. I don't even know who my father is. I know you will find a good place for him and that's something I could not do. I hope Leena will forgive me for the clothes I took. And I took the dollar

19

I found by your cash register. I don't know where I'm going, but I didn't want Jackie to be along when I can't take care of him. I may try to hitchhike to Bentonville, or somewhere. Thank you, Margie.

Hmmmm, well that was that. And the little fellow was no dummy. He undoubtedly missed his mama, but likely not the person who had hurt her, or he may have remembered that he sometimes had an empty stomach, but no longer. He was a square shooter for one so young. He faced his future with chin up and eyes open.

No dumb kid. Keith was the person who did not yell at him or kick him, and had food, and, not to be overlooked, talked with him and rewarded him for obedience. He quickly learned that if he wanted to stay in the diner, he must sit on a little stool and then he could have a cookie unless it was time for eggs or something else.

And, little by little, he filled out his skinny little body and Keith kept putting off the trip to Berryville to the Boy's Home. Leena quit reminding him.

She had plenty to do. She kept the eggs gathered. Also, she was in charge of producing new little chicks when a hen went "broody." The little boy was no trouble to her. Keith's problem.

Chickens actually interested Leena. Nature had determined that some should be mothers, and when a hen seemed to be in the mood, she might hide her nest away from the hen house and try to fill it with eggs that could not be gathered.

Leena was good at finding a broody hen and producing a nest of eggs for her, and also covering her over with an "A" house to keep her dry and away from the coyotes. Eventually she would produce fluffy, yellow balls with matchstick legs and tiny beaks that tried to peck out the eyes of their fellows. Then Leena would let the mama hen out of the "A" house so she could teach the chicks to forage for insects.

Simple equation. Eggs meant chicks and chicks grew into chicken dinners. Chicken dinners eliminated the necessity of deciding what was for lunch. Also, a lot of insects went into the chicks, instead of only the leaves of the vegetables eating holes in them.

But today Leena would fix up the silly little vehicle that belonged to Miss Lillian. Scooting herself under the car was no trick because of the height of the wheels. Skinny wheels they were, with no tires to speak of. The driver felt every rock or dip, bad as it it was a hay wagon.

Shouldn't anyone ever be caught up here in the mountains in a contraption that belonged on the smooth streets of Eureka Springs. Some folks never learned.

Let's see, now. Diagnosis was difficult from some people. She had been faced with words like "It makes a wiggly noise when I step on that pedal." Or, "Why do the wheels go that way when I turn this thing this way?" Or, "There's a funny noise back there." What kind of a noise, she asked. "I don't know! Do noises have names?"

That was the ladies, but the fellows were worse. They were embarrassed to say to her that they hadn't a clue about what was wrong. What's to be embarrassed about? Whatever it is, do they want it fixed…or don't they?

Miss Lillian was one of those who said the wheels didn't go the right way, and for once, she was right. Jiggly, rocky mountain roads jar this or that loose. Now that she had found the immediate problem, she spent a bit of time looking at other potential trouble spots.

While totally absorbed, something jarred the working platform, and a scratchy noise followed. Leena started to crawl out from under to see, but she met a sizeable person, squirming his body along to crawl under.

"Grady O'Keef! What in the world are you doing?"

"Just tryin' to spend a minute with my girl."

"Then get on out of here and find her."

"I found 'er. I located her when we were in the sixth grade and I got a crick in my neck from lookin' around a mess's red curly hair. Like to'a threw my spine out'a joint."

"I'm not your girl."

"Sure you are. You just won't admit it?"

"Wouldn't that tell you somethin'?"

"Yep. Tells me I got'a keep on keepin' on and bein' patient."

"Wastin' your time, you are. You ain't the only fellow around."

"Of course I am. Otherwise, where at would be the other fellow?"

He had a point, there. She resorted to her well-used excuse. "I ain't got time for gaddin' about!"

"I know you got no other fellow, 'cause all the girls from school are married and on their second kid. No other fellow worth his salt'd wait around like I do."

"Aw, get on out there and run your grader. Ridge road is gettin' so rough the wheels are fallin' off these little carts."

"I done graded all the way up to here, and I got hungry. I aim to stop over to the soup kitchen and see what's on."

"You already know what's on. Same as it's been for two years and countin'."

"Yep! And that's what I like about it. Why don't you crawl out from here and let me take you to dinner?" Tired old joke but it worked sometimes.

"You only take me there 'cause you don't have to pay for me over there."

"I always pay for my food. This time I'll insist on payin' for yours. Is that a deal?"

"All right, but first you got'a do somethin'. While I hold this thing-a-ma-jig in place, you scoot out and get me the blue handled wrench from the tool box."

As he began to scoot out, he wondered, "Why blue handled?"

"I marked it. It's the one that usually fits everything that goes wrong."

After a shuffle and a rattle, he announced, "I got it."

"Then hand it here."

He stooped and thrust the tool toward her. "How long is that gonna take?"

"No time. Done. Get out'a the way and let me up."

He did, and stood back to watch. He knew what was coming.

The bulky-clad, coveralled figure stood upright, removed greasy gloves, drew the zipper from chin down to belly and stepped out. There stood before him a well-formed lady in a pink and blue dress with pink, embroidered collar. With a twist and a shake, the hood-thing came off her head and the red-gold curls sluffed out into their natural shape.

He watched with a small smile. Man, oh man, what a sight! He almost felt that he should pay her for the performance. Or at least manage a bit of applause.

Then she broke the spell. "Well, let's go! Are you hungry or aren't you?"

With her right hand in his and his left arm around her waist, he moved toward the edge of the platform. "Watch your step, Miss. This here's a ten-inch high platform."

She looked at him and rolled her blue-green eyes in a sarcastic way. "Oh, thank you, sir. I wouldn't want to trip."

It took about a dozen steps to reach the front door of the Soup Bowl Diner. And luckily the table was empty.

In his best and most polite voice, he asked, "What'll you have, Miss?"

No need to answer. On its way to them was two bowls of vegetable soup, and from somewhere came the lovely crackling sound of ground meat patties now being browned on the miniature stove.

Through the window it was plain to see the horse-drawn grader that pulled the gravel stones back up from the ditches and smoothed them out across the road. A good, all-weather road was Ridge Road. A dozen years ago, it was mostly loose rocks and dirt that turned to mud in the rain and flowed down the mountain in muddy rivulets. All that was gone.

The gravel stones and the grader were a very much appreciated up-grade. The grader operator ground his way up and down kills all the way from Wishbone Hollow to Kings River which split the county in half. Another grader came from Berryville to the river and returned.

Carroll County Arkansas was the only county in the state, possibly in the whole of the United States, that had two county seats. That had happened before the solid bridge was built over the river.

It just didn't do to have half the county without a county seat that could actually be reached, and neither town would give in to let it go. So, in true "can-do" Arkansas fashion, two county seats were formed. Worked good. So far.

Grady O'Keef was the lucky critter that got the grading job. Very few applied, because the driver must be out in all kinds of weather and on the road overnight. He must find grazing grass for the mules, though he carried chopped corn on the machine. Also, he must find food for himself.

So here he sat with the attractive lady.

Soup, hamburgers and coffee. They appeared to be any courting couple, while the mules attached to the grader flung their manes about scattering the flies.

The fact that GRADY operated the GRADER was a favorite joke from one end of Ridge Road to the other, as everybody had met Grady sooner or later either going west or going east. And everyone was happy to see him as he always made the road a lot smoother than it was before he passed by.

But then the lunch was over, and he had to get on the road again. "I promise you this. When they get me a grader with a motor, I'll arrange to have all my break-downs here."

She rolled her eyes and swatted him on the shoulder. "Git on out'a here. I got work to do."

She watched the grader as he ground his way past the diner/fixit shop and disappeared over the hill, then went back to Miss Lillian's vehicle. It would be washed and the velvet seat covers brushed. Something she always did. Couldn't hurt to do something extra.

Then she stepped into her shop and wrote out the ticket. She didn't charge based on the time a job took, she just charged for knowing what it took to fix it. Worked out well. Just now, competition was a lot of hilly miles away.

UNCLE KEITH

Burley Collins, lawman, had watched Grady grind his way up the hill and wave as he passed. He would be going on down to the Soup Bowl and he had good reason. So many of the passer's by stopped in at his roadside stand for cider and jerky, but not Grady. He headed for the diner. He waved jauntly and passed by taking his noise and dust with him.

For good reasons, Grady gave his business to the diner. All the better to keep his eye on Leena and not let her forget about him.

A small smile passed over the lawman's weatherbeaten lips. A fellow had to do whatever he had to do when he had his eye on a girl. Girls like Leena, and his Annie Jo…they were scarce and he'd had to do a few things he wouldn't ordinarily have done if it hadn't been for her. Didn't hurt him a bit, for a fact.

He had another reason for being interested to see Grady go by. The pleasant faced fellow with the fiery red hair was also just nosey enough. More than a few times he had stopped in to report something that seemed out of the ordinary along the way. The lawman in Burley Collins was always alert for trouble that could happen so suddenly.

Jackie, fed regularly and given all the milk he wanted, filled out into the ways a two-and-a-half-year-old should be filled out. He adapted himself quickly, a trait that was likely born in him, to the ways of the Sullivan household. Leena, he loved and needed, but it was Keith that he adored.

He followed along when the goats were milked, he watched the hand-operated separator that separated the milk from the cream. He watched the chickens being plucked of feathers. He took his toys, ordered by Keith from the Wards Catalog, to his assigned corner of the diner to play. Keith was not permitted to get out of his sight.

There had been hours of discussion as to what to do with him, as it was certain that Keith was not going to give him up. Keith had considered what he should be called…turned down Daddy…and finally settled on Uncle Keith. Sounded more reasonable for when he grew up. Eventually the boy settled the question in his own way, and Keith became Papa.

But still, something had to be done. Humans had to be legally named and counted, and surely Jackie was not the only tot caught in this web of human wrong decisions.

There were letters to the proper persons in Eureka Strings as to the first way to go. He would have to bring to the county seat all the information he had about the child, an affidavit from a respected neighbor (that would be Deputy Burley Collins) that the child was well treated, and that Keith's information was correct.

An outright adoption was not possible under Jackie's circumstances and that seemed strange, but Keith could be assigned "loco parentis" rights, meaning he was to be the legal person in charge of the child, and that no one else was held responsible. The name of another respectable person was needed, in the unlikely event that something happened to Keith. That would be also Burley, and he would do whatever had to be done.

And then, with that all done, Keith must come to the county seat and bring the child. He would receive a name and a number and assigned a birthday if he didn't have one. This happened more times that one would hope for.

The diner and the fix-it shop were shut down for the space of three days and the trip was made. Leena permitted no one to drive the truck but herself, so she was obliged to go along.

The little fellow looked to be about two and a half, so his birthday was assigned as December first. His "local parent" was Keith Sullivan, with the alternate of Kathleen Sullivan, and his name was assigned as Jackson Keith Sullivan.

He was taken to the clothing store and outfitted in flannel shirts, overalls, summer shorts and underwear. Also sturdy shoes and socks.

After ice cream cones all around, the Ford flat-bed truck headed east and began to successfully attack the mountains of Ridge Road. The exhausted little boy went to sleep across Keith's knees, and the adults breathed more peacefully now that his presence was legal…or at least as legal as possible.

The local government was happy to make this type of arrangement, as there were so many that must be assigned to "homes." Happiness all the way around. It was always good for a kid to be wanted.

The little fellow with the dark skin, black hair and eyes was assigned to parents with red, curly hair and blue-green eyes. No problem. A lot of folks got mixed up in the their looks. There was, however, a good bit of interested speculation as to his linage.

His absentee father could well have belonged to the Ouachita tribe that had occupied the Arkansas mountains since the dawn of time from before there was an Arkansas. Or it might be of the Otoe tribe from the northern border of Arkansas and southern Missouri. Or, he might well have been from the northern part of old Ireland. No one knew, or cared, but the situation was interesting, nevertheless, and provided conversation.

And Jackie was no dummy. From somewhere, he inherited the ability to learn quickly, and insisted on stories being read to him regularly.

And it was shortly after this trip that Ole Mr. Phillip Stanhope, the legal owner of the wonderful Ford truck, needed a trip to Wishbone to see the medical person who assigned the aspirin, three-way cold medicine and the medicated petroleum jelly for treating minor scratches and rashes.

He must stay overnight, as the trip itself was hard on him, and he checked himself and Leena into the small hotel for the night. Being somewhat responsible for him, Leena had insisted that their rooms be adjoining. She had used the trip to replenish her gasoline supply by filling the six cans that were tied to the bed of the trunk, but the old man had remained in his room.

During her shopping, the old man had requested to be left in his hotel room, and that might have been a red flag to Leena, but she had her own errands to attend to, and was just as glad to do them alone.

They enjoyed a good supper at Mr. Stanhope's expense and retired early. The next morning, Leena gassed up the truck and stopped by the hotel to pick him up, and he was ready and in good spirits.

The old man was not great on conversation, so Leena occupied herself with her own thought, humming this or that tune from her childhood, and often making up new verses to amuse herself.

Half way home the old man adjusted the small pillow she always put in for him, and leaned back to "rest his eyes." As usual. And before noon she had pulled in at his house. She spoke to him and received no answer. She turned to look at him, eyes closed, hands limp in his lap. She looked long into the pleasantly wrinkled face, all wrinkles relaxed more than would be expected in a nap in a jouncy truck ride.

It didn't take long to realize this ride would be had last he would take in a sitting position.

Her blood ran cold for the unexpectedness of his passing. He had seemed to enjoy the trip and the evening at the hotel. He was tired, but then he had enjoyed an awful lot of birthdays. She didn't know how many. Didn't matter. A person's time came when it came, and obviously this was his.

He'd made his preparations and given them to the lawman in a sealed envelope. The truck was Leena's and the attractive twenty acres that adjoined that of the twins was to be given to the two of them, along with the house and everything in it.

He wished to be buried on his property, had left no family that he knew of, and had outlived all his friends. Lawman Burley notified Preacher Phil Darkhorse who came and with a few locals who knew the old man, his body was laid to rest, and he was sent on to his eternal home.

Now there would be the house to rent, as an empty house attracted bums and transients, and so often burned down with nobody living in them. Offer it for rent at a small fee and get someone to take care of it. Shouldn't be empty long.

Leena would miss him, but her thoughts of him were of gratitude, for how would she have learned about automobile engines if he had not needed help with his truck?

And automobiles would be in the future of Ridge Road in a matter of a few years, just as the twins were the future of the residents.

They came home from the laying away to find a strange man seated on her work platform. His car was back down the road, and it had had a fit, or something, he said. Anyway, it wouldn't run and he had heard someone here could fix it.

Leena nodded, and told him, "That'd be me. I'll get my chains and we'll go get it." The Ford flat-bed had a job to do. A couple of chain hook-ups and the disabled vehicle would roll right along onto Leena's platform.

Not so!

The fellow who said his name was Billy Brown pointed her down toward Wishbone for a couple of miles, and indicated a small side road.

"It's down there." And he pointed.

Leena's red flags arose. She'd been here and done this before. She cautiously turned the blue flat bed into the road that did not appear to have a disabled car in the yard.

He clarified. "It's around back."

Leena nodded. She stopped the truck and got out. She lifted the lid on the tool box attached just behind the truck cab. "Need to get the chains ready," she said, by way of explanation.

He stepped out and came around the car behind her. "We don't need them chains, Sweet Pie. It's just us down here, hidden-like. We're fixin' to have us some fun!"

He put his hands on each side of her waist. "Turn around, Sweetie."

She said, "You bet!" She had just felt into the box and gotten a good grip on the club that was part of an oak tree. In a flash of movement, she whirled around and wacked him a lick on the side of his head, cutting into an ear and bringing blood.

Her next grip came up with the short rope that she used to swat him in the face, and then tie his hands before he had a chance to realize he could actually make two of her in size. *Who would have thought...how did she...wow!*

"Get yourself up on the flat-bed and lean against the cab. We're goin' for a ride and have us some fun. You see this here rope? One end is on you and the other end will be tied to my steerin' wheel. You thinkin' on jumpin out'll put you down on the road to be drug all the way to the Burley Collin's Bistro."

Having no choice, the fellow decided on her idea of fun, and climbed awkwardly onto the truck bed, still trying to comprehend what had happening. *How'd she do that? She must'a got so strong from turnin' them wrenches and bolts.*

Leena climbed aboard the driver's seat, once again being thankful for such a high-end vehicle that didn't have to be cranked to start. Just pulling the choke and turning the key set the engine to purring. She took a deep breath of pride, and again thanked old Mr. Stanhope. He bought the best, did Mr. Phillip!

Leena backed out of the little side road and headed back up the road to the Bistro and Lawman Burley. She wheeled into the spacious frontage of the Bistro, and was greeted by Ugly Face, the bloodhound, with a flap of her rag-like ears. Deputy Burley Collins was not far behind, wearing a small smile behind his stern, lawman look.

This was not the first time she hauled in some young sport for the mistake of thinking she would be easy pickings. When was it going to get around among the hopeful squires that Miss Leena Sullivan made her own choices of company?

This one, like most of the others, would be put in the "cage," his onsite jail, made of oak logs and a couple of iron-bared windows. A few hours in the eight feet by eight feet cell, along with a bit of a lecture, usually took care of the problem. So far he had never had a repeat "offender."

By cuffing him and leading him away, Leena had done her part, and with a wave to Miss Annie behind the counter of the roadside stand and a pat on the velvet head of Ugly Face, she turned back to the fix-it shop.

There were no fix-it jobs for today, so she decided to weed the chard and the radishes. She hoped for a prospective renter of Mr. Stanhope's house really soon. It was becoming a nuisance for her, and a real trial for Keith who had to make the daily trip back into the woods to milk the half a dozen goats, for milk they certainly did not need.

They'd advertised the house on the advertising tree over by the roadside stand. Anyone who wanted to know anything checked in regularly to read the thumbtacked messages, wants and for sales and trades. They decided, Leena and Keith, that they'd advertise that the goats went with it, to possibly attract a family. If the renter didn't want to bother with goats, she'd just sell them by staking them in front of her shop with a sign.

She parked the truck and went in to diner and sat at the counter.

"No disabled car, huh! What he wanted was just you?"

"Yep. Burley's got 'im now. Could you dip me up some beans?"

He set the bowl before her, with a message. "The girl down the road who raised bloodhounds has a runt pup she'd like to give to Jackie. I thought I'd check with you. The little fellow may not be housebroke."

"Tell 'er to bring it on. Little boys need a dog, especially the ones alone. He'll have to grow fast to stay ahead'a the dog. Ugly Face was a runt, remember? Now she's about the size of'a butcherin' calf."

"Good job. We need a dog and old Pippy tried, but she just wasn't dog enough. And she got too old." Pippy was now about a foot under the grass, the spot marked with a pointed stone.

Leena finished her beans and announced, "Goin' to the garden," and she was gone.

THE WANDERER

Keith opened a Mason jar of canned beef from the last butchering. He chopped the pieces of meat into fine shreds and set them aside. The regulars would be by, and if there were leftovers from the beef there would be sandwiches.

The three old fellows trooped in and settled around the tiny table. One announced, "Grady's a'comin' up from the river. Kickin' up a dust that'll mess up the washins' on the clotheslines line all the way to Wishbone."

"Yeah, and clog up the noses'a old folkes."

"Better'n havin' pot-holes the size to hide an elephant!"

"Noticed Burley had 'im a prisoner in his pokey."

"Did Leena haul 'im in?"

"Yep. That girl ought'a get a bounty on them fellows she brings in for teachin' the bums a lesson."

A head full of red curly hair popped through the door. "Leena in here?"

"Nope. Garden."

"Thanks." So he'd have to pull a few weeds before he enticed her into the diner for double chocolate cake. Cheap at the price.

He approached the garden and called out, "You seen my girlfriend?"

The answer came, "Nope, she hasn't been here. Maybe if you pull a few weeds, she'll be here."

"'Speck maybe I'll just do that."

The mail hack pulled up in front of the diner. Lanky, long-legged and balding, the postal delivery man stepped down from the gasoline powered vehicle newly purchased by the postal service. Paul Mannford entered the diner.

"Hello, Paul, what's a'goin' on?"

"Hunger, mostly. I'll have beans and a beef sandwich. Maybe pie…I'll decide. Seems everyone on the Ridge got mail today. Even you, Keith."

"Imagine that!"

After decades of almost no delivery of mail to rural areas, the gasoline engine made its way into northern Arkansas. Of course, the cities had had automobiles for a long time, but delivery to the hills had been sketchy.

Now the "gas-buggy" plowed its way across Ridge Road and its many mailboxes twice a week. A long way from Wishbone to King's river and back did the trick.

The advent of the mail order catalog had the most pressing effect on his job, because of the multitude of packages to be delivered. But now that he had the car called a "mail hack," it was a breeze.

Amelia and Jacob Atkins met when they were six years old and expected to leave the safety of their homes to attend that strange thing called a school. And they couldn't get it over with in one day…it was going to be EVERY day and how could they possible manage it? For two shy, protected children it seemed insurmountable.

They took a look at each other as a kindred face in the excited traffic of the school ground, and the face they looked at was very much like their own. Anxiety, very near to fear, was instantly recognized in the other person. In a moment, the bond was made.

They somehow survived the first grade and the grades after that, but their friendship was tied with many knots.

At ages eighteen, they were married and set up in Jacob's father's business. Atkin's Upholstery, Mattresses, Pillows and Overstuffed Chairs.

As the years passed, and the parents went on, the business became Jacob's and it did well enough to support a large family. The only problem being that the family did not appear.

It was not of concern at first. Early twenties was for getting started in life, and the children would come. Sure to.

The thirties came, and the concern began. Everyone had children. Why, Ridge Road was fairly crawling alive with children of all ages, and they were the subject of much comparison, discussion and concern among their parents, but Amelia and Jacob had seemingly escaped that puzzling concern.

The absence of children even affected their social life, for if you had no children, how could you possibly sympathize with others when their kid did something stupid…even dangerous?

It was just months before their fortieth birthday that Amelia came down sick. That meant a trip to the herbal woman, Old Bessie Cravens, who was the precursor to going to a real doctor way down in Garland Community. No use to make the trip if Bessie could fix the problem.

The wrinkled old woman looked at Amelia with sympathy. She was indeed sick, but she would do what she could. She mixed the herbs carefully, calling on her knowledge of each one, and put them in a quart jar sealing the lid down firmly. Her price was high, but the Atkins were happy to pay it if it only gave Amelia a bit of relief. She charged twenty-five cents for the herbs (and her knowledge of which were required) and five cents for the jar, refundable upon return.

"Now this here medicine needs to be made into tea and you drink it the first time you put feet on the floor in the mornin'. Then rest in bed for an hour or so. I could'a give you somethin' better but not in your condition."

Jacob was alarmed. "Condition? Is it that bad?"

The old woman nodded sharply, and set her sagging facial skin to wobbling. "It's gonna be bad for a while, on account'a her age."

"But she's not even forty? When'll she get better?"

The old women's mouth firmed, and her eyes quenched shut as she thought. "I'd say about five and a half to six months."

Jacob stared in horror at the old woman. "Only six months?"

The old woman shrugged and stated, "Well, most womenfolk think that's long enough."

"Long enough to live?"

"Of course not. Havin' the right care it don't have to be fatal."

"Right care? Where'd we go to get the right care?"

"Oh, there's folks around. If ya can't find no other midwife, bring 'er on down here."

Now Amelia came alive. "MIDWIFE! Did you say MIDWIFE?"

"Sure did. Most woman don't want to have a baby alone. Helps to have a friend or someone who knows somethin'."

Jacob leaned forward as though to ferret the truth out of her. "Are you sayin' she's…. ???"

"Sure is. You sayin' you didn't know?"

He shook his head sadly back and forth. "No. After so many years we'd done give up. But…are you really sure?"

"Sure as these old mountains is made out'a rocks. Course, this should'a been took care of years ago. Birthin's easier on the young."

Then Jacob, "Oh, Miss Bessie, we tried."

And Amelia, "That's the honest truth. We tried and tried."

The old woman nodded agreeably. "Well, I'd say you finally got 'er done."

With hands shaking with excitement, Jacob paid out and took his wife back to the buggy.

And Miss Bessie was right. In due time, she was the expert who delivered a pink and screaming creature into the arms of her father, who stared at her mother as though she'd been the one to paint the Mona Lisa.

And a name must be produced. They'd hardly thought about a name as they'd hardly thought Miss Bessie was right. So now they must think.

They passed on through Rhoda, Dorcas, Abigail and Susannah. They paused a bit on Mary and Elizabeth while Miss Bessie held her pencil ready to make it legal, if they could just decide.

Both parents looked down with incredulity at the pink creature. Amelia looked up at Jacob. "I've got it. We must name here Sharon. Remember the Rose of Sharon the prophet Isaiah wrote on in chapter 35...first verse? About blossomin' "as the Rose of Sharon"? That's our little girl. Sharon."

"Not Rose?"

"No, too many Roses bloomin' up and down the Ridge. She's Sharon." And Sharon she was.

Sharon was a scrawny little being, and not much to look at but no one would mention it to her parents. Over the fence gossip had a field day with it.

"That baby! After nine month's a' work and a few hours a' labor and that's all they got."

"Yeah, a body'd think the angels'd bring a beautiful baby, long as those two had to wait."

"Maybe the beautiful ones was all gone. 'Cause you and me, we only got pretty ones."

That brought laughter, but the whole of the community was happy for them. The Wards Catalog got a lot of business because of small Sharon. Amelia spent happy hours perusing the worn pages of that book searching for at least one more thing to order for her.

Postman Paul Manford could count on at least one package a week to be delivered. Even Sharon's own swing came with the mail, with bulky rods and springs.

And the Ouachitas who had occupied the mountains before her made a board with tie strings to hold the baby in, and they hung it from a tree so it would move in the wind and turn to give the baby a variety of sights. That swing worked for many generations, but times were different now. No cradleboard for Miss Sharon Atkins.

Sharon was never a dimpled baby, having skinny arms and legs and a pixie face. She was never sick, and brought her parents all the pride and excitement their forty-year-old bodies could manage.

She started school at the appropriate age, and did well though she was still no beauty. Well dressed and shod, she was, but the skinny arms and legs and pixie face seemed there to stay.

She had friends and she did what the class did with no special mark for herself. However, there was a Christmas program at the school when she was nine years old. The teacher at that time had a flare for the dramatic. The program was moving along as most Christmas Programs did, when, at the time of the New Baby, an off stage voice began to sing "Hark and Herald Angels Sing." Who in the world was that with the clear and beautiful tones? And then when small Sharon came onto the stage dressed in white with crepe paper wings still singing, she paused beside "Mary."

With hardly a break in tempo, she changed to "Away in a manger no crib for a bed, the little Lord Jesus laid down his sweet head."

At this point several smaller girls with large stars tied to their foreheads came in and looked at the baby while Sharon sang, "The stars in the heavens looked down where he lay. The little Lord Jesus, asleep on the hay."

The audience, composed mostly of family members who were required to attend, were aghast at the purity and clarity of the girl's voice. Even those without a musical bone in their bodies could tell she was something special.

Then she broke into "Star of the east, oh Bethlem's star, bringing the wisemen who came from afar…." From the back of the room three boys, clothed in their father's shirts with towels appropriately wound their head, came bearing brightly wrapped "gifts."

Applause began with a few mild claps and mounted into a roaring acclamation as Sharon's voice continued. "While shepherds watched their flocks all night all seated on the ground. The angels of the Lord came down and glory shone around."

During this song, every other child who was not in the first part came in wrapped in white sheets and helped Sharon sing.

She didn't need help. Her parents were dry mouthed, agog. Their daughter. Their precious jewel had come into her own.

Within days, the whole of Burnt Tree Junction knew of the heavenly voice of the Atkins' homely daughter. They knew how she tied up the Christmas Play as beautifully as with a gold ribbon with her singing.

As for "coming into her own," Miss Sharon had no plans for that but sank back into her place at the back of the groups. That was all right, though. She had made the neighbors listen and look at her, and that was enough.

At age twelve, Sharon wanted a horse of her own. Not one of the plow horse or the carriage horses that pulled the buggy. She wanted her own animal that she could cover with a blanket and ride anytime she took a notion.

It took a bit of time, but Jacob finally located a young filly, just broke in to be ridden and he would have paid any price. The filly was jet black and had a perfect white star on her forehead, and Jacob certainly paid extra for that, but what did he care?

Sharon named the filly Star because the white star in the black face reminded her of a starry night. She learned to get aboard the animal without mussing up the blanket. She and the filly seemed to have had an instant understanding as they went tearing around the farm, frightening her parents almost out of their wits.

She and the filly remained close friends for years. When Sharon was fifteen, the change happened. Like a butterfly from its chrysalis, her pixie face rounded out and created a hint of a dimple in her cheeks. Her arms and legs began to look like girls' legs, and her body left no doubt that she was a girl.

She and Star ventured up to Ridge Road, so the animal could take a good run without going up and down hill. She stopped in for refreshments at the Soup Bowl, and the sight of Keith Sullivan completely filled her baby blue eyes. He had been three years ahead of her in school and had been a wiseman in the play, and she had seen him a lot, and now he was all grown up and he had done a good job of it. She found no fault in any part of him.

It didn't hurt her opinion one morsel to see the six-foot-something, broad shouldered Irishman wearing an apron over his neatly ironed khaki shirt and pants…that he, himself, had ironed. He lost no appeal by bringing her a bowl of vegetable soup and a handful of crackers. Among the crackers was a chocolate-raisin-oatmeal cookie that he normally gave only to children.

She was smitten. She ate and watched him go about his kitchen duties. About half way through the soup, she was joined by a fellow of about four years, who climbed into one of the chairs. He was not supposed to do that, and must stay in his "play corner" but he couldn't very well see this person from there. He was munching on the cookie and looking at her, so she told him, "Hi there. Have you come to keep me company?"

He nodded, and noticed the cookie. "You got a cookie! That means my Uncle Keith likes you." And after a pause, "I like you, too."

Keith barely recognized Sharon, but noted that she had done well with her time. In fact, she had made excellent use of every year. Dressed in a plaid, full-skirted dress, she had arrived on the back of a beautiful, spirited filly who was, at present, tied out front.

Hmmm, he wondered, *would she be coming back?* She seemed to be enjoying herself, so it was possible.

She came back, and on her third visit, in which she wanted only pie and coffee, he brought it to the table and went back for another cup of the fragrant brew for himself. He did something that he had never done during the almost five years of the business. He stood behind one of the chairs and ask, "May I sit down?"

A smile and, "Yes, please do."

Papa Atkins was on Ridge Road. He had two reasons for being there, one being a legitimate need to visit Deputy Collins. The other being to find out what his daughter was doing and where was she going. That was the responsibility of a parent, no matter how old the child. Wasn't it?

He found out, and heaved a painful sigh. He wouldn't accost her in front of other people, but he really needed to say something. He turned it over and over in his mind, searching for this or that way of reducing the shock on Amelia when she knew.

Deciding on no good way, he just blurted it out. "Brace yourself, my dear. I have bad news. Our daughter is keeping company." He prepared to comfort her with words about how he could take care of this problem, and she looked squarely at him, questioningly.

"What is the bad news?"

"Why, it's that she's seeing a boy!"

"I know. She's visiting Keith Sullivan…you know, we knew his parents before they were killed."

"…uh, yes, but she's going to his place. A fellow ought'a come and ask permission to see the girl."

"He can't. He's runnin' a business. And let's think back, did you ask my papa if you could court me?"

"This is different," Jacob stubbornly insisted.

"What's different is that she is ours. Otherwise they are the same. She's a girl and he's a fine, young fellow. Would you prefer that she settle on one of the hoodlums that run up and down the ridge? Them that form gangs and irritate the homeowners?"

"…uh, well…."

"By the way, what did you want with Deputy Collins?"

"Oh, it was nothin'."

"It was somethin' or you wouldn't'a been gone so long."

"I didn't want to worry you. It's just that we lost a couple'a pigs from that last batch, and I wondered if he had his eye on any gang, and did he need help with the hoodlums."

"Oh, were you going to invite them in to see our daughter?"

Jacob drew in a deep breath, and let it out again. "You win. I understand."

Then she softened. "I know how you feel. Sometime we're gonna lose her and it may be soon. But you know what they say, children are not possessions, just borrowed jewels."

After the time that Jacob joined her at the table, Sharon spent a lot of time at EAT AND GET GAS. Sometimes she was pulling weeds or hanging wet clothes on the clothesline with Leena. Or possibly hunting for mushrooms after a rain. Or chatting with her while she adjusted the something-or-other on some four-wheeled vehicle. A time or two she was asked to climb into the driver's seat to push this or that pedal as instructed by the voice from below.

After she had another birthday, her parents should have been ready for the next request from her. She wanted her own car. Her shooting Star was not enough any longer. Still fun, but that was just fun for one, and how many interesting places could she go with him...like Wishbone or maybe Berryville? None, actually.

She let her request be made known, and then kept quietly out of sight. They'd need to talk it over, of course, and she should be patient. But the thing was, she not only wanted a car...she wanted a certain car.

Leena had a little Ford, shiny black with a glass windshield and roll up windows. Just think, if a person started out warm and took along a warm brick, he could ride in comfort...maybe all the way to Wishbone!

"Think of it Mama, warm all the way, and you could go shopping without ordering from the catalog."

"Tell me why Leena had that car when she has the blue truck she takes everywhere.?"

"She traded for it. She had a buggy she got from Mr. Stanhope, and when a fellow left that car with her to be fixed, he was so mad he said he's swap even-steven for a horse and buggy. Leena said, 'Fellow, you got a deal.' So he rode away with the buggy and the little black Ford stayed with Leena. She had it fixed in no time.

"She said he forgot he had to put oil in the something or other. It burned up a whatever, but Leena had an extra one hanging in her shop. Mama, you ought'a see that shop. Two whole walls are nothing but hooks and nuts and washers and filters and even sacks of bolts are hanging. She says it's real handy 'cause when there's an empty hook, she's knows she's out'a whatever should be hangin' there, and she'll get another next time she goes to Wishbone."

Amelia Atkins could just picture a wall filled with greasy, black whatevers, and a few shiny gadgets. And here her daughter was smitten with those smelly, noisy, rattling things that were full of "whatevers" and she actually wanted one..

But her second thought was, the purchase of a car would tie her to the EAT AND GET GAS, if only to be close to the fix-it girl.And the red-haired diner owner...he would be there close. Mama was no dummy. Her Sharon could definitely do worse, so they must check out that little black Ford. It could hardly cost more than the horse did.

Not only that, the first time Mama was whisked down to Wishbone in a little over two hours, and brought back the same day she asked herself, "Where has this been all my life?" Of course, for the first years of her life it hadn't been perfected like this one was.

And she hadn't had a driver like she had now.

RENT HOUSE

There was still that house to rent, and it had been posted for almost a month. Its biggest problem was that it did not have Ridge Road frontage that so many people liked, but Keith was getting tired of milking those goats every day, and what does a body do with all that milk?

The pig helped a lot, and the Sullivan family had baked custard a lot. Couldn't serve it in the diner, of course. The milk overage was a one-time situation, Keith hoped, and the customers must not get used to it. He had pared down the menu as much as possible, and if he didn't have what the customer wanted, they could just run over to the roadside stand for cider and jerky.

A young fellow came along and wanted to see the place. Leena was not impressed by one lone fellow. How long would he be there? She really wanted a family, but there was Keith and that eternal milk, so she agreed to show it to him.

He told her that his ma had sent him to see it for her, and if he thought she'd like it, she'd see it for herself. Leena knew he was lying, but she really wanted someone in the house. She'd rent it for nothing, except when folks got something for nothing, they thought it was worthless and tore it up. At least that was what she had been told.

So she walked back down the little road, with "Bob" chattering constantly about how sure he was that his ma would like it. He was a sizeable fellow. A couple of inches taller than Keith, and a few pounds heavier. He had a day's worth of whiskers, but then some men grow them that fast, and his clothes were passable. There was a chance he was telling the truth, or something close to it.

She put the key into the lock, and he followed her inside. He glanced around the room and pronounced it perfect. Maybe Ma wouldn't like it but he sure did, and he slipped his arms around her waist from the back. His right hand held a length of rope.

She yelled, "Cut it out!"

And he said, "Ah, honey, you don't mean that. It's just you and me in here and there's a lot of fun to be had in this big old empty house."

Leena looked down to gage the position of his right foot. She lifted her shoe (Montgomery Ward's Best Ladies Shoe, split-leather calf skin, with the fashionable Cuban heel) and positioned it over the toe of his leather shoe and came down with all of her 120 pounds. She felt the leather "give" under the pressure and heard him yell in her ear.

"Ouch! You little…" and he released her waist to reach for his injured toes.

Leena whirled around, lifted the baby Walther, 22mm, from her pocket, aimed and shot, sending the bullet into the pine of the wall paneling. All that was visible was the shiny, pea-sized circle of the metal end of the bullet.

She grabbed up the rope and demanded, "Hold out your hands."

He hesitated; surely this wasn't happening.

"Move or I'm gonna get nervous, and when I'm nervous I can't aim to miss like I did just now. It takes practice to miss a target like you."

He decided he'd hold out his hands. With one hand, she whipped the rope around and around his wrist, clenching in a half-granny knot. Whole granny knots took too hands, but he couldn't even get this knot to his teeth.

"All right, Mr. Bob or whoever you are. Back out through that door and walk backward up the road we came down. I'm right back here where you can see me good enough so'a you'll know me next time you see me. Remember, don't make me nervous."

It happened that while this was going on, the three older fellows were attending to their domino game but startled at the gunshot. It would have been hard to miss what it was. They jerked their heads quickly to Keith who waved a dismissing hand. "It's just Leena. She's showin' a fellow the rent house."

"Leena…? Alone…?"

"Yep. She didn't need no help."

"Are you sure? We'll watch the place for you?"

"No need. She's all right."

"…Uh, how can you be knowin' for sure?"

"One shot."

"Yeah, we heard it. That fellow looked big from the window. She might need…."

"Naw, it was just one shot. If she'd'a needed help, there'd been two shots. She'll be a'comin' along here in a bit."

It took a while. One can stumble over a lot of unseen rocks and grass clumps while walking backward. When they reached the fix-it shop, he was instructed to back up to the flat-bed. Then to stretch out across it and lie on his back. He hesitated, obviously considering his options. She upended the gun, wavering her hands as if nervous. He decided to lie down.

Three wrinkled anxious faces were pressed against the diner window, watching and unbelieving as the fellow stretched out on the back of the flat-bed, and allowed her to tie him down.

"Lay still there, Bob. Remember how I get when I'm nervous."

With load straps from her tool box she tied one across his feet and another one across his belly, attaching the hooks in the edge of the truck bed. These were the same hooks that held her gasoline cans solidly in place.

She stretched another strap across his shoulders and pulled it tight. "Now, Bob, this here strap is stretched tight, and the hooks are a bit out of place. If you squirm about, the strap's likely to slide up and be across your neck. You don't want that."

She stared at the silent man for a long minute. "And now, just so's you'd know. I'm tyin' the other end'a your rope around my steerin' wheel to be handy. If you squirm yourself loose, you'll be drug along 'cause when this here truck gets to goin', I have a hard time a'gettin' it stopped. Understand?"

He nodded carefully. By now he understood and didn't want that strap across his neck.

Another single shot rang out over the mountain.

The fellows jerked their heads back in to the diner. "Another shot. She need help now?"

"We can watch if you need to…."

"She's fine. That shot was to tell me she's headin' over to the junction to dump the fellow off with Burley. He needs a little coolin' off spell in Burley's pokey."

The men watched the Ford flat-bed fire up, puff a bit of exhaust, and ease out onto Ridge Road.

One unbeliever turned to Keith. "You mean to say this here happens often."

"Pretty often. Often enough for us to develop a signal. She's got a fair amount of 22mm shells in the other side'a the shop. Saves time, and if there's only one fellow, she'd not likely need help. There's been a time or two I needed to signal. Got a couple'a bullets stuck in the wall over there."

The men waved their heads in unbelief, and returned to the domino game. Keith added, "When you got a business a'goin' and a purtty girl next door, you got'a be careful."

Paul Manford came through the door and tossed a letter across the counter toward Keith. Something was up. Not that he was nosey about people's mail…fact was, he didn't care a wit. But he did care about people and he had delivered a letter to Burley that was addressed in the same school-girl printing. It had said,

For Mr. Burley Lawman, Burnt Tree Junction, Rte 62,
Ridge Road, Arkansas.

Crazy looking address.
Then here was one for Keith in the same writing, addressed to:

Mr. Keith at the Soup Bowl Diner, Rte 62,
Ridge Road, Arkansas.

Whatever was written in them must be very important and it's a wonder it got here. Should have had "Eureka Springs" in the address.

Well, anyway, they got here and he got them to the right persons. That was all that was any of his business.

"Got any beans left, Sullivan? Pass me the chile peppers and a cup'a that stuff you call coffee. Scoop me up a hunk'a that cake, too, will you?"

THE LETTERS

While postman, Paul Manford, consumed his chile and cake, Keith looked at the address on the letter in puzzlement, but also apprehension. Couldn't be anything but bad. It was several hours before he could actually open it. But finally:

Dear Mr. Keith,

I am writing this to warn you of something that is going to happen. The man who beat me up and turned me out is going to do something with Jackie. I am hearing that he plans to grab him and hold him until he gets money from you to get him back. Then he is going to kill him and leave the county so the law can't catch him. I have heard that you are keeping him, and that is what I hoped for. I know this man but I do not know what name he will be using. He will wait for a good time to do it and it maybe will be a month, or more. When he is determined to do something he does it. Will you be really careful with Jackie so he does not grab him? I know I am nothing but Jackie can be something if he gets to stay with you. I love him very much. Please be careful until the man is caught. Margie.

Down the road short way, Deputy Burley Collins opened the letter with the strange address. Precisely printed letters like a third grader. It read:

Dear Mr. Lawman,

I am writing you so you will know that something is going to happen to the little boy Jackie that lives with Mr. Keith at the Soup Bowl Diner. I have heard that the man who beat me and threw me out is planning to grab Jackie and carry him off so he can collect money from Mr. Keith. He isn't going to give him back when he gets the money. He is going to kill him so he will not be recognized and then he is going to leave the county so the law can not find him. I don't know when this will happen but I believe it will because of how I found out. There are some folks who wanted to help me and they couldn't go to Mr. Keith because he might not believe them. I don't know what name the man will be using. Likely it will be one I have not heard and it may be a month or more before he does it. but I really believe he will. I know Mr. Keith will need your help when it happens, so I wanted to let you know. Please help. Jackie's mother.

The deputy returned the letter to its envelope and tucked it into his pocket. This was going to take a bit of thinking and planning, and certainly a trip to the diner. A cup of steaming hot coffee anytime of the day was one thing the roadside stand did not offer.

Bartley Wilcox also had some thinking to do, as well as a few other things. One of those things was to stop over at the Soup Bowl Diner for a sandwich. He had heard that they were quite tasty and worth the money.

The thing was, he was a thrifty Scotsman, and he lived just a bit down the road and a ways up King's River. Just trot along home and there was food aplenty. His Louisa was a first class cook. But, face it, he had to get a picture of what was going on and what he could do about it.

So he saddled up his trusty stallion, Pistol, and he and his four-legged buddy would trot on up the hill to the Junction. He'd passed it many times, but never felt the need to stop…or even give it a second look other than marvel at the small businesses that had sprung up along Ridge Road.

So he passed it again, and noted the fix-it shop. Not that he'd ever felt the need to drive one of those things that fed on gasoline instead of grass, but to do what he needed to do might involve more help than he had suspected. Anyway, he needed to check out the immediate neighborhood, including Lawman Burley.

He urged Pistol into a canter and passed by the EAT AND GET GAS, allowing himself the customary chuckle at the choice of a sign. There were a couple of horses tied in front of the Soup Bowl Diner, indicating customers at the counter.

Next door was the fix-it shop with the light blue Ford truck parked on the wooden platform generally used to repair automobiles. Was the Ford ailing? Seemed so, but it was in good hands. Everyone seemed to agree on that. He passed on by and proceeded for a mile before turning around.

When he again reached the fix-it shop, he saw a lanky redhead in an attractive, full-skirted dress with a pail of what seemed to be soapy water. One hand held the sponge and the Ford's hood and fenders were getting a bath. Intrigued by something he could not yet define, he slowed down a bit to admire the scenery. He'd heard, on the mountain grapevine telephone, that at least two young sprouts who overstepped their appreciation of Miss Leena took a ride over to the lawman for a lecture on how to treat a lady… regardless of how she looked or what she did for a living.

Rather amusing, but he'd never find himself in that position. His Louisa wouldn't stand for it. Little did he know how wrong he was.

Also, on down King's river from Bartley was a fellow named Robert LePrey. His ma, with French ancestry, chose the name "Robert" for her son, and insisted on the French pronunciation of "Row-Baer," accent of the "Baer." When the lad entered school, he fell heir to the English pronunciation. At Ma's insistence, the teacher attempted and the fellows at the school tried for "Robber" but finally settled on "Bear."

The lad, who was tall for his age and who had a build that created thicker shoulders, was finally happy with his name. So Bear it became and it stuck to him on into his adult life.

Bear LePrey, being strong and ambitious, went to the mountains as a logger, a job for which he was highly talented. His strength made him valuable on the ax to bring down the trees and also in dragging them down to the river where they were collected and used for cabins or tied together and sent down the river for another customer. Log cabins had everything going for them... inexpensive to put up, warm in the winter, cooler in the summer and, if oiled every few years, could last three lifetimes.

Having no place to spend his earnings, Bear accumulated a rather large fund. Then one day he realized he was logging his life away, so he took his earnings and left the mountain. He'd have a little fun before he got too old, and his fun centered around anything that wore a skirt.

It was said by neighbors, if a goat could get into a dress, Bear LePrey would be lining up to buy it hay. The objects of his attention were not always agreeable, but mostly were convinced by the baubles and attire he could afford to buy. It did not occur to him that money really does not last forever.

Inside the diner Keith Sullivan watched through the window which he kept sparkling clean. He had a very good reason for watching for anyone he didn't know.

On the mountain communities like those along Ridge Road, a person was often more known by the horse he rode than on how his face looked. Keith had seen the black stallion go by at a canter, and remembered seeing it once or twice before, but not often. He had no knowledge of who the rider was, but when the animal came back by after the space of a half an hour, red flags flew up in Keith's head.

Would that be the kidnapper who was scouting the place with plans to grab his little Jackie, who played on the floor with toy animals ordered from Wards catalog? Lying on the floor beside him was the half-grown bloodhound pup. When the pup first arrived as a gift from the breeder, she was admired for her ears, already beginning their length. For a few days she remained nameless. The four-year-old wanted the exact right name and it hadn't occurred to him yet.

"Aunt" Leena was stooped down beside Jackie stroking the long ears of the pup, and she commented, "So silky! Her ears are just like silk!" Jacky had never heard the word but he loved new, pleasant-sounding words, and "silky" fit the bill.

He turned his coal black eyes toward his "aunt" and exclaimed, "That's her name, Silky."

"Surely, now, Jackie. You don't really want her named Silky, when she is going to grow up to be a really big dog."

The four-year-old looked sternly at Leena. "Her name is SILKY!"

So that settled it. Silky it was and it was not much worse than what they called the bloodhound that belonged to Miss Annie at the roadside stand. "Ugly Face" was there to be her bodyguard, but so often she was pulled by the lawman for duty to track down a criminal.

The boy and the dog were fast friends, once she got past the puddle-on-the-floor stage. And Keith glanced down at the boy and the dog on the floor where so much time was spent. The boy needed to be able to play outside, but Keith couldn't bear it unless he or Leena was there with him. There was the kidnapper, for goodness sake! And who knew when he would strike.

Deputy Burley had come over a time or two and waited until there were no customers. This thing with the kidnapper qualified as a legitimate threat, and he and Keith would need to compare notes on strangers hanging around. And Keith was in a better position to do so.

This time the black stallion trotted on by with the rider's head hardly turned toward the diner. Just an innocent stranger, but why would he pass by and return so soon? Forgot something? Or casing the place for the best plan? It was very worrisome. Margie had indicated he might not be recognized.

Well, he'd remember the fine-looking stallion the next time he came by, unless he was somewhere else in the diner or concentrating on the cooking. Indeed, it was very worrisome.

Bradley Wilcox trotted on by the windows and disappeared. Keith went onto other things. Running a successful business took attention, and in his case, attention to the customers. If the place and the food was not pleasant, they might not come back. Repeats were the mainstay of the business, like the three old gentlemen, the postman, Grady O'Keef with his grader, and a few others.

Bradley Wilcox had a head full of thoughts. Jackie's mom, Margie, (though that was not her real name) had assigned him as a watchman over the son she had to loose. She'd wisely informed him of her new address in the distant town, but did not leave her son without on-sight watchfulness. Who better than a cousin to be assigned that duty?

Rather like baby Moses who was placed in the river. His mom could not stay and watch what happened with his, but his big sister, Miriam, was an able guard, and enabled Moses' mom to be the one to rear him.

Bradley had been two grades ahead of "Margie" and was assigned to "watch out for" her. He was laughed at and made fun of because he could not stay and play after school. He must see that his cousin got home safely. That worked well until Bradley was pulled from school to help out in the fields when he completed the sixth grade, and that left fourth grade Margie with no protector. It was her misfortunate to have been born beautiful, and at an early age attracted male attention. At first it was flattering, and then it was frightening. She'd have to get smart really fast, but it was hard to do.

Bradley thought and thought about the current assignment. He really needed to talk with the lawman, but he must be very secretive. He must not be connected in any way with Keith, Jackie or Deputy Collins. Neighbors were very smart about adding two and two and getting a variety of answers. Also questions. Like what in the world was Bradley doing with the lawman? Coming to see him in the dark of the night might be an answer, but he had a family to take care of and work of his own to do. *Keep thinking, Brad,* he told himself.

Then when he had almost reached King's River and prepared to turn north, the idea hit him. It was so funny and so workable that he roared with laughter, making Pistol slow down and turn his head around to see what was going on.

What he thought of would require the help of Miss Leena and the blue truck. He'd have to give it a lot of thought and work out the fine points, but he was good at that. He'd do it! Absolutely, he'd do it!

JOANN KLUSMEYER

BRADLEY WILCOX

Margie had been a pretty baby and got prettier as time went on. It was a family concern and that was why Cousin Brad was assigned as watchman, but as Margie finished school it became from hard to impossible to keep up with her. Her beautiful innocent face was a fatal attraction, and the rascals of the area found her the way a dog wolf finds a mate.

It became a mark of social success to have taken Margie on a walk without a brother or cousin following. And a walk with Margie should end up with some kind of sparkling, dangling object for her as a gift.

And Bear could afford objects, at least at first, but Margie was hesitant to be seen with him. Partly her family warnings, and partly her own survival instinct made it difficult for the huge French man.

Things got a little bit easier, but it was all because of another young man who lived farther upstream. Tommy was what would have been called a real looker, with a rugged jaw line and the beginnings of a handsome nose. Being with Tommy, even without shiny gewgaws that he could not afford to give, was possible because he was so good to look at…and the other girls thought so as well. A social plum, so to speak.

This went on for a while, and then she became strangely reticent. She stayed at home and tried her hand at cooking. It was a puzzle to the family until her figure began to become rounder and rounder.

"But, Mama, we was just goin' for a walk. I didn't know what Tommy was thinkin' a'doin'. Then when I said, 'No, Tommy,' he didn't believe me."

Then the word had gotten around with the other fellows, and they didn't believe her either. Who knew who the papa was, for sure, but she hoped Jackie's papa was Tommy, the beautiful.

Bear LePrey wasn't blind. He'd just wait it out and her folks'd be throwin' her out. That's when he'd be right there to catch 'er. At least that was what he told himself.

But the family didn't throw her out and in time there was a fine-looking baby boy. Margie named him Jackie. That's when the shiny, sparkling gifts began to come. And Bear wanted nothing but

51

to sit in the porch swing and talk with her. He seemed to have an unending supply of money, and he was going to put up a cabin on his papa's land. He'd like nothing better than to make a home for Margie and the little boy.

So he moved her in, and there wasn't any preacher close, but what did that matter. Margie was not a talented cook, and the other drudge work of a mountain woman did not appeal to her, so Bear decided to beat some sense into her. It wasn't easy and it took a lot of beatings.

She stood it for almost two years before she developed the escape plan. Bear kept such a close watch on her activities that she was just about smothered, but cousin Bartley was considered safe. Maybe he'd be able to talk some sense into her…maybe show her a way out. Money was getting a bit tight in the LePrey cabin, and that made tempers burst into flame more often.

When little Jackie went crying to his ma when Bear had Ma crying, that did it. Cousin Bartley was going to help her find a way out so Bear, who couldn't yet locate a preacher, couldn't find her, beat her, and bring her back. She couldn't even go home to Papa. Papa had promised to shoot to kill if he ever got Bear in his gunsights, and if that happened, Papa would go to the jail over in Eureka Springs. Papa shouldn't have to pay for what was her fault.

So she and Cousin Bartley thought and thought. She obviously couldn't take Jackie with her, and if she left him with Ma and Papa, Bear would cause trouble.

So the brain of the two of them landed on Keith, the upstanding owner of his own business and not hampered by his own family. If they could find a way to leave him there, Keith would either find a home for him, take him to the Boys' Home over in Berryville, or keep him. They both hoped Keith would keep him, but Margie must go far away and go fast.

About three, turned out to be a bit longer, days at the Soup Bowl would do it, and then Bradley would come by and wait in the dark woods until she had a chance to slip out. He had a horse ready for her, and they would be at Wishbone by morning. They'd rest a day, and head on over to Eureka Springs where there was a good north/south railway.

With the money she took from Keith's cash register, she could buy a ticket, and go south. Alone, she'd be able to find something to get by on. And it'd worked, but this this other thing came up.

Bear ran out of money and he found out where Jackie was. He was so mad, he announced to the world and everybody what his plans were. He'd get a lot of money from the rich fellow who obviously liked the kid, but then he couldn't let the kid live because he knew Bear quite well. He would remember the beatings, and by now he could talk. Too bad! He'd have to die, and there were miles and miles of woodland in which to leave him, and the animals would take care of the burial. Good plan. The thing was, Bradley heard about it as did Margie's whole family, but Bradley was the only person who knew where she was.

She could only communicate with him through "pick up" service that the country post offices had. Address the letter to the post office, and they would hold it until someone asked for it. It might lay there a week or two as Bradley could not make the trip every day.

So that is how he knew that Bear was going to try to kidnap Jackie, and Margie did not know what name Bear would be using while he scouted out a way to do what he wanted to do. In addition to height and hulky shoulders, he had brains. The trouble was that he didn't often use them, so they were in good shape to plan the heist of the kid.

Now was the time for Bradley, who actually had other things to do than protecting a cousin, to get his plan in first class order and decide on a way when he could carry it out.

This was a day that yet another prospective renter came, wanting to look at the place for rent. Keith took a look skyward as though seeking help from above. He was TIRED of milking those goats, and daily he threatened to turn them into chile stew. Good thing he didn't.

The prospective tenants were an older lady, a younger lady and a pair of children. Leena groaned to herself, as there did not seem to be a man to shoulder the cost of the rental. But it had been over a month, and everyone she showed it to, just loved the house, the cellar and the barn, but they did not like being off Ridge Road.

Leena did, however, agree to show the house, yet again. Luck was with them. It was perfect for them, and did she say there was a large cellar? Wonderful! They really needed a large cellar.

Leena asked, "Your husband. Will he be movin' in with you?"

"Oh, no, Sweetie. He had a tiff with a lawman who laid 'im out. We put 'im in the ground nigh onto nine years ago."

Leena nodded companionably. "And the children's papa?"

The older lady was quick with the answer. "Nope. Son took after father and it got 'im twenty to life. Nope, we take care'a ourselves." And before Leena could ask another question, the lady continued, "You was a'sayin' there was goats to come with it?"

"…uh, yes, but we can do somethin' with 'em if they get in the way." The thought ran through her head at what Keith would like to do with them…and he didn't even need the meat.

"Oh, no. Them goats was part'a why we wanted here. 'Course, bein' off the road is good, too. I don't like the dust a'flyin' around the cheese makin'."

"Cheese making?"

"Sure enough. We'll likely have to pick up a couple more goats, to make sure we got some a'milkin' all the time. We make the cheese every day, and store it to ripen in the cellar. Where we was livin' it was a good setup, but way back in the woods and hard to get down to Wishbone. On top'a that, the people's kid wanted the house."

"What kind of cheese do you make?"

The younger woman decided to talk. "The real name is feta, but there's them that call it goat cheese. We sell it down in Wishbone. We wrap it up in that shiny red paper and the summer people really like it. We needed the cellar to store it in, and we was hopin' for a place handy like this that didn't have a kid wantin' it. Movin' is hard work with all our equipment and no pay."

Long speech, and then she had to run after a small boy who was getting close to the well.

Cheese wrapped in red paper. Sold in Wishbone. "You know, Miss, what is your name?"

"I'm Elsie and that's Martha with the youngens. She's my daughter-in-law."

"Well, Miss Elsie, I think I may know about your cheese. We buy it a lot in a round pattie, with smooth red paper around it. I just love it."

At this point, she might have offered to pay Miss Elsie to take the house, but Miss Elsie was ready. "Miss Sullivan, we'd like to move in right now. I got your $7.00 for the first month, and when we get goin' anytime you want cheese, you just come on down here and eat all you want. It's like my Martha said, movin' is hard work and we don't want to do it again. Later on, we might ask if we can buy this place."

Leena nodded. The deal was set, and if Keith had his way, he'd set a price and sell it right now. Or maybe give it away.

And now the Sullivans had new neighbors.

GOAT CHEESE

Leena left the new tenants to their own devices and hiked back up the hill, hoping this would be the last trip for a while unless she was carrying a few pounds of cheese.

At the top of the hill a grinding sound caught her attention. Looking to the west she saw Grady just topping the hill. How about that! She was looking for a break…but what was that following him? He had been using two mule teams to give one a rest, also to double up on the steep hills. But Ridge Road was level at the top. What was that team of mules behind him pulling.

Something black. Small. Pretty light, the mules were not straining at all. Oh, for goodness sake! She recognized the black top of Sharon's car.

Grady was grinning fit to split his face when he stopped. He guided the other team of mules on up into the yard, and Leena cleared the wooden platform for her.

"Don't' need that," Grady told her. "This lady just forgot that cars don't eat grass. I came onto her a couple'a miles back, gas tank dry as a desert."

Sharon, who had rode in the car to steer it, stepped out smiling in a bit of embarrassment. "Forgot to fill the tank in Wishbone."

"No problem. A lot of my best customers forget to fill their tank. I'll bring you a can."

Grady took it from her hand and filled the tank of the little black car. A pull on the choke and a turn of the key and the trusty little motor roared into life. "Now, Sharon, remember this. Cars do not eat grass, and this is what happens when a car is hungry. It stops. Speaking of hungry, I'm going to the diner."

Seated around the little table, Leena broke the good news to Keith.

"Guess what? No more milkin' goats for you, brother. It's rented and I got the rent money right here." She handed over the coins and took a bite of pie. Spicy apple with a flakey crust. Perfect. Keith was good with pies.

"Not only that," she continued. "Our tenants are the people who make those cheeses wrapped in red paper down in Wishbone."

Sharon nodded, "And you could sell toasted cheese biscuits made with that cheese. My mom makes them with leftover biscuits. I'd bet your customers would like 'em."

Keith glanced out the window. No black horse going by today. Jackie was still on the porch with the dog. Keith had thought of actually tying him to the door knob on a leash, or something, so he wouldn't forget and wander off. But how could he really do that? Tying him up...like an animal? The neighbors would likely have him drawn and quartered for child cruelty. He'd be better off to wish Silky was older and knew she was supposed to protect him.

But it was like someone said, "If wishes were horses, then beggars could ride."

Jackie decided to come in, the floppy eared dog trailing after him.

"Papa?"

"Yes, Son?"

"There's a old bigger worm outside."

"Bigger worm? Worms won't hurt you. Just leave the worm alone and go away."

"The worm wanted to play with me. I left him and he came over to me."

"The worm came after you?"

"The old bigger worm. He came to me and I came in the house."

56

"Son, listen to me. How big is the bigger worm."

At last the boy had Keith's attention. He spread his four-year-old arms just about as far as they could reach. "He was this big!"

"Surely not! Worms don't usually grow that big before the birds eat them."

"I'll show you. Come see."

Keith decided it was a good idea to look at this enormous worm. The centipedes in the Arkansas wood and could get rather big, often as long as a forearm. Jackie didn't need to be stung by one of them.

"Jackie, was the worm orange...with a lot of legs?"

The serious, little face went back and forth in a pronounced "no." "He was the color of a stick. No legs at all."

That was it. Keith excused himself from the lone coffee drinker and went out. He followed the child to a bare spot where he had been playing with sticks and little rocks. "There!" said the confident little voice. "And there he is, waitin' for me to come out to play."

Keith drew in a horrified breath as he gazed on body of a snake. Just a harmless garden snake, but it might have been a rattler. He stepped back, in a moment of indecision, and the bloodhound pup, Silky, stepped forward to sniff.

Hmmm, good time to make an example of this snake. He stepped over to the garden fence and picked up the hoe. With a well-placed whack, he severed the head of the reptile. The headless body writhed and twisted and Silky's inherited urges came forward.

She rushed toward the writing reptile and snapped at the twisting body, shaking it furiously, and then jumping back. She stared at the results of her efforts, and the writhing had died down a bit. After a moment of what appeared to be contemplation, she attacked again with another vicious shake.

If Keith had been offered a present of a new suit...a new cook stove...or even a car of his own, he would not have been more pleased. He had been concerned about his inability to train the dog to do what she was born to do, but just look at that dying snake! It was just a harmless rat snake, and would only need to have been chased away if it had not been for Jackie looking on. The boy must be instructed on the difference between snakes and worms, but Silky deserved a reward.

"Jackie, come in the house and bring Silky. She deserves a present."

And to the dog he said, "Good dog! Good dog! Come Silky." And he patted the velvet head. Boy and dog trotted after him back into the house and on into the diner.

Keith reached into the pantry and scooped up a small handful of ground meat and put in it her dish. Silky looked at the meat and then at Keith, and back at the dish. Keith encouraged, "Good dog!" and with his toe he nudged the dish closer.

Silky seemed to understand, and the meat was gone in one swoop of the sizeable tongue.

Keith reached into the pot where he was preparing vegetable soup, and forked out a meaty bone. "Here, Jackie, take this outside for Silky, and stay with her for a while. But don't bother with worms and snakes until I have time to tell you about them. OK?"

With a pleased grin, the boy disappeared with the dog!

Keith's lone coffee drinker had been interested in the interchange, so he explained, "The pup thinks she killed a rat snake, and I rewarded her. Next time it might be a rattler." Then he admitted, "I was surprised that she did it. She's just a pup."

The traveler drained his coffee mug and stood, "Well, I know about bloodhounds, and she was just doing what she was meant to do. You have a good dog there."

Keith continued with the soup to have it ready for the lunch diners. There'd likely be ten or twelve persons who wanted a bowl of vegetable soup, rich with beef broth, at the giveaway price of five cents. He didn't make much on the soup, but diners often wanted pie or cake afterward.

When you have a business, you have to notice those things. And every so often there comes a customer who leaves you the gift of advice. Such as the one today.

As the man closed the door behind him, Keith called out, "Come back, sir."

And then he turned his mind to the boy and the dog. And Burley Collins. He nodded with the decision in his mind. "I'm going to have to find a way to train that dog. Ain't no way I can afford to look after the boy every minute, and he's got no ma. It's somethin' I got'a do."

It was a week later than Leena came in bearing a red-wrapped package about the size of a half a dozen saucers stacked together. Cheese. The fancy kind they sometimes indulged in from Wishbone. He recognized the wrapping.

Leena was full of excited smiles. "I got an idea from what Sharon said. Our new renters say they'll sell us cheese for half price if I come and get it. I looked at it and I think it'll fill about ten biscuits. It could make a new item, if they aren't too much trouble to make."

Keith sighed loudly, but nodded. Yes, he'd thought about it, but one of the hardest things about a tiny diner was holding down the menu size. He knew of the delicious things he could make, but the walk-on trade just would not support them.

However….

"Let's try it. Things are quiet right now and I have six biscuits left over from yesterday. I can find something else for the dog."

His sister nodded. "OK. First we slice the biscuits open. How much cheese do you think?"

He thought. "Maybe a quarter of an inch. It's pretty rich and any more might be too much and ooze out. But you can't put cheese side down on the grill. Too hard to clean off."

"Hmmm, how about a skillet with a lid, and heat the biscuits before putting in the cheese."

"Yeah, the big iron skillet, and just leave the biscuits there until we need one, and then grill the sandwich on both sides of the outside of the biscuit."

"Let's try it." The huge, family-sized skillet was heated and slid to the back of the stove to keep warm. Four sliced biscuits were put into be warmed. When toasty and softened, a biscuit-sized slice of cheese was added, and they were put on the grill.

Two pairs of interested eyes watched and steam and smoke arose. Dribbles of cheese peeked out around the edges. Maybe too much cheese. But the dribbles did not reach the smoking grill.

Time for samples. Too hot! Ouch! Melting cheese fights back!

At that moment Sharon walked through the door. "Cheese biscuits!" she announced. "I'd know the smell anywhere."

"Well, pull up a stool and have one."

She ate the entire biscuit without words, while Keith and Leena nibbled and eagerly waited for a verdict.

She wiped the last crumbs from her face and announced. "I think you got a winner, here, if you can figger how to make a profit on it."

"Does it taste like the ones your mom makes?"

"No, she makes them in the oven, but these are better. The cheese doesn't burn. Could you make a profit on five cents each?"

Leena shrugged and turned to Keith. He nodded. "Sure could. Maybe give a few away as free samples. Maybe to Grady, Paul, and maybe the domino players. I wonder what these things are like when they get cold."

Sharon shook her head. "Don't look at me! None have a chance to get cold with my papa at the table."

"All right. There's one left. We can try."

"How about, if it works after it gets cold, folks might take one or two with them for a lunch, later." Sharon started to pour herself a mug of coffee, but dumped it instead and started over. That was the problem with selling coffee...keeping it fresh...but fresh coffee had to stay on the menu even as a loss. No question one way or the other.

It was as Sharon and Leena were preparing to leave the diner that the black stallion passed by on a brisk canter as if on a business errand. And then he came back. He tied the stallion near the road and strode briskly toward the diner. Stepping inside, he handed an envelope to Keith explaining, "Note for the lady. I can't be seen with her. Read it and give it to your sister. In private."

Before Keith could respond, he was out the door and leaping aboard the horse. He would have been too far away for Keith to hear him when he said, "Come on, Pistol, we got'a get out of here."

With a full gallop, the horse and rider were out of sight.

With a hesitation born of apprehension, Keith slowly withdrew the paper from the envelope and read it.

THE REQUEST

He unfolded the paper and read.

Miss Sullivan, I have a strange request to ask of you. I must pretend to be someone I am not, in order to help save little Jackie. You will understand when I explain. When my ma explained Ecclesiastes 10:20, to me, she said that I must never think I was not overheard when I told something secret, or that I might be repeated and often falsely. I think that might be the start of the sayings around here, that "the walls have ears" and "a little birdie told me."

The fact is, I cannot be seen with you except if you do this to me.

I am aware, as everyone else is, that you have a way of handling fellows who get fresh with you, and that that you haul them over to the deputy.

I need to talk with the deputy about my part in saving Jackie, but I must not be seen talking with him as a friend, but only as a prisoner. This is because of safety to my family and the fact that person who wants to kidnap Jackie lives somewhat close geographically. I know the person you know as Margie, and I know she wrote to you and to the deputy.

In order for me to talk with the deputy, I must appear to have been hauled in for reasons of being fresh with you, and you must tie me to the back of the truck so I can be seen to be at the deputy's house against my will. I will be hoping that someone sees me being hauled in for a lecture on how to treat a lady.

I care a lot about Margie and Jackie, and there'd be no way to know who his pa is, and whoever it is, he does not want it known. But I do know that the kidnapper, who may appear under any name, is not the pa.

So I might leave my horse, that is well known in my neighborhood, tied close by and in sight. There may be other ways to get this done, but I really must talk with the deputy.

I would like to have stopped in at the diner and got a peek at Jackie, but that would be unwise until this person is taken away. Jackie knows me too well.

The rider of Pistol, the coal black stallion.

Keith read the note twice, re-folded it and returned it to the envelope, which he put in a pocket. It was a very important document, and, somehow, he believed it.

Keith asked, "Leena, could you grab that Bible over there and see what it says? Ecclesiastics 10:20."

Leena read: "Curse not the king, no, not in thy thought; and curse not the rich in thy bedchamber: for a bird of the air shall carry the voice and that which hath wings shall tell the matter."

They nodded to each other. That was about what they figured it said.

The folks now say "the walls have ears." And it seems King Soloman agreed with them.

And it was true about Leena and the blue truck. She'd made no secret of her method of disposing of unwanted attention onto Deputy Collins for a lecture on how to treat a lady.

Jackie took Leena by the hand and insisted, firmly, that she come outside and see the snake worm that Silky killed. Silky tried to process all that happened, and she might not have known the seriousness of the lesson, but she positively knew that she done the right thing with that strange creature.

She also knew, in her thoroughbred mind, that what she did was for the small human, and was approved of by the large humans. She felt the intense satisfaction of a creature who realized it could do what it was born to do. She moved closer to the boy and pressed her large head against his hand, and the small hand moved to her head and silky ears. She could still taste the raw meat that had been her reward.

The girl and the boy returned to the house and he gathered his wooden animals and the blocks he used for fences. He could invent innumerable games with them. Keith, when he had time, enjoyed watching him place the painted, wooden animals in positions and talk to them…and also explain to them why he did what he did. The way Papa explained things to him.

That boy needed something else to play with. His own toys had been long gone, so Keith must get himself to the Wards Catalog and see what they had. He needed something he could create with. Something that took more of his mind. And he needed a wagon. Maybe for Christmas, but he needed something sooner.

Maybe a new story book to be read to. Maybe…well, he could talk with the deputy's wife. Annie Jo seemed to have the answers to a lot of questions. Maybe tomorrow when Leena could sit in at the diner.

While down the lane to the renthouse, activity was going full blast. Two more goats had made their ba-a-a-ing way past the house, urged onward by the daughter-in-law. These two ladies were hard rock serious. They were setting up a business they knew well, and if things worked out as they hoped, it could become theirs, "lock, stock and barrel," as the old saying went.

They had made shelves for the cellar, and even spoke of digging another one, if she, Leena, had no objection. Keith agreed, stating if he had a minute to spare, he'd help dig.

Keith made a little "granny sign" for the counter stating a new item was being tested. Biscuit toasted with feta cheese. Maybe good when cold for lunches.

Leena, who had never seen the "coal black stallion," waited for someone to come to be hauled into the deputy. Didn't happen right off, and all the time the operators of EAR AND GET GAS were on edge.

And there was Silky. In her young head, she knew she did the right thing. She had been feeling, for some days, that there was something she should do, but that maybe she was already doing it because the humans treated her well. She stayed close to the smaller human, as the others seemed so active, and how could she stay with both of them? These thoughts were not active and thought-out, but more of a deep, mild unrest…watching for a reason for the unrest.

But now she knew. There was a job for her, being born a working dog, and her job must be with the small human and against the creature with no legs. She felt that the creature was dangerous, and that she should watch for her own safety. Nip, shake and fall back. Take a new grip and shake again. It felt good, and she had been given the tasty reward.

Perhaps this was not all she should do, but it was a start and she would watch for another opportunity.

Grady thought about the new, gasoline powered graders that did not need mules. So far they had been available only on short runs that kept them close to repair facilities. A road grader was a hard working piece of machinery.

His route, being one half of the Ridge Road extending from Eureka Springs to Kings River that split the county, was one he had wanted and he had wanted it particularly because of Leena. This way he got to pass the TIN-LIZZY FIXIT every week or so, and it was important that he remained in her mind. And he didn't intend to do this forever. The money was good…it had to be because the living conditions were deplorable.

Eating cold food, sleeping wherever night time caught him. Each time he thought of asking or a change, he remembered why he wanted it in the first place. There were a lot of girls in the world, and a number of them were attracted to him. Maybe it was because they knew his job paid well, and that he had no time or place to spend the money.

He, also, had no time to properly court a girl in the way most of the girls expected to be courted. There were some that would see that he had placed himself between the skillet and the stove, and that a job like his should be done by some old codger who had nothing else to live for.

Not as a paying job for a young man.

But he had never been seriously attracted to one girl other than Leena, whose head he had looked around to see the black board. For one whole school year he sat there and considered himself lucky. He told himself that he was acquainted with every hair on her head. Keith made a good friend, but Grady fully intended to make him a brother-in-law.

Meanwhile, he ground his way up and down Ridge Road and cared for two pairs of grey mules. One thing about the job, though, was that it gave him a lot of time to think.

There had to be a way out of the rut he was in. Up and down the road, getting absolutely nowhere. Always repairing what travelers and the weather did to the Arkansas soil, adjusting the blade to draw back into the road the gravel that made the road travelable in the November rains. And all of that wouldn't be so bad, if he just had a place to live.

It was very important job, and it was one he wanted and not only because of the girl. The four animals, a pair in front and a pair following behind were the engine of his life, propelling him along almost like a part of his family. Unbelievable, actually.

Even for a fellow with no living parents, the mules made a poor substitute, but nevertheless....

And life went on, so to speak.

BEAR'S DILEMMA

Bear LePrey had a lot on his mind. Felling trees on the mountain with a lot of men had its pluses, but he was now twenty-five years old and that seemed to be some sort of a sign post...a time to take stock of what he had and didn't have, what he wanted and how could he go about getting it.

It had occurred to him several times since Jackie's mom had peeled out in the middle of the night, that surely she...or the boy... should be made to pay. He couldn't find the mom, and that was not for want of trying, so it seemed it had to be the son. Something must be made to give back the cost of what she, and others like her, had extracted from him in disappointments and aggravations.

There was the mountain lumber-jacking that should be an answer. Joining a crew of lumber-jacks and working there for a couple of years would furnish a sizeable nest egg. He was no dummy. He could add up a few figures, but he just couldn't set his mind to going back to the mountain, and be away from girls for that length of time. One didn't get ahead by going backward.

So grabbing the boy was the next most palatable plan. He had nothing against the kid…rather cute, actually…but Jackie was not his and the kid's next best use would be a as lever to get money.

The dummy who operated a diner (for goodness' sake!) over on Ridge Road seemed to have fallen for the kid, so how much would he pay to keep him? Ridge Road west had not in his preferred location. He would rather go east to Berryville, so he was not personally acquainted with the diner.

And of course there was that other thing. The Deputy Constable lived up on the bluff that overlook Blue Lake, and he was not to be toyed with. That star on his chest gave him the right to track down anyone he thought was breaking, or even bending, any law. Had his own temporary jail, Bear had heard. Right there on the mountain bluff. So that had to be figured into any plan Bear came up with.

Too bad the kid wasn't still a baby because then he might not have to kill him, but a four year old…and at that age a little boy would remember him…especially as he had lived in the house with when he was two and almost three. So the kid would have to go, and Bear was against killing, unless it was someone who stood between him and what he wanted. There should be no one left alive to recognize him.

Now only one problem existed. How was he to get the money without being seen, but, as he was no dummy, he just had to plan it out. There would be a way, it just took a little time, and time was what he had.

There was that old way. He could demand that the money be left in a rotten stump, of which the Arkansas woodland had a'plenty. But no, there'd be someone watching. He had to do better than that. Days passed.

Keith needed to make a trip to see the deputy, and he had an additional reason to go. There was Annie Jo, the wife of the deputy, and she had access to the latest Montgomery Wards Catalog. Jackie needed some new toys, and Annie was so helpful. Anyway, that was a place to start.

He was lucky…he caught the deputy at home. Not only at home, but sitting in the shade by the roadside stand, enjoying a glass of cool apple cider. Keith joined him, and Annie brought another glass of cider.

"Burley, I'm sorry to put this on you, but it seems others did it for me. This thing about my little boy is just about to get me down. I watch everyone that goes by the window of the diner, though I don't know why. I wouldn't know him if I saw him. And I keep thinking and thinking on how the kidnapper could to it, but there's just too many ways.

"I know a fellow that knows more is going to see you. Leena brought you the letter he wrote to us. I don't know him, except for his black stallion, but he seems to be contact with Jackie's mother. This here problem has just too many sides to it for me to get a hold on it."

The deputy listened and nodded, then said, "All problems have too many sides. Every lawbreaker has his own set of sides, and they're all different. We just have to play this by ear, and make sure someone is watching the boy all the time.

"I may know more when the black horse rider decides to create a scene for Leena to have to bring him in. Likely we'll get a physical description, because it seems the fellow knows 'im."

Keith sighed from frustration, and moved on to an easier subject. "I wanted to talk with your wife about toys. Jackie needs something more than a dog to play with, so maybe a book or two, and some toy that takes time and a bit of brain power to play with."

Annie, of course, heard every word, being close by in the stand. "Come on over here, Keith. I have exactly what you need."

He came, and looked at the picture in the catalog. It seemed to be a lot of little sticks in different lengths with notches in them.

She went on, "I know what you're thinkin'. Those sticks don't look like a thing folks'd buy, but those are perfect for little boys, and even my daughter likes them. They are called Lincoln Logs, after the president who was seemingly born in a log cabin. You can see they're notched just like real logs used to build houses. The lengths of the logs are different.

"There's a paper with some suggestions of things to be made, but Jackie'll have a hundred other ways to play with them. There's fences, towers even miniature furniture that can be made. I'd advise you to buy the largest set, or you'll have to reorder soon. If I had a little boy, I would order him two of the largest sets. Believe me, these are wonderful!

"And you mentioned books. Let me loan you a couple for you to see if he even likes books. Not yet five, as he is, and he may not be ready for words. But there's one thing I'm sure of. He'll love bein' read to out of them. The best place for books'd be the book store in Wishbone. They sort'a specialize in kid's books. Got everything there is to have! Even a really nice Bible story book with a lot of pictures."

So Keith went home with a pair of well-worn, well-read books. Goldilocks and The Three Bears and Little Red Riding Hood. Hmmm, well, he'd see how it went. But the logs, now, that was sure to be a real winner, and he did as she suggested and ordered two sets.

He also had a promise of the Christmas Toy Catalog that usually came in late August so toy orders would get there in time for Santa Claus to bring them.

He had another little chore to attend to while Leena was watching the diner. It was clearly time for Jackie to have his own room. There were plenty of rooms in the big house, and there was the small bed that Keith himself had used. It was full length, but narrow. It would fit well in the little room where his grandpa had spent his last days.

Jackie would be five in the fall, and that was the time that he could start to school. But Keith felt a prickle of fear roll down his back and up his arms. School! Imagine! And he would be away all day and not in Keith's protective care.

But then...he assured himself...the evil monster would be caught by that time and spending time behind bars. Either that, or buried. If Keith had his choice...but no, he mustn't think of that.

Jackie watched the big bed work its way down the stairs and into the little room where he kept his toys. The empty room, he had thought in his mind. If he was there, it wouldn't be empty. He liked the word, empty, the way he liked Silky, and a few others. Happy was a nice word, along with delicious, otherwise (other eyes!) and peanut butter. He loved words...some even better than others.

When the bed was placed by the window, and new sheets and quilts spread on it, he giggled, climbed on and stretched out. Silky watched, then stepped down to the foot of the bed and hoisted herself onto the quilt. No more sleeping on the floor beside the bed of her human. She could now be right at his feet, and she would know every move he made, and when he got up. Maybe this whole move was made so she could take better care of him. If that was so, she was quite appreciative.

Then Keith took over the diner and set Jackie on one of tall stools that he must not play on. He showed him a little book, a four-year-old sized book.

Jackie opened it up and saw the picture of bears. One, two, and three.

Two fingers on one hand and one on the other. That made three.

There were words, and Papa did not offer to read them. So Jackie would just have to insist. "Papa, what is the name of that word?" and his small finger was jabbed at the page just under the first word.

"That word is 'Once.' It means 'one time.'"

"What's the name on the next one?"

"That's 'upon' and it means 'on top of' or 'at the time of.' Understand?"

Jackie nodded hesitantly. He put up one hand with the fingers spread. "Five words. One for each finger."

Keith nodded. This was getting interesting. "All right, Jackie, it says 'Once upon a time there.' See, five words."

Jackie nodded. "Now another five."

Keith obediently read, "Once upon a time there lived three bears. They lived…."

Jackie closed the book with a decided pat, and slid down from the tall stool. As Keith watched, wondering, Jackie disappeared and called.

"Aunt Leena! Where are you?"

"I'm, here, Jackie."

Keith followed Jackie as he ran up to Leena, in her room. "Look what I have."

"Oh, you have a book! That's nice, Jackie."

"NO! It's not a book. I have words."

"You have…words…?"

"Yes. Listen." And he put the book on the side of her bed. Leaning down he opened the book to its first page. Jabbing his finger sharply at each word, he recited. "Once upon a time there were three bears. They lived…."

Aunt Leena was speechless, so he tried to help. "See, the three bears are right there. Lookie at the pa, the ma and the baby. That's what it says, 'Once upon a time there were three bears. They lived.'"

By now, Keith was standing behind him. Leena looked up and put her "shhh" finger to her lips. Pretending to be confused, she pointed to the word "time." "Can you tell me again what this word is?"

With remarkable patience, he explained. "That word's name is 'time.' That means 'when,' I think."

"And what's the name of this word?" She pointed to "They."

Jackie looked at his aunt and frowned, amazed that she didn't know. "That word says 'They.' I think that means all of them. All three of the bears."

Then his aunt made everything right. She scooped him up and into her laps and told him, "Jackie, I think you are a wonderful boy!"

Jackie knew what wonderful meant. Sometimes it meant cookies, but this time it meant kisses, which were almost as good.

Aunt Leena looked up at Keith. "Mister Sullivan, I think you have your work cut out for you, tryin' to stay ahead'a your kid!"

Keith read the story with Jackie pointing to each word. Ten words in a row were just about his limit of current memory, but he was fascinated with them all. He demanded that the whole book be read to him again, and when they came to "Goldilocks" he shouted it out before Keith had a chance to say it.

Well, that took care of that. There would very soon be a trip to Wishbone to visit the book store. It would be three weeks, likely, before the Lincoln Logs arrived.

THE CHEESE BISCUIT TEST

The three afternoon gentlemen darkened the door of the diner. Finding their table taken by a traveler idling over his coffee, they sat themselves on the stools at the counter. Reluctantly.

The first man picked up the "granny sign" and read about the cheese biscuits. "Make me up one'a them things. I'll test it out for ya."

As Keith lifted one to the warm biscuits onto the grill, the second fellow said, "Give me one'a them, too. Make it two, 'cause this other fellow'll here, he'll want one."

First man nibbled at the edge of the dripping cheese. "Tell you what, if you got'a a big bowl, put this in it and fill it up with vegetable soup."

Man number three commanded. "Make it two more."

So Keith lifted the three cheese biscuits into three bowls and filled the bowls with soup. The four of them watched as the broth, rich with beef and tomatoes, seeped into the soft biscuits, soaking them apart and allowing the cheese to melt and seep out, creating flat, golden bubbles on the surface of the vegetables.

Spoons were passed around, and man number one stated, "Just as I thought it would taste. My ma made this, but here cheese was different. This is better. She invented it so I wouldn't drip soup on my clean clothes."

While he spoke, a stream of broth spilled from the spoon onto the sleeve of his shirt. Oops!

Man number two commented, "She was not successful, was she?"

Man number one ignored this comment and spooned the steaming concoction into his mouth. Some comments do not deserve a response, and this one was summarily ignored.

Fortunately, the usurper at the table decided to leave in time for the three men to have their domino game. It would have been inconvenient for everyone if they had been forced to play their game on the counter.

Keith watched them and wondered, would that cheese biscuit deal work out with the chile beans? He had a sneaky idea that it would be tried.

But next there had be that trip to Wishbone that would produce an even dozen books similar to Goldilocks and the Three Bears. Also a small wagon, that he could pull inside the house.

There'd be a big one for outside, as soon as this kidnapping fiasco was over, and Jackie would be safe in the yard.

THE ARREST THAT WASN'T

It had been six painful weeks since the receipt of the note from black stallion rider, and Keith had watched daily. It even occurred to him that the "rider" might even be the kidnapper pretending to be a friend, but then here he came.

It had taken many a "heart to heart" talk with his Louise for Bartley to feel he could do what he had promised to do. He assured her that he was playing a part, and that she was the only woman in his life, and would always be. He told her that it was temporary, and he was telling her so that if word got back to her, she would know what was going on.

But that she could not say anything, at least not yet. The plan could give itself away. But when the kidnapper was caught and sent where he belonged, she could say all she wanted to say to everyone that she had known all along, and it was just to catch a lawbreaker. She could say that her Bartley was assisting the deputy over on the Ridge. That they would be safer, now, that a certain scum and been wiped out of Carroll County.

Or she could say anything she took a notion to say. He saw no other way to do what he knew he had to do.

He rode the stallion past the EAT AND GET GAS and turned around and came back. He guided the horse to a prominent place near the work platform. He strode into the TIN-LIZZY FIXIT shop and told the proprietress that now was the time, if she could manage it.

So after a reasonable length of time, he emerged with both hands tied behind him, and was frog-marched to the blue truck. He scooted up against the back window glass and sat quietly, as Leena attended to a great number of "little duties" inside the shop.

They mustn't rush through this, because it wouldn't hurt at all for someone to see it and send it along on the grapevine telephone. Leena took her time leading Pistol to the truck and tying his reins to her steering wheel. That way, if she moseyed along in third gear, the stallion could easily trot along beside.

In due time, she came out and fired up the truck's trusty little engine. She drove slowly back up the hill to the roadside stand, Pistol prancing proudly beside.

She pulled in at the roadside stand and announced her presence with the truck's musical horn, "Ooouaogaaah! Ooouaogaaah!"

Deputy Collins played his part, and ceremoniously marched Bartley Wilcox into the log pokey plainly visible in his yard.

The deputy waited until after dark to visit his jail cell.

Bartley greeted the deputy with an apology. "Sorry to do this to you, Deputy. I just couldn't think of no other way to talk with you without gettin' myself in trouble for seemin' to be on the side'a the law...which I am."

"Think nothin' of it, my friend. The star on my shirt gives you the right. So tell me about this person."

"Yes, sir. This is what I think. I think it'd be Bear LePrey that'd be tryin' to get even with Jackie's ma in the best way he can, and to get a little money to skip the county. I could be wrong, but the local grapevine is a'sayin' he's been strange, lately, and is for certain plannin' somethin'.

"He's a'thinkin' that somethin' that affects Jackie would affect her, cause the news'll get to her, somehow. The fact is, I'm the only person that knows where she is, and she won't even talk to her folks without me deliverin' to 'em by hand. I have to go to Eureka to hear from her, and it's startin' to be a bother, but I'd do it for Jackie.

"And I don't want nothin' to cost Keith Sullivan any money, after him a'takin' on the job'a raisin' that boy, the kid bein' my second cousin by rights. His ma is truly grateful for him doin' it, and I think she said somethin' like that in her note to him."

Deputy Collins listened without comment. "You're quite sure it is that person, Bear LePrey, that is plannin' this?"

"Yep. I'm believin' he's the only one with skin in the game. Other's are glad enough that Jackie's with Keith, at least the ones that know, and you know how words get around."

The Deputy nodded. "I know you mentioned he could be using any name, so could you give me a physical description of him?"

"That'd be easy. He's a big fellow, did a lot'a lunberjackin' up on the mountains. He's maybe a couple'a inches above you, and a lot thicker in the shoulders and arm muscles, he got that way a'swingin' an ax and forkin' logs around to get 'em in the river. When it comes to muscles, he's in good shape."

They talked for a while longer, and the deputy asked, "Do you want me to let you out of jail now…or wait till mornin'?"

Bartley grinned. "Maybe wait till mornin', if you don't mind. Say about noon so you'll be givin' me time to learn my lesson. I need to learn to respect purty girls."

They both had a small chuckle and Bartley added, "It took a while to make my wife understand this was the only way, and when we catch 'im, then she can tell the world the whole truth.

"Fact is, one thing that frightened me about even tryin' to help is that I got kids'a my own, and if Bear took'a notion, and thought I was a'talkin' to the law, he wouldn't be above grabbin' up one'a my youngens. Right now, he ain't much carin' where he gets money from…just so's he gets it. My Louisa, she's a smart girl, and knowin' that helped her to think that me pretendin' to get put in your pokey was a good thing."

The deputy nodded his understanding.

Bartley continued, "Right good-thinkin' girl, is my Louisa. Me and our youngens make up her whole world, if she ain't content with it, then it'd be a surprise to me. I'm a lucky fellow."

The deputy nodded again, "I understand about that. You and me…both of us."

Shortly after noon the jail house door swung open and the two men came out. Burley told Bartley, "Now your horse is here, and I won't wave good bye to you in case some birds may be watchin'. You needin' to pass on any information from now on, just manage to leave it with Keith.

"Seems from what you say we'll be needin' all the eyes we can get. If we need trackin', I got Ugly Face here and she's been tested. She's as good as they come."

Bartley muttered, "Thanks," and swung astride the stallion. A familiar nudge of the knee against Pistol's ribs meant gallop, so he did. His hooves beat against the hard earth like the hounds of hell were after him, appearing to get away from Burley as far and as fast as possible.

The brother and sister were relaxing over a cup of tea in the empty diner. Good smells issued forth from the stove in preparation for the lunch regulars.

Jackie was snugged up to the little table with his head in a book, pointing to and pronouncing the words he knew. He called for help on a new one.

The two at the counter traded glances and thoughts as they so often had. "Readin' by sight. I'm wonderin' what the teacher'll say about that when he starts to school. "

"Not much she can say. A body can't really unlearn to read. She'll deal with it, and a bit of phonics won't hurt 'im."

"Also, there's this. He loves learning new things, so chances are he'll love phonics, and that'll help 'im later on. I've heard'a youngens havin' a memory to learn by memorizin' the words. Our grandpap, you know, said some folks were taught to read out'a the Bible, that bein' the only book they had."

"Right, and it must'a been a chore findin' the size 'a words to learn on and maybe borin' to the kid before he could make sense'a what he was readin'."

A few sips, then, "I'll say this, I'm doubly glad I ordered the Lincoln Logs. Maybe that'll get his head out'a the books before he goes blind. They ought'a be here any day."

Then Leena. "You know! He don't even know his abc's! He's just remembering shapes."

Keith nodded. "Yeah, and won't he have fun learning the abc's! It might take him a whole afternoon!" Another relaxed sip as he lazily stared out the window at the road. "Hmmm, I see another horse I don't know. Don't know the rider, neither, and it's a fancy, high-end saddle."

Leena turned quickly and caught the back side of horse and rider. "Did he look this way?"

"If he did, he was really sneaky about it. If it was him, he'll likely be back by in a few minutes. I only know that either there's new people down the road, or he's someone who is closer to Berryville than Eureka. I'd'a remembered that horse."

The two siblings locked glances. "Do you know what?"

"I do! The direction he came from, he was bound to meet Bartley at a gallop. I wonder if they spoke?"

"I wouldn't be surprised. They know each other, and now Bartley's plan may be good. Bartley was obviously galloping away from the lawman."

"I'm startin' to be certain that is the person. I'd for sure know that horse, and why would he glance this way if he wasn't hungry?"

Leena smiled. "Yeah, I know. You know horses like I'm fixin' to know automobiles. In Wishbone I find myself saying, 'There's a Chevrolet, or a Locomobile…or a Runabout…or a National…or maybe a Lane.' New automobiles with new names are hatching out everywhere like fleas on a dog's back."

Keith nodded recognition of her comparison and kept his eyes glued to the road. He had one of those feelings. He hoped the fellow would turn full face, but he didn't. It was less than ten minutes that he came back by, and only took a couple of quick glances. "Casing the joint" is what the little "cops and robber books" would say.

At this point Keith would have "bet the farm," as another saying went, that the rider on the chestnut mare was the one who wanted to grab Jackie, who was now at the table reading for about the fourth time the story of Goldilocks and the Three Bears.

Who cared what the book said, or of the plight of poor Goldilocks who got caught house-breaking. The challenge for Jackie was remembering what the name of each word was.

Silky had to go outside to answer to nature, and she lifted her nose and moved her head sideways, swinging her ears to bring more scent to her nostrils. She picked up on a new scent among the many she was exposed to, and she cataloged the new scent in her very capable brain.

The human riding on the animal passed on by without having an effect on Silky's small human. While she was out, she took a turn around the house, and into the edge of the woodland. There might be another of those legless creatures snooping close by…but there wasn't.

A body had to get a little exercise, and the small human didn't come outside very much. Silky went all the way out to the road and there was a lingering trace of the new scent. A mixture of horse and human. She sneezed air through her nose to get a fresher scent. Sure enough, a totally new one.

She lapped up water from the pan below the pump spout. Water put there especially for her, she knew. Finally satisfied, and rested, she came to the front door and scratched with her thick-clawed paw. The door magically opened by one of the humans… didn't matter which…and she stretched out on the floor close the small swinging feet of her human.

LINCOLN LOGS

Bear LePrey put his horse into a gallop and headed for Kings River and home. He had seen what he had needed to see. The EAT AND GET GAS was set back from the road just far enough to create a place to leave horses. Trees were cleared back, and he'd have to take closer look and scout the place better before he actually did it. It'd take dark time to do that.

And the thing about Bartley, how'd a body'd think he'd go after that red-haired girl? Him with that Louisa who's just as purty. And a farm that pays so well. Why'd he risk that…? Oh, well… Bear had his own concerns and no time to bother himself with Bartley's stupidity.

Deputy Collins had made a trip "down under the bluff" where he kept his animals. It really wasn't "under," just straight down, but not as low as Blue Lake. Everything was in order, and the apple trees were loaded with tiny, green apples. Future apple cider and apple pies. And jelly.

He dropped by the roadside stand for a glass of cider before going on to the next thing to be done. Annie Jo had news.

"Couldn't tell for sure, but I'm thinkin' the future kidnapper just went by to take a look at us and at the diner. Beautiful chestnut mare and expensive saddle. Big fellow with thick shoulders and a wide hat. He actually looked like a logger."

"Makes sense. Havin' brains like Bartley said, he'd be sure to look it over a time or two. He hasn't said where he wants the money put, and that may be holding him up. When he figgers that out, it'll be time to watch out."

Ugly Face stood and shook her folds of skin into a more comfortable position, circled the ground twice, and spread herself across the cool dirt. She closed her eyes half way to keep out some of the flying dust and rested. By now, she knew she could be needed at a moment's notice, and she needed to be rested and ready.

Bear LePrey put his mare into an energy-saving trot and headed for the house of his parents. Would he ever be glad to get away from there! They expected him to help out with everything being done while he stayed there. What's the sense in that? Well, it was just a matter of time, and his ability to determine a safe place for the money, without himself being caught when he tried to collect it. That was the holdup, but he'd figger it out. Folks might say he was ugly or that he was mean, but no one ever said he was dumb.

Then Paul Manford and the mail hack delivered the Lincoln Logs. Keith had thought about how he would be giving them straight to Jackie, but then hit on an idea he really liked.

He waited until the little fellow was absorbed in his books, and that the diner was empty of customers, then he quietly spread out one of the sets across the counter.

Jackie worked a while and came to a word he didn't know. "Papa, what is the name of this word?" He was holding the place on the book, and ordinarily Keith would go to him. Today he didn't.

"I'm busy, son. You'll have to bring the book over to me."

Jackie obediently slid off the chair and brought the book. When he saw the pile of little brown sticks that Keith was fitting together, his eyes and mouth flew open like they were put on springs. He carefully placed the book aside.

"Can I help?"

"Hmmm, well, we can talk about it. Do you think you know how to play with my toy?"

"You could teach me!"

Good answer. He lifted the boy to a stool and proceeded to put log on log and make a little square pen. Jackie picked up the same size logs and did the same. "I can do it," he proclaimed. "I can already do it."

"All right, we'll do it together until someone comes in. Then we'll have to move them to the floor."

"We could move them now, couldn't we? Then we wouldn't mess up what we made."

"Good idea. Go bring the little wagon and we'll put the logs in it."

No sooner said than done, Deputy Collins arrived and took a seat at the counter. "Annie thinks she saw him. Rides a chestnut mare, she said, with an expensive saddle."

"Right. I saw him, too, at least I suspected. Didn't see 'im in the face, though, but why would that matter? If he gets his way he won't be facin' either of us."

"But we still have no ransom note. Don't see what we can do until then."

"Wish I knew what was going on. School starts in a couple of months and I don't see how I can let Jackie go until the kidnapper is caught. He'll be terribly disappointed."

"Surely it won't be that long."

It was when Jackie had been put to bed, and Silky took up her post at the foot of his bed, that Keven realized what had to be done without delay.

When Jackie went to school, whenever it would be safe, he would have to have transportation. The EAT AND GET GAS was located about half way between school districts, so it meant that a school was less than two miles away.

It was actual about one and three-quarter miles and a bit far for a five-year-old to travel. It was also a fact that about half the children came on horseback, and all schools had a maintenance area for the animals.

On thinking on which horse to select, there was hardly a question of which was best. It should be Sparkle, a pony with a gentle disposition and who was a good ten inches shorter than the preferred height for horses. She was born with small light spots of hair among the dark brown, and someone thought she was reminiscent of a starry sky.

Sparkle was eventually shortened to Spark or Sparky. She would be the one Jackie could handle best, and maybe use for a couple of years until he acquired more skill and longer legs.

So Spark it would be, and tomorrow would be the day to begin. So with that weighty matter settled, he could permit himself to go to sleep. Surely every good parent had gone through these moments, but that was the responsibility…and pleasure of rearing a child…wasn't it?

And Jacky slumbered peacefully in his new room. It was ideally suited, being at the back of the house and away from a lot of household sounds. It had a wide window along the south side, and caught the coolness of the predominately southern summer breeze. His old grandad had made good use of the room for several years before going on to his reward.

And now, it belonged to Jackie and his toys…and Silky. The dog had taken her place at his feet…there was plenty of room. She could lay with her head almost in line with the sill of the window, and be favored by the summer breeze.

It was on this moonlit night that Bear decided to do his scouting, his reconnoiter no less important than a regimental scout sounding out the territory for his commander. He purposely chose the moonlight rather than a flashlight because he knew that a sneaking person was much less obvious in natural moonlight than a person with a flashlight.

Reason number two, a flashlight spotlighted only what was within its circle of light, and Bear required a wider spectrum. He need to check on window size, ease in raising and who (or what) occupied the room. As well as determining where the kid slept.

He first noticed the window screen that kept out the night bugs, and that it was the old fashioned type that had two hangers at the top and one hook at the bottom to keep it from flapping. Perfect. He could remove it without a sound.

And the window. It was opened a perfect eight inches from the bottom to direct the breeze lower in the room, and the heat of the attic would cause the convection that would pull the cool air in. July and August in Arkansas were hot, stuffy months.

So, with sharp eyes attuned to the dim star light and the half moon, he examined the window closely, and could hear breathing inside. A lump under the white sheet. Wonder of wonders! This was actually the child's bedroom, and there he was…soundly sleeping. Could anything be easier! Luck was surely with him for this would be like "taking candy from a baby," so the saying went.

He was sorely tempted to ease up the window and grab up the kid this minute. But he forced his breathing to remain calm and his hands to be still at his sides. Do not "jump the gun," as the saying went. Many a battle was lost because some one person was trigger happy. Also, he was not dressed as he would be, and did not have the sticky plaster for the kid's mouth. He did not have the horse stationed where it would be, and he had not checked out the direct path that he would take through the woods.

He would not use his best horse on the first part of the venture, as he was much too valuable. That animal would be tied and waiting and ready to carry the pair of them across King's River.

For going through the woods he would need one of his pa's carriage horses. He would be stashed at a spot for easy boarding, and be rested and ready to find his way through the dense vegetation for the next couple of miles.

But everything looked perfect for the operation to succeed. Imagine! The kid lying almost in the wide window on the far side of the house! Nothing could have been better arranged.

He nodded to himself with intense satisfaction as he slipped quietly away and disappeared into the dense growth of trees. Then he would cut back toward the road, where the stallion would be waiting…likely tossing his head in indignation with having been left behind, and hidden in the trees, no less! He will be fired up and ready to go, and horse and rider would be out of the neighborhood and range of the deputy in mere seconds.

Silky's sharp eyes watched the proceedings outside the window, and her young age filled her with doubts. *Do I announce the presence of this stranger, or do I let the humans sleep? Is this person a danger…or a friend?* She knew who he was from the mingled scent of man and horse after the chestnut mare had galloped first up… then down the road. But then the rider had gone away causing no notice among the humans, but his scent remained filed away in Silky's highly bred brain.

And now, here he was again. He had not awakened her small human, so perhaps he was expected and just doing his duty. Perhaps the larger humans knew he was about, and not a problem. So Silky lowered her large head onto the white sheets and breathed in the soft, summer air from the south window, her eyes relaxed at half-lid, ready to spring into action. Nothing happened this night.

But something did happen. The ease with which this part of the operation could take place was now known to Bear. The next thing would be how to make sure the adults and the dog would be somewhere else and not in the room when it happened, and for him to quickly get the sticky plaster onto the kid's mouth. Minor details. The perfect plan would come to him.

All in good time.

RIDING LESSON

Sparkle, now called Sparky, was mildly interested that she was chosen when Keith came into the pasture. Mostly the human would have need another of the several horses, and that was not a problem. She would just lower head again and feel around with her sensitive nose for her favorite blades of grass among the less favorites. The trained tongue circled her favorites and omitted the others. But this time was different.

Keith came straight at her, and he brought a carrot, sweet and orange, fresh from the garden. Sparky knew about carrots, but mostly they were not for her. She understood, and continued to be content with the sweet grasses. But this time was different, and the carrot was for her. Keith even broke it into three pieces so it would be easier to chew. He waited while she chewed the vegetable, and he patted her neck and spoke to her while she chewed. She accepted with mild interest as the saddle was put on her back, and the straps buckled under her belly.

She would have followed him anywhere, but she was led just up the house and he stopped. She stood quietly and content as the bridle was put on with the bit inserted into her carrot-stained mouth. She'd been trained to this by the very person who was with her now.

Beside her was a small human looking on with a mixture of concern, apprehension and fear, along with a bit of anticipation and excitement.

A real horse…not a little wooden toy in the Lincoln Log pen. Not only that, he was going to be put on its back just like a grown up. He would be there all alone, but Papa would be beside him. It would be all right.

"Now, Jackie, I'm going to lift you up and onto Sparky's back but I'll be right here beside you. We'll see how you fit in the saddle today. Tomorrow we might use just a blanket, and you'll like that better, I think."

The boy felt himself being lifted up and over and he widened his feet to accept the little chair that was on the horse's back. He'd seen, of course, many riders on horseback, but it had never occurred to him to see himself on a one, but here he was. Sparky turned her head as if to see that he was properly seated, and Papa patted her nose and told her it was all right. She took a step forward.

So, here he was, riding on a horse. Papa seemed to think he could do this, and surely he was right. This seemed to be part of the preparation for attending school, that magical place where all sorts of new things would happen.

They circled the house two times, and he was lifted down. The ride seemed to be over. Uncle Keith said, "Now we pat Sparky's face and thank her for the ride. You and she must get acquainted and be friends so she will understand when you tell her something."

When he tells her…? How could that be, but he patted the long brown face and she blew a puff of air at him. He startled back, but Papa steadied him with a hand on his shoulder. "Don't be afraid. She was just answering your patting. She was saying, 'I know who you are and I like you.'"

"She said that?"

"She sure did!"

"I didn't know you knew how to talk horse!"

"It's not hard, son. You'll soon learn. Just like you learned the names of words in a book. You'll have fun learning a lot of new things."

Keith said and did all of these things with a cloud of apprehension and dread settling around him like a soggy coat feels in the rain. He truly believed the person called Bear was planning a kidnapping. It was just too preposterous to not be believed. It was necessary to keep the dread from his voice, because Jackie did not need to be concerned as well. It was not his duty to keep himself safe…it was the duty of a father. Then why did Keith feel so inadequate?

The next day Jackie was given the carrot and in unsteady fingers he reached for the broken chunk of carrot. He forced his fingers to remain in place as the large teeth were exposed, and the long tongue encircled the orange stick of vegetable. A smile of satisfaction and accomplishment spread across his face as Sparky chewed the carrot, losing only a bit of juice from the corners of her mouth. He did it! He'd fed the horse, and she ate just like he knew what he was doing.

Keith surveyed the short legs that could not in any way reach the stirrups, no matter how high he shortened them. What was he to do? He couldn't be with him for an hour or so during the morning and mid-afternoon to get him to and from school. Those were two of his best hours in the diner. Every day. Well, that was tomorrow's problem. Today he rode without hand holding.

"Now, son, these straps are called reins, and you hold one in each hand. If you want her to turn this way, you tightened the rein on this side. And the other way is the other rein. And when you want her to start walking, you say, 'Git up!'"

With the sound of the known direction, Sparky's feet began to move, and Jackie's eyes widened and his grip tightened. He balanced his taut little body to match the sway of Sparky's steps. Keith smiled. If he could just get on and off, they'd have it made.

Three times around the house, and then down the lane toward the rent house, turn around and come back. Jolly good show!

But the show was over. Had to be. He had to get into the diner to relieve Leena. A gas vehicle of some sort had pulled into the yard. Since it was actually running on its own power, it must be here for gas.

Leena escaped the diner with a half biscuit in her hand. Yep, there was the Pierce Arrow, the most expensive auto available in the mountains, and the biggest gas guzzler. After having been caught empty a time or two, and made to suffer the embarrassment of being pulled in on eight equine legs, the driver had found a place in the tiny interior of the auto to carry extra gas.

While Leena watched, he poured the last drops of gas from his can and exchanged with her for the five gallon full. Leena did not sell partial quantities…either you wanted five gallons, or you didn't get any gas from her. Simpler that way.

Before he paid, he mentioned, "I've got a different sound, like a squeak but not a squeak. Wouldn't have took note of it, but I smelled something."

"Smelled? Like what?"

"Hmm, well, like burning without smoke."

One of Leena's worse problems was the customer's inability to explain a sound or smell. "Bring it on up on the platform. I'll take a look."

The driver, Ervin Wheeler, asked, "Will it take long?"

Leena sighed inside. One of the most asked questions was "How long will it take?" The next most asked question was, "How much will it cost?" She wanted to shout back, "How do I know until I see what's wrong?" But she didn't.

"Bring it on up and I'll check. Then I can tell you more."

She slipped into her handy coveralls that covered just about every inch of her body. She pulled on her tight fitting rubber gloves and squirmed under the auto. It took about three seconds to smell the problem. Hard to describe but a definite problem. She felt around and spotted the "hot spot."

Mr. Wheeler squatted nearby, as though watching her would speed up the discovery. She used to invite customers to have a cup of coffee in the diner, but realized they thought she wanted them out of the way so she could damage their precious auto and charge more.

So he waited in an uncomfortable position while she unscrewed something or other, and squirmed out bringing the greasy part.

"See this? It's wore down, and it's lopsided now. I'll bet the auto was driving jerky. The operation manual says to check the oil regularly. I know it's easy to forget, but when it runs out, this happens. If you didn't come in now, you would have ground into the next higher assembly." She tried to use "manual" words when she could. Made her sound like she knew something.

"If you had, it would have cost a bundle and took a long time. As it is, I have oil, and I have a replacement one of these. It'll take about fifteen minutes. Do you want me to go ahead?"

He did. She disappeared into the Tin-Lizzies Fix-it door and reappeared with a shiny new "one of these" and a can of oil.

"I'll just change this out and show you about the oil." She could have said, "Here's the oil. Surely you know where to put it." But she didn't. It seemed customers preferred to be thought of as dumb, rather than just negligent.

She put the remainder of the oil in the box where he kept his gas can and charged him out. On the whole, he was glad to pay it. It was a very expensive car, and it was good feeling to tell the world he could afford it. If it had been the "next higher assembly" he'd likely have had to leave on a borrowed horse, and wait until a part could be brought in from Wishbone. Such indignities were to be avoided if possible.

Mr. Wheeler backed carefully off the platform, just as another car pulled into the yard. A lady was driving. Can you believe it… women driving? So unladylike! He backed up to Ridge Road and headed on down the gravel to the east.

Miss Samantha Harding greeted Leena happily. "Needed gas. But I'm starvin' dead away. I hope the cheese biscuits aren't gone." With a finger wave, she disappeared into the diner.

Leena hoisted the five gallon can to the auto's gas tank and poured about four gallons. She checked the tires as she knew Samantha would want done. A nick in the rubber. Not bad but needed watching.

She wrote up a ticket for the five gallons as was her rule. Samantha wouldn't care. Her husband furnished money so she could spend it. She handed over the cash and climbed in the seat. Waving merrily, she was off.

Leena loved customers like Samantha, and she was getting more of them all along. Ridge Road took forever with a horse and buggy, but the gas buggy got them there in jig time. And there were those regulars who expected and appreciated reminders and suggestions. That was a lot better than having to learn about the guts of an auto engine for themselves.

The thought of the cheese biscuit made Leena hungry. Maybe there was one left. She settled into one of the three chairs so she could have a view of the driveway.

Paul Manford wheeled in with the postal van. He stepped down and headed for the diner so she stayed sitting. Maybe he just wanted gas…or maybe nothing. He stepped inside and announced he was double hungry and he'd take two beef sandwiches, if you please.

Keith pleased. He split the buns and piled on the shredded beef.

"Toss in a hunk'a that cake, will ya, and some coffee. And Miss Leena, I got a job for you. Had myself a flat on the road, and changed it out. If I'd'a had a tire pump, I'd'a aired it up and tried to make it in, but I think it may have picked up a nail. Horseshoes don't hold their nails forever and they kick 'em off right in the road. Anyway, if it's fixed up on my way back I'll pick it up, otherwise next time. They make us carry two spares out on these long routes."

The sandwiches and cake appeared before him, and the coffee was not far behind. It was pleasant to watch a man eat when he enjoyed his food, and the postal carrier did enjoy his food. Not an ounce of fat on his whole body…maybe it jiggled off on the rough roads.

Leena did have a tire pump and the air whistled out when she tried to find the leak. Just turn the tire around and listen for the whistle. A little of the special glue and a rubber toothpick poked in the hole took care of it. Wait a few minutes and pump it up again. The postal service was charged regular fee.

Paul finished the food and came out. "Change out the gas can, too, if you will. All that's left in there are fumes."

She did, and there was more than fumes, but it wouldn't have gotten him very far. She dumped the speck of gas into the last sale of 4 gallons. Bit by bit and eventually she had another can of gas. It all helped. Need to make a profit somewhere or why stay in business?

She counted the full cans and knew a trip to Wishbone was imminent. Maybe restock a few other items that all the cars used. Bolts, clamps, hoses, radiator leak-fix, rubber toothpicks for tires. She'd see what Keith needed. Always flour, sometimes another thing or two.

Jackie came trundling into the diner with his Lincoln Logs in the miniature wagon. He liked to play where there were people. "Aunt Leena, I rode on top of the horse. It was fun after I stopped bein' scared."

"Good for you, Jackie. I never did really get over bein' scared. I had to buy a truck."

Jackie fitted the log shapes together and commented to no one in particular. "When I get big, I'll have horses and trucks and other things."

Keith's mind added, "That is, if I'm successful enough to keep you alive until you get big."

SECOND LOOK

Bear would like to have stepped into the Soup Bowl Diner for a cup of coffee or something. He thought better charged up that way, but he couldn't do that. He couldn't even get a glass of cider at the Bistro.

He did, however, think about horses as he road along. His favorite horse would be saved for the final getaway when he had the money in his hand. Until then he would appropriate the use of his parents' animals. There'd be the careful carriage horse for the first part, and that would be Prince. Being totally black would make him more invisible. Then he would change to a faster animal like Zipper. Old Zip would get him to wherever he had stashed the kid.

He'd just walk right now through the wooded area and select a path among the many. It would be dark when he had the kid and he wanted to be sure nothing would go wrong.

It was after he had wound around a bit and decided to head back to the road that a sight filled his mind and body so greatly, he could hardly breathe. This part of the mountain, not being where he had often been, he was surprised to come suddenly upon an old cabin, seemingly unoccupied, and apparently hadn't been lived in for some time. There was an animal shed, a privy, a tiny smoke house, and a cabin that appeared to have about three rooms.

The whole place had a feel of being deserted, grass growing right up to the doorstep. Also the road toward Ridge Road was grown over with saplings of persimmon and ash. When he could breathe again, he paused and stared as one would stare at a beautiful painting.

This could not have been more perfect if he had arranged it himself. Just pop the kid in the house and lock the doors, and tend to the next problem.

How to get the money? Hmmm, well, that would take more thought.

His best thought so far was to have it delivered to the Wishbone post office for pick up by...who? Maybe Simon Simms....

The problem with that was the distance from the Junction to the town of Wishbone, taking at least three hours on a fast horse, and then what if it wasn't there yet? Reason told him that he could only leave the kid alone for so long. There'd be a search for him and the locals would know about this deserted cabin.

There should be a better plan. How did kidnappers figure all this out, anyway?

GRADY O'KEEF, OBSERVER

The last days of June were real scorchers. No rain for the last month and the ground was dry as powder, especially in the ditches bordering Ridge Road. Too bad for someone whose job it was to scoop up the dust containing the flint gravel that had washed into the ditch, or flung there by the tires of those little gas buggies.

Grady pushed the mules forward by promising them grass at the Soup Bowl Diner. The fine dust arose in clouds and he thought he could feel it filtering down his shirt collar and through his hair. Had to be…it was settling on everything else.

Near the top of the hill, now, and an effort must be made to be presentable…or maybe half presentable. At least he wasn't wet with sweat because the hot wind dried sweat as fast as a body could make it.

From his pocket, he extracted the comb, and leaning forward, sought to remove as much dust as possible from his hair. Nothing could be done for the shirt but to take it off and shake it, then put it back on. He spoke to the grader's conveyance, "Git on up there, you lazy skin full'a bones. We got'a make time."

The mules heard him and saw what was sure to be the destination, and they quickened their steps a little. They turned, without direction into the grass beside the Fixit Shop and began to mouth the dusty blades. Like the humans, the mules did what they had to do.

He entered the diner quickly closing the door against the flies. Pesky little buggers just sitting there flapping their wings, waiting to get in. He plopped himself on a stool and announced. "Got so much dust in my throat I can't even swallow. Gimmie a bowl of that chile and maybe it can cut through my throat it. Don't mind so much eatin' dust but I shore don't like it in my throat."

Keith had set the steaming bowl before him before he finished explaining about the dust. For the umpteenth time, Keith wondered how it was that something blazing hot as his chile could be relished greatly when the weather was so hot. Oh, well…chile was one of his money makers.

Grady was well aware that he was valued somewhat for his ability to pass along news, and he had a couple of little items to pass along. Or maybe just get help to make sense of them.

One was that a strange horse and rider had been seen. Not that he knew every horse in northern Arkansas, and any horse and rider could use Ridge Road, but when one goes and comes one day and goes and comes again in the same week, it was noticeable. Grady had so little to think on while pulling gravel up from the ditch back into the road that he noticed. A sharp mind had Mr. Grady O'Keef, and any of his teachers and most of his friends would say he was capable of much more than road grading, but they would not be thinking of his reasons for keeping the job. That job with the grader helped him keep tabs on Miss Kathleen Sullivan.

So he announced the presence of a strange horse and rider, and wondered if there had been a new family move close to the Ridge without his knowledge. That would have been difficult.

So he stated the fact of the different horse, and was met with silence that was unusual. Ordinarily some comment, however trivial, would be made but there was nothing out of the mouth of either of the twins.

Hmmm, well…there was that other comical rumor going around that he knew was not true, but it made conversation. It seems that Mr. Bradley Wilcox, who he knew quite well, was put in Burley Collins' pokey for a cool-off period. The fact that Bradley would put himself in that position was absurd. That straight-up-and-down Bradley always did things the right way and never got into trouble.

So Grady knew for certain that bit of a silly rumor would bring words of some kind out of one or the other of the twins' mouths, but he was wrong. Silence again, as they went about their business, and little Jackie played with his logs and animals.

All right. If that was the way it was going to be, he'd just tell the rest of it but he'd wait until Cecil Green finished his pie and left. Then he'd find out what in the tarnation was going on when he told the last part of the Bradley incident.

Strangely, the powerful spices and the stove heat of the chile had cleared up the discomfort in his throat, so he could try the berry pie. Pretty classy pie. He decided not to comment, as he had often, that Keith would make someone a good wife. Something was going on here.

Cecil Green was forking up the final crumbs of pie crust, and gulped the last of the coffee that was now cold. "See you folks later."

Keith responded, "Sure thing, Cece." Only three or four flies managed to get through the door, and Leena picked up the swatter to take care of them, sending them on to wherever squashed flies go.

After a pregnant pause, Grady looked at Keith and then at Leena and said, "Alright, friends. What gives? I was gonna say it was rumored that Bradley must'a been sayin' things to Leena that she didn't like, for her to haul him off to the pokey. I'm smart enough to know that didn't happen, and if it did, Louise Wilcox wouldn't have none of it.

"So you folks gonna tell me what's wrong?"

The twins looked at each other and answered each other with a slight nod. Grady was going to have to be pulled into the circle of information. Partly because he was too smart to be left out, and also because his eyes and ears could be of value. He was in position more than anyone in the western side of the county to see what was on the road.

Keith refilled Grady's coffee, and with somewhat coded words, as Jackie was playing nearby, he was brought up to date.

Grady listened with his head in a perpetual nod. He'd known there was something about the Bradley story that was not being told. And the fellow on the strange horse, who was not a Burnt Tree Junction resident, also made sense. He had, indeed, been casing the place to make his plans.

"Where do you reckon he was aimin' to put the item he stole till he needed it? A cave, maybe?"

"That'd be my bet. I can't remember any vacant farm houses around here. Land's too valuable here to let go idle."

"Maybe way off Ridge Road? Likely wouldn't be past Kings River. If it was a cave, it'd be anybody's guess as to which one, or maybe one that nobody but him knows about."

"Anyway it's good to know that us and Burley guessed the right person. Wore a big hat, too."

Grady drained his coffee. "Well, that grader don't run itself, and the mules got enough'a Leena's grass to make a few more miles. I'll be off and keep a peeled eye for anything else."

"Yeah, and if you got a chance, check on any empty sheds or something someone knows about."

"Will do."

Grady had hardly cleared the hill when a little black car pulled into the yard. Out stepped Sharon, pretty as a picture. She let in only one fly. It didn't last long.

"Wheeou, hot out there," she commented. "I saw a dust cloud down the road. Grady must'a stopped by. Any new rumors?"

The twins eyed each other once more. Like Grady, Sharon seemed like family, and it's hard to keep secrets from family.

Leena began. "It's not really a rumor, but you need to know something. Come with me and I'll tell you while I bring in the washin' before it collects any more dust."

So Sharon heard the whole story while the dry clothes came off the clothesline.

Leena finished with the admonition to tell no one. "Just you and Grady, Burley and us are all who knows, except for Bradley Wilcox who's helpin'. It'd sure help to know when its gonna happen. Jackie can't be watched all the time. Can you even imagine someone bein' so mean…who would steal a little boy and kill him…just for money?"

Sharon paused, thought a minute and faced her friend. "Tell me this. What job is facing you the hardest?"

"Huh?"

"I can help. What's the next jobs you don't have time to do?"

"Oh, I was just talkin'. There's no call for you to help…."

"Tell me immediately." Sharon demanded an answer with her best stubborn chin protrusion.

Leena relented. "Alright, you asked for it. The sweaty bed sheets need to be changed and washed, I've run out of gas cans, the okra pods have to be picked today or they'll be too big and hard. Keith needs to train Jackie on horseback and a car is coming in at 1:00."

Sharon paused a minute. "Got it! You head on down to Wishbone right now. I'll strip the beds and wash the sheets. When Keith needs to leave, I'll sit in the diner. I can't cook but I can serve and collect money. When the car comes in, I'll pick the okra pods. I know how to dry them. What else is bothering you?"

"Nothing today. But you don't…."

"Sure I do. I have nothing to do at home, and I'd likely be here bothering you anyway. So get in your little blue truck and get with it."

She did. In less than an hour she was back with the filled gas cans, just in time to meet Grady walking in leading a limping horse.

"Need a favor," was his greeting. "Mule stepped on a round rock and pulled a tendon. Got'a leave him somewhere and borrow a horse. I know you got no mules, but it's a regulation to have two teams. Your horse won't have to pull...just be there."

"Uh, well, ask Keith about which horse. I'll take the mule and...."

Sharon broke in, "I'll take the mule. I know what to do. My horse is all the time doing that while coming up the hill."

The surprised Grady handed over the lead, and Sharon disappeared with the limping mule.

Grady was thoroughly out of sorts. Maybe the hottest day of the year, and he had mule trouble. What if he hadn't been close by the Fix-it Shop? "Leena, I got business to talk over with you when I get back from this run. Don't get scared...it ain't about you and me. That's already settled. It's about an engine."

"What about an engine?"

"I'll tell you when I get back. It'd take too long now and I got three mules about a mile down the road bein' all alone and I hope they're still there. I got'a get a horse and gallop on down there."

Within ten minutes, he was gone in a trail of flying dust, seated bareback on the shapely back of Racer, a young appaloosa stallion.

Sharon was up to her elbows in soap suds. "Got anything else you want thown in? Got good sud."

"Yes. Dirty towels in the diner."

"Got it. Now you get busy on the next thing you got'a do."

Leena unloaded the gas cans and grabbed a sandwich just as the little Rover Runabout was pulled in behind a pair of mules with a man on a horse following along. In the Rover was a pair of teenage boys. "I was comin' in with a problem with the brakes, and the bloomin' key got stuck and wouldn't move. Hope you know what to do. I got'a get goin' on an errand, and the boys'll take the mules home. See you later." And he was gone in a trail of dust.

Leena was momentarily taken back. Brakes she knew. Happened all the time on these hills. But the key, that was another problem. To the two teenage boys she said, "Pull it on up. The mules won't hurt the platform."

They did.

The wet items were on the clothesline. In this heat they'd be dry in an hour. Sharon was slicing the okra pods into little half inch wheels into the drying pan. A day in the hot sun and they'd be shriveled and dry and perfect for flavoring winter soup.

Sharon also brought in the squash that had allowed to be a bit too big, but they would still fry for lunch. That had been a "job" that Leena had forgotten to mention.

Leena donned her coveralls, hot and sticky. No clean spare. "Hey, Sharon, you still got that sudsy water?"

"Got it! What goes in?"

"Cruddy coveralls."

"Got it!"

Leena handed over the coveralls and attacked the key problem. This was her first time for that problem. Have to probably open the whole dashboard and work from the backside.

Grady, on Racer, had thought while going a mile in a minute. An idea had been mulling around in his mind for a while, but just had not yet come to a head. He was not ready to give up the route, but something had to be done. It was 1910, after all, so why should he be working with pre-historic equipment?

First...he'd have to lay out his plan to Leena, and it would depend solely on her answer, which way he could go. Here he was twenty-two years old, and he was good and tired of what this job required him to do.

Within minutes, Racer had him back at the grader and three mules patiently waiting, switching their stubby tails and rippling their skin to keep the bothersome flies on the move.

Sharon led the limping mule to the shed. Now, where is the liniment? And she'd need some binding cloths to pull the strained ligament into place, and to hold the healing liquid on the tear.

Arkansas roads and trails were made of rocks, often worn smooth. Sprained ligament happened to every horse, sooner or later.

Mule taken care of, she fed him a cup of corn and left him tied in the shed. As she passed by the garden, she scooped up a dozen overripe tomatoes. Leena was apparently on a long job so she'd just get the meal started. Cooking was not exactly her thing, but she knew what to do. First the diner.

"Keith, Leena said you needed to be gone with Jackie for a while. I'm here to take over."

Keith removed his apron and handed it to Sharon. "Thanks. Come on, Jackie. We've got to see Sparky."

The three domino players came trouping in. They stared, startled at the lovely face of Sharon, instead of the stern one of Keith.

Sharon greeted them. "Come on in. Don't worry, I didn't do the cooking. Keith just had to be gone a while."

They settled around the little French table. "Thought we'd go for the soup today. What kind is it?"

Sharon took a taste. "Tastes like chicken with sausage. Squash, peppers, carrots and peas. That suit you?"

A few affirmative nods. "We'll take it. Put it over a biscuit, will you?"

Leena loosened a few screws and removed the dash on the Rover. With a longer screw driver she was able to poke the back side of the key and loosen it enough to remove it. Then she examined the key. Undamaged, but also the wrong key. She tightened the inter-workings that she had loosened, and reattached the dash cover.

Now for the brakes. Likely forgot to keep them lubricated like the manual insisted, but she had replacements in stock. Hmmm, stock was getting low on some items. Have to take care of that on the next gas trip to Wishbone.

Her thought strayed. Wonder what's got into Grady that he needs a "business" meeting? Whatever that is. What did she have to do with his business? Oh, well, he'd be back and hungry. She had other things to do.

Sharon was in the diner so Leena pulled the dry items off the line and folded the aprons and towels for the diner. *Still wonder what Grady wants with me....* She guessed she'd have to keep on wondering, as he wouldn't be back by for two days.

Bear LePrey was antsy. He needed to get this thing rolling so he could clear out of this dumpy bit of houses and people and find some place worthy of his presence.

Mounting Zipper, he went again to the Junction just to make sure. He'd check out the diner, and then go through the woods on the way Zipper would have to go. Best the horse had been through on that path before, because it would be dark when it happened. Also, he wanted another look at the abandoned cabin. That looked like the answer, but he still didn't know about how to get the money.

Delivering the ransom note would be easy. Just fasten it to the mail box. Couldn't put it inside, because the postal route man might pick it up.

All he could think of was to send the ransom money to the Wishbone post office to hold for pick up. But that was so time consuming, and he'd have a brat on his hands. Didn't want to kill him until he was ready to skip the country.

Old Zip wasn't fond of trailing through paths with low limbs, but he managed. When they reached the cabin, the animal was rewarded with a cup of corn...which he didn't often get. Bear knew it was best, when possible, to give the animal good thoughts about a certain place. Like folks said, he wasn't short on brains. Just didn't always use them.

Zipper munched corn in the shed while Bear examined the cabin. Looked good. There was an old fashioned latch lock that could be fastened from the inside or out, and operated on a latch string through a tiny hole through the door.

He consulted the almanac on the moon position, and in three days there would be a quarter moon, just what he wanted. Just enough light to get around and not need a torch. So three days it was, and he'd raise that window just enough to pull the kid through. He'd have the sticky plaster on his noisy mouth before he woke up enough to cry.

With a smile on his face, he collected Zipper and gave him a friendly pat on the rump. All was in order.

THE BUSINESS MEETING

Two days later and Grady was back. This being a business meeting, he insisted it be done in the Fix-It Shop.

"Miss Leena, it's this way. I find myself at a crossroads, and need to ask you a couple'a questions."

"Fire away," came the invitation.

A deep breath and a sigh. "I see tin lizzies hatchin' out like flies in the springtime with every name under the sun. What's a Hupmobile, for goodnew sake?"

"It's a...."

"I don't want to know. I do want to know how you know how to fix what goes wrong."

"Easy. Repair Manual."

"But there's so many different kinds."

"Not really. Mostly the guts are the same, just a different kind'a bolts or door handles, and a different name plate. All of them have a combustion engine that don't change much. There's only so many ways to be different."

"So you could repair most any auto that pulled in."

"Hmmmm, well, maybe. Some might take time, and might have to wait till I get a new manual."

"So the manual's the answer."

"Sure is. The companies want the cars to be fixable, so they can keep sellin' 'em."

"Next question. You ever see the road graders with engine, like they use on city streets?"

A shake of her head.

"Thought so. But there'd be a manual somewhere. Those things'd break down occasionally and have to be fixed."

"I guess so."

"So if I got a hold of a manual, and showed it to you, could you tell whether you could fix it or not?"

"Uhhh, maybe."

"So I gotta figure out how to get one."

"That's easy. You just order from the company that prints 'em up. Likely cost you a dollar and a half. I can do it for you."

"Good! And there's another thing. I want a bill made up to turn in on my problem. Add up the linament, the boarding fee for the mule for the four days, and the cost of loaning Racer."

With a toss of the head, she dismissed the order. "There ain't no charge for all that. Keith wouldn't hear to you payin'."

"Wouldn't be me a'payin'. It'd be the state. The mules and the grader don't belong to me, it belongs to them, and they pay when something happened. I'm tired of takin' favors when it ain't my fault or my property. And, say, add in the cost of the grass and corn for the mule. I want to get some attention."

Leena studied the serious face of Grady. Surely she qualified for a question of her own. "Why?" she asked.

"I'll tell you why. I want one of those motor operated graders. I could grade all the way to Berryville in half the time, and that would cancel the need for a grader there. The company would save money, and I'm going to tell 'em so."

"Why do you need a manual?"

"I don't. You do. If I have trouble anywhere between Eureka and Berryville, you'd be one to fix it."

"But...."

"No buts. I've made up my mind. I'm not giving up the route. You might forget who you belong to."

"Well, I...."

"Of course you will. How different could the engine in the grader be than the engine in all these cars you take on? 'Course you might have to stock more gas cans."

Leena could think of nothing witty to say while mulling over in her mind what he just said. Her? Repairing a grader? Well, there'd been a time or two when he brought in the horse-drawn grader with a stripped chain, pebble in the gears, or maybe a bit of oil on the wheels. No charge. *Grady says that will stop. Well, we'll see.*

TONIGHT'S THE NIGHT

The Farmer's Almanac said a quarter moon tonight, and it wasn't raining. So, tonight must be the night. He had to get this right.

He saddled Prince and Zipper leading the fast horse to the house just in case he needed it. He'd actually decided that the vacant cabin would be the place to stash the kid because it would be easy to lock him in. A lot easier than a cave and no one close enough to hear him bellering.

He smiled to himself as things seemed to be going so right. And he really needed the money if he was going to go on down south, and he had convinced himself that he was entitled to it, as much trouble as he was going through to get it.

He tied Old Zip in the shed with a cup of corn. He led Prince into the trees on the path he would use when he came with the kid. It might get Prince excited if the kid screamed and yelled, but that would not under the mouth plaster. Darkness settled in the dense woods. It was time.

Leaving the horse a couple hundred yards away, he crept silently as a puff of smoke up to the place where the kid would be sleeping. Going to be easy! Easy as a piece of cake!

Stopping first at the mailbox, he fastened a note to the lid and crept away. He wasn't happy about leaving the money in Wishbone, but could think of no other way.

Silently he removed the screen and set it aside. Carefully, he lifted the window up, and it slid quietly on its runners. Two bright eyes behind folds of hairy skin were watching his every move. The sensitive nose had caught the scent, and Silky was immediately alert. She remained totally still, hardly breathing.

Deep down under the wrinkly skin was the conviction that she was going to need to do something, but she didn't know what. Edging forward on her belly to get closer to the window, she watched the movement outside. The moon gave just enough dappled light through the trees to see the human. It was the big human.

She watched as the hand reached inside the window and patted gently on the sheet, feeling for something underneath. The slight movement of the sheet caused the little boy to shift his body closer toward the window, and the hand jerked quickly out. The human outside the window moved away.

So far, so good. Her human was safely asleep. She lay alert and staring at the open window still sniffing in silent whiffs at the hated scent. What did she need to do? Instinct whirled around in her fertile mind. What? What? What was expected of her to do for this human?

Jackie signed gently and drifted back into sleep, but the scent was still outside. Silky was not going to relax until it went away or one of her persons came and told her to do differently.

Bear wrung his hands in indecision. The kid was a light sleeper, and it would take precious seconds to get him outside so he could slap on the plaster. Maybe if he reached in with both hands, but that would take a higher window. So be it. He lifted gently and the window went up to about a foot and a half. Placing the plaster on the sill where it would be handy, he slowly put both hands through the window.

Silky now thought she had an answer...or at least part of one. She reached her head forward and clamped her jaws down firmly on one of the hands and the big human made a small sudden sound. Now Silky had another decision to make.

In her strong teeth she could easily crack through the bones under the skin, but should she? After all, this was a human and not a rabbit or raccoon. She just held still for a few seconds, and then opened her jaws. She was still where she could reach either hand, if it came in again.

It didn't.

Bear clamped his mouth shut and bore the pain. That hated dog that was always with the boy was in the bed. Of course it was. He should have known. In the pale moonlight he examined the hand, and could see the red of the blood. Teeth cut through the skin. Didn't break the bone, though. Skin heals.

Holding the hand away from himself so the blood would not drip on his clothes, he made his way to the patient Prince, standing like a statue by the tree.

Leaping astride, he rode to the cabin where Zipper waited. He put Prince in the shed and locked the doors. Dumb animals could just wander off if they weren't penned in.

He went into the cabin and sat down on the bare floor. His hand ached and throbbed, but the bleeding had seemed to stop. It was time to do some thinking, because this plan did not work. His mind began to play around with ways to get rid of that beast. Gun shot, probably the best. Catch the kid outside and one bullet would do it. Then he'd have to wait a week or two before he tried again.

Silky worked her way closer to the window to get a better view, as the scent began to fade. She huffed through her nose to clear the scent so she would be ready if the human came back. Her movement aroused the boy who turned over again and put his arm around her neck. Yes, her mind told her, she had done the right thing. The scent was going away, and the hands were not coming through the window.

She lowered her head onto her paws and rested, but her eyes were not totally shut. Summer mornings in the mountains come early. Silky was careful to remain motionless, not to disturb the small human that was hers.

When he was awake, the pair of them crawled from under the sheet and down to the floor. Jackie pulled his wagon of logs along as the pair made their way to the kitchen where everyone would be.

"Papa," Jackie greeted Keith. "Did you know that Silky can open the window to get cooler? I think she got too hot where she was sleeping."

Huh? Keith was alert. "Silky opened the window? I don't think so, Jackie. I think I opened the window so you would both be cooler."

"No, Papa. You opened little," and he spread his hands about 4 inches apart. "Silky opened big," and the hands were spread clearly a foot and a half a part.

"Opened big? I would like to see that. Can you show me?"

"Come." Leaving the wagon, but with the dog close on his heels, they went to his room. "See? Opened big. Silky got hot."

Yes, it was opened "big" and that was certainly not the way Keith had left it. And what was that stain on the sill?

He leaned across the bed, and Silky jumped on the bed and sniffed the stain and issued a rumbling growl that started in her throat and rippled through her lips.

Keith stared, motionless with total and abject fear. It was clearer than the nose on his face what had happened. His little boy could have been taken except for the young bloodhound. Whoever it was left blood and the blood was not from the dog. New plans had to be made, and he had to go see the lawman.

He was silent around the boy. Why disturb him when he thought he knew how the window got opened. Clever dog, huh!

When he could do so without explanation to Jackie, he stepped outside and came around to the window. Footprints in the loose dirt. Large footprints, and there on the window sill was a sticky plaster, such as are put on horses to keep medication on a cut, skin snag or sore.

That comleted the picture. The kidnapper was prepared for little boy screams. Keith followed the scuffed trail to where it was obvious a horse had been stationed. Chills ran down his arms. Very good plan this person had made.

The weary Bear finally dozed, and laid over on the floor. He was awakened by a pair of irritated horses still tied in the strange barn. He would have to have a better plan.

It was later that the mailman, Paul Manford, came in for pie, and slid a note toward Keith. "Didn't have mail for you, but thought you'd want this taken off your box."

"Thanks, Paul." One more piece to the puzzle.

Keith nodded and took the note without offering an explanation. He'd just remembered what he meant to do, and when Paul left, he did it.

Calling Silky and the boy, he took the dog to the bedroom and motioned her to get on the bed. He reached across and patted the window sill where the blood stain remained.

He patted the stain and Silky growled, deeply and meaningfully, and Keith patted her head and said, "Good girl, Silky. Good girl."

The pair padded after Keith to the diner, and he reached into the cooler and took out a small glob of ground goat meat. He put it in Silky's dish and patted her again. "Good girl, Silky."

The raw meat was gone in an instant and Silky wagged her tail in appreciation. Once more she had done the right thing… the thing her insides told her to do. And once more she had been rewarded.

GRADY, THE GRADER

The manual came in a week. Leena expected it. That printing company gave good service to customers, and she had given them a lot of business. If she got a minute, she'd look over the directions. Couldn't be too bad, and if what she could do would lighten Grady's job, no problem.

Today she needed to go for cheese, and a little billy goat needed to be turned into chile meat. He was getting so mean and kept getting out of the pen. Being hot weather, the meat would have to be taken care of in a day.

Sharon came early. "What do we do today?"

"Oh, Sharon, don't think of it. You were such a help yesterday, you've done enough."

Sharon was a stubborn person when she wanted to be. "If there is still jobs piled on you, then I haven't done enough. I was bored at home anyway."

Leena gave up. "If you're sure. I'll take Jackie with me for cheese, while Keith gets the goat in the butcher hoist. Then you can help cut up the meat, put together chile spices, and help fry down the patties."

"Good. I'll watch the diner until Keith gets back."

Grady had spent the week putting words together in his mind to make the case that the Earthworm Grading and Plowing Company would be ahead to put an engine grader on the long routes.

No place to repair breakdowns, they had told him some months ago. Well, he had the answer to that. There were repair shops in Eureka, their home base, and in Berryville, belonging to another company. Now there was also a repair shop across the road from the roadside stand called Uncle Burley's Bistro. That was going to be a surprise to the Earthworm people.

By mid afternoon, the little billy goat would cause no more trouble unless someone ate too much chile. The ladies had mopped a lot of sweat but had two lards crocks filled with the meat patties and packed in the grease from the frying. Good way to keep meat from spoiling for several months.

Sharon had taken time out to make the evening meal. Meatloaf and baked sweet potatoes in the already-hot stove. Cornbread and a peach cobbler had shared the hot oven.

Summer is still light at 7:00 PM and Sharon turned the key in her little car. That horrible hill was dangerous in the dark. Likely as not, a deer or stray razorback hog would wander out in front of her. Had to get home before dark.

"Thanks so much," she was told, whereupon she tossed her head and insisted, "It was nothing. See you tomorrow or the next day." And she was gone.

"What in the world would I do without her help," Leena moaned later.

"Good cook, she is." Keith was working on his second helping of cobbler.

"Good at everything. I've been thinking on something, and it'd be up to you to do it."

"You think I need more to do?"

"No, but you'd do this best. You got a full time job and I got more'n I can do right by, and Grady's tryin' to get me more to do. What we need, you and me, is a wife. Sharon is so good at 'wife' things. But if you don't like her, we need to put an advertisement out on the note tree at the junction. 'Couple needs a wife. Apply at the Eat and Get Gas.'"

Keith paused between bite. "Oh, come on now! Be sensible." But he was grinning at the thought, just the same.

"Brother? Listen to me. I'm being about as sensible as I can be. Should I be the one to look for a wife?"

That had the pair laughing as they so often did in their almost twenty-two years, but there was a grain of truth in it. Leena's business had increased until she hardly had a minute and the diner had to be tended regularly, or the regulars would stop coming.

On that note, Leena cleaned the kitchen, and Keith prepared for the next day. Thoughts were racing through his head. He'd already thought of the increasing demands on time. And Jackie would have to be taken to school for the first two or three years.

Just how could a pair of talented young persons get themselves in such a work-weary position?

Now Sharon…well, face it. A girl as talented and beautiful would certainly not settle for a fulltime job with the only pay being a fellow who would love to have her beside him. And if he actually asked her and she had to turn him down (and why wouldn't she?) what would that do to the friendship with Leena, and would Sharon feel like she shouldn't be around anymore? This took some thought.

His last duty of the day was to make the cookies. Whatever part of yesterday's cake and pie that was left over was dumped in the huge mixing pan. With the appearance of the pan came a small boy, working himself up onto the high stool to watch. This was clearly an act of magic to see Papa make cookies out of pies and cakes.

And Papa had to decide what little bottles of spicy powder were to be opened and added to the big mess. Then six (fingers on one hand and a thumb) eggs were cracked open into it, along with a big scoop of honey. It was mixed round and round, and if was too hard to mix, a pint of peaches or berries was dumped in.

If it was too soupy, left over biscuits could be added, but usually it was oatmeal that was served for breakfast.

Around and around it was stirred, and Papa had to taste it sometimes, and there were times that he let Jackie taste to see if it was "good" yet.

Then there were two big flat pans and the mess was dipped out into little piles and set in the pan. The pans were put in the oven, and out came flat cookies where the piles had been.

When they cooled down, there would be a cookie for him and for Silky but they had to take it outside because Papa had already swept the floor.

THE GRADER MANUAL

Leena's mind could not seem to settle down. There was that manual and she'd hardly had time to look at it, and Grady would be coming by wanting an answer from her.

Weary as she was, she lit the lamp and turned the pages. So much of the wording was familiar to her. And there were pictures. Pictures of the guts of the engine powered grader from many different angles, with little arrows pointing to numbers, and the numbers were in paragraphs of words. Like "This is a 'whatever,' and it does this and that. It needs to be replaced every 'whenever.' And, "This part of the 'whose it' must be oiled to perform well and avoid wear."

Then there was the part she liked. "If the complaint is 'this,' then the problem is likely to be 'that' or 'the other.'" That was the life-saver to the repair person. She read them through until her eyes would stay open no longer.

"Yes," she would tell Grady, of course, but there was still the problem of time. Clearly she and her brother needed a "wife," and her choice would definitely be Sharon, so she'd just have to start working from another direction, if her brother was too shy and humble to step up to the plate.

With that final thought, the next sound she heard was the roosters crowing.

Grady listened to the answer to his question with an expressionless face. He'd known the answer (knowing that Leena could not resist a puzzle, and that she was addicted to the metal and iron guts of the combustion engine.)

Then he nodded. Now it was crunch time and he would have to meet with the big wigs of Earthworm, and that was going to be no easy persuasion. Who was a peon like a country driver to advise the bosses how to run their business?

But Grady O'Keef had one important thing going for him. Grader drivers came and went at just about the same speed. Those who stayed on as he did were the gold of the operation. The driver who had been with them the longest was Grady O'Keef, and he was the ones who made the fewest complaints.

They knew, of course, that the time would come that he would want off the road. It was difficult to rear a family while on the road and next to impossible to find someone to share it with him. So when he requested an audience, no one was particularly surprised. Would a small raise keep him on the job…or maybe a larger raise?

That section from Eureka to King's River was a rough one. Hard on mules as well. The King's River to Berryville was easier, but still the young men stayed three or four months at the most, and most of the "quits" came in midwinter. That small cab had no way to be satisfactorily heated.

Grady was dressed in his best clothes, and nervous as a cat… but not that he would be fired. He just really wanted a grader with an engine. Was that too much to ask?

"Good Morning, Grady," he was greeted. "What can we do for you?"

Four men of an age were seated in the room facing the chair where he was presumably supposed to sit. They wore mildly expectant faces, with just a trace of "Let's get this over with," and a bit of curiosity. There was just a touch of "Why were we all called into this meeting with a grader driver?"

Grady opened his mouth to "Sirs?" And at this point every word of his much rehearsed speech disappeared like dew in the sunshine. Finally he dredged up with what he had hoped to put in the middle of his speech.

"What I'm here for is that I think I have a way to save Earthworms some money, maybe quite a lot. I've been over two years in the cab of that grader taking care of it and the two teams of mules. They have become my family, in fact, as I must find food and shelter for them before caring for myself. I manage the run from Eureka to King's River and another driver has the run on to Berryville. I know you know this, but there are a few things that might not have been mentioned.

"I grew up on Ridge Road west, and have had a lot of friends who have fed your mules, and put me up for the night just for the sake of friendship. No charge to me or Earthworms. Time has gone by now, and a lot of new people live there, strangers to me.

I cannot go to a stranger and ask them to feed my mules on their grass, especially now when the heat is so great.

"My answer would be to change out the mule drawn grader for one of the engine operated ones. The big picture would be that engine would use gasoline instead of oats and grass, but there are a lot more.

"Just this week, I had a mule step on a round rock and sprain a tendon. I walked him back to the nearest place to board him, and hired a horse to take me back to the stalled grader where the other three mules waited, and could have been stolen. Mules are valuable, I know you know."

He paused for breath, and the man who sat behind the desk motioned him to wait. "Ed, would go get the others?"

Then there were six men watching him and the desk man told Grady to continue.

"Yes, sir. The mule had to be treated by the owners of the establishment and was down for four days being cared for and fed. That created an expense for Earthworms. I hitched the horse to where the mule had been, but you all know that horses and mules do not pull the same way.

"I paid for the use of the horse, and turned in the bill. I have to quit using the few friends I have left.

"Here is what I suggest. An engine driven grader could handle the whole run from Eureka to Berryville, eliminating the need for a driver, and also a pair of mule driven graders. The driver, me in this case, could spend nights in either city and not along the road, which is dangerous for one man alone, or in the homes of friends, and I don't have many left.

"There would be mechanics at both ends of the line in the event of difficulty. And then...."

"Wait," interrupted Desk Man. "What about breakdowns midway?"

"Thank you, sir. I was just gettin' to that. Up at a place called Burnt Tree Junction, about half way to King's River there's a fix-it shop owned by a very able mechanic. There's no way you'd'a known, but we got gas cars runnin' up and down the ridge, now, needin' gas and bolts and things, and a lot of times a lot worse problems.

That mechanic has a good business, and getting' better all the time, and would be able to take on maintenance and emergency repairs for a grader. I already check it out."

Desk Man again. "That is news. Who is this person?"

Grady nodded brightly. "You'd likely not heard'a this owner, name of L. A. Sullivan. Sullivan is a local and been there for years. Fixes up Fords and Chevrolets, and Hupmobiles, Runabouts and all sorts of gas buggies. Has a room full of rods, screws, belts, and drills, and also grease, gas and oil."

Desk Man again. "Hmmm, well, continue."

"I'm about done unless you have questions. Bottom line fact is, I like gradin', and I'd like to stay on workin' for Earthworms. I'm hopin' for a way to continue that. I did a lot of figgerin' while drivin' along and I'm thinking saving time, boarding costs, value of mules and the problem with keepin' a driver on the Berryville run might well outdo the cost of an engine driven grader."

He paused. What else could he say? And there seemed to be no questions.

Desk Man took over. "Thank you so much, Mr. O'Keef. We have some talking and thinking to do, and we'll get back to you."

Grady managed a non-committable smile in the direction of the men and told them, "Thank you so much, sirs." And with that, he turned and left, closing the door softly.

As he stepped out of the Earthworms place of business, a sudden weakness hit his knees almost putting him down on the brick-paved street. It was over. For good or bad…for plus or minus…for up of down, it was over. Done. Past. No more planning how the speech would go.

He'd done his best, and had managed to keep from saying "She is a very good mechanic," as he had thought he might. Knowing that a twenty-two-year-old lovely lady was the mechanic would, for absolutely certain, kill the possible deal.

When he managed to get strength into his weak knees, relief filtered down upon him like a spring shower. It was over. One way or the other.

He checked into the wonderful little diner in Wishbone and bought a mug of steaming, strong coffee and a cinnamon roll.

Their cinnamon roles were about the size of the steering wheel of his grader and covered with sugar, spice and everything nice. Very popular.

He sat on the little wire legged chairs like the ones in the Soup Bowl Diner. He stared at the people passing by the big front window and worked on the cinnamon roll.

His thoughts began to whirl around in his head with dizzying speed. How long before he heard back from the Earthworm people? Maybe never…? If the "never" happened, what would he do? He'd been through this over and over, and hadn't found an answer. Driving the grader was all he had ever done that paid decent money.

What could he do? He might raise mules for sale. He knew about everything there was to know about those cussed animals, but with the onset of the auto, how would that effect the need for mules…or horses either, for that matter.

He spent a whole hour and a half at the tiny table on the chair with wire legs, and nothing was settled in his mind. Time to hitch up the mules and climb back onto the cramped seat of the grader.

The graders had sort of a cab for necessities, and there was a shelf bed that let down for times the driver had no other place to be. Not very comfortable, was that shelf, but the worst was that it was just about two inches shorter than he was. Absolutely no stretching out, and a lot of head bumping. He was TIRED of that bed. He was tired of cold, dry food, and tired of eating dust kicked up by the Austins, Runabouts, Hupmobiles and Fords.

He'd just about had it. As a popular saying went, he had just about "got his bucket full" and he was just about to empty it on something or somebody.

In spite of his sketchy attention, the lovely, talented Leena would not be around forever. Let's face it, that was the tap root of his whole problem. Seeing her for short sketches of time just wasn't cutting it anymore.

As the mules leaned into the traces and pulled the grader up out of Wishbone onto Ridge Road his mind was made up. It was now June, and by the last of September, he would be doing something else, or he would have the engine driven grader.

THE OPEN WINDOW INCIDENT

Keith was so upset and frightened that he could hardly remember how to scramble eggs. Something had to be done, and he didn't know what. The boy's bed had been temporarily moved in to his own room, and the mattress placed on the floor.

Jackie, the good natured, thought it was like a picnic getting to sleep on the floor in Papa's room. He loved having a papa. Why not! Every little boy needed a papa, even if he had to borrow one.

Keith reminded himself that it was not a permanent solution. Al right in an emergency, but was not right for the long run. If it was winter, he'd just be moved upstairs where it was warm, but in the summer it was more than warm. It was scorching hot.

He tried to keep his mind on the diner and the customers but it was practically impossible.

And on down the road Grady was hailed by Paul Manford, postman. After the "howdy's" Paul explained. "I got a message that needs to be left with Keith Sullivan. I don't know him, but I know you're thick with those two, so you'd be the one to tell him.

"I don't know too many folks west'a the river, but I know everybody on the east side. I know Bear LePrey really well. Went to school when he did, and us fellows had a lot of trouble tryin' to include him in our games. Wanted everything his own way. Seemed like he enjoyed mading trouble. Acted like he was doin' us a favor to play with us.

"From what I hear, he ain't changed a lot. Keith Sullivan'd not know that Bear was dog bit pretty bad on his right hand. That dog, likely tryin' to protect the kid, got Bear's hand in its teeth, but it didn't bite hard or Bear'd not have a hand left. He got lucky, but he don't see it that way.

"Fact is, he's pretty mad at the dog and wouldn't be above takin' a pot-shot at 'im. I'm knowin' those dogs are valuable, and even if he wasn't, Keith'd not want'a lose 'im. So if you'd pas the word when you get a chance, I'd appreciate it."

Grady nodded agreement. Good as done, and the two fellows parted with a friendly two-finger wave. Paul fired up his engine and left a trail of dust that settled onto the mules, Grady's head and shoulders and the road grader.

Grady watched until the car was out of sight. Chin thrust and lips firm. He'd eaten a lot of dust in his life, and likely would eat a lot more, but he decided it would not be while climbing the hills in this grader.

Leena tried to cheer her brother. "We'll think of something."

"I don't know. I can't even think if I salted the soup."

Leena sorted out a soup spoon and dipped it into the fragrant, bubbling liquid. "You salted it."

Then she leaned onto the table, chin in her hands, also thinking. Grady had just dropped in to mention that he had talked with the big-wigs, but didn't know if or when he'd get an answer. Meanwhile, she decided she'd take inventory of her needs for the next trip for gas. So many things to be done, but she just couldn't bring herself to do them.

She drew a mental picture of the side wall where so many items hung. There was the top bar that was almost empty...hey, top bar.

"Keith! Listen up! What if we clamped bars just inside the window, maybe six or eight inches apart. Then we could reach through to raise and lower the window but no way could Jackie be taken out. What'd'ya think?"

"Bars. Like on a prison window. Hmmm. But where'd we get the bars?"

"Right off the wall of my shop. I got clamps and screws and a big old screw driver. We can have those bars on before you take the pie out of the oven."

"It's two pies. Sold out yesterday. Twice I had all seats full. I can't take this."

"You don't have to. I'll get the bars and you be ready to man the screw driver. That'll take away one thing that's worryin' us."

Five minutes later they had tacked six bars over the window, stretching from the top to about five feet down. Keith was forcing the screws into the solid oak walls.

Jackie asked, "What's that for?"

Leena fielded the question. "To make your window look pretty. Do you like them?"

He thought a minute. "I like them. I just figgered it was to make little boys ask questions, like most other things."

At this point Sharon stepped in. "Keith, you got customers. I took care'a them. I took the pies out 'cause they were tryin' to burn. Do you want me to cut cut 'im? Lawman wants a piece."

"Yeah, cut 'im a piece. I'll be there in a minute."

Jackie said, "Silky, do you like that new window?"

Silky did.

Keith went back to the diner and Leena gathered her tools. Sharon followed her to the shop.

Packages of screws and bolts and clamps and rubber washers were all over the floor. It appeared a tornado had just struck it.

"Look at that!" Leena invited. "Keith was about to go berserk and I was in a hurry to get the bars. I was about to count stuff anyway. Gotta make a trip to Wishbone."

"Why is Keith berserk?"

"Too much stuff fallin' in on us at one time."

"What kind'a stuff?"

"Scared about Jackie. Too many customers at a time. Too many goats to milk. I got a new customer, and Grady may have more for me. I got no time to do things like I used to."

"What'll you do?"

"Don't know." And an idea struck into Leena's head. "It's all Keith's fault."

"How so?"

"He needs to find us a wife. He ain't even lookin'."

"You both need a wife?"

"No, one'll be enough if it's the right one." Leena was sorting "like" items from the pile and grouping them together in heaps on the floor.

Sharon stood behind her, watching, and trying to make sense of her words, just after wondering about the almost burnt pies. A wife? And Keith isn't even lookin'? What was going on at this place that was always so well run?

She asked, "What kind'a wife does he need? Do you know?"

Leena leaned back on backside and propped her hands behind her. "Yes, I know. He needs someone like you only just for one thing."

"What one thing?"

"Maybe two things. First off, she mustn't be pretty." (Leena wanted to say "beautiful" but that would be too much.) "So you can see you're safe. That lets you out."

Sharon, puzzled, was silent for a couple of minutes. Then, "What's the other thing?"

Leena turned to face Sharon full on. "She must be very disagreeable to get along with, and likely a sorry cook."

"Why doesn't he need those two things?"

"He needs them, but he knows he isn't worthy of anything so grand. He's just a diner cook with a little boy to raise. Not only that, he has that terrible red hair that won't behave, and doesn't want to see any fancy food on the table."

"How come?"

"He knows that he is not worth the person who he would like so he mustn't look for someone like that. There is no way she would agree to be with him. And he works so many hours, he doesn't have time to look for the ugly, disagreeable, horrible cook that he knows he deserves."

Silence…as Sharon studied this strange person sitting at her feet. Then the strange person said, "Sharon, grab a hunk of paper and a pencil over there on the shelf and write this down. Brackets, fourteen. Belts, three. And let's see, gear grease…."

Leena counted and Sharon wrote. Keith took Jackie for a riding lesson and Sharon manned the diner. Too many customers, huh? She'd thought that was the object of a business. He just needed more stools and another bar.

Now if he moved Jackie's play area, he could add a bar here that would take four, maybe five, stools. The stools could be slid under the bar when not needed. She filled four biscuits with the feta cheese and put three in the warming oven while she ate the fourth one. The three regulars came in.

"Hot out there, did you know that? Gimmie a chile with one of them cheese sandwiches under it."

Actually, she sold three of the mixtures and collected ten cents from each of them. Leena came in and poured herself a mug of coffee. "Gonna wait until morning and go to Wishbone early. Gotta get gas, too."

Sharon watched. "Got a question."

"Shoot...."

"Just how ugly would that person have to be to suit Keith?"

"Pretty ugly. You'd never make it in a million years. Why, you couldn't even be mildly disagreeable if you tried, and you couldn't even let the pies burn." She sipped the scalding liquid, smiling inwardly. Things were going just as planned.

"And you remember that cheese thing you made with the pimentos and tomatoes? He hates stuff like that on the table. He only ate three helpings. He'd rather have had mashed potatoes fried in cakes."

Sharon might be beautiful, but she was not dumb. She knew exactly what was going on and she had to decide what to do with the information. This was getting serious.

"Leena, can you picture another bar starting from the window and going back to Jackie's toy box?"

Leena nodded. "And the wall scooted back about three feet."

"Five more customers?"

"Maybe eight."

BOARD MEETING

Down in Eureka Springs the decision makers of Earthworms met at the big table. Big table meant big decisions or changes.

Bits of conversation flew back and forth. Changes were hard to decide on and even harder to make. But the thing was, it was now 1910 and it was a new day. The combustion engine was at the bottom of it, and road graders had just come on the market. The first ones had a bit of trouble, but corrections were made. It took a strong engine to pull gravel up from a ditch and spread it across the road while trying to haul up another load from the ditch. Along with continuing to move forward.

The last purchase, however, was looking good. It was now on a downtown route, clearing the road for a new grocery store. The driver really didn't like the job, but hoped for a better one with Earthworms.

Talk.

"I ain't seein' a reason for change, of acount'a one complaint."

"Maybe, but look who complained. Our best driver."

"Anyone can be replaced."

"Did you see the size'a the boarding bill we got? Can't keep havin' that."

"That was only one time."

"Did you fellows take note'a what O'Keef said?"

"Yeah. He's been spongin' off friends. Give 'im a raise to shut 'im up."

"Not that easy. He wasn't wantin' money."

"Let 'im quit if he don't like it!"

"And replace 'im with two that won't last two months?"

"I thought what he said made sense. Seems he gave it a lot'a thought, and we've never been out there where he is."

"Good mechanic, he thinks."

"I say let's let 'im stew a while. He might'a just been lettin' off steam."

"Not Grady O'Keef. He's gonna leave if he don't get what he wants."

"Leave? Surely not. Been there for over two years not complainin' about the conditions."

"Yeah and it ain't been 1910 before, and things are different. That young fellow's gonna leave if he don't get an engine drawn grader. Mark my word."

And comments flew for better than an hour, and Desk Man let them fly. He already knew what was going to be done. That new grader was going to Ridge Road, the Berryville driver was going to bring his grader to the short, downtown run, and the new guy was coming to the office to be available for emergencies.

And that's exactly how it happened. Desk Man motioned to a young fellow among them. "James, fire off a letter to that young fellow out on Ridge Road. Tell 'im to come in to see me next time he's down this way."

"Yes, Sir! Right away, Sir!"

And the board meeting was over.

BEAR RIDES AGAIN

Bear LePrey was just about as angry as a man his size can get, and that's pretty mad. That dog had actually cracked one of the bones in his hand, and he'd likely have a stiff ring finger…that's what the horse doctor down the road told him.

It ached all the time and drinking willow tea didn't stop it. It had to be dressed and Ma was pretty angry with him for letting a dog bite him when her son was just trying to pet it. Just too friendly and good natured, that boy of hers was.

"Told you, son. Leave them strange animals alone. You never know when they got the plague, or somethin'. And they all got teeth."

Seems he couldn't do a thing with just his left hand, not even putting on his socks. Nothing except find his mouth. He could eat right well, it seems.

But he was bored. Nothing to do but wait for his hand to heal. He could ride the horse, though, but he wouldn't take a favorite animal. He was sure he'd never ridden Zipper down Ridge Road past the Bistro. Bear was well aware that men were known by their horses fully as much by their appearance.

Zipper trotted amiable down past the roadside stand and then the Eat and Get Gas. Bear took a quick glance and there was that brat playing in the dirt of the yard with that hateful dog laying not five feet away.

Catching him outside playing alone was going to be hard to do. That dog was stuck to him like a coat'a paint. Well, he'd just have to keep at it.

None of this was Bear's fault, of course. If that stupid Margie had not taken the kid and cut out in the night, he wouldn't have to do all this, and he wouldn't have been bitten by that bloodhound. Clearly her fault, and now she's gone to who knows where. Got shed'a the kid, though. Should'a done that earlier.

He rode on past the junction to the road down to the fellow who makes log cabins. Time to turn Zipper around and head on back. Nothin' to be gained by lookin'. Already done that.

He'd hardly turned around when he noticed the road grader making its way up the hill. A fresh furrow of dirt and gravel came up with the first blade, and was leveled out by the second one. The driver, redhaired fellow, was standing on the machinery with his back turned. Just as well. Bear would just as soon not be seen on the west side of King's River.

Grady had just moved off the driver's seat to pretend to check something with the blades. The truth was, he did not want Bear to think he had seen him.

Bartley Wilcox had just stopped him earlier in the day to report that Bear was about…riding a different horse, but still wearing the huge hat. Now, how smart was that? He also reported that Jackie's dog might be a new target of Bear's rage.

Seeing Bear was turning around, he slowed his mules to let him get away. Then, at the junction, Annie Jo waved him over to report that Burley had seen Bear on a different horse.

If Bear had only known how he was being watched! But all he could think of was how he was going to get it done.

Leena was under a Stutz Bearcat checking a bent axle. Sure enough, and stingy old Mr. Bedford was going to be angry. But that's what happened when he let his spoiled son drive an expensive car. She could fix it or not. He would part with twenty-seven dollars, or he could just wobble on down to Wishbone and pay more. Likely wear out a few bearings on the way. He was just lucky she had one in stock. Axles were pretty much alike, and these mountain roads were murder for certain parts. Axles included.

All Leena could think of was when was Grady going to get news so she'd know. She was frustratingly torn between actually wanting to work on the grader, and being already overworked by details. So many sweaty clothes in the summer and so many vegetables to be put by. Keith was going to have to do something soon.

Truly, the twins needed a wife for all those pesky little things that took so much time. As Keith seemed to feel that he did not deserve the person he'd really like, and as he had no time to seek and court the one he clearly deserved, his wife-hunting was at a stalemate. That meant the search would shift itself to the able shoulders of his sister.

She'd had an idea, and it might still work. It had been late yesterday that she had mentioned that the community of Tribbey had a wedding. The school teacher got married and that left a vacancy. Certain propects were notified when that happened, to see if there was someone the area who qualified and was interested.

When she mentioned the wedding, Keith had nodded but had not responded. He had enough things to think about, without thinking about Tribbey's school problem.

Leena had waited an appropriate length of time and mentioned, "You remember when Sharon took the test for teacher certification?"

No answer. Another short wait.

Then she added, "The school board notified Sharon to see if she was interested." Ha! That got his attention!

He took a breath and signed, wearily. "Is she gonna take it?"

"Don't know. She's gotta do somethin' 'stead'a spendin' all her time takin' care'a us."

Silence. But he was totally alert on the inside. Sharon gone? Surely not. But yes, she had to do something. She was barely two years younger that he and Leena.

Leena yawned noisily and stated that she was headed for bed. Tomorrow was another day.

Keith settled into his over-stuffed chair so he could more comfortably grovel in the depth of anxiety, and mentally added Sharon to his list of worries.

Jackie and the bloodhound settled happily in his cool toyroom/bedroom with the fancy decoration his family had put in his window.

Bear had wisely given up nighttime snatching of the boy, and had gone on to other plans which included getting rid of that ever-present dog.

Grady spent a comfortable night in Wishbone, the new grader being parked out on Ridge Road. There was no chance of it being taken, as it would not move without the motor running, and that took a key which was resting safely in Grady's left boot.

He drifted off to sleep with the words of Desk Man playing themselves through his mind. He'd been greeted with the chummy greeting of, "Come in, son, and sit." He did.

"You sure educated us with your talk. I'd never read that book that came with the new graders, and neither had anyone else. Imagine not waiting for a breakdown to make repairs.

"That book actually did say that regular maintenance checks were to be made after two months or 150 miles, and it gave a checklist of the most likely items to check, just like you said.

"So, I'm giving you the keys, and you can learn to operate it on the way back to Wishbone. I'm sending our mechanic with you to answer questions, and to bring back the mules and your old machine.

"Another little secret that you mustn't let get out is that our money counters put their heads together and realized we were working a bit backward. It was decided that long routes like yours and about four others would benefit more from those machines, and the others used here around town with greater accommodation for the mules.

"So, you have my thanks, and an upgrade in your pay, but don't let it get around or others will be swarming me with their own suggestions."

Mr. Desk Man winked and grinned at that last admonition, but Grady felt sure he actually meant it.

So Grady had stopped in Wishbone and had a wonderful meal at the diner at the hotel. He'd checked in and stretched luxuriously on the stuffed mattress and decided he would have a mattress of his own and no more sleeping of a one-inch pad of feathers, themselves crushed into dust.

Bear made a little stop at the shed where the horses were gathered. Which should he take to make the trip through the woods? His last choice had been Prince, and that was still a good one. Prince knew he was a carriage horse, and valued for his appearance of a lifted head, arched neck and measured steps.

There were a lot of trees and low-growing limbs in the woodland behind the Eat and Get Gas. Maybe Captain would be better. A bit smaller might fit better among the trees. Git-away speed would not be a factor because he would just look for a good aim at that dog and get him with one shot.

The way sound ricocheted around the hills and caves, it would be a few minutes before anyone would locate the direction of the shot, assuming they actually heard it.

That done, then he could concentrate on the boy without that evil dog to bother with. He was told by Ma that in another two or three days he could get rid of the protective bandage, and that he had better be more careful about petting strange dogs. It don't do to be good to some dogs and even some folks.

Well, Bear already knew that.

ONE MORE PROBLEM

Grady, being mentally and physically exhausted over his last several weeks, had slept in on the wonderful mattress and had breakfasted royally on diner coffee and a pair of the mammoth cinnamon rolls.

It was early afternoon when he rolled in to the parking place at Eat and Get Gas. He grinned happily as he shut down the motor and pocketed the key. No mules to consider!

Leena had just crawled back under the Morse Minor to change out this and that, and the greasy parts were liberally caked with road dust. There had to be a better way of cleaning than she had.

She had just been pulled out from under by her renter. "So sorry to tell you, honey, you been so good to us, but we got'a move. We got us offered a place down by Wishbone that's got spring water piped in. This bein' such sudden notice, we thought we'd leave a store'a cheese in the cellar, and would you put a price on these seven nannie goats? They seem to have took to us, and they're good producers."

Leena was momentarily stunned, thinking the rent house problem was settled, maybe forever. "Uh, well, yes. Thanks for tellin' us and for the cheese. I'll check with my brother on a price for the goats."

She had just crawled back under the car and realized she needed more soapy water. She then scooted out and stood up, shaking the loose coveralls in place, and saw a bright orange monster occupying the driveway. WHAT in the world was that!

But when she saw Grady appear from around the corner, she knew she was looking at her new charge. This was the new creature she would be totally responsible for. So much bigger than she had imagined from the picture.

She decided Mister Morse Minor with the dirt-caked guts could just wait a little longer. With a fluid and practiced motion, she zipped down the garment and stepped out of it. She yanked off the cap and shook out her hair.

She met the wickedly grinning Grady, and hauled him into the diner. "I got'a have coffee before I can look that monster over."

Grady allowed he could stand a cup also.

Leena tried to clear away the most recent problem from her mind. She had no intention of asking Keith about pricing the goats. He'd say "Take 'em for free. No, I'll pay to have them gone." No deal. Maybe a swap out for more cheese, or…she'd think of something.

She blew the steam from the cup and announced to her tale mate, "Renters leavin'. Got a better place. They just told me."

Instead of a word of sympathy, what she got from Grady was, "Hey, that's wonderful! Just perfect."

"WHAT!!!"

"You just got a new tenant. Me. I'll rent it and move in the minute I can, and I don't want any goats."

"You'll…what…?"

"I was fixin' to look for a place. No more sleepin' rough for me. Bed with eight inch feather bed, that's what I want. I'm ridin' in style. Got the route from Eureka to Berryville and a raise, and you got the scheduled maintenance check, and whatever you want to charge."

Leena decided this took more than a cup of coffee to think about. "Keith, would you slide me down a slab of that cake. Applesauce, it it? Good!"

A saucer and fork came scooting down the counter with a piece of spicy brown cake riding along. She picked up the fork.

"But I thought it was going to take days before you found out anything. And you can be in a house every night?"

"Sure can. That thing has an engine that moves it right along, and I got a mechanic that can keep it doing that. Here's a secret for you. Wouldn't'a got it so easy if it wasn't for you."

"Me...?"

"Yeah, you. L. A. Sullivan, Mechanic, that's you."

Leena settled for a dollar a piece for the seven nannie goats and 120 pounds of cheese that would only get better with age. Grady watched impatiently as their plunder was loaded on wagons. It would take him about seven minutes to move in and install the borrowed mattress until he could get his own.

THE WIFE

Keith glanced occasionally out the window toward the road. Sharon should be coming along, and he'd see if she would sit in the diner while he took Jackie for a riding lesson. Thought he'd go up the road to the catalog store and order about six new bar stools. The new shelf was temporary until a better board could be found, but it worked. Right now it had kitchen chairs, but they were about six inches too low for comfort.

And there was that nagging thought in Keith's head. Sharon might be gone? No! Sharon had always been there, at least for the almost four years that the diner had been opened.

Sparky also glanced up occasionally. It was always the other horses that went out and came back, and she was usually left behind, but lately it had been different. The tiny human had been riding on her back, and it almost always had a piece of carrot, or potato. Sometimes an apple.

It was a nice break from being inside the same pen all day, every day. She looked up again, but nothing yet. A few more bites of grass, and maybe....

Jackie had his toy wagon full of logs, and was standing at the new bar building this and that. Beside him on the bar was the book of children's poems, a gift from Sharon's childhood.

Jackie loved words. He loved happy sounding words and words that had sounds alike. He first noticed the sound-alike words when he thought of "eat meat." And "bug rug."

When Aunt Sharon read her little stories, she made the end words sound happy, and they both giggled and laughed.

"Simple Simon met a pie man." He'd announced, "My papa is a pie man but he isn't Simon. But he can bake a cake. Who can make a rake?" Words were such fun.

But Aunt Sharon wasn't here so he couldn't ride Sparky or read a book. So he built towers with his logs and waited.

Bear had brought Captain up Ridge Road, and walked him back to the abandoned cabin. He tied him there and walked toward the diner. Carefully using the paths, and not stepping on dead leaves to crush them, he slipped along, moving up close enough to see the back yard. Maybe the dog would come out to tend to nature, and he could get a shot.

Sparky saw the man, but she knew he was not the one who would take her for a ride, so she continued nibbling the grass. Then, here came the right person.She watched to be sure, then ambled over to meet the man who patted her and held to her mane while she walked along beside him.

Bear watched, and a sigh of disappointment escaped his lips. Not today. Keith was taking the pony for a riding lesson for the brat, and the dog would go along. Better luck tomorrow.

He carefully retraced his steps, but he was glad he came. There was a flattish rock in a good position for him to watch the back of the house. The rock was about the size of a double bed, and almost as flat. He could wait on that rock and hardly be seen unless someone was looking right at him. Maybe not even then.

He made his way back to the cabin and led Captain back to the road. Mounting, he put the horse into a gallop and headed toward King's River. He could wait. Sometime the time would be right, and he would do what he must do.

Leena cleared the breakfast table and washed the dishes. She picked a basket of tomatoes and sorted out several for lunch, peeling the rest into a large canning kettle. One couldn't have too many canned tomatoes. Maybe Sharon would see the ones on the table and get an idea. Maybe.

Sharon moved a stool behind the bar and opened a new book she had just bought. There were two persons at the table but they seemed to have what they wanted. Keith and Jackie were gone and she had just finished sweeping the floor of tracked in dirt.

Leena dipped the scalding hot tomatoes into jars, filling five of them, and then putting them in the cooker to boil. Time for a break. She helped herself to coffee and sat in one of the chairs beside Jackie's book of wonderful sounding words.

She had just sold Paul Manford a five gallon can of gas and he had whispered, "The Bear is out. Riding a little tan race horse. Thought you needed to know." She thanked him and waved goodby, then added the empty can to the three others she had. Another trip to Wishbone for gas would be soon. And it was going to take even more to feed that orange monster that had crept into her life.

Leena fingered the rhyme book and a thought struck her. "Sharon?"

Sharon looked up from the book.

Leena continued. "Another thing that ugly person must have is a hatred for little boys, and must never give him gifts or let him get to likin' her."

Sharon put the book aside. "Do you suppose he'll ever find that person?"

"Not if he don't start lookin', he won't."

"I got another notice from the school board. Eakley's havin' trouble getting' someone, it looks like."

"Givin' it more thought?"

"Hmm, well. My ma is afraid I might. That's way over past Berryville, and they don't want me so far away."

Leena nodded, sipping coffee. So far, so good. Ma and Pa Atkins would do their part.

The fellows returned, Jackie flushed and rosy-faced from excitement. "Aunt Sharon! I rode Sparky! All the way to Uncle Burley's!" He grabbed her arm and tucked it around himself. Then he saw the book she had been reading.

"Aunt Sharon! You got the wrong book. This is the good one!" And he tucked the rhyme book into her hand.

Leena rinsed her cup, put it on the hook and left the diner. Jackie was doing his part. Now, if she could just get through to Keith.

Keith thanked Sharon, and watched her leave with Jackie and the book. *Such a beautiful girl, and she won't last a minute in Tribbey. Or Eakley, either. The fellows a either place will gobble her up like a rattler gobbles a frog.*

Sharon sat Jackie at the table and told him to pick a poem he wanted, and she would be right back. She stepped to the garden and pulled two green peppers and two pimento peppers. She searched until she found a young turnip that had not gone bitter.

She returned to the kitchen, and Jackie had picked a poem, and was puzzling over one of the words. "Aunt Sharon? What's this word?"

She looked. "It's 'trundle' like being pulled along and making noise."

She chopped the onion the skille with butter, and the four leftover breakfast biscuits broke into small chunks. Into the browned bread chunks, she added the four chopped peppers and the sliced tomatoes. She stirred thoroughly and put half in a casserole dish, spread a layer of goat cheese, added the bread mixture, and then a thick topping of cheese. It was too soon to bake it so she set it aside and took the five jars of canned tomatoes to the cellar, still warm from being boiled.

Jackie was working on a poem he had never heard read. He liked to do that to see how many of the words he already knew.

Green beans. There could be a few pods of the new crop. They'd be young, sweet and tender. She'd just check it out.

Jackie brought his book and followed her. She might take a long time, and he'd need to know another word. As she searched along the row for enough to make a meal, he walked beside her with the book open. "What's this word?"

"That's 'fountain' like a stream of water that bubbles up."

She found enough green beans, if she just added a couple of chopped potatoes to fill them out. Then she'd get the broom and attack that cob web that appeared across the window. What in the world is a "cob"? Is it that spider that has four pairs of legs instead of eight legs spread evenly around its body? Maybe so. They made a funny web, hard to see unless the light was just right. Anyway, it had to go.

The regulars came in and occupied the table. An old couple with a little girl stopped by for a sandwich and two men on a horseback came in. They opted to sit on the low chairs at the new bar.

The postman stopped in for his favorite desert. He eyed the blackberry pie and the lone bar stool and opted for cake and took it with him. Just too crowded in there, and that strange little kid would likely spill milk on his uniform.

GATHERING MUSHROOMS

Leena was crawling around inside a National Runabout reinforcing the flimsy stalks that held up the roof. Ridiculous construction. If a surrey, which was essentially a moving tent, was needed, then a surrey should be used, not the roof of what was supposed to be a car.

However, the complaint of the owner was that it jiggled when she drove it down the lane to her home. Of course it jiggled.

The road jiggled. It had been hacked out of pure stone. So the "mechanic" was reinforcing the rods and installing a bracket at the base of each one trying to make it appear that was the way it was made.

While sweating and straining, she promised there would come a time, and maybe sooner than anyone thought, that she would turn down dinky little jobs like this. Right now, she still needed the gas, oil and tire trade of these customers, so she took every job, even patching oilcloth roof leaks.

Keith was speculating on whether there would be enough of the berry pie left to make cookies, or would he have to add a pint of berries from the cellar. Cookies were a must.

Sharon had helped Leena with the washing, and had commented that the weather was right for mushrooms, her ma had said. Shower after a dry long spell often brought up mushrooms under the oak trees, if they had a bed of dried, rotten leaves.

The land down the hill behind the Eat and Get Gas had just about every kind of tree imaginable, so there were certainly oaks, and they would have dry leaves because nothing had disturbed the trees since the time God created them.

Washing finished, she located a large basket and headed out down the sloping rear of the diner. Jackie, bored with toys and books decided he would go with her to "help."

He was told, "Go ask Papa and say we're going to be in the woods." He came bouncing back excited that Papa had said "Yes, be sure to mind Aunt Sharon."

Good luck! The first tree did, indeed have mushrooms and they were gently pulled, and the stubby root replaced in the ground for the spores to remember to grow more when the weather was right. There was another tree very close that looked even better.

Leena finished with the Runabout and was waiting for the first coat of paint to dry, so she took a shovel to the garden behind the house to turn the dirt for planting fall peas.

Not far away on a slab of volcanic stone sat a person waiting and watching with eager anticipation.

Absolutely every pore in his body oozed with irritation, aggravation, anger and hatred and the product of this ooze created a cocktail of loathing and self-pity. He WOULD have that boy and make the world pay for its gross mistreatment of him.

He had also spent more time on that rock than he thought he should have had to. Each day he presumed that would be "the day" and it aggravatingly had not been. So today he waited in the after-rain steamy air and watched the area behind the hated house.

He saw Sharon come through the back door followed by the boy. He saw the boy dart back into the house and return with the vicious dog.

Sharon turned her face toward him while she waited, and the late afternoon sun dappled through the leaves with sparking rays. He stared, mesmerized with a realization. That girl they called Sharon was absolutely beautiful…even more than Margie had been.

Standing there, her hair bunched on her head and a look of expectation on her face, and he knew he must possess her. He also knew it was the wrong thing to do, because she was not a part of his careful plans. He was prepared to deal with the boy and the dog, but not an adult, but he could not stop himself.

He followed silently on the slightly damp leaves, moving only when she was turned away, staying behind a tree trunk. He was very skilled at hunting in trees. That was where the deer liked to hide, but they did not hide from him.

So interested were Sharon and Jackie that they did not look his way as they knelt to gather the small globes of fungi for the basket. The boy squealed with excitement when he found another patch, and waited for Sharon to tell him if they were big enough to gather.

The kidnapper was now so close he could see the basket and the mushrooms. He could see the shine of Sharon's hair and the satiny blue of the tie that kept the hair in place. He could see the smooth line of her chin when she turned to the boy. Lovely. So beautiful it made his stomach hurt!

Called for a change of plans. So now how to actually do it. Sharon obviously loved the little boy, and he could use that. He had a small 22mm Walther in his pocket in easy reach to use on the dog. He'd have to work fast and use the element of surprise as he shot the dog…grabbed the boy…and make Sharon believe she must not make a sound or the boy would die.

In his befuddled brain, he was certain it would work. It had to. It had cost him too much time and aggravation not to. It was clearly his turn to have something good to happen to him.

While he was poised to act, the huge grader came down the little lane on the other side of the house and stopped at the back house. He watched through the trees as Grady left the machine and went into the house.

From the corner of his vision, he saw Leena stand and look in the direction of Grady's house. Just then Jackie squealed in excited joy at an exceptionally large mushroom.

Leena turned toward the scream, but Bear stood as still as a tree trunk and Leena again turned to her garden. After about a minute, he again stood and located Sharon and the boy. Still in positioned correctly.

It was now or never. Bear watched for Sharon to stoop and turn away from him and he dashed forward and grabbed Jackie around the waist holding him tightly with one arm. He should reach for the gun but had to put his hand over the boy's mouth and somehow place the plaster on his face. The dog had been aware of the hated smell, and had snaked around and leaped at the back of the person almost knocking him down, but grabbing a mouthful of clothing. There she hung, but Bear now had the plaster and as it hit the brat's face, it let out a muffled scream.

Leena heard it and told herself, Jackie was having the time of his life with this new game and she continued to turn the soil of the garden row.

Sharon turned and gasped, and she was told in a throaty whisper, "You make a sound and I'll choke this brat." Jackie was squirming and kicking with rage and trying to scream through his nose.

"Lady, mark my word, I will kill him and then you. You will follow after me on this path and you will not say a word." So that's what she did.

Leena rested for a minute against the hoe handle, and heard no more excited squeals…and not only that, the last squeal sounded more like a bee sting than the sight of a large mushroom.

She turned and her eyes searched through the trees but saw neither of them. Dropping the hoe, she dashed through the gate and down the path. In minutes, she saw the basket of mushrooms. She whirled around looking in every direction and saw the last glimpse of the blue hair ribbon through the trees….

She wheeled around as fast as she could, dashed through the trees and slammed through the door, grabbing the Henry Repeating Rifle from over the door. She yelled through the house, "Keith, go get Burley. Jackie's been nabbed."

Keith heard and looked at his three regulars and the postman. "Paul, go get Burley. Jackie's been kidnapped."

Leena fired two shots in the air. Signal for help. Grady grabbed the gun he must always carry and tore out through the trees toward Leena's signal.

The kidnapper had a good lead and knew where he was going. He slipped through the trees and headed down hill toward the cabin, dragging the dog behind him…her teeth still attached to the seat of his pant.

Silky knew she had to do something, and wasn't sure what, but she was hanging on to the mouthful of coveralls and pockets until she figured it out. The man tried to reach around and swat her with his hand, but was unable. Silky wondered if she should let loose the cloth and grab for the hand, but decided she'd hang on to what she had.

At the cabin he ordered Sharon to open the door and go through and close it after him. He edged through the door trying to hold the kicking feet away from him, and the flying fists out of his face. Who'd have thought the kid could be so strong?

Paul fired up his mail hack and drove down to the roadside stand, honking the horn and yelling for help. Annie Joe heard him yell "kidnapper," and she ran to the gong she used to signal Burley that he was needed.

The lawman appeared in minutes with a horse and a large bloodhound dog, her ears flapping like butterfly wings. He yelled to Paul, "Where at?" and the mailman answered, "Behind the house, I think."

Keith had grabbed the first horse he had seen, and jumped on, guiding it with knees and a tap on its face. It happened to be Flossie, and she sensed urgency and galloped like the hounds were after her. Keith had heard Grady drive in, so he would be behind the house. That meant someone should go down Ridge Road and cut back north, and that would be him.

Two people he loved…Jackie and Sharon. His heart tried to beat out of his chest, it seemed. Anger tore his breath from his throat. He dug heels unmercifully into Flossie's heaving sides and her hoofs pounded the gravel road. He tried to think how far they could have gone so he could determine when to head into the trees.

Inside the cabin Bear began to realize he had likely bitten off more than he could chew but he was not giving up. Sharon was staring at him as though he was the devil himself, seeming to be more angry than frightened. She should be frightened. He wouldn't hurt her if she could just manage a few tears, and be more respectful. That's all he wanted, respect and obedience. Margie never learned that.

Silky looked around and there were no open doors, and the room was not large. Here was her chance. She loosened her grip and leaped at his back, knocking him forward.

The instant he was in the leaning position, she took another grab at the side of him that was closest, and closed her mouth on about a half a pound of flesh. He screamed and whirled, flinging Silky away but she scrambled her feet on the split log floor and circled looking for another bite.

Bear, with his hands full of the kicking Jackie, tried to aim the gun. Silky had not been taught what a gun was but she didn't like the acrid smell of it. When the man removed a hand from Jacky to aim the gun, the boy slid down to the floor.

When Silky saw the gun where she could get at it she snarled and leaped with all her teeth showing. She knocked the gun to the floor growled and leaped toward his throat. She missed, but grabbed a mouthful of coverall buttons and front pocket.

Sharon scooted across the floor and grabbed the gun. She shouted, "JACKIE! Go through to the other room and shut the door. Lock it." She did not take her eyes off the man as she backed up to get a better aim. She fired two shots from the Walther, whizzing them on either side of Bear's head.

Exhausted, Bear just stared at her. Jackie got mixed up and went out the wrong door and found himself outside all alone in a place where he had never been. He looked around at all the trees seeming to close in on him and screamed the loudest he had ever screamed.

Keith had left the road and was ducking through the trees having no idea which way to go, and the sound behind him was surely Burley and the dog. Ugly Face sniffed the strange scent mixed with the smell of gunpowder, which she knew so well. She raced thought the trees crossing the path where Bear had dragged Silky behind him. That was also a scent she knew.

Following the scent toward the cabin, she let out a few barks of "treed," which was the universal dog signal the the quarry was pinned down and the human could proceed.

Silky perceived that the person with the gun, whom she knew so well, was now in charge, so she stood back snarling and lifting her furry lips at the taste of the same blood she had tasted before.

Bear was bleeding from the back side, with blood running down his legs and into his shoes. Sharon knew she had control, so she could afford to wait and not hurt him worse than he was already hurting. Her two shots would tell help where she was. If help didn't come, she would eventually shoot his legs and take Jackie home.

Help came.

Grady caught up with Leena and her rifle. They followed a path of scuffed leaves left by Sharon. Keith, followed closely by Burley, came down what had been the road, now full of sprouts and small trees. The horses ducking under limbs and the men laying flat to keep from being rubbed off.

Ugly Face smelled Silky inside the cabin, but couldn't see where to get in. She knew Jackie only slightly but knew he was not the enemy. Jackie grabbed Ugly Face by the neck and hung on, and boy and dog saw the men on horses break through the trees.

Jackie yelled, "In the house, Papa! Sharon's in the house!"

The men dismounted and opened the front door just as the breathless Leena and Grady entered from the side door.

The four rescuers stared at the Frenchman standing with hands down at his sides and blood soaking the back of his clothes. Sharon stood with the Walther aimed and did not take her eyes off him. She stood where the late afternoon sun shone bright squares of light on her and on the split-log floor. Beautiful blue ribbon held her bright hair away from her face. Her cheeks were rosy with color from the excitement.

Keith stood looking at her as though he could never stop. He was prepared for injury or possible death, and she stood like a statue, fully in charge. WHAT a lady!

She had saved herself and his little boy and he had some serious thinking to do. He'd not be the first fellow to be turned down, but he now knew what he wanted and he'd never get it if he didn't ask.

Burley took the rope that he always had on a sudden trip like this, and tied Bear's hands behind him. With the help of Grady and Keith, he hoisted Bear across the saddle, dead man style with his bloody backside toward the sky. It would have been inhuman to make him sit for the ride.

Flossie had now heaved breath into her powerful lungs and willingly accepted the lawman on her back as she and the other horse made their way back to the road. They had obviously done their duty and could not walk home in honor.

Keith and Grady walked back with Leena and Sharon as Jackie bounced around them chattering excitedly.

Sharon pushed all the praise of the capture off onto Jackie. "Jackie couldn't scream or bite, but he used his feet in a wonderful way. He was just tall enough that the way Bear was holdin' him, he could kick where it would hurt the most. All I had to do was wait till Jackie hurt 'im bad enough."

And Keith tried to apologize. "I'm so sorry that had to happen."

Sharon answered with wide questioning eyes. "Why? Why'd you be sorry? Be glad, 'cause now you don't have to worry about Jackie anymore."

As they got closer to the house, she suggested, "Is anybody hungry? I got that cheese casserole set back pickin' up flavor, and there's green beans with taters. Blackberry dumplings? Be ready in twenty minutes."

A few more steps and she added, "No mushrooms, though. Maybe tomorrow."

Leena smiled under her breath. "'Atta girl, Sharon. Pour it on!"

They might get a wife after all.

Jackie was too excited to eat. "I kicked and kicked but I wanted to bite 'im."

Keith ate like a condemned man consuming his final meal. Bite after silent bite, staring into his plate. Grady was a chatter-box of comments, and none of them about the new orange Monster.

Sharon passed around her perfect cornbread, and Leena tried to eat with her fingers crossed. Maybe…maybe….

LATER

Leena and Grady were in the "rent" house, now with its new tenant who proudly pointed out what he liked. "Off the road, see? And I'm be keeping the Monster right here. Cellar full of cheese if I get hungry. Close to the well for water. No goats!..." On and on as though Leena did not know the house from inside out…including the bullet hole in the wall with the bullet still in habitation.

"See here? I got everything I need. A wonderful house, a new machine, more money…. Everything! So now, what'd you think about it?"

"Think about what…?"

"You givin' up all that nonsense about not bein' my girl. I can give you a house, a new job and I can afford all the furniture you want to buy, except for one thing."

"What's the one thing?"

"I get to pick the mattress. It has to be eight inches thick like the ones at Wishbone Hotel."

"Never been there to see it."

"That'll change. Is it a 'yes'?

Leena paused and considered the matter. "I reckon so, except for one thing."

"What's that one thing?"

"The Monster will never be parked on the driveway. That's for my blue truck. You have to pull around in front of the house."

A deep nod of Grady's head. "Done!"

The matter was not so simple in the Eat and Get Gas. Kevin returned to the diner and Sharon followed. There were things to do, such as the close-of-day clean up required of every eating establishment, and he had now had to make the cookies. Even after a kidnapping, life, as they say, went on.

He took out the big pan and dumped in the last of the chocolate cake, and the lone piece of pumpkin pie. Sharon watched Kevin's face as he made a silent decision. How would he fill it out?

Sharon offered, "If you need fruit, there's left over blackberry dumplings. I'll get them."

He nodded and waited, long stirring spoon in hand.

She returned, dipping about half the dumplings into the bowl. "Enough?" she asked, spoon poised.

"One more spoonful."

He whirled, then he turned to her. "Sharon, when I knew that beast had you I was so scared I could hardly breathe. I was certain he'd kill you and the dog and take off with Jackie."

Sharon waited.

"You've been such a help…and a pleasure…and…."

Sharon waited.

"I wish I could give you what you deserve, but it seems I can't. I'm only me and not likely to change. You have so many choices, why would you choose me?"

Sharon waited, dumpling bowl in one hand, dipping spoon in the other. The house was deathly quiet. Jackie, totally exhausted and run down by the excitement had leaned over his pile of blocks, and was sound asleep. Silky lay at his feet, one floppy ear over Jackie's right shoe.

Her eyelids were closed down to a tiny sliver of brightness. One move of the foot and she would again be on guard. She was totally satisfied…as she had never been in her short life. She had done what her insides had told to her to do and how she had her small human back where he belonged. She drew a long breath in through her sensitive nostrils and let it out in one audible, relaxed breath. So good it was to feel the way she did.

Keith half-heartedly stirred the cookie mix a couple of times and turned to Sharon. "And there's Jackie to consider…."

Sharon nodded. "Yes, there's Jackie. Aren't we lucky? Jackie will be such fun to watch grow up."

Keith's heart actually skipped a beat and he put the ladle into the mixing pan and turned to her. "Was that a 'yes'?" And he held his breath because it couldn't possibly be true.

Sharon's calm reply. "Was there a question?"

"No. There really wasn't," and he wrapped his arms around her, dumpling bowl and all.

The cookies finally got into the pan and into the oven. After all, life goes on and cookie dough must not be wasted.

It was a month and a half later that Preacher Darkhorse made them a pair of couples. And the Monster was parked where it was supposed to be. Right in front of the rent house.

Lawman Burley Collins had made one bit of effort toward the comfort of the injured. He had furnished a pan of warm water and a soft cloth, along with a jar of the wonderful stuff called Vaseline Petroleum Jelly.

Bear could just barely manage to spend the night on his stomach, or walking around thinking of what he could have done better. The lumber logging camp might look really good before morning.

Paul Manford was pleased with himself for his small part in it all. He might have done more, but the United States Postal Service expected him to deliver mail, not play private detective.

He did, though, feel a small sense of "pay back" for the time Bear had caused trouble among the fellows at school. The school boys had learned one thing, though. All the world was not like themselves and their parents, so be on the alert. Bear had been a good lesson on what not to be.

Bradley Wilcox could, now, bring in his last load of meadow hay for winter animal feed. Maybe he'd done the last thing he could for his cousin and he had great hopes for her. She had sent a message that she was heading down south toward Little Rock, because she had a line on a good cooking job. She'd always loved cooking.

Only Bradley knew that she was telling him that she was going north to Joplin, Missouri, being about the same distance as Little Rock. And he knew her "new job" would have something to do with making ladies' hair keep up with the styles. He was well aware that she hated anything that had to do with cooking.

And a smile played about on his face as he thought of Louisa's "I told you so" pleasure of telling everyone that she had known all along that her Bradley would never get himself in trouble…he was just helping the lawman.

Also, one other little thing. He could now freely stop in at the diner for a coffee and a chat whenever he pleased. Also, he could take a peek at the handsome little Jackie, actually a cousin, once removed, or something like that.

Grady told himself that it would be good that he no longer had to try to notice what horse Bear was riding, or to get information on him to Burley. He had a good hot breakfast at the diner, washed down with three cups of coffee. He crawled into the Orange Monster (as his Leena called it). No mules to feed and harness!

He hoisted a five gallon can of gas into the cab of the Monster. He'd not need that much, but there might be a dry gas tank somewhere along the way. He'd give them just enough petrol to get to the Fix-It Shop.

He stepped into the cab and inserted the key. A beautiful roar, and then the Monster settled down to a comfortable purr. This was the life! Also, only one night a week would be spent away from the "rent house" and his best girl.

Preacher Darkhorse received a gratuity of $5.00 for the ceremony. He usually got $1.00. Not only that, he was almost forced to take the butcher pig, a young, quite round Hampshire, a breed said by many to have the best hams. The noisy little animal was just perfect for butchering.

He also had the immense satisfaction that he was permitted the legal authority to bring such a wonderful ending for those two young twins at the Eat and Get Gas.

Keith felt that he should actually walk very carefully as he went about his duties. He was obviously dreaming, and he was determined not to wake up.

Sharon had a bit of sympathy for the plight of Tribbey School, but glad its answer had not been her employment. She also had a few more good books for Jackie, and a few more recipes to put on the table for these appreciative people who absolutely needed her…a situation she had never before enjoyed in her whole pampered life of being the only child of well-to-do parents..

Leena crawled into her coveralls (now clean) and scooted under the hood of her current assignment...that touchy little StutZ Bearcat. Its trouble was that it had too many fancy "advancments" that dropped off or shook loose. No matter, it just made more money for her shop.

A smile of satisfaction came with the realization that they now had a wife like Sharon, and she, Leena O'Keef, would no longer be bothered with the pesky details of running a house.

Mrs. LePrey shook her head in amazement that her Robert (Ro-bahr) was in the pokey down on King's River. He was always such a good boy...never did a thing wrong in his life. It was all the fault of that girl called Margie. No good...that girl!

There were now two French tables in the diner, and the three afternoon regulars approved. They were now assured of getting one of them. Not only that, there was Keith new "help" and a body'd have to admit, she was a picnic for the eyes.

Lawman Burley Collins delivered Bear to the County Constable, Ike, down on King's River. He rode away and told himself, "One down, and about a hundred to go." He stopped in at the diner on his way home, and there was only empty seat. He took it and had a slab of cherry pie, almost as good as his Annie Jo could make.

Constable Ike slammed the metal door of the pokey shut with Bear inside and told himself, 'What would I ever do without Burley Collins?'

Sharron Atkins
Amelia-Jacob Atkins.
Old Bessie Cravens
Grady Okeef
Ole Mr. Phillip Stanhope
Jackie...Margie
Kathleen Leena Sullivan
Keith
Duke Washburn
Lillian Landrum
Burley Collins

Paul Manford Postman
Bradley Wilcox
Bear LePrey
Racer, borrowed
Zipper belongs to Bear

PART II

THE HONEY TREE

THE HONEY TREE IN THE YARD

S he leaned against the garden gate looking at the forlorn garden of late September. Bare okra and corn stalks, stringy tomato plants with a single ripe tomato hanging limply, and pumpkin vines yellow and brown with their orange globes exposed to the world.

Pumpkins that should be gathered and preserved in the cellar. Wonderful pumpkins that did not have to be canned, and cheerfully contained their spicy goodness inside until needed, even if that was months away.

But all that did not seem important to Victoria Spencer who was, at this moment, contemplating her own future. And lack of same.

For Victoria Spencer, the future was a deep, dark tunnel and she had no way to turn around and go away. The ladder on which she had built her life had been whisked away from under her, and she was hanging in space, doomed to fall through the tunnel of darkness.

"Miss Torie? MISS TORIE!" A shouted voice came to her from the road. "Torie, your horse done pushed the fence over and is a'grazin' in the ditch."

"Thanks, Uncle Hank. I'll come and get 'im." And then where would she put him, and how could she repair the fence?

The old man came into the yard uninvited. "You're needin' help," he stated as a matter of fact. "I could bring up a couple'a fence posts in place'a the rotten ones. But there's others a'leanin'.

I'll bring this critter on in for ya." He left to get the old horse, leading him by the mane.

"Thanks." It was so hard to accept help when she and Bradley had made such a complete and self-sufficient pair. Together. But now, there was no Bradley. And nothing was complete any more. A lot of plans for things not even started.

It was so appropriate that, at this moment, the life within her belly decided to turn over. No pain yet, but she well knew it was coming. Maybe 3 months away if she was lucky. There was much to do first.

"Momma?" a voice came from the house. "Momma, where are you? Missy done pulled on the dresser scarf and stuff fell and broke." Luke was a faithful reporter, and what would she do without him? He'd be five years old at Christmas and looked so much like Bradley that it brought on tears of loneliness.

"I'm coming," she told the voice. "Just don't let her pick up any broken glass." Now why did she say that? There is no way he would have let her be cut on the breakage. No matter how exasperated he was at the two year old, he just sighed and patiently took care of her.

"Uncle Hank, if you would, just put that evil beast in the corral. I'll be so much obliged for the fence posts. I got'a make some decisions on him. I'd feed 'im to the buzzards if I didn't need 'im for the buggy."

The old man came through the gate leading the horse. He sought for words of sympathy to bestow on her. "Some critters is just plain born ornery, and there ain't no changin' 'em'. That grass he was after is dusty and tough and he had much better eatin' down by the creek."

Torie Spencer, age 23, entered through her kitchen door and into the bedroom. There really wasn't anything actually broken, just scattered. Hairpins, comb and various dresser items, along with a bowl of safety pins and buttons. Luke was putting the buttons back in the bowl and Missy was putting hair pins in her mouth.

Torie took over the job of retrieval after folding the scarf and putting it aside. From here on for the next years, she would do without her lovely embroidered scarfs on the furniture.

"Luke, honey, I'll do this and you go gather the eggs for Momma." Luke, relieved from the tedium of the buttons, was gone like a vapor of smoke and the door slammed behind him. Egg gathering was a job he loved.

Floor litter picked up, she retrieved her daughter and went to the kitchen. Food. Supper. She sighed long and loudly. If it was not for the food, the producing of and the preparing of, and the absolute necessity of, she might just survive. No matter. Potatoes, fried, and eggs, boiled, made a usual supper favored by her brood. She had plenty of both.

Later, the children in their beds, Torie blew out the flame in the oil lamp. *Save oil,* she told herself. Besides, the thinking she had to do could be done in the dark as well as in light, and without bothering to change into her gown, she stretched out across the hand-pieced quilt on her bed.

Think, she instructed herself. *Make at least one good decision before you go to sleep. Decisions are all up to you, now.*

Winter was coming, and the wood supply was in, thanks to Bradley having looked ahead. Also the stored vegetables in the wonderful cellar he had dug three years ago. She'd need to get a hog butchered, but a neighbor would do it for halves. She'd need kerosene for the lamps and maybe salt, matches and likely a few more things. There would be enough money to pay for those…but what then?

Yes…what then?

THE NEIGHBORHOOD

The sad plight of Torie Spencer was sudden and continuing conversation in the neighborhood of Enterprise, located on Ridge Road in northern Arkansas. Here it was, the beginning of fall and Bradley Spencer was buried in the church yard leaving a pregnant wife and two small children. It made no sense at all.

It was obvious that the community would need to step up with help for her, but what help would be most needed right now? There needed to be talk.

The Tuesday Quilting Club that met at the church was the place where many things that were done and planned and the talk got started. There were not many problems that happened on an Arkansas mountain that the ten or twelve ladies could not solve. But Bradley's death had been a shocker to them all.

Two weeks ago he was hale and hearty, taking care of his family, and then he was gone. Without doubt, he passed on from something he caught over at Eureka Springs when he delivered his wagon load of honey jars. Came back feeling poorly, woke up sick, and was dead by nightfall. Made no sense at all.

According to the local medical pronouncement, it was seemingly something called meningitis or some such word that no one knew of and could hardly pronounce, but it was always fatal and he was gone. And it was said that other cases of it had happened in the city.

So, now back to the subject of his widow. It was clear, from words in the Bible, that widows and orphans became a responsibility of the community. So get with it.

Gracie Jones, the sort-of leader of the quilters, brought up the subject as the ladies were gathered around the latest quilt.

"Has anyone been to see Torie?"

Small hesitation, then, "I think Uncle Hank has been by. He replaced a couple'a fence posts for her."

Then others joined in.

"Well, she can't just be left there alone, can she?"

"What can we do? She has everything she needs but Bradley. He had left her with the important things like food and wood. Of course, there's all those bees…."

"Torie can handle those bees. Bradley taught her that the first year they had them boxes. Brought most of the boxes over from his Pa's place in Bentonville. Brought bees with 'em."

"I don't understand bees. They sting. I don't see how she does it?"

"It don't seem to bother her none. Anyway, there's money in 'em."

"Yeah, if you can get the honey over to Eureka Springs."

"And how'd she do that with a baby and two toddlers?"

"That Luke, he ain't no toddler. Almost five and he starts school come fall."

"Yeah, and I hear he's a good hand to look after Missy. She'll miss him when he goes to school."

"She don't have to let 'im till he's six. It's the law."

"I'd reckon that's so. With a newborn and Missy'd be 3 by then. He'd be a good help."

Gracie brought the conversation to the most immediate problem. "So what about her layin' in? There's no one at the house to come and ask for help, and none of us are able to just go and stay there a'waitin'. It'll be early spring with everything goin' on in the gardens."

Silence for a space of time. Babies didn't come scheduled, say at 2:00 on a Monday. They came when they jolly well pleased, be it rain storms or night times. All of that was known without being said.

"One good thing, though, she's been through it before. Chances are she'll know when she starts to need help."

"Who'd she get to notify?"

"I don't know, but here's a thought. Uncle Hank seems to take it on hisself to handle this sort of thing. Bein' the closest o her, he might be the one to check in to see how things are a'goin'."

There were nods of approval. Best idea yet, and it relieved the busy ladies of the immediate problem. Torrie being only six months along gave them time for a better idea later...perhaps. The busy farm ladies had few periods of no activity. Cooking, canning, butchering, washing clothes, and dealing with kids left few idle periods, and the sacrifice of a few hours on a Tuesday to get away, were necessary for their sanity. Hence, the birth of the Quilters.

And in this way for the ladies of Enterprise, dealing with the plight of Torie, while dim and dreary, took second place to what was being prepared for the evening meal. If Uncle Hank was to be the plug that staunched the immediate need for decisions, then so be it. What else did he have to do?

The ladies began to put away their sewing, wash the teapot and draw the quilting frame up to the ceiling out of the way of a Sunday School class that would be using the room on Sunday. The topic would undoubtedly arise again next week.

Torie awoke with a raging headache in a quiet house. Too quiet. The barn was within hearing distance, and the irritated moo of the milk cow was plain to hear. How had she managed to sleep so late?

A cup of her precious, expensive coffee (that she would certainly have to give up) would get her started, and she could get that milking done. Most important that she take care of the cow. And if she'd hurry, she might be back before the kids woke up.

If it was Missy first, she'd wake Luke and he'd watch over her. Luke, her pride and joy. And there was school facing her for next year, and being barely of age, she could hold him back a year to help at home.

He was so looking forward to going. Holding him back would be hard for him, and could she actually do that to Luke? Why should he have to pay for the calamity that had befallen her family? Also, why, for that matter, should she? But it had happened and that was that.

The aroma and warmth of the coffee was comforting, so she took a last quick sip and closed the door softly. She had a nanny goat about to produce a baby in about a month. Goats were easier to manage than cows, so maybe she'd need to make a change…but then what would she do for the calf to butcher for beef?

Everything on a farm seemed to be woven into one tight mat in which when one string pulled, the whole thing seemed to unravel. And the main string was generally a tough man to hold things together. A tough man like Bradley. They had planned their family together, based on the fact of his being there, and now he isn't. Nothing was fair about that.

The steady beat of the thoughts in her head kept time with the splat, splat, splat of the milk streams into the steel milk bucket. The friendly nanny, Elsie, nosed Torie's neck and shoulders from the back as if to remind the human that her time was coming.

Everybody's time was coming!

Thoughts continued. Baby goats also produced meat, quite tasty if they were butchered young. That was a thought. And chickens reproduced themselves if permitted to do so. Food had to be the first thought.

There had to be a way to go forward, and she must find it. In true Torie fashion, she would work out her own problems. It did not occur to her that she was the subject of Tuesday Quilters conversation.

As she stripped the last of the milk from the cow's udder, she turned her thoughts to the bees. With winter coming on, and the honey flow over, she had some time there. Nothing pressing, and that was a blessing. Tending to the bees and the hives themselves would be exactly no problem; it was just everything else.

When she had married Bradley, he had bought the twenty acres on Ridge Road (with house, barn and fences) with his savings from the bees on his father's farm. The bees were moved in to the bee garden almost the same instant that she and Bradley had moved into the house, and they had gone from there.

The honey bees had their own pasture, one that was sown with tame and wild flower seeds for their sake. It was Bradley's intention that the bees furnish the ready cash to cover items not produced on the farm, like clothing and such. Torie had agreed that it was a good plan. The best, actually, as were most of Bradley's plans. The six original hives had done well, and then when his pa had passed, he made the long trip to bring over the other six hives.

They bought pint jars by the hundred and lined them with slabs of honeycomb. They filled in the spaces around the comb with the liquid gold that sold so well to the summer visitors in the resort town of Eureka Springs. But Eureka Springs was a long trip away.

She turned the cow and goat into their own pasture, not the one with the bee hives, and picked up the pail of milk. The farm was a definitely like the mat, skillfully woven together with Bradley's energy and dreams, and it worked out beautifully…until it didn't.

Bradley took the energy and dreams with him when he went, and that was the string that had held the mat from unraveling. Oh well, more later, but now there were hungry kids and a lot of clothing to wash. Later there would plenty of time to worry properly about everything.

Uncle Hank lived on a forty-acre patch of ground with which he did nothing that did not have to be done. Garden for vegetables and animals for meat and water for the washing of his clothing and himself when absolutely necessary. He'd given 'the best years of his life' to the law enforcement in town. The law enforcement now produced enough cash to live on. What else did he need?

He'd never felt the need to take on a wife. Any lady that he would be happy with would surely not be happy with him, so he let it pass and was content to admire the ladies from afar.

In this way, the section of his land that adjoined the Spencer's was left fallow to do as it pleased. Grass for the cows, and a lot of flowers from seed the north wind that blown over the fence…he guessed. Anyway the twenty acre strip was alive with flowers in their season, and the flowers were alive with the Spencer's bees. He rather liked it that way.

This fact was not lost on that lovely Victoria who awarded him with a jar of her honey every few months or so. *Even-steven*, he thought. *Tit for tat.* Besides, he had nothing, really, to do with his life except that few things he did for others, and it seemed that he might now have a chance to fit in somewhere in Torie's life. Even if it was just keeping her fence together.

So when Gracie Jones came to him with her request, it fitted right in with his own plans. Yes, he would be glad to keep check on her, and when her time was nearer, he'd find a reason to see her daily…just to make sure she was still up and around and the kids were well.

That would fit comfortably into his day. Today, however, he hooked his horse up to the blade he used to cut hay and he would bring down the old flower stems along the border fence. That would shake out the seeds into the ground before the winter birds got them. Bradley's idea, so he guessed it worked.

He'd learned that bit of information from Bradley on one of the 'over the fence' chat sessions. So when he mowed down his own flower stems, he'd go offer to bring down the flower garden patch that held the bee hives. Yep! That's just what he'd do. Bradley was not here to do it.

A 'nuther thing he'd do was to invent a need to go to Eureka Springs. He went, every so often, just for the thing of it. His own cooking satisfied him quite well. He'd learned a lot over the years, but a few days in the city gave him a choice of excellent eating places. Made a nice change, it did, and he'd just make that little trip down in a week or two.

Miss Torie would likely have a few little things she needed, and he'd have the buggy with plenty of room. He'd tell her when he went over to mow down her flowers and blooming weeds. That way she'd have time to have her list ready.

THE NEW SCHOOLTEACHER

The teacher of the little school in Enterprise community was leaving. After twenty-three years and a whole generation of children having been taught, she decided to go over to Siloam Springs and live with her sister. Her meager savings and small teacher's pension would serve her well.

The news was met with oh's and ah's by the community and speculations abounded over and over. Who would they get next? And would the small size of the school attendance affect the quality of the person they would eventually get? Miss Eldridge had been an excellent teacher, expecting nothing from the community but the attendance of their children. Teaching them and making them behave like humans should was the job she had chosen and she was well able to handle it, but now that was over.

The Tuesday Quilting group tried to handle the catastrophe over their needles, cookies and tea. Needles threading through the brightly patched cloth brought their thoughts to the problem.

"I just can't believe Miss Eldridge is a'leavin' us. Seems like she's educated this whole strip of Enterprise and it looks like we expected her to go on forever."

"Yeah, and who'll we get to replace her?"

"And will the Simmon's be willin' to board 'er, like they did Miss Eldridge? Sure hope they're not tired'a doin' the boardin'. I'd hate to have to take a turn at it."

151

"I'm thinkin' it won't be a problem. The state started payin' $12.00 a month and that much money goes a ways with a family. Just for them furnishin' a room and food, that'd leave a good profit."

"Unless she's a lot'a trouble, like wantin' a horse for her own use and things like that. There's not many places close enough to just walk across Ridge Road. Like with the Simmons.'"

Eventually, Gracie Jones tried to steer the conversation to Torie's plight, but the teacher situation was new to the community and needed to be thoroughly discussed.

Grannie Tolbert snipped off the end of her thread and reached for the spool. A thought had been working around in her ancient head and she was wondering if it was time to bring it up. She'd lived long enough to know that one person's anxiety often became another person's answer. That one person's plight could be often be turned out to be what another person needed, and she thought she had a plan.

She cleared her throat, and looked around. They all knew Grannie well enough to know that the cleared throat meant she had something to say, and so often, what she said made sense. There was silence as all eleven faces turned to the old lady with the wrinkles of experience portrayed in her features.

"Been thinkin'," she began. "Iffen we got'a get a new teacher who'll be needin' a place to stay, bringin' government money along with her, where'd be a better place for her than with Torie Spencer? She's got room, and she could use the money, and how much food could one lady need?"

Grannie looked around at the interested faces and felt that she had a 'go ahead' to continue. "On top'a that, if it would be a problem with her kids a'bein' a bother to the teacher, there's that honey house. We can't know if Torie'll continue with the bees, but that that machinery needed for the honey'd fit in one'a her rooms. That'd give privacy to the teacher when she wanted it."

Hmmm, this was an interesting idea. Like the killing two birds with one stone, and take care of both birds. Conversation started.

"How big is that little honey house, anyway? I never did see it except from a distance."

"Two big rooms. All thick logs and partitioned off with shelves built in against the walls."

"Should be easy to keep warm, anyway."

"And far enough away that the kid's noise wouldn't bother 'er, still close enough for meals."

"Do we know if Torie's gonna keep the bees?"

"For sure. I know that. Bradley taught her how to act with 'em and she just took over. She's even caught wild strains that cluster in the trees. She just smoked 'em with her smokin' cab and scooped 'em into the box."

"For a fact, you say!"

"For sure! I watched 'er do it. She said they were too interested in protectin' the queen to want to sting her. Said that'd keep 'em quiet till she had a chance to decide where to stop and make a new hive. They couldn't think'a stingin' 'cause they didn't have no hive to protect yet."

"Well, in that case...."

"The plan'd work all right if she'd go along with it. She might not appreciate us buttin' in."

"The way I see it, someone is going to have to 'er, sooner or later. And if the fellows'd give her a day'a work, they'd get that machinery moved into a room and outta the honey house and have it done."

"There's somethin' else. If the government knew the teacher'd have a choice of a private cabin, we might get the best teacher."

"Maybe, but we don't know what was the best teacher till she gets tried out in our school. Either way we go, it'll be like buyin' a pig in a poke. We'll see what we get when we get it, and I'm not sure Ridge Road'll have a lot of drawin' power. We think it's great since it got graveled, but maybe the teacher wouldn't care about that."

"Well, I can say one thing. Torie's about as close to the school as we could ever get. She was even sayin' it was going to be good for her Luke to be able to walk by hisself when he starts."

"So what do we do now? Talk to Torie?"

"I'd hate to do it. Maybe she wouldn't want us to be so nosey."

Grannie Tolbert clear her throat again. All eyes turned to her, respectfully. With a half-smile that shifted her laugh wrinkles to one side, she said, "I sort'a got a 'bee in my bonnet' on that."

A chuckle rippled around the edges of the quilt at Grannie's play on words about having an idea. Torie's bees, for goodness sake!

Gracie came up with the invitation. "What's your bee, Grannie?"

"I'm thinkin' Uncle Hank'd be the one for that, him bein' the closest to 'er, and bein' on such friendly terms. He's worked with the public and had to get good with his words. He'd think of a way so's to be polite and all."

Of course. It was plain as the noses on their faces, and the ladies gave unanimous consent. It would be for Uncle Hank to do it, and for Gracie to inform him of it. Things important as this must go through channels, and Gracie's man was on what passed as a school board.

For a teacher to be presented with a whole cabin of her own, it was offering a rare plum. How many folks had an extra building unless they were keeping a hired man for farm help? Good help had to be paid for, and a place like the honey house would be very good pay.

The sewing group was now able to discuss supper menus and new recipes with a clear conscience. A problem had been thoroughly and properly discussed and a decision made. Problem closed, if Torie just went along with it.

Uncle Hank brought another three fence posts to replace another spot where the horse had pushed against the fence. He looked toward the house and there was lovely Torie hangin' wet clothes on the line. Hank smiled softly to himself.

Lookin' back, if he'd'a took the time and trouble to get a wife, he might'a had a daughter about like Victoria. And here she was, a girl without a pa and he was a man without a daughter. And he had it right here under his nose, and look at that little boy, chasing around and trying to catch the fall butterflies on the purple asters…being about the last of the planted flowers to bloom.

There'd be a few flowers blooming even after frost. Bees were working on them until the end, maybe dreading when they would have to go on partial hibernation.

THE ACCIDENT

Merrill Brooks leaned back in the comfortable chair while he was being measured. He studied the pair of legs stretched out before him, one with a nice leather boot and the other with no foot.

It was a thing of nightmares to remember what happened at the railway switch yard where he worked. He was crouched under the edge of a car attending to an adjustment when, up the track, a catch slipped, or something, and it sent a handcar shuttling down the rails toward him. He saw it coming and knew what it could do, but that knowledge did not help him actually move away quickly enough.

The only thing he could do to keep from being crushed was to sacrifice a foot, which he did, entirely as a reflex action. He pushed himself back across the gravel and drew in his legs. The right leg made it intact, but the left was a bit slow.

The rim of the cart met the top of the rail and removed his foot from his leg as neatly as if a surgeon had done it. Or maybe a butcher removing the head of a slaughtered animal. At first he felt nothing but stared at the amount of blood…then the pain hit so hard it took away the breathe that he would have used to scream.

A co-worker saw it all and screamed for help. The medical person, who must always be present, was there in an instant binding Merrill's uniform pant leg to his flesh to stop the blood. He was carried to a nearby rail car and taken on a flying trip to the hospital.

Merrill did not remember much after that except for the fire in his leg. Blazing explosions happened with every heartbeat. And then the pain was gone, and so was he. He was kept under numbing medication for the day, and when he awoke the next morning, he had a lot of medical company. He was told he was so lucky to have had help so close by, and for the cut to have been so low on his leg. There would be very good prosthesis made in a few weeks, and crutches would be issued for use until then.

He would be pensioned (paid off) by the railway, and he could think on retiring or doing something else that could be done without a lot of walking. What all happened had been enough to throw a lesser man into a depression from which there was no climbing out, but not Merrill.

When one door was closed, look for another door. For a fact, he was not particularly thrilled at his job with the railway anyway. It put him on the road a lot, and he was expected to work in any kind of weather. A troubleshooter was subject to being on call by everyone but himself. He'd sort of fell into this job because he was good at it and was handy.

So now it was time to look around. Managing the crutches was relatively easy, but it left no hands for carrying. This was going to be taken care of in time, but what to do with himself until then?

Casting his sharp mind about, to all he had seen in his almost thirty-two years, he started with his time at school as a boy. There'd been that certain teacher…and he had challenged young Merrill to perform and not sluff off just because he was able to learn in a short time. Keep his mind busy, he was told, or it would wander off, and that would get him in trouble. And the teacher told him he was too smart to let that to happen.

Merrill remembered watching his teacher after that. Watching the way he did his job, and how the class looked up to him, and how interesting he made his lessons. He had a way of making every student feel that he was special.

Merrill had wondered at the time if that would be something he liked, but then he had somehow found himself as a troubleshooter for the railway. The job paid quite well. Trouble and more trouble, and nothing but trouble. It was rather like a doctor who always had to deal with sick people because he chose that job.

As he practiced with his crutches, he thought and thought, and the thought that bubbled up most in his mind was the memory of that teacher who had influenced him so greatly. His name was… uh…Hmmmm, why couldn't he remember the name?

As he was clicking down the sidewalk in his crutch practice, he passed the huge brick building titled ARKANSAS BOARD OF EDUCATION. Almost without his thought, his crutches turned him into the doorway. There were three steps up, and he had been advised to practice on steps, so he did.

He clumped down the marble hall to the ornate door with a person behind it. He didn't care much who it was, as he was just passing the time. Wasn't he?

He maneuvered his way through the heavy door (something else he needed to practice on) and approached the first desk. The person looked up with a forced smile and advised, "The applications are here on the desk and the desks are for your use in filling it out."

"Uh…applications…?"

"Yes, sir. We have qualifications for our teachers and the application is necessary. If you need help getting located with your crutches, I'm ready."

"Uh…no. I am supposed to practice, but so far it's taking both hands on slippery floors. If you would bring the application and a pencil to the desk, I can take it from there."

The attendant nodded. "I'd be glad to, sir. Just have a seat and I'll bring it."

He did. Thoughts were tickling inside his brain, wanting to talk with him. *Just look where you came to,* his brain said, *and you are filling out an application for a job you think you would really like. See how I helped you?*

Merrill printed his name and all other pertinent information in the assigned spaces. He really had no academic education beyond high school, but he stood out head and shoulders against most persons to whom the eighth grade was graduation.

The attendant watched slyly as Merrill worked on the printed form. Then he slipped away quietly and returned. Another man came through the side door and chatted with the attendant until Merrill was finished.

Merrill started to rise, and somehow get the application to the front desk, when the second man approached.

"Please keep your seat, sir. We can chat a bit. Have you ever taught school before?"

"Uh…no."

"Then why do you think you'd like to try it?"

Hey, this was going to be good. Since he wasn't going anywhere anyway, and was just practicing, why not enjoy someone to talk to. So he leaned back and told of the teacher he had liked, and he did not miss any details.

His listener said not a word nor asked a question until he finished.

"Mr. Brooks…is it? I'd like to tell you our situation. Your qualifications are adequate and we need a teacher badly. One of our city school teachers had a medical emergency and she will be unable to return, and at her age, she is not likely to survive.

"With all our sympathies aside, we have a class with no teacher. You may not be interested, as they are very young children grades 1 to 3, and they are now being taken care of by various mothers. We would like for you to accept this offer, and it will give you an idea of what it is to teach children as you have never been there or received the necessary academic help."

Merrill Brooks stared at the man as though he had appeared from outer space. They were offering him a job! It was now "crunch time" and a yes or no was expected. He swallowed twice and asked. "Sir, I'm on crutches, do you think that would be a problem?"

"Not with us, it won't. I can set you up to start next Monday, giving you time to get your breath and be ready. The teaching material is here and I can let you have it right now. I can put it in a satchel that you can wear over your shoulder.

"By the way, I am Elliot Martin, Superintendent of Schools in Northern Arkansas. I can give you the address of the school. It's within a few blocks of where we are now, and I can notify the school principal that you are coming. I will leave it to you to do any explanations you see fit."

"Uh…thank you very much. I appreciate the chance to try this and I'll do my best to be adequate."

With a wide smile, Mr. Martin told him, "I'm thinking you will be more than adequate and hope we will be assigning you permanently to a school to start next September. I'm so glad you stopped by, and I'll bring the books and meet you at the door over there."

Mr. Martin indicated the door Merrill had struggled through. And now, if he hurried fast, he could be out the door and away before the needed papers arrived. He grinned at the idea, and posted his six-foot-two body beside the marble doorway.

Later, in his room, he sat wearily into his best upholstered chair. What did he just do? What in the name of God's green earth was he thinking? But he remembered that his foot and the crutches had seemed to take over, making the decision on their own. That should make it plain that he didn't need to know why it happened this way, because Somebody obviously did.

On the prescribed Monday, the six-foot-two stranger entered the room and looked at the nineteen children. So small. Children came so small that he felt like a giant, and obviously looking like one to the children.

He put on his most friendly smile. "Hello, fellows and girls. I'm the new teacher and I want to ask you one question."

The room was pin-drop quiet. "I want you to remain in your seats and not run away because I can't run fast enough to catch you."

The older, third graders looked at each other with puzzled frowns. Did he mean that…that the class could run away if they chose? Then they looked back at the giant facing them.

"All right, you've had time to think about it. How many of you will stay in your seat and not run away? Let's see you raise your hands."

All was quiet, and then one of the bigger girls shyly raised her arm about halfway up. Then another, and a couple of boys bravely raised their hands the full length of their arms and waved their finger.

A smaller boy, obviously a first-grader, stood up. "I won't run away, sir. I want to see what you're going to say next."

A giggle started and it grew into a full blown laugh. When the laugh died down, Merrill sat himself behind the teacher's desk and asked, "Now we'll begin. My name is Mr. Brooks, or you can call me teacher, whichever you please. And you will tell me your names and I will write them down. And tomorrow, you must sit it the same seat where you are sitting in today, or I might call you by the wrong name."

That brought on another giggle and then a laugh. The new teacher knew now, beyond the shadow of a doubt, that he had this class in the palm of his hand. He had them in the same way that his own teacher had captured him. He opened the material that had been given him, and started on what he thought might be interesting.

Being seated had paid him back by making his leg ache from lack of circulation. Just a twinge, but he didn't have time to coddle his foot (or the lack of same). He had nineteen pairs of eyes glued on him, waiting for what he would do next.

And this was the way he had become a teacher, and he had already forgiven the stray cart that had forced this decision. He might even reach the point of thanking the errant cart, so pleased he was with this beginning.

At the end of the year, he was given his option of four spots. He could teach a class in town, or there were three rural openings. He took the offers home with him and studied them carefully. Here was where he must not make a mistake, as he planned to stay there for the next twenty years at least.

Eventually, he could arrange for his own lodging, but at first he must check into the lodging the community had prepared to give him which was a private room in the house of a resident, and all his meals would be included in the contract.

For two of the locations the room was described as private and quiet, and one of them had a separate two-roomed cabin with separate facilities, but he could take meals with the family if he wished. When he considered the number of books he would be taking with him, there was no question of the place he would take.

Was he, by chance, allergic to the sting of bees? No? Well, then his contract would indicate as much and say that he was to be given the two-roomed log cabin with a heating stove and other furniture near the family home. It was also within easy walking distance of the school.

He had now received his prosthesis, which was what they called the artificial foot. It was rather like a boot, and should fit is such a way that it did not slip off. Compared to the crutches, managing the boot would be a breeze, maybe, and he could dispense with the crutches, though he was advised to keep them… just in case. No problem.

Something to look forward to, for sure.

THE BEE HIVES

Victoria Spencer was now three weeks past the burying of her husband, her soul mate and life partner who left so suddenly. So now she must look forward and make decisions for four people.

Time to take stock of the have's and have not's.

As previously stated, Bradley, in his wonderful way of being prepared, had, at the time of his demise, already prepared for the winter with wood. It was stacked in neat ricks just outside the kitchen door. He had left a paid-for house, twenty acres, a going bee-keeping business and a small savings along with the proceeds of the year's honey sales. One hundred and forty-three pints of honeycomb and liquid honey had been delivered to the three honey customers in Eureka Springs. Sold at twenty cents a pint and subtracting two cents for the jar made a profit of $26.74 for the year. Not bad but was slated to be better. That had been the intention.

Most of the work was done by the bees, of course, but there was the processing and bottling which took a good three days of hard work. Then there was the cleanup. Honey was very sticky, but by the time Bradley returned from Eureka Springs, Torie had cleaned the "honey house" from wall to wall.

The farm big house had consisted of a four bedroom house, a generous barn and the honey house which was located across the yard snugged up against the fence around the bee pasture.

The bee pasture contained the twelve hives scattered around in the two acre plot dedicated to the production of flowers of every kind that would produce nectar. The fertile Arkansas soil and the southeast slope of the land was like a bright pieced quilt top. Adding to its brightness was the swarms of butterflies whose wings created a dizzying movement all summer long and produced no income at all in return for what nectar they stole.

Bradley, in his dedicated mind, planned the income, and it was working perfectly as planned. But now…no Bradley.

And there was the honey locust tree. It just appeared one spring a few years back. The birds must have been responsible for the seed, as there were no other known honey locust trees on the Ridge. And the fact was, that tree would not have been allowed to survive if it had come up in a field instead of in a fence line. The fence between her land and Uncle Hank's land had a three strand barbed wire fence and Uncle Hank mowed both sides of the fence to keep down the weeds.

Somehow, the sprout of the tree had sprung up and was missed by the mower and by the nibbling mouths of the goats until it grew tall enough to protect itself with its own thorns, sharp as daggers, and spaced up and down the limbs and trunk.

It was surprising that Uncle Hank had left it, as the root may well have extended into his property, but it had escaped him until it was six feet tall and produced its first honey blossoms. White flowers were grouped in bunches like grapes, and hung down in the same way. The first year the clusters were small, but from then on the tree expanded like a child's balloon, with the flower clusters hanging twelve to fifteen inches in a swaying perfumed curtain with a distinct aroma of expensive perfume.

From the very first, that aroma was irresistible to the bees who crawled in among the small flowers buzzing their wings pulling sweet nectar from the blossoms.

By then it had attracted Uncle Hank, as well as Bradley (owner of the bees), and a memory popped into the grizzle haired head of the older man.

"As I live and breathe, that there tree is a honey locust, and I ain't never seen one in this neck'a the woods. Had a lot of 'em down farther south…called 'em honey trees. Seems those flowers flavored the honey in a way that folks liked."

The men also noticed that while the tree seemed to be directly under the fence, it swayed to the east to come around the first barbed wire strand, and grew up to the next strand of wire, and swayed back to the west. Then to the east again, in a weaving pattern.

Now it was a full grown tree with a trunk the size of a stove pipe, but it was still woven within the fence, being on Bradley's side for the first and third wire strands, and on Hank's for the middle strand, and maybe most of the root. The men playfully discussed this phenomena of nature, and who it actually belonged to... deciding, finally, that it belonged to the bees who were ready to defend their rights to it with their lives.

Maybe it flavored the honey, but who could tell for sure with all the other varieties that were mowed down and reseeded each year.

But that was in the past, as Bradley was. And the honey tree was far from the mind of Bradley's widow.

Torie lifted her chin and firmed her lips as she gazed out of her kitchen window. She would make it alone. Somehow, there would be strength.

Quiet as a shadow, her son crept up behind her and watched for a whole three minutes. Then, "What're you seein', Momma?"

Torie drew in a breath and turned to her son. "I'm seein' our future, son."

"What's a future?"

"It's all'a the tomorrows in the world. We get them one at a time, and use them up. So today, the eggs are your future, so go get them, and then we'll find something else to do."

Wordlessly, he picked up the wire basket and left. The large flock of chickens occupied one wing of the large barn, locked in at night to protect them from coyotes and other hungry beasts.

So now, selecting a sheet of paper, actually the back of a sales brochure that appeared in the mailbox. She numbered one to five, and decided five decisions was the most she could manage in a day. Scheduling activities had been Bradley's job, but now was hers.

1. Stop starting every day with tears, and plan for the bee pasture.

2. Make a needs list to send with Uncle Hank.

3. Make arrangements for help butchering the hog.

4. Render out the bee's wax and get ready to make candles.

5. ??

Somehow her mind could not center on number five, but it was sure to appear before the day was out. Of course, she must make long-range plans but not all today.

Luke appeared with the eggs, at least a dozen and a half of them. Maybe she should have made number five be to figure out how to make the wealth of summer eggs last into December to March. Why did hens regularly slow down their laying in the winter?

"How about we make cookies the first thing, Lucky Luke?" The stove was still hot from preparing breakfast, and heat must not be wasted if possible. Another stick of wood would make enough heat to bake the cookies.

Oatmeal cookies were a wonderful container in which to hide a lot of eggs and made such handy snacks for everyone. Oatmeal, honey, eggs, spices and baking powder and a lot of stirring to moisten the oatmeal.

"Get out the pans and get your spoon ready. The next job is yours."

Luke giggled and found the step-on stool to increase his height. He was good at dipping a spoonful at a time and spacing them in the pan.

Turning the job over to him, she dressed Missy and made the beds. Yesterday's washing had dried on the line, but had yet to be folded. And folding reminded her of the saved diapers. She must count them and maybe add to them. Christmas and the baby's appearance were the next sure thing to happen to the little family.

Next came the "want" list for Uncle Hank. Oatmeal, sugar, kerosene, matches, baking powder, and, oh yes, the seed for the tall yellow clover that bloomed late when many other blossoms were past. The many blossoms of the tall clover were a favorite of bees, it seemed, but the seeds held high on the stalk as they grew, and were also on the menu for winter birds.

Uncle Hank dropped by for the list, and looked carefully at her walk and overall shape while she was occupied getting him a cup of tea for his journey.

He nodded his head in agreement with himself. Things were progressing, but, please Lord, no twins. She has enough to do.

Hank's job in law enforcement had given him an eye for details, and babies were such stubborn little cusses, they came when they came, with no regard to the convenience of their parents. All of the cops were required to take a brief course on spotting details and remembering them. Emergency childbirth was among the lessons.

The cookies had come from the oven just in time to add a couple to Hank's tea. Luke watched the cookies being eaten by Hank, smiling with pride that they were perfect, as usual. And he did it!

Hank left to join the horses and wagon and he would be taking on his journey a cookie in each hand as a present from Luke. The slow, methodical rhythm of horse hooves on gravel, along with the steady grind of the wheels, was very conducive to thought. His best thinking had often occurred on the trips to town.

The latest thought was on the visit from Gracie Jones and her husband, Herman. They appeared stiff and important looking as though their message had deserved an honor like a presidential address and grateful attention must be paid.

Herman began. "Bein' a close neighbor to Torie, you'd be knowin' what she's got ahead'a her, and we're here to help what we can. Community duty, you know."

(Yes, Hank knew, better than they ever thought.)

Herman Jones continued. "Our quilters set their minds to what could be done, and they came up with an idea we're passin' around. 'Course she's been left provided for and not like a charity case, but maybe we have a plan to help."

(He was right. Torie was NO charity case. She, herself, would be most angry to be considered as one.)

Eventually Herman, with the prodding from Gracie, came up with the real reason for the visit. "You know, of course, that Miss Eldridge is leaving the school this year, and that brings us together to make a decision. Also, the Simmons's have decided they do not want to board a teacher anymore. With their youngens gone now, they'd like to be free to do some going on trips and such."

(Did anyone other than Herman care why the Simmons' felt they had done their job? *Get to the point, Herman, before your wife has a coronary. I'll pretend I don't know why you're here.*)

Gracie's elbow gave a gentle nudge, and Herman continued, "So we've got to find another place for the new teacher, and being close to the school would be a plus. The state is going to pay $13.00 a month for her keep, and we got to thinkin' that even if Bradley left his wife in good shape, it wouldn't last forever."

(Hank nodded deeply, hoping the nod would be considered as encouragement to finally get to the point.)

"So we got to thinkin', that is, the quilters did, and they came up with this plan. Miss Victoria is in an excellent location, bein' within sight'a the school, and havin' a lot of room in her house. But what was even better, they thought of the honey house. The equipment kept there could easily fit in a bedroom, and the house could be prepared for living in. Maybe put in a stove, bed and table. Could be that these things could be found to be available around the community. We're generous to a fault, you know. Gracie and I still have the couch and chair we replaced when we painted the parlor. We could donate that."

(Hank heaved an involuntary sigh. *At last! Now go on and tell me that I have been chosen to tell Torie she is the new boarder for the teacher.*)

"So we was thinkin', all of us, that you bein' close to her, so to speak, you'd be the best to explain it all to her. We'd have no trouble rounding up help to get it done…like movin' the heavy stuff. We all know she's got more on her than her pockets can hold."

(Well, he was right on that. And the plan was an excellent one, killing two birds with one stone…as the saying went.)

Now it was time for Hank to do his part. "Certainly, Herman. I'd be glad to lay out the plan and let her think on it. Of course, we're not gonna push her into anything."

Gracie came to life and assured him, "Oh, no, we wouldn't do that to her!"

(*Of course not. Mostly because Torie would not permit herself to being pushed. But it IS a very good plan, and I'll make that plain.*)

Hank's visitors stood, making it clear that their mission was fulfilled and they were ready to go. Hank stood with them and offered his hand to Herman to shake. "I'll certainly do what I can." And they were gone.

Hank settled himself back in his easy chair with a fresh cup of coffee. He smiled to himself as he reviewed the visit. Good folks. Quick to help others in the community. All up and down Ridge Road were the folks best referred to as "the salt of the earth" without which the earth would be utterly tasteless. Or so, went the Good Book.

They were righter than they even knew, that he, Hank, was the best choice for this chore. Sometimes he even thought of that lovely girl as his own daughter, unfortunately born to another man.

As he rode along the road and gazed on this house, and then that house, he knew how fortunate he was to be able to retire in such a paradise as Enterprise.

Torie sipped the last of her tea, cold now, and rinsed the cup along with Hank's cup and hung them on their wall hooks. Missy was working on the cookies, one in each hand, as her breakfast. Luke was placing them carefully in the cookie jar, leaving the jar lid off. All heat must be out of them first, or they got soggy. He'd learned that the hard way.

It was time to issue orders. "All right, youngens, today we start on the pumpkins. First we count them, and then we bring them to the cellar on the sled. I think the sled will hold five for each trip." She held up her hand with all fingers spread. "Five pumpkins."

Luke held up both hands. "Five and another five. Two trips. See? Five, six, seven, eight, none, and ten. See? Missy, ten pumpkins."

Torie had to smile, tolerantly, "Luke, darling, it isn't eight, none, ten. It's eight, NINE, ten."

"Oh, yeah. I forgot. Missy, it's NINE, ten."

Missy had put both cookies on the table and lifted both hands.She swallowed and said, "None, ten."

"No, Missy, it's NINE, ten."

Missy nodded. "None, ten."

Torie told Luke, "Let it go, son. She'll learn."

Out in the garden with the sled the work began. They counted the huge golden globes and agreed on eighteen. That was a lot of pumpkins, but they, along with the oatmeal, made wonderful

167

cookies and pumpkin custard, which also hid a lot of eggs. She would need to make good use of that filling food.

Two trips to the cellar today. Torie and Luke pulling the sled and Missy riding on the largest pumpkin. Enough for today. Two more trips for tomorrow for the other eight, and maybe one or two that had been missed on the counting.

TELLING TORIE

Torie Spencer moved from day to day, trying not to look ahead. She reached December with her unwieldy body still responding only to great effort. It was time to start thinking what she must do today or could leave until later.

She divided an older sheet into ten pieces for diapers. One just couldn't have too many of them in the winter. Drying indoors made the air so damp, and when rains started, it seemed they never stopped. Neither did the need for dry diapers.

The community had a very capable midwife, so it was said, but Torie had no way of notifying her all the way down to Garland Community when the time came. So she pushed it from her mind, as she did a lot of other things.

Uncle Hank stopped by for something or other just about every day. What a help he was! She talked with him about letting the cow go and keeping just a goat. Or maybe two goats so their milking periods would overlap. Hank said, "Let me think on it first."

He thought and came up with a plan. Yes, keep a goat or two for milk, but also keep the cow. Let her have a calf every year, and let the calf stay with her in the pasture to consume all the milk she produced. That would make an excellent calf to butcher, or to sell. Torie certainly had enough grazing space to feed the cow, and if she didn't have enough, he'd open the gate to his back pasture and the cow could go there with his horses.

"Think on it, Torie. It don't pay to get rid'a things too fast. Cows don't have to be brought in and milked if they have a calf with 'em, and a bit of shelter in the field. Goats, on the other hand, are easy to milk, but need a barn for shelter. And they don't require much purchased food."

Torie thought on it and agreed. It was always easy to get help on the butchering if she offered half the meat as payment. That took care of one problem.

On to the next. The baby. All of the happiness at the first of the pregnancy turned to apprehension and a bit of dread. It just wasn't meant to be this way…but it was. *Face it, Torie.*

Christmas drew closer, and Hank appeared every day doing one thing or another around her farm until he actually saw her. Then came the day he didn't see her, even though he spent a half an hour mucking out the barn. Good exercise, that was.

He tapped on the kitchen door and it was opened by a wide-eyed little boy. "Momma's sick."

"She is? Is she in bed?"

"Yes. I'll show you."

When they reached the bedroom, Torie was standing, having heard the knock on the door. Hank swallowed hard as his eyes traveled down. She should be with the midwife right now. It was time for him to take command and use his experience and training.

"Torie, I want you to lay back down on the bed slowly and carefully. Is there a way we can remove the children comfortably?"

Torie edged toward the bed. "Luke, sweetie, I want you to go to the kitchen and make a cookie picnic. Fill a jar with water, and Uncle Hank is going to take you and Missy to the honey house for a long, long play time. If you get sleepy or tired, there's the quilts to lay on." At the end of this speech she was breathless from the force of the contraction.

"Uncle Hank, there's a fire in the stove at the honey house. They'll be OK for a while." She leaned forward, hands on the bed to meet the force of the next pain. As Hank turned to do as she had suggested, he saw the puddle form at Torie's feet. Water broke. Not good news.

"Into the bed, Torie. I'll be back. Don't be afraid."

After settling the children with their toys in the honey house, he ran back to the house, heart pounding. This had always been a dread. So many things could happen.

"Torie, my dear. Listen carefully. There is not time to get help for you. If I tried, you would deliver before I got back. Better I stay and help. Don't worry, I've done this before. Twice, actually. All cops are trained in emergency births and it happened more times than one might imagine. Babies come when they come, and yours is going to be here before two hours pass."

Torie groaned and held tightly to the bars on the iron bedstead. She had no words to argue. Help was help. Grabbing a moment between pains she told him, "Bottom drawer. Baby things."

Hank nodded. All things in good time. Seeing a quilt chest, he opened it and removed four pieced brightly colored quilts. Spreading them on the floor, he reached for her hands to help her move.

Training had told him that the floor was best, better than the bed if he was alone. Solider and easier to move around than a double bed. Easier to clean up. A hard floor meant nothing to a woman in pain. It would be the farthest from her mind

Torie moved to the floor without comment. He held her hands as he eased her down. The next pain made her gasp.

Hank, with nerves tingling up and down his arms, pretended he was on duty, and had been called to this emergency. Which he had, actually.

"Breathe fast five times and stop. Then five more times. Count them. Don't worry about what I'm doing. Just concentrate on breathing."

One, Two, Three, Four, Five. One, Two, Three, Four, Five....

On the afternoon of the thirteenth of December, a loud, irritated yell echoed against the rafters of the room. Torie's baby girl tested her lungs on a prolonged scream against the ills of a world that had yanked her from her warm bath.

"Torie, you have a little girl! I'll get the blankets and wrap her." He now opened the bottom drawer of the bureau and grabbed up a pair of flannel blankets. So unprepared he was! Where were the scissors and a tie for the cord? So embarrassing. He hurried to the kitchen and came back with a knife and spool of thread.

The house rang with the wonderful music of a newborn human, as Hank wrapped the small copy of humanity and put her in her mother's arms. *So, now what?*

Torie, her pain subsided, was a help. "Uncle Hank, a rubber sheet in the bottom drawer. Water in the stove reservoir and pan hanging on the wall. Wash clothes in bottom drawer."

Thankful for the nudge, he had her back in the warm comfort of her bed, the soiled floor quilts rolled up and out of the way. The pan of warm water and cloth were brought and Torie reached for the cloth.

"Put the water on the stand here, and I'll clean her up."

The baby's yells had died away and were replaced with hiccups, always a good sign that everything inside was working. Hank stared at the woman and the baby and marveled at the strength of her and others like her. They did what had to be done. God did a good job when he gave childbearing over to women.

Then he touched knuckles to forehead as he remembered. *Time of birth. Must be recorded. Let's see, it was about 10 minutes ago...or maybe 15 minutes.* Time had seemed irrelevant in a situation like this.

Torie finished with the cleaning and snugged the baby under the covers where her father had spent many nights.

"Her name is Katie," Torie volunteered. "Katie Elizabeth Spencer. Bradley Spencer, your daughter is here."

Sadness along with the joy. Hank recorded the name and date and estimated the weight. Everything looked perfectly normal.

"Should I check on the children?"

Torie shook her head. "Not yet. They're good for an hour at least, and sometimes they just go to sleep on the quilts."

So he went to the kitchen and poked up the fire. The both of them needed tea or something. Maybe coffee. He filled the steel percolator with water and the basket with grounds. Within minutes it was perking merrily, sending forth fragrant steam.

With warm mugs in hand, they looked at each other. "Thanks, Uncle Hank. I'm so glad you were here."

He nodded graciously. "I was meant to be."

With amazing strength, Torie arose from the bed the next day, and unceremoniously added young Katie to her burdens.

Luke was most impressed at the ability of his wonderful momma to be able to produce this other small human. He curled

Katie's fingers around his own and grinned with pride at the baby's perfection. "Look, Momma, eyebrows! And fingernails!"

Torie knew from experience that a baby bottle would become necessary. She filled the bottle with warm water to get the sucking started. Katie was most obliging for a few sucks and then pushed it away with her tongue.

Next came half milk and half water, and Katie approved.

Uncle Hank took care of the milking for the next two months, and supervised the birth of the nanny goat's baby. The appearance of the kid meant goat's milk would be available for Katie. Everyone was certain it was best for babies. Maybe it was.

Gracie Jones appeared as a forerunner to the welcoming committee. She brought all the diapers she had collected. They were old and soft, the best for a newborn's thin skin. She gave Torie every chance to say the honey house would be remodeled for the teacher, but Torie said nothing. Obviously, Uncle Hank had not kept his promise. At least, not yet.

She told Torie that others would stop by next week, but don't think of entertaining them. They would bring the refreshments. The world would be better with more of Gracie Jones's, who quickly stepped when it was inconvenient for others.

In March, Uncle Hank brought over his garden plow and horse. Spring gardens must be planted. Peas and turnips should have been in the ground. And Torie was out there planting and covering. Time, tide and death waited for no person, and spring garden planting surely fitted in there somewhere.

Then came cutting the potatoes for planting. The seed potatoes were already beginning to sprout, and she could get five to eight plants from every potato.

It was after a morning of planting, and she and Uncle Hank retired to the kitchen for food. She had set beans to cooking, and there was cornbread alongside. Hearty food for working people.

Hank decided it was time. "Torie, when the children go to play and Katie dozes off, we need to talk a bit."

Being forewarned, Torie was apprehensive. What could be the problem. Was Uncle Hank ailing? *Oh, please, no!*

He began. "I guess you know that Enterprise is losing the school teacher."

"Miss Eldridge? Oh, no!"

"Yes, she's decided she has enough, and is going to go live with her sister. The School Board has checked around, and think they have a new teacher coming, but there's another thing. The Simmons' have decided they have had enough of boarding teachers."

He paused as Torie digested the happenings so far. Not surprising that she didn't know what was going on. He was about the only other person she saw.

Torie wondered what was coming…was she expected to board the teacher along with everything else? But then, she did have the extra bedroom, but how could a teacher stand to be around three children under six? Didn't they need time alone…or something?

"Well, I could…."

"Wait, my dear. There's more. While checking around and finding no one, someone's bright eyes lit on your honey house. Of course it is well known that you will continue with the honey production. That is known, but there was a suggestion that if the honey equipment was moved to your spare bedroom, the honey house would be ideal for the teacher, and perhaps she will be a person who likes to take care of herself."

Torie considered this, lower lip caught in her teeth, as though trying not to say what was on her mind.

Uncle Hank added the clincher. "The state is going to pay $13.00 a month, year round, instead of the usual $12.00. That is because this teacher has something or other wrong with her foot that makes her not able to walk distances, I hear. Of course, my information is third- or fourth-handed. I may be wrong on that. Anyway, she has been judged well able to teach and to get around without help and she is young enough that it will be hoped that she'll stay a while."

Torie's agile brain began to add things up. Twelve months times $13.00 dollars was more than $150.00 a year. Tickles went up and down her backbone making her shiver. An answer? Could it really be an answer? And what was wrong with having the honey equipment in the bedroom? It would certainly be handier.

Hank again. "You don't have to make up your mind yet, but the sooner they know, the sooner they can cinch this particular teacher who seems to want a country school. I understand she has turned down a city school and another one or two."

To Torie, it was sounding better and better.

He had one more thing. "If this works out with you, there will be help in the form of muscles to move the equipment. Also, there will be donations to take care of the cabin furnishings. A living room couch and chair, a bed and two chests, a table with three chairs and a stove are already promised. But I notice you have a stove in there. Would it need to be moved with the equipment?"

Torie nodded. The stove definitely was needed.

"Not a problem. A stove has already shown up. I'll let you think for a while and be sure. That means you'll have another person on your land and it will likely be that she'll have company occasionally, being only thirty-two."

"I can't see that being a problem if she can stand bees. They're there, you know, but mostly interested in attacking flowers, not people."

Uncle Hank nodded. Definitely relieved. "This particular teacher has a horse and buggy but that should not crowd you. She might even have a dog, but your little terrier might like the company."

This was still sounding better and better to Torie. Maybe the teacher would be a human who could provide an occasional minute of adult conversation. "Yes, go ahead and tell Herman Jones I'll go along with it. I guess it starts in August?"

"As far as I know, yes."

It was about March and planting time that Merrill Brooks had finished mulling over in his mind all his teaching options, and settled firmly on the school in Enterprise community, located on Ridge Road. He even liked the names of the community and the road.

He spent a pleasant day looking at conveyances and settled on a buggy. The single seat buggies were sporty and sharp looking, but he wasn't sure what he would need to transport, so he settled on a double seater.

The horse he bought was named Trumpet, for some reason, and he even liked that. He had four months to look forward to the move and to settling into a community. Being a part of somethings. Making friends to spend time with.

And now, with his new "boot" which he pointed out to his little class of first, second and third graders, he would enable him to catch them if they ran away. It started off the day with a giggle which he always tried for. The little buggers were such fun, and their achievement was already above the guidelines set for their grades. And he had two months of teaching them left before summer break.

Mr. Martin, the super of schools, had confided that he would like to clone Merrill into about a dozen others. He always knew that teachers were born, not made, and that maybe education made one a better teacher, though that could be debatable. For one who was not born to be a teacher, the job of teaching children was all up hill. And it shouldn't be.

THE BEES

It was on a warm May afternoon that the moving crew descended upon Torie's farm. Two wagons brought the furniture, and a wheeled cart was furnished for moving the heavy honey straining equipment.

Luke was excited, almost ready to burst, because he thought they might also be bringing the teacher. Such a wonderful thing was going to happen. He would participate in the wonderful thing called school that was going to happen to him in September.

School! The magical place where anything could happen and he would have the teacher in his own yard! What a status symbol!

The early gardens were popping through the ground and the bee pasture was green with flower buds of every size and shape. Torie watched them daily for the expectant flush of blooms by April first. They were honey in the making. Bees were already testing the breezes for the summer's work. Butting a head wind could be very tiring.

Torie had collected the fall honey and returned the frames for the bees to continue work. She seemed to understand bees. They never attacked her. They were not eager to give up their lives to protect the hives but they would if they had to. Unlike soldiers who had a chance of surviving the battle, a honey bee gave her all when he stung a human. His life would be over. Her life was given when she decided to sting.

If she had a chance, Torie would have twice as many hives, and fill them with swarms that had split and followed a new queen on her maiden flight. It was fascinating how it happened. The swarm buzzed closely around the new queen until she chose her castle and kingdom.

Her scouts would be circling far and wide in search of the very best place, and when the queen chose to rest on a limb, her subjects crowded around and pressed close. And enemy would face many stings before he reached the queen and endangered her, and the five would experience many casualties.

When someone rushed to Torie with the news of a new swarm, she rushed just as hard toward them to calm the swarm with puff of smoke and scoop to transfer them into a container. As quickly as possible, the container was placed before the door of an empty hive.

The door may have temptingly been baited with honey if there was time, but the weary swarm was usually quick to see the opportunity and crawl through the low door. If they deemed it satisfactory, they would encourage the queen to take a look. And how could she ever refuse such lavish furnishings of many frames ready for the little hexagon of wax cells to be filled with honey?

Each bee, at some point in its short life, was a guard, a worker, a scout and a producer (somehow!) of both wax and honey. If a thief robbed the honey early enough in the year, the hive merely made up the difference and still survived the winter on their own product.

Positively fascinating and amazing for something about the size of half of a lady's thumb! Who is it that could not be an admirer of the honey bee?

But the honey house had to be emptied. The bees were definitely not happy with the activity of so many humans and their strange smells so close to their hives. This activity attracted some of the scouts, who were ready to fight, and unfortunately, several lost their lives in the battle, but the work went on.

By late afternoon, the change had been made, and the two large rooms of the honey house were made homey and comfortable enough for any discriminating lady teacher. It had been a labor of pride and it was the hope that this teacher would appreciate the effort and settle in. It was truly the best that could be had by rural teachers, and she would undoubtedly see this.

It was hard for Luke to understand that the beloved teacher would not appear for months. Sometimes it's hard to be only five years old.

And while Merrill was uniquely happy with his little class in town, his heart had already proceeded ahead of him and dwelt on Ridge Road and his own school. The one he had never seen. A long-distance love affair, so to speak.

There was a small, emergency building on site, he was told, that was intended for an unexpected overnight stay by the teacher, or as a refuge for a child who became ill or might be contagious.

The little building was twelve by twelve feet, containing a tiny stove and a pull-up table that was a shelf to be let down flat when not in use. There were several small shelves for necessities and maybe a book or two. The bed was a narrow affair, with no head or foot frame. The shack was, in fact, only an emergency shelter.

It all sounded good.

The summer went on. Torie, with her last bit of desperation at not being to able to care for her children and do what had to be done, consigned young Miss Katie to a backpack sort of arrangement patterned after the baby carriers in other countries.

She took her naps aboard her mom who manned the hoe that removed the weeds. Children had to grow, and so did vegetables. Somehow the summer passed.

MERRILL BROOKS, TEACHER

Merrill gazed with pleasure on the shining coat of his new horse. Who cared what name he was called in a past life; his name was now Sultan. The light brown shone gold in the sun, and his trimmed mane was free of tangles. And most important, he fitted so nicely between the shafts of his buggy.

The tall wheels of the buggy were new, and the leather upholstery was well cleaned and oiled. A day in the hot summer sun would set the oil so it did not rub off. His spare belongings were packed into two sizeable suitcases and the books were packed into many boxes that had been picked up at the grocery store.

Standing back and looking at it, he was astounded that his whole life of thirty-two years could be comfortably packed into a horse-drawn buggy. But then there just hadn't seemed a way or a need to accumulate possessions. He was never in one place long enough to enjoy them. Perhaps this fact fertilized his love of books...they went along uncomplainingly wherever the railway sent him. They were as content within their covers as he was in his way of life. Or so he thought.

He realized now, not without a bit of horror, that he was almost grateful for the cart that took his foot. Otherwise, he would have undoubtedly still have been Mr. Fixit, on call to any calamity. He would be nothing more than a useful tool to be used when needed, then put away until needed again.

He had been an expensive tool for the railway, and the money was good, but when that was all one had, what good was it? Now, however, he could use the money to prepare for the rest of his life.

He had found things to do in town until his teaching contract went into effect. Now it was August, and he could show up at his new home.

His horse and buggy were shipped by rail to Eureka Springs and he rejoined them at the station. The map said to go east through town until he reached Highway 62, otherwise known as Ridge Road, so named because it twisted around trying to follow the high road on the mountain ridges. Occasionally it had to go to the valley, but then it climbed back onto the ridge again.

From Eureka Springs, he passed through Wishbone Hollow. What a picturesque name! He continued on by the small town and began to climb higher. It was a very long and hot day but he knew he was getting near. There were several small named communities, not really cities, and eventually he would get to Enterprise.

The sun was very low but still he watched the scenery go by and admired this and that. At one place he even saw the spacious-looking log house that seemed to have just grown up out of the woodland. There was a big barn and a smaller cabin, likely for the parents of the owner of the house. How appropriate!

He drove on, and consulted the hand drawn map. He had to be close. He was to meet members of the school board at the school house, and wait over night in the small emergency cabin. Tomorrow he would be taken to his new lodging.

And there on the right he saw it. It was so perfect, it should be on a calendar. The red painted building, windows down the sides, belfry rising from the roof over the small welcoming porch. Just as he'd thought it would be.

He instructed Sultan to turn in at the driveway, and the horse was more than ready. It had been an uphill climb all the way. When he turned in at a driveway, Sultan snorted approval and whickered a greeting at the other waiting horses.

Merrill guided the buggy toward the tiny structure that must be the emergency cabin. He was met by two of the local school board, Mr. Herman Jones and Mr. Clyde Albright.

They watched him descend and came forward, hesitantly. Merrill stepped forward and extended his hand. "Pleased to meet you, Sirs."

The hand was accepted, but the pair of eyes searched the buggy that seemed to have no persons waiting to get out.

Herman Jones spoke up. "Did you come alone, Sir?"

"Uh…well, yes. I have no family."

"But we were expecting…."

"The thing was, we were here to greet Miss Brooks. Would you tell us your name, Sir?"

"Oh, I was sure you knew. I'm Merrill Brooks. I have the contract to teach classes in this school." Was he talking with first graders?

"Oh…uh, well. Would you excuse us to have a word?"

"Certainly, Sir," and he retired to the buggy seat. WHAT was going on?

Mr. Albright was shaking his head vehemently. His mouth formed the word "NO!" and his eyes were blazing beneath shaggy brown.

"Right. It won't work. We should have been told."

"Did we ask?"

"No, but who'd have thought to."

"What'll we do? We can't find another place in a day. No one is interested. Boarding the teacher is a rather confining duty."

"But Torie…there alone with those youngens? It'd never do."

"Right. Anything could happen. Surely there is a mix-up somewhere?"

"But what about now? He, I mean she was meant to spend one night here. What'll we do?"

Merrill was becoming irritated. He alighted from the buggy and approached them. "Sirs, is this or is this not Enterprise?"

"It is, but…."

"If there's a problem here, perhaps you could guide me on to the cabin, which I understand is ready."

"Well…sir…? You see there's a problem."

Merrill was very tired, or he might not have spoken so sharply. "There's not a problem with me, I can tell you. I can show you a copy of my contract. That's all I want, and I'll sleep on the floor if it's not ready."

"Well, sir, it's not that easy."

"All right, I'll sleep in this little outhouse, and you'll take me to the cabin tomorrow."

"But there's a problem. The cabin isn't ready for you."

Merrill again, "Where is the cabin?"

Both men shook their heads. "It doesn't matter where it is. We can't take you there."

Merrill had at this point really HAD it. "Look, fellows, I'll sleep in this thing tonight, and I'll give you a day to get this sorted out. If you can't, I am turning my horse around and heading out back to town. You choose. Now open up these doors for me and I'll see you in the morning."

Herman Jones poked the key into the lock with a nervous hand. "Sir, we might not be here early in the morning. There's an errand we have to take care of."

The exasperated teacher bit his tongue against a few well-placed remarks, promising his brain that it could use them tomorrow when things might be clearer. These dumb heads knew he was coming and could assume he would be tired. So what was it with the errand to take care of...?

Mr. Clyde Albright stepped inside the shack and lit the lamp. The cabin having been shut up all day in the sun, was itself an oven from the August heat.

The two men could think of no apology or a graceful farewell, so they mounted their horses and trotted down the road.

FIRST DAY

Merrill stepped inside the little cabin. Small and stuffy, and it was definitely not made to house a six foot two inch man of average build. He practically met himself coming and going. The tiny bed occupied a corner and was a scant two feet wide. It was possible to walk around the bed if one turned sideways.

He stepped out and shut the door. He unhitched Sultan and led him the schoolhouse porch and fastened him to a post. He took grain from the buggy and fed him.

He rutted around in his luggage and brought up a roll of bedding that had traveled many miles with him. He had debated on whether to bring it along, but now he was glad he had. He rolled it out onto the porch floor and seated himself on it, leaning against the schoolhouse door.

Sultan's crunching of the corn in his feedbag made Merrill hungry. He searched his mind to remember the choices. There were crackers and sardines, a cheese sandwich, two candy bars and a stick of beef jerky. He also had water and two apples.

All put together they weren't much of a meal, but he started in. As tired as he was, if he got really full, maybe he'd sleep through until morning.

As he munched along, he kept seeing that little log cabin he's seen back down the road away. Could that have been it? The one he was contracted to get? He was willing to bet it was, and if so, what was wrong that had to be fixed in the morning?

In his whole life he had never seen two grown men so utterly dumb struck. Surely they were not an example of the people he had chosen to be with? Couldn't be, or Mr. Martin would have warned him. Or maybe Mr. Martin didn't know.

Finally, near morning, he went to sleep, but was awakened early by Sultan's snorts and the trees full of birds. Also an orchestra of katydids rubbing their legs in the trees.

Breakfast. Sultan would fare quite well, but all Merrill had left was an apple and part of the jerky. Hmmm, well, he could go back down the road and beg at someone's house. That made him grin in spite of himself. What an introduction that would to the person who was planning to teach their children! But then....

He ate his apple and chewed on the jerky. Sultan enjoyed his feed bag full of corn. Tossing a saddle onto Sultan and leaping astride, he managed to land the saddle. He'd been practicing a lot, but there was no way to keep the boot from just dangling. It wouldn't fit itself into the stirrup. No problem. Sultan was getting used to the lop-sided load.

He turned back down the mountain toward the neat house and the log cabin that he had seen yesterday. He could get a closer look riding on Sultan than from the buggy. He was soon there, and pulled the horse up to the fence.

He found himself looking at the largest flower garden he had ever seen. They were everywhere, with hardly a path between them. Early fall butterflies, the small golden ones, flitted here and there, dipping into the tall, yellow clover blossoms and the purple fall asters. Bees buzzed busily from flower to flower and then zooming off to the little hives. He was so fascinated, he almost forgot he was hungry.

Sultan nipped at a clump of grass and lifted his head to chew. He spotted a horse about two fences over and whickered a greeting. The other horse whickered back. A small boy came from the big house swinging a wire egg basket.

A lady appeared from nowhere (maybe a barn) and walked toward the house with a pail. Morning activates.

Sultan whickered again and the lady turned and looked his way. She hung the pail of a post and approached him.

"Good morning. Is my horse out again? I heard yours greeting someone."

"I don't think so. He sees the horse in the pasture."

She looked back at him. "Were you looking for someone? I don't remember seein' you before."

"I'm a stranger," he admitted, "but I really admired your little log cabin. Do you ever rent it out?"

"Uh...no sir. I'm sorry but it's spoken for."

Merrill felt his skin prickle from excitement at being, at least seemingly, to be right. *Be brave, Merrill and say it,* he instructed himself. "It wouldn't, by chance, be waiting for the new school teacher?"

The lady jerked as though startled. "Why, yes, it is."

"Then you may be seeing me later. I'm the teacher."

"You...are the...teacher...?"

"In the flesh."

"But, you...."

"Ma'am, it's just a guess, but I am presuming that you were expecting a lady teacher. Well, I'm no lady as you can plainly see."

"But you were...not met...by anyone? Mr. Jones was...?"

"I met him last night but he was confused at meeting a man. I didn't know the reason for the confusion then, but now I know."

Torie finally remembered her manners. "You can't have had breakfast yet. Why don't you come on in and see Mr. Jones later. I can have breakfast ready in minutes."

His stomach made an appropriate comment in the form of a rumble. "I could really do that, and be grateful." He guided Sultan up the ditch into the road and came through the gate as she held it open.

In a matter of minutes he was seated at the table with the lady and two small children in front of fluffy biscuits, gravy with bites of sausage mixed through like a flock of mallard ducks feeding in the lake. And alongside was a heap of scrambled eggs with a tall glass of fresh milk.

They were finishing off with a fresh cup of garden tea when there was a sharp knock on the door. When it was opened, there stood two men staring from Merrill to Torie and back again. They seemed to be speechless.

Merrill helped them out. "Glad to meet you fellows again. I was going to try to look you up, but this makes it easier. I had a little time this morning so I thought I'd check out a place to live. That little building in the school yard was too small for a fellow of my size.

"Uh, well…we didn't…."

"I know. You were expecting a delicate little lady and you got me. If you want to change your mind just say so, I have other places I can go. I chose this one because of the separate house. As you can see, I'm much too big to be boarded in someone's house."

No response from the confused men.

"It seems I found the cabin, so I plan to move in today. It's perfect for the present time, but if I continue here, of course I could be making other plans. If this is not satisfactory, tell me now. I've just finished a lovely breakfast and I'm going to the schoolhouse for my buggy. I can meet you there, or not, as you please." And with that, he stood, smiling amiably, and looked at the startled Torie.

"I thank you for the lovely breakfast, and if this does not to work out, I'll drop over to say good bye."

He walked past the men and out the door. The speechless men struggled and finally found words. "Now, Miss Torie, it really won't work to have him here. We'll find a place."

"Why won't it work?"

"Because…well, the community will not accept it. It wouldn't be right for him, a man…."

"What does the community have to do with it? He looked at the house and likes it. All of this was a community project, so let it be."

"But…well, we must get on over to the schoolhouse and deal with this. Good day, Miss Torie."

"Don't you worry, Miss Torie. It'll be all right." And they were gone.

Torie watched them leave. A bit puzzled, of course, but perhaps it would get clearer soon. But for now, she breathed a sigh of relief. This arrangement would comfortably solve what was an impending problem for herself and her children.

DECISION TIME

The two men, being of the same mind, had nothing to say on the way to the school house. They just put their horses into a trot and arrived just as Merrill was hitching Sultan to the buggy.

"Mr. Brooks, we sincerely regret this situation, but you see Miss Torie is a young, attractive widow, and you…a fellow living in her yard…well, it just wouldn't work. Do you see?"

"No, I don't see. Would I also be kept from renting a house next door to her…or maybe across the street? Do I look like a murderer, or worse? The school board obviously OKed this deal, and Miss Torie was cordial and friendly, so I don't see the problem you seem to see. But here's the way it is. I will remove the problem. This problem will not last more than the ten minutes it takes for me to attach my horse to all my worldly possessions and pull out onto the road.

"Time to make up your minds, my friends. I have my contract right here and handy, and I can tear it to bits in a second. The president of the school board will not take this lightly. He really wanted to place me in town, but I chose Enterprise. Under these circumstances, you would be unlikely to get a teacher for this year, but that would be your choice."

The two men watched as Merrill climbed into the buggy and clicked to Sultan, who whickered softly at the other horses, as he turned toward the road.

The two men suddenly found words. "WAIT! WAIT! Let's give this a try. It's just a little misunderstanding."

Merrill called a "Whoaa" and Sultan stopped. He turned full face to the two man and looked them up and down.

"Thank you, gentlemen. I'll be here on Monday ready to teach your children. But I must say this, the minute you are unhappy with me, just let it be known and I'm gone." A click and

Sultan was moving away. Merrill even had the unmitigated gall to wave cheerily to them as he reached the road.

Within minutes, Merrill Brooks was moving into his new home. He insisted that he didn't need the offered help, so Torie went on with her many duties, after advising him that lunch would be at twelve o'clock.

Back in the house, Torie was faced with a demanding five year old. "I think that man is the school teacher. I like him."

Torie nodded. "I think he is, too, son. At least for a while."

"No, Momma, for ever and ever!"

Torie smiled at his insistence and told herself, *May it be so.*

The new teacher shook out the bedding and spread the bed. He rearranged the couch and chair and drew up a bucket of water for the kitchen. The well was handy…practically on his doorstep.

He surveyed his furniture. Small table with three chairs. Generous cabinet with a smattering of dishes and a drawer for the silverware. All along the west wall were the bookcases. Entirely adequate, and much above most of the bachelor pads he had inhabited over the years. This could be looked on as a real home.

He had save the chore of the placing books to the last so he could enjoy it. His boxes of books were handy on the floor, and he gazed on them with pride. They, in fact, had been the road map of his life so far.

Being on the road so much, and not having the chance to develop friendships, he had turned to books and made them his friends.

Documentaries, how-to books, histories of the world, old English poets and a few classics. It became a habit for him to find books about new things. He wanted to know everything, and was well on his way to doing just that. Books were so satisfying, so comforting and they were always the same. They did not change their words as so many humans changed their minds.

Books were also agreeable about how they were treated. They occupied the shelves as they were assigned and did so without complaint, they rode along on the swaying train when he desired, and they waited patiently in the rented rooms ready to comfort him in his few leisure moments. They could be ignored for years, and they would still share their knowledge without complaint or demand.

He knew he would be spending a lot of his time in the kitchen at the table, so the wall of shelves was perfectly placed. He could always look their way, recognizing their covers like the faces of old friends, if he'd ever had any.

He looked out the window at the late August garden. He practically lived in the flower garden, and bees buzzed overhead like rising funnels of summer heat. Butterflies flitted among them like so many colored threads in an intricate embroidery pattern.

What is this thing with bees? He knew, of course, about the honey, but there must be a lot more to learn. Maybe Miss Torie…? No, he would not bother her. He would not be dependent on her in any way and add to her duties. He'd be going to Eureka Springs occasionally, and of course they would have a library, or maybe a bookstore where he could buy information on whatever he wanted to know.

He had hopes that Enterprise would have some friends who could accept him, at least casual ones, but that seemed unlikely, at the moment. The books on the shelf, however, were a certainty. Yes, he would find a book that explained all about bees. There could be a lot more to them than Miss Torie was using. That huge flower bed would surely feed a lot more of them. He'd more about know later.

And Torie Spencer moved on with her life, comforted by the income of $13.00 a month which was more than adequate for her needs. She would be able to put back some of it in jar…a habit taught her by her late husband. But now, harvesting the honey was the next big item on her list. This would be the first year of managing it alone.

Not only that, her helper, Luke, would be in school and not available to pacify his sisters. Another thought, it had seeped gradually into her mind that here, now living in her yard, was a male figure for her son. A boy needed that. It was one thing she was sure of, and he would have had that if Bradley had…*oh, Bradley! I know you didn't intend to leave me alone, but…*and then her resolve kicked in.

She mentally shouted at herself, *STOP THAT, TORIE! YOU KNOW WHERE THAT SORT OF THINKING LEADS! YOU CANNOT AFFORD THE TIME TO BE LOLLYGAGGING AROUND. BRADLEY IS NOT COMING BACK! HE CAN'T! HE WOULD WANT YOU TO MOVE ON, SO DO IT!*

Having chided herself thoroughly and reminded herself of the recent periods of depression, she squared her chin and laid out the honey production equipment. The bedroom was a bit cramped for working room, but it would at least be very handy. She could deal with that, and when there were the jars to go to Eureka Springs, she would also deal with that.

A bucket of soapy lye water bubbled on the stove…the routine cleansing of Katie's ever-present diapers. There would be another year of that before she could be trained.

And she must find time to make more soap. Hog fat and lye water. Amazing to her how those two items made soap that cleansed away grease and lye. Just one of those fascinating quirts in nature.

Keep moving, Torie. Time to pick the late tomatoes and can up a few more jars for the cellar. Of all vegetables, tomatoes were the backbone, the thread that held together many of the family's favorite dishes. So many things could be made of them. Dozens of soups, casseroles when blended with cheese (and oh, yes. The cottage cheese needed to be made. Right now.) And tomatoes straight out of the jar and served cold made a tasty summer dish, along with potato salad and boiled eggs. Not to mention sliced raw in a plate to eat alongside whatever else was served.

She had held the cranky Katie back from a nap hoping she would sleep longer, but now she kept going to sleep in the highchair. It was the time to get started with the work…and where was Luke?

She stepped to the door and called, "LUKE! LUKE! I NEED YOU!"

"Here, Momma." And he came running from the door of the honey house. Torie frowned and sighed. How could she tell him that the new teacher was not his possession and still allow whatever friendship the man had to give? And him also a close neighbor? Well, that small problem was for later. Tomatoes were for now.

"Luke, bring the sled around, and we'll get the ripe tomatoes."

There'd likely be a couple more flushes of tomatoes before frost, and she needed all she could can. They were so reliable. An extra mouth, now. But likely no more than Bradley's had been. It was something she had to get used to…again.

The sled carried the three bushel baskets, ready for what would be gleaned off the ragged old vines, and Missy rode gleefully on the sled. Missy was now three and must be weaned away from being the baby and getting to ride. She was not likely to go along with being forced to help. That was going to be hard to do.

"Now, Missy, you only pick them when they're red. Not the green ones like this. Only the red ones."

Missy nodded agreeably. "Red," she said. Well, they'd see how that went.

Tomatoes counted up fast, and the baskets were full in a half an hour. Boiling them down for the jars would take the rest of the day, but other things could be done in between.

Too bad Luke couldn't reach the clothesline.

DECISIONS

Merrill placed the books carefully within his own system. Beautiful covers on some of them. For a while, he had an audience, but then the little fellow was called home by his mom. Polite little guy, and packed as full of questions as a sardine can is full of fishes.

Speaking of sardines, there didn't seem to be a grocery store for miles. He was going to have to get food supplies as he did not intend to be a bother to Miss Torie when he needed a snack. She had enough to do.

Small knock at the door. And there stood Luke with a huge, red tomato in each hand. "Momma said these were for you, and that I had to come right back. So, bye!"

Putting the tomaotes in Merrill's hand, he turned and ran back. Not very happy, it seemed. Mama needed him, it seemed.

When Torie got into the mess of peeling the tomatoes, she didn't need Katie squalling in the background. Luke was very handy with her so that would take care of her for an hour. A lot could be done in an hour.

Oh, yes, the cottage cheese that had to be stirred constantly. She'd get the stool and have Luke stirring until Katie woke up.

Nine full jars of tomatoes lined the kitchen wall when lunch was served. They had to cool before going to the cellar.

Lunch consisted of brown beans and ham, sliced tomatoes and cornbread. Merrill thoroughly enjoyed it, but knew he had convey the fact that he did not expect it, and he must not hurt her feelings by letting her think that her food was not good enough. He'd have to think about the best way to say it.

Also, he must make that trip to Eureka Springs, and it was not a one-day round trip. It would be an over-nighter and maybe he'd have time to look for the bookstore. He needed the supplies for at least one daily meal in the cabin. With the breakfast Torie served, he would very well 'batch' on the other two. It would surely work out, at least for a while, and he could plainly see that she needed the monthly $13.00.

This was Wednesday, so if he went tomorrow to Eureka, he'd be back on Friday in time to be ready for school on Monday. Sultan would not be pleased with the trip for he was happily grazing in the pasture with the resident horse, who seemed to have no objection. There was grass enough for all.

The day passed with no sight of the school board members. It seemed they had decided to let it go.

On the way to Eureka Springs, Merrill had a lot of time for thinking. Nineteen students, and three of them in the eighth grade. Two girls and a boy. For a lot of families, it would be a sacrifice to let a boy have all eight years of school.

His small neighbor, Luke, would be a starter this year. Five year olds were really not expected to do much, but it gave them a good start by giving them a idea of what was expected. They could hear the others recite and learn a lot that way.

While in town, he'd look for large sheets of paper and some kind of dark marking pencils. He had an idea for visual presentations. There would be so few in each class, they could share books so that was not a problem. He was greatly enjoying the pleasant mixture of excitement, satisfaction and a sense of completion which was sure to have a great effect on his immediate future, and possibly long term.At age thirty-two, it was time he was thinking past day to day. Time to grab the reins of life and dig in.

On Tuesday of this week, the Quilting Circle had met, as usual, but they had the wonderful bit of news to excite them.

The lady teacher they had arranged for turned out to be a man! What a trick to play on the community, but nothing was said to the indicate the ladies were concerned. After all, the contract referred only to the "teacher" and the "community." So, what was the problem?

The fact of the $13.00 payment to Torie totally erased the need for the community to do more for her. She was a self-sufficient lady, and could easily be insulted by help that assumed she could not do for herself. Everyone knew that. They were sure she would do nicely. Several of the ladies had passed along gently used baby clothing which was welcome. It was a thing done for every one of them. Out grown clothing might well be passed around to 3 or more families before it wore out. Especially for those as young as Katie.

But here was the big, and most interesting, subject of conversation that arose in the minds of the ladies.

Torie, an attractive twenty-four year old, and a male boarder who was thirty-two years old and had no family. Speculation was great.

"Imagine that! A man teacher!

"Wonder if he's any good at teachin'?"

"Doesn't matter. We have to take what we can get. Ours might be the smallest school in the whole world."

"And he's livin' over with Torie."

"Uh, well, not really with her. He's in that bee house."

"Ain't that in her yard?"

"It's a big yard. But she's supposed to feed him. I'll bet he eats more than a lady teacher would. I'd hate to have to cook for an extra mouth every meal."

"Speck he eats more'a Bradley did?"

"Maybe not, but…."

"But if it's in the contract, how would it be extra?"

No answer.

"Well, anyway, I'm glad she's gettin' paid good. We don't need to worry about her no more."

"Or bother her."

"I wonder why a man teacher took a job all the way out here? So far from anywhere?"

Gracie Jones fielded this one. "He told Herman that he had a four choices and close this one."

"Do you think it might be that he knew about Torie? And her bein' alone, and all?"

Gracie again. "No, I know that for sure. He just said he couldn't stay in the little shack…that it was too small for a full sized man. He slept that first night on the porch of the schoolhouse, and then lit out to search for the log cabin he was promised. He found it, too, and Torie gave him breakfast."

"I suspect he didn't want to live in a family house. Too many women and kids, I'd think."

Grannie chose this moment to clear her throat. "It'd seem to me that we may be lookin' for somethin' that don't exist. Bein' located in the same yard don't make a lot'a difference to a fellow intent on harmin' a lady. Why, he could live over in Garland, and still make trouble, or occupy one of her rooms and be safe. Seems it'd be well to give the man a chance."

Gracie agreed. "You're right, Grannie. We'll save that for when we have a reason to doubt 'im."

So Eloise took the hint. "Did you notice that baby, Katie? She has her papa's chin dimple."

"I wonder if that dimple reminds Torie of Bradley all the time."

Grannie again. Bad throat problem today. "I'm thinkin' she'd not need a dimple in the baby to be reminded of what she lost."

"I don't know how Torie can stand it. Bein' alone with those three kids all the time."

"Seems like she had no choice."

"I'd say she may be too busy to remember that she can't stand it."

And the men of the community had a bit to say.

"Why wouldn't the state people have said that our teacher was a man?"

"Don't know, but maybe to them a teacher is a teacher, man or woman. You wouldn't think of then sayin' 'we have a woman teacher for you.' So they must consider 'em completely interchangeable."

"But they ain't."

"Well, I, for one, wouldn't have that job no matter how much they paid. Imagine all day and every day with a couple dozen youngens and their everlastin' questions."

"A teacher's supposed to have the answers to questions."

"Huh! The way I heard it, he came off a job that paid three times as much. Quit 'cause he hurt his foot…or something."

"Yeah, and it makes 'im walk funny."

"I'm ready to put up a five spot that says he don't last the year. Got any takers?"

"Mr. Brown, if'n I was a bettin' man, I'd take you up on that. I got a feelin' that we'll be seein' that fellow around here for a lot of years to come."

"Maybe so. I just hope he's as good as Miss Eldridge at teachin'."

"Reckon how he likes bein' there with Bradley's wife?"

"I thinkin' on how Bradley'd feel."

"Think on what you said. If Bradley could feel anything, he would not be gone."

"Right!"

"I wouldn't say Bradley was in a position to feel one way or another. But that's where the separate housing was located and that's what Mr. Brooks wanted, or he'd go back to the state school board for a transfer."

"And a'nuther thing, no one else on the Ridge was wantin' to board a teacher."

"I sure wouldn't have."

"You're sayin' we had no choice?"

"Not if he wanted to stay here. And it's already too late to make changes. School starts in a week and man, oh, man, am I ready!"

"If I recall right, that log cabin is practically in the bee patch. Reckon how he likes that?"

"I heard it was in the contract if he was allergic to bee stings. Said he wasn't. You know, some folks pass out and maybe die from stings. Seems he OKed the deal knowin' about all them hives"

And on Friday, Merrill Brooks got an early start back up Ridge Road. He was a bit disappointed that he had to leave Eureka Springs so soon. Next time he came, he'd try to arrange an extra day to just look around. He didn't half see the places he'd like to have seen.

His buggy was loaded with staple groceries for a week. A baking pan and another skillet. Flour, sugar, salt and pepper, and such as that. He spent most of the short amount of time looking for the large paper sheets he wanted as teaching tools for the first grades. No paper big enough or tough enough, and no cardboard that would hold up. At one point he ducked into a diner and stared into a cup of coffee. There had to be answer. Many times he faced problems that had no answer in the manual, or maybe he had a part that didn't fit, or old machinery that no longer had repair parts, or an emergency forced him to make do in a hurrry. Coffee and thinking had pulled him out of all of them.

In all of those times, he had stared into his coffee and enlisted the help of his brain. *Brain, what would you do here?* So when the paper he sought was not available, he thought, sipped, thought and sipped some more. *Brain...? Where are you...?*

All right. There was no paper, but paper didn't last well anyway. Wooden boards were too bulky. Maybe cloth...uh, heavy cloth...NO! Canvas! Canvas could be easily cut into the sizes he needed and would allow letters and numbers to be painted on. It could be rolled up to store and would last for a generation. Not only that, if he didn't need that one panel anymore, paint it over with white paint and use it for something else.

Got it! Coffee and thinkin' always came through for him. He'd just have to see that he always had coffee in his little log house. So, where would the canvas be?

Tent maker, that's what he needed to find. When the waitress came to fill her coffee, he asked her, "Ma'am, do you know if this town has a tent maker? I'm lookin' for a large sheet of canvas."

She thought for a second. "You don't need a tent maker, you need the lumber company that sells sawed buildin' planks. He's down toward the river. Go down the street and take a left. You'll see 'im. Hawks Building Material."

"Thanks so much." He sipped the last cup of hot coffee so fast it almost scorched his throat. Mustn't let it waste, though.

The twelve-foot square sheets of canvas, three of them, folded nicely and a gallon bucket of white paint would turn the tan canvas into white. A quart of black paint and a small brush would do the lettering.

He was so pleased with himself that he checked into the hotel for the night and woke up before the sun. He had breakfast in the diner and had a lunch packed for the road. Sultan was reluctantly headed up the hill to Ridge Road.

If his teaching panels were three feet by three feet, each sheet of canvas would produce sixteen panels each, and twice as many if he used both sides. He did it! He and a cup of coffee did it again. And he had the same thrill of achievement as he had when fixing a problem for the railway and getting a breakdown back on the rails again.

He was easy on Sultan climbing the hills, letting him slow to a walk, and it was almost dark when he reached his cabin. He left the buggy loaded and pulled it into the side of the shed that Torie said was his. Sultan got a cup of corn, and the green pasture, and Merrill hauled his groceries to the cabin by the armload.

He dug down in his plunder for the new coffee percolator. Time to celebrate and break it in. The heavenly aroma filled the log cabin and eased out into the yard just in time to meet the platter of food coming his way.

At the door she said, "You weren't back for supper, so I scooped some on the platter for you. Just in time for your coffee."

The plate held chicken noodles heaped onto mashed potatoes and the platter was hot from being kept in the oven for him. A bowl of canned peaches rode along on the tray. Merrill accepted it gratefully.

"Miss Torie, ma'am, would you, by chance, have a taste for coffee?"

"Coffee is my top favorite drink. Tea is good, coffee is better."

"Then may I offer you a steaming mug of it? I have a whole pot to consume, and coffee has never been known to keep me awake."

"Me, either," she admitted shyly.

The tiny table with three chairs held the tray easily, along with two coffee mugs.

Torie eyed the groceries. "I'm sure you know that food comes with your contract?"

"I do, yes, and thank you. The fact is, I rather enjoy cooking on occasions, and I don't want to interfere with your schedule, especially for supper. Of course, I'll be takin' my lunch to school, and I'll make it myself. Bein' alone so many years, I sort'a got in the habit. Please don't think I don't like your cooking. It's wonderful."

Torie could have enjoyably sat at the little table for another cup of coffee but she didn't. This sort of thing must not be allowed become a habit. There are rules for fellows and gals, and they must be obeyed. She knew them well. The cabin was HIS house.

She left after the last sip. "Breakfast is next, and I'll expect you."

THE ABC'S OF BEES

Merrill busied himself unpacking his purchases. Surely this was not all he needed, but he'd soon make another trip to the quaint little town in the valley.

He caressed the cover of the book ABC'S OF BEES. He'd searched the shelves of the little book store for as long as he'd had time for. There were a lot of interesting choices, but his mind was firmly set on the subject of bees.

Finally asking the useless question, he was told, "Oh. Bees! Why, I believe I might just have one book, but it's in the back. I'll get it."

It had taken so long that he was becoming concerned. He had to be on the way, and yet had things to do, but here she finally came, carefully wiping the dust from the cover. The book had a black dust jacket and was clearly over-sized, measuring ten by twelve inches. That meant a lot of good reading, and if he was lucky, maybe a few drawn-to-scale illustrations.

"I found it!" she announced happily.

Merrill, always being interested in details, wondered, "Why was it hidden in the back room?"

The young lady with a toss of the head, admitted, "Well, the book was not alone back there. It's a space problem, really. You see how little space I have, crowded in between two buildings. I reckon I am lucky to have any space at all, but there's the tiny room in back that has the books that have been proved to be slow sellers. I've been here goin' on four years, and you're the first to ask about bees. Mostly folks learn about bees from their pas or someone else in the family."

Good answer. He counted out the money for the book, but couldn't help asking, "Suppose I come back here before too long, maybe I could slip quietly into the back room to see what you have. Would that be possible?" One never knew until they asked.

"Oh, yes, sir! Anytime and spend as long as you like!"

That excited answer intrigued him more and more. But the sun was climbing. He needed to be on the way.

So now, though it was late, he flipped through the pages. Words, graphs and drawings! Exact what he loved. But he sadly put it on the shelf. Tomorrow was another day. He would plan to give himself over to the book.

He awoke to country sounds. The crop of young chickens had a few cocks who were trying out their morning cry, announcing their sex. The familiar "Er-er-er-erah" with a falling volume at the last, came out "Er-erah." Merrill blinked himself awake and told the young cocks through the window, "I'd not be out there braggin' fellows. You're just announcin' yourselves to be ready for the stew pot."

The answer came through clearly. "Er-erah!"

He hauled himself out of bed and looked at the clock. What happened to the time? He must have been totally exhausted. It was almost 7:00 and breakfast time.

Poking up the coals in the stove, then scooping fresh grounds into the six cup percolator, he added water. Miss Torie obviously likes coffee, so if he can just get the fire going, he can add his part to the breakfast.

When the perking stopped, he lifted the pot and one mug and headed for the big house.

At the kitchen, he found the door open because of the heat, so he announced himself, "Good morning!"

"Come in!" was the invitation. "I'm putting it on the table."

He entered and took his assigned place after setting the coffee pot on the still-hot kitchen stove. "This thing makes six cups, just right for sharing," he announced.

A voice from another part of the house. "Momma, you want me to hold Katie's bottle?"

"No, son. She's been tryin' to hold it herself. Give her a chance."

"OK." Then, "No, Missy. You're messin' the drawer all up. I'll get your dress."

There came a squeal of objection.

"Momma, she's holdin' her hands over her head and won't let me put her dress on her."

"Missy, let Luke help you, and then come on in here."

The two children trooped in together and took their places, Luke on the chair with the block for height and Missy in the highchair. Luke's eyes brightened as he saw Merrill.

"Hi," he greeted companionably.

"Hi, yourself," Merrill responded.

The bowl of fried potatoes scrambled with a lot of eggs appeared on the table alongside the biscuits and gravy. Milk was served to everyone.

As Torie sat down, Luke asked, "Me?"

At his mother's nod, he bowed his head and folded his hands. "Dear Lord, please bless this food. Amen. " Then raising his head brightly, he said, "Missy, take your hands out of your plate so I can give you potatoes."

Where upon, Missy clapped her hands against her ears and giggled. Obviously, this was a practiced game.

The observant eyes of the teacher spotted the white coveralls hanging on the wall, and the hat with the veil nearby. Obviously this was to be a bee-keeping day. Torie, noting his glance, explained.

"Thought I'd start in with the bees today while Luke's here to watch the girls."

Merrill responded. "Good thinking. Can you do it alone?" He could hardly see how he would be a help, but politeness demanded that he ask.

A quick nod, and then, "I can. I've done it before. It's just that when I start, I can't watch Katie, so I need Luke to do that. Missy thinks Katie should be able to play with her. Katie can't get out of the crib but Missy can get in, and Missy hasn't learned yet that 'no' means 'no.'"

Luke, with a mouthful of potatoes and egg, nodded agreement. He obviously knew the drill. Been there before, no doubt.

What other comments Merrill would have made, he decided keep to himself. He'd just wait and see. This should be an interesting day.

As much as he would have liked to observe the bee thing, he realized that he would not be appreciated and likely be in the way, and he really needed to work on his canvas panels.

He rolled out the canvas on the yard and measured three feet, and with a straight board, marked a cutting line. After a few minutes locating his knife (he really had to create some kind of order on where things were) he sliced the sheet into sixteen panels. He only needed four for today, so he rolled the others together and put them away. He thinned the white paint with lamp oil and spread it on the canvas with the brush. It soaked in nicely and would dry quickly. He'd like to have both sides painted white before noon so he could begin the lettering.

The snow white figure in the hat with a net vail moved about visiting the various hives. She carried a bucket, presumably for the contents of the hives which would be honey and wax honeycomb.

He'd know more if he'd read the book, but the jiggle of the wagon had made that impossible.

The bright sun of the late August morning did its work on the panels and they were dry on both sides by 10:00. Jolly good timing.

Stretching a sheet onto his small table (it was a fair fit) he began to apply the black lettering. After his experience with last year's class, he found third graders to whom cursive was a foreign language, and they tended to just connect printed letters with a short mark thinking that would work. It didn't. Third graders must be able to create readable cursive, so he had an idea.

If he lettered, Aa Bb Cc Dd, and so on, even the first graders would see that the printed letters had 'cousins' that were written a different way and they would not be shocked later when the teacher expected more. Even the other grades might be able to benefit if the former years' teachers had not stressed it. Cursive was necessary.

It crossed his mind that if Luke had not been otherwise employed, he'd likely have had an audience. He was really looking forward to teaching such a bright little mind.

While the thicker black paint was drying, he whistled for Sultan, pocketed the key to the schoolhouse, and went for a short ride. It really should not have been necessary to ride, as the schoolhouse was in sight of the cabin, but walking in the prosthetic boot was tiring, and he had decided he needed to practice riding. Sultan did well with a lopsided load as soon as he realized that's how it would be, but his rider was not so confident. Maybe he could re-invent the stirrup to fit the boot…or something. There'd be a way, when he got around to thinking on it.

The foot, now, was an interesting appendage. Hard round bone in the heel to take the first pressure of most steps…all but tip-toe. Then there was the arch that was the pressure releaser that eased the knee muscles. The ball of the foot was very good for balance, and then there were the toes. That big toe was far more important than one would think. It seemed to be part of the "kick off" for taking a step, and it worked well when kneeling. All the toes together were important in the "send off" for taking another step.

He'd learned all that while researching after the accident. There was one other thing and it was one of the things he missed most. That setup of bones and cartilages in the ankle permitted swivel in several directions, and the prosthetic boot just didn't get the hang of it. It created a swinging movement that was purely unnatural, and his research indicated that the unevenness could cause back problems.

That's when he decided that Sultan's four legs would take care of as much of his walking that he could manage. He tied Sultan to the porch post of the school…likely wouldn't even need to time him later.

He turned the key and spread open the padlock. He pushed the door open with great anticipation. Ah, there it was, a picture book classroom, evidently left in this way by Miss Eldridge, who was so loved by the community.

There were desks, twenty-four of them, in perfect rows of four each. A surveyor with his equipment could not have made a straighter row.

In the center of the room stood the teacher's desk with a blackboard behind it. On each side of the blackboard there was a book case with a few well-worn books. Definitely needed more. The teacher's ruler was lying in the chalk tray of the blackboard. It was like a picture from a magazine. Typical Country Schoolroom.

He attempted to move a chair and was amazed to find that it was bolted to the floor. What in the world does that mean? Were the desks subject to being stolen? It was going to take a wrench to lose them from the floor but it would have to be done. The pattern of the rows was totally wrong. A blind person could see that.

Also, he wanted his desk across the corner in front of the back outside door. It didn't make sense to be sitting directly in front of the chalk board and in the way of the student's eyes. A shove instantly revealed that the desk, also, was bolted down.

Hmmm, nothing could be done today, but he still had another day before school began. Tomorrow, he would get over here with his wrench (as soon as he found it) and create a whole new pattern.

Another thing, the desks were two sizes, but there was not much difference. He could picture Luke in the smaller of the desks, with his chin barely over the writing surface. Something had to be done and he knew what it would be. Maybe not at first, but as soon as possible he would make a picnic table with benches along both sides that would fit the five- and six-year-olds.

Yes, that must be the first job. Why, Luke could barely see over one of these desks! How did Miss Eldridge manage that? Miss Eldridge must have used blocks or books or something to raise the smaller ones but nothing of the sort was laying around. Blocks could not have been comfortable for small bottoms.

First decisions made, he took a tour of the outside. If the fenced in portion was the boundary for the school yard it outlined a comfortably large space, but where were the seesaws and swings? A "skinning" bar would be nice and there was ample room for several pieces of play equipment, still leaving space for a downsized softball diamond.

Head whirling with ideas, he headed Sultan back to the pasture. Time for more thinking, and maybe he'd remember where the wrench was.

Torie hurried with the job, but it was obvious that she could not finish with all the twelve hives today. It was not fair to Luke to leave him in charge for more than about four hours. Then it would be lunch and the girls would be put down for naps. Maybe she would then take another swing at it.

She'd cross her fingers that next Saturday would also be fair, and she could finish. Right now, she had buckets of the sticky syrup, and a lot of jars to fill with honeycomb. Then the spinner that extracted the last of the honey would have to be turned on and it was noisy. She'd need to wait until after naps.

All of this could be done. It would just take scheduling. So now, what was for supper? The garden still held a few late choices, so a casserole made with cheese would work. While still in her white coveralls, she pulled a few carrots, some onions, a few late pods of okra that seemed tender. A handful of green beans and some late kale to shred into the broth. Along with seasonings and cottage cheese on the side, it would be hearty enough for a man. A quick side of deviled eggs and a pan of biscuits would do it.

And tomorrow, she would mix the leftover biscuits and cornbread with sausage for a meatloaf. Tomatoes, onions and okra alongside. And maybe she could find a cantaloupe or two to add to canned peaches and plums for a fruit combination. Or maybe peach cobbler would be better, and certainly more filling. The school teacher was not a small man, and likely needed the extra food. All it took was planning and remembering the contract.

The honey equipment being in the bedroom was handy, but a bit cramped. She'd have to work out something better, or just decide to live with it. The honey preparation only happened once a year.

She carried water, cleaned jars, washed the floor of spills, carried out dirty water and wiped the jars and set them in a row. Sixty of them. A big day's work and she smiled at herself with satisfaction.

Each sparkling new pint glass jar held three generous slices of honey still in the comb. It looked simply beautiful but, for the money, it was not the best buy for the regulars. She had emptied only five of the twelve hives, and, believe it or not, bottling with the honeycomb was the easiest part.

She had turned the handle of the centrifugal container to extract the golden semi-liquid and had carefully lifted by the spoonful to fill the sixty jars to the top with the golden semi-liquid flowing around the slices of honeycomb.

The next batch (more like the next two or three) would be pure strained honey which was what the knowing customers always bought.

Honeycomb wax is a thing of beauty, but it is not edible. It's messy to try to eat, and takes up space. The Spencers learned from experience that the store customers wanted a small number of jars with the comb, but their money makers were the strained, full pints with the shiny, gold colored lids. Some of the stores tied a bit of colorful ribbons around the lids to attract more attention.

But the added value to Torie and Bradley in the strained honey was that they could keep the wax. There were dozens of uses on the farm for the wax, from keeping leather soft, to treating any leather item that had stitches, to making candles and a few other things that needed lubrication..

But the most important value was leaving as much of the wax as possible attached to the edges of the honey frames. The bees required time to make honey, but also it took their time to make more wax to create the cells. If wax was provided for them, they would use that, and leave more time for money production.

It made Torie exhausted to think of the next probable eighty jars that would all have to be strained of wax. One really earned the wax but no job was easy. They had decided, she and Bradley, but then....

So there were at least two more days like today, more likely three or four, and they need to be soon. The bees have to have time to replace the stolen sweet. The last of August had been designated by Bradley, and it had work out. They had time to get the honey jars to the stores for the Christmas trade, and then for the summer visitors.

It seems incredible that one can be too tired to go to bed and to sleep, but here Torie sat at the kitchen table, elbows on the table cloth and chin resting in aching hands. Not only was she tired in body, but she was worn ragged in her mind. Too much thinking. Everything still too raw and bleeding. Too much newness hitting her in the face.

The idea of the money the honey brought was fighting with what she was doing to harvest it. With careful spending, the $13.00 a month would get her by, if nothing unexpected happened. But it always did. That's why it was called "unexpected."

All the people she knew, all up and down Ridge Road, knew to expect the unexpected...and then figure out what to do with it.

Bradley had carefully planned on using the honey as a reliable money source, and it had been that way. But then Bradley had always been there to make it so. So what about the plan....

Torie felt the tears trickle down on her fingers. *Oh, Bradley! I can't go on...I really can't. Why didn't you take me with you?*

At that moment, 10:00 as it was, there was Katie wanting her final bottle. Suddenly screaming as though a diaper pin was sticking her. It happened every night, but she was reliable and when she got the bottle, she went on to sleep until morning. One could safely say, though, that number three child was not long on patience.

Torie pushed against the table to hoist her exhausted body upright. The bottle was full and was setting on the still-warm stove. She took it to Katie's crib and handed it to the tiny clutching fingers. Once more she had been relieved/grateful that her babies had to be bottle fed. A half hour of nursing might be more than she could stand, and she might go to sleep sitting up. Maybe even drop the baby.

Back to the table for a last cup of tea to make her sleep, she sighed and forced her mind to be blank. Tomorrow would be better. It had to be.

Then a gentle night breeze from the north wafted the aroma of fresh coffee through the door. The new teacher had made his evening coffee. Why so late, she wondered. Did he also have thinking to do? Was he nervous about next week? She'd heard that this was his first teaching assignment.

Six cups. He had complained that his new pot refused to make only two cups and have it taste right. So there was clearly enough coffee for Torie, and there would be an adult face to look at and an adult voice with words that were not a question or a complaint.

NO! She would not let this aroma tempt her. She could not go to the honey house for a bit of conversation and a tempting drink. She could not…and she would not…go. She would get past this. She had no choice.

She took a long drink of the tea and set the cup down. She could actually afford the luxury of coffee for herself, but that was not the whole problem. Loneliness required another adult face and no amount of love for her children took the place of it.

She placed the half full cup of tea on the table and moved toward her bed. There were worse things than making honey all day. And she would rise above this loneliness. Bradley had been gone for exactly one year. Another year or two would make a big difference.

Of course it would.

BEDTIME COFFEE

Merrill Brooks made his six cups of coffee, and sat himself at the table with the new book, ABC's OF BEES. A new book was always satisfying, and a cup of fresh coffee made it perfect. Of course it did.

He saw a light in the kitchen window of the big house. *Awfully long day for Torie, huh. Oh, well...* and he opened the book. He looked at the lighted window again. While he was looking, the lighted window suddenly went dark.

He still stared. *Merrill,* he told himself. *This cannot go on. Those two fellows in the school yard a few days ago were sort of right. Now it's up to me to do something, but I don't know what. But one thing I'm sure of, I am the cause of this lady being up and working half the night. It's got to stop.*

Having chided himself properly, he returned the book to the shelf, dumped the last three cups of coffee out the door and filled the pot with water ready for breakfast.

He crawled between the sheets and listened to the crickets in the trees, and a few night birds conversing. Merrill had experienced a lot of thought periods and sensations in his years of travel, but loneliness was never one of them.

Strange, why it should creep up on him now...just when he had things going his way! What does one do about a problem like that? Was he missing the noise and activity of the city? But no, otherwise he would have stayed there.

But Merrill was always the problem solver, so he must just get at it. Loneliness must be cured! That could be tomorrow's project.

The new teacher awoke the next morning in time to scoop coffee in the percolator to make its six cups. He poked up the fire in his stove and set the pot in place on a burner while he dressed for the day.

Sometime in the night it became clear to his subconscious mind that this would be the day of decision. He had clearly stepped into water that was too deep to wade out. He must now swim.

He put on a smile and headed to the big house with the coffee pot. Marvelous aromas blended with the coffee in a way to melt a man's heart. Nevertheless, things would change, though he would clearly be the loser. He could make passable biscuits, but not like Torie's.

He casually mentioned that he would be away at noon, and she offered a lunch of biscuits stuffed with egg. He could hardly turn her down, now, could he?

Bringing Sultan in from his green pasture sealed the deal. No turning back now. Climbing aboard (it was getting easier to manage his boot) he headed the stallion toward the schoolhouse. His answer had to be here. Tomorrow he would start classes.

First he visited the little shack. It couldn't have been as bad as he had remembered it, but when he stepped inside, he saw that it was worse. It had absolutely no redeeming factors, and was a total waste of space on God's green earth. God could never have been the maker of this miserable pile of lumber. It had to come down, but what would the school board fellows say? He'd have to go about this delicately.

Stepping off his two and a half foot casual step, he measured from the front of the shack to the thick woodland. Fifty feet. He measured from the side and it was forty feet. It was obvious that if the shack was not there, a perfectly decent building could occupy the space without taking an inch from the playground.

While Sultan munched on the fresh grasses in the edge of the woodland, Merrill sat himself down on the front porch of the school. If he looked toward that corner, what did he see? It was the same thing he saw last night, and early this morning, and seeing it now made it seem possible to achieve. A log cabin stood there…if only in his mind.

It was totally possible for a building, forty feet by fifty feet, to set in the corner of the school ground as neatly as a diamond is set in a gold ring. It would be made of native logs and chinked between the logs like his two-room cabin.

There could be adequate living space in one end and still leave a spacious room for many events. Christmas parties, school productions with parents in attendance and other events. An everyday use could be when it was used as a lunch room for the children to spread their lunches on tables and eat together instead of separately each in his own screwed to the floor seat. It would create a change of scenery for them, and on rainy days there could be indoor games. It would surely beat reading or drawing while at their desks.

Even if the attendance reached as many as thirty students, it would still be quite adequate. The first part of his problem was solved. He now had a project to occupy his mind and protect from loneliness, and he would have a place to live, at least part of the time. He must not totally leave the two-room cabin or Miss Torie would lose her boarding pay.

Now that he knew of an answer to the problem, he must figure on how to manage to get the building. Money was not the problem. His insurance from the railway would take care of it, surely. He wasn't sure what the cost would be, but it would be at least ninety-five percent labor.

Trees were everywhere, just waiting to be felled and skinned into a smooth shape, and there would be those who did it for a living. He needed to find out who built the cabin, but he must not ask Torie. She must have nothing to be concerned about. Maybe the fellow next door would know…being an older guy who seemed to care so much about Torie…? He'd work on that.

So now, what to do in the meantime? Oh, yes, there were those bolted down desks. Back to the cabin for the tools…also the painted panels. He needed to devise some sort of rack to hold them in place, and it must be moveable. He'd pencil in some plans but nothing solid. Would there be a place to get planned boards…there must be a mill somewhere close. He'd have to check around.

The lumber in the old shack would do perfectly for the panel rack and the table for the four- and five-year-olds. A shame he couldn't use it. At least not yet. Maybe there would be a loose board or two around Torie's place.

Back on Sultan and a short trip up Ridge Road. It was a spur-of-the-moment thought, but he really wanted to check on his surroundings and there might not be time later.

But as he turned to go up Ridge Road, he met Uncle Hank out for a ride. "Howdy, neighbor!" The older man waved a hat at him, and Merrill turned Sultan toward him.

"Yessir, fine day isn't it?"

Hank responded, "Goin' for a stroll, are you?"

"Wish I was. I was just needin' somethin' I forgot over to the cabin."

"How'd'ya like that little honey house?"

"Wonderfully adequate, friend. Who'd there be around here who does such beautiful work?"

"Wouldn't know about that, myself. The fellow to ask'd be Burley up top of the hill."

"Top…of the hill? I wasn't sure this hill had a top?"

Hank chuckled at the obvious joke. "Ya keep goin' three or four miles and you'll a get roadside stand that'll say Uncle Burley's Bistro. Folks around here call it Burnt Tree Junction ever since a tree got burned by lightnin'. French fellow that drives a spice van named it. Burley sort'a keeps a finger on the whole strip from Eureka to Berryville, bein' that he wears a star."

"The law man, huh?" That piece of information will be good to know.

"Deputy Constable, he is. From all angles he's a honorable man. Can't say that for all lawmen. Well, I'll get on off, knowin' you got errands to do."

"Thanks. Good to talk with you, sir."

Uncle Hank turned his horse toward the hill and Merrill headed for the two roomed cabin. A glance around noted that the white coveralls were now in the flower patch. Hmmm. Well, he'd asked if she needed help. She likely wondered what kind of help he'd be.

Later, wrench in hand, he began to attack the bolts on the chair legs. It turned out to be a tiresome job and the routine of it took the place of the loneliness. Almost. Well, that was not quite right. It really didn't help much at all, but that was not the purpose. The purpose of this labor being to space the chairs so he would have better view of each student, and to have the smaller desks closer to him.

Another thing he thought of that was needed was a small platform for the teacher's desk. It gave the teacher more of a positon of importance and also was in better view of the students. He really needed some dimension lumber, somewhat planed smooth to remove splinters.

Smooth planed lumber. Hmmm, those bee hives were handmade, just as he had seen in the book ABC's OF BEE'S. Obviously they would have been made by Bradley. The fellow seemed not to buy what could be made. The more he saw of Bradley, the more he admired him.

So, that being the case, he would have tools, and likely a stash of scrap lumber.

It would be like what he had heard of quilters. The leftover cloth scraps and the quilts never seemed to come out even. Builders and boards would be the same. He'd need to look around in that huge barn and see what he could find.

About twelve o'clock his stomach began to make itself know. He mopped his sleeve across his sweaty forehead, and remembered the biscuits. The wonderful biscuits Torie had insisted he take. They would still be in the saddle bag that was still lying across Sultan.

The stallion was contentedly grazing in a sunny patch of clover when Merrill took the biscuits from the bag. Warm. They were sunshine warm and highly fragrant. Light and fluffy and stuffed with eggs that had been fried with the bacon. First class sandwiches. Three of them.

He could have eaten six, but he was grateful for the three, and went back to work. Tomorrow was the big day.

When he had scooted the desk and chairs the way he thought he wanted, he went outside again. Once more he stepped off the corner where his mind could already see the solid walls of the new log building that was auditorium/lunchroom/rainy day playroom/ and adequate living quarters for the most particular teacher. How can efficient can one get!

Time now to give thought as to how to bring up the subject of the building to the two-man school board. He'd decided in the night that it should be thought of as a community project, though he planned to foot most of the bill. A timeline should be about Christmas, giving the community time to learn about him, and for him to be certain Enterprise was the answer to his dreams.

That left four months to spend in Torie's yard. Either that, or work out a way to exist in the shack…but no, the shack must come down.

Torie had started her Sunday with a story from the Big Book of Bible Tales for Little Children. It was the one about Daniel in the lion's den, a favorite of Luke's, though Missy could not possibly imagine a lion, though the picture was very plain.

"It's just a big, big cat," Luke told her but she surely did not believe him.

There was no way Torie could have managed the distance to the meeting house. She'd had to make peace with that thought many months ago. Of course it was a commandment to "remember God's day and keep it holy." But there was also the explanation, that if one's ox (livelihood) was in a ditch (in trouble) there was a reprieve. Get him out of the ditch!

Her bees were not "in a ditch" but they were on the verge of stopping their duty of making honey if she did not remove her share. Hence, coveralls on and Luke in charge of the house, she attacked the next two hives. The bees could certainly be 'oxen in the ditch' as they buzzed dizzily around her, their senses dulled by the smoke from her smoker.

The honey from these hives would be separated as much as possible from their combs and that was labor intensive. She reasoned that two hives would be a day's work. And she'd somehow manage the other four hives, one each day during nap time.

She was accustomed to figuring out how make do when things did not go right. Another benefit might be that if she was tired enough after it all, she might just hit the bed and go to sleep, and thereby avoid loneliness. And avoid thinking of Bradley. That surely had to stop.

Also, if she closed the kitchen door tightly, perhaps the aroma of coffee might not be able to invade. Sure, she had coffee grounds, and could certainly make her own, but somehow when filtered through the mountain air, the aroma picked up something else. What? She did not know, nor did she want to think about it. Dangerous thought, it was.

Her pails full of the liquid gold, she returned to the kitchen at eleven o'clock and found Luke and Missy building towers with the blocks, and Katie sitting beside them jabbering and drooling from her teething.

She'd heard that "every good and perfect gift comes from above" and she had believed it. So when she saw the various abilities of her firstborn, she lifted her head and told the angels, *Thank You for Luke.*

She was joyfully greeted by a pair ready for lunch. Somehow Momma meant lunch, regardless of the timepiece. Biscuits chopped up fine and browned in the skillet. Honey, butter and a bit of spice heated warm in a pan and poured over would work. Tall glasses of milk for each.

This might be a good time to introduce Katie to the table. Weariness notwithstanding, she re-diapered the little girl and sat her on her own lap. Missy was about to lose possession of the highchair and she was sure to be unhappy about it. She would need a booster block like Luke's.

Katie sang and cooed, and chewed her fingers while watching her mother eat. Then came the bite that was tucked into her own mouth. Wide eyes looked at Momma with horror at Momma's betrayal, and her talented tongue removed the foreign substance with a pronounced "Pathooey!"

Torie set her on the floor with the blocks, which promptly went into her mouth. Evidently Katie was not ready for food and to each his own. Perhaps the blocks tasted better. She had no complaints from the other two but Katie was her own kid…right from the start.

And there was supper coming up. When she got into the honey stickiness, she'd not want to stop until she was through, so start supper now.

Baked potatoes would do well and while the oven was hot, cook a pumpkin custard. Such a filling way to use those huge orange lumps in the cellar. That was also a way to hide a lot of eggs. Eggs!

"Luke, son, did you gather the eggs?"

"No, Momma. You said not to open the door. I didn't."

"Good boy, but now go gather them. And when you pass the garden, pull up about five green onions."

What else for supper? Breaded tomatoes. Butter the last of the biscuits, chop up an onion and slice in a dozen small tomatoes. Pop it in the oven. That, and cottage cheese should make the meal.

Now, to attack the straining of the honey. It looked like there would be about twenty jars. A good day's work. She began the grinding of the wheel that spun the honey out and the wax in, making it easier to collect.

Merrill finally found that he had run out of duties to keep him away from the cabin, and he and Sultan ambled on home. There wasn't time to go "to the top of the hill" to see "Uncle Burley." Also, an early visit was more likely to find someone at home, and he hadn't yet decided what to tell a person why he wanted to find a builder of a log house.

He stepped into his cabin, still perfumed slightly from the black paint used on the letters. He still needed a rack or some kind of an easel for the panels.

After releasing Sultan into the pasture, he ventured into the barn. Tools, if Bradley had them, would likely be in the feed bin behind locked doors, but they were not locked. The door opened with a touch. Maybe country folks don't steal.

And there on the wall were hooks and a shelf and just about every tool imaginable was there. Some he didn't even recognize. *And look there on the floor.* A lovely pile of scraps, plenty for the easel and also the teacher's platform.

In addition, maybe the little table for the four- and five-year-olds. It wouldn't take much space for maybe six children. Maybe even eight. It would be up in the corner opposite his desk so if the little ones decided to whisper to each other, it wouldn't disturb the others.

He sorted out what he'd need, but did not remove it from the feed room. It did, actually, belong to Torie. Ha! Look at that! There were the unassembled parts of some of the bee hives! He recognized them from drawings in the bee book. Could he manage to fit them together? Hmmmm, well…later, maybe.

A little thread of curiosity flitted merrily through his brain, along with the book shop in Eureka Springs. What books would there be hidden in the back room of the bookstore? He'd save that in his mind as a surprise to look forward to. Right now, he had his plate full of ideas to be worked out.

Speaking of plates, he recognized the unmistakable fragrance of potatoes baking, blended with something spicy. Pumpkin pie? How does she do it…the bees, the children and, of course, himself?

He'd sure like to have that easel for the first day, but there just wasn't time. There was the blackboard and even a bit of chalk that would have to do. Could there be more supplies, somewhere, maybe in the teacher's desk? He hadn't thought to look.

Small thoughts were having trouble finding room in his head with all the very large ones taking up space and multiplying.

Back in the cabin, he wearily stretched out on his sofa. It was the first time he actually sat on it. Hey, it wasn't bad. Good cushions. Plenty good enough for company if he ever had any. Yeah, that was a laugh!

TORIE'S WOOD SCRAPS

Small tap on his closed cabin door. Luke's voice.

"Momma says come and eat if you can, or would you like it brought here? But I want to say, please come."

He decided he could come, the aroma of the potatoes and the spicy something or other was driving him mad.

Sure enough, there was the baked potatoes, split and filled with butter. Chopped green onions on the side. Some kind of tomato casserole that smelled spicy, and the still warm pumpkin pie on the cooler part of the stove. Well, anyway, it looked and smelled like pumpkin pie.

By now, he knew to bow for the evening meal. "Dear Lord, please bless this food. Amen."

The lunch biscuits having been gone on some time ago, he sniffed from the fragrance that the blended fragrance of the food had been properly blessed. As was requested by Luke.

Luke brightly announced, "I get to go to school tomorrow."

Merrill gave him a smile, "So do I. Maybe we can go together."

The boy dissolved into giggles. Mother intervened. "Son, pay attention to your food."

The pumpkin "pie" had no crust, but it had cream to pour over if desired. Katie poked an experimental finger into her mother's pumpkin custard and then into her mouth. A frown and an irritated whimper.

Missy was having no trouble with her bowl of custard and cream. Saucy little thing, she was, and if things went well, she'd be in his school in two or three years.

He brought up the subject of the stash of scrap wood. "I noticed a lot of wood scraps in the feed bin. Could I use them for an easel I need for the younger students? And maybe some of the other pieces for this and that?"

"Absolutely. Take what you need I'll never use it."

The summer evenings were long before the sun totally disappeared. With the five year old looking on, he created the three legged easel and wondered how he'd get Sultan to put up with it on his back. But then there were also the panels. Clearly a trip with the buggy.

"Luke, go ask your momma if you can help me take the rack to the school. If we hurry, we'll be back before dark."

He was gone like a puff of smoke, and quickly back. "I CAN! I CAN!"

It was a bit of trouble getting the buggy out of the barn and hitching Sultan as he had other activities in mind, but since it had to be done sometime, better now. His passenger was so excited he could hardly remain in the seat.

A half an hour and they were back. The crickets were screeching and the night birds conversing when he told Luke, "Thanks for the help, buddy. See you tomorrow."

Merrill drew up a bucket of water for a bit of a bath and decided his day was done. In the lamplight he selected the bee book and set the percolator to perking. Tonight, he would drink his coffee and read about bees. Whatever was wrong with him had to stop. He had always found comfort in books and he still could. So much for that old loneliness thing than kept hovering around him!

He sipped the coffee and read, not realizing a word he had read. Thoughts going ninety miles an hour in the whirlwind of his mind and had completely erased a whole three pages of the text.

He refigured the stepped-off dimensions and drew a sketch showing where the building would be placed in relation to the school house. The back part of the new building would measure almost twenty by forty and that was almost as large as the cabin, and it would still leave a large room about thirty by forty for other things. That was huge, compared to what they currently had.

And tomorrow was another day. He needed to get some sleep.

Strange thing. Sleep remained aggravatingly out of reach. Could he blame the coffee? But coffee had never done that to him before. Finally sheer weariness took over, and he slept.

In the big house, weariness and exhaustion finally took over, and the closed door shut had out the aroma of the fresh coffee. Almost.

The first day of school dawned sunshiny bright with a promise of being hot and sweaty. After the usual hearty breakfast, and lunches of biscuits and sausage put in the lunch pails, the teacher and his pupil boarded Sultan and were on their way. Luke, jittery from excitement, held to the teacher's belt, as instructed, fidgeting and chattering like a young monkey exploring a tree.

Merrill would have loved to have walked to the school, and he would have except for the accident. But the thing was he needed to start the day with his foot fresh. He didn't so much have a limp, more of a hesitation, due to having no ankle. It was becoming patently evident that Sultan would have to do most of his distance walking from now on.

Several children were already waiting near the porch so he had an audience as he unlocked the doors and company as he adjusted the printed panels on the easel with outsized C-clamps. He was not happy with using "C" clamps, but he would come up with better fasteners later.

When all were settled, all nineteen of them, exactly the size of his class in town. He piqued their curiosity about the panels but refused to explain them. "Not for today, students. Big lessons start tomorrow. Today we get acquainted. I'm Mr. Brooks, but I'm sure most of you will refer to me as 'teacher.'"

He placed them in the order he had planned. He had three eighth graders and one seventh grader. Five first graders, and the others sprinkled in the grades in between. There were a couple of brother/sister pairs. He didn't like that particularly…it might tend to hinder freedom of speech and there would be the usual tattling. But he would manage, as he had managed all his life. He wanted to handle all school related situations by himself, but one dealt with what one had, and the fact was, children mostly had a pair of parents.

Nineteen names were a handle to remember, but he had made a seating chart and could refer to it, and take it home for further study.

The first day was without problems and he was even more eager than ever to begin, but the "bee in the bonnet" syndrome was affecting him strongly. He just had to find out more of how this community worked, and who was in charge of what.

He told Luke that he would drop him off at his front gate because he had an errand. Also, he must tell his momma not to expect him for supper, as he would be late, and would take care of it himself. *Only fair*, he thought.

Sultan, well fed and rested, was in fine fettle, and gladly trotted west up Ridge Road where they should locate a roadside stand, whatever that was. Merrill gazed, with interest, at the civilization that had drawn itself to Ridge Road. Every quarter of a mile, or so, there would be a farm…huge barn and animals about. In between were small businesses offering this or that service or product. Also, there were lanes that branched off the road, clearly leading to other homesteads.

There was the Herman Jones Cattle Ranch. Huge barns and hayfields. Many hay fields were in the process of being cut and put by for the fall. Most crops in, but a lot of hay was still being harvested.

Which brought up another thought, what would Torie use for hay? Two horses, two goats, and the one cow were left. Winter was coming…but the hay production was not a concern of his. Whatever they had done in the past would surely be done this year.

Clearly not his business. *Let it alone,* he chided himself. *Remember what we decided, you and I.* But he wasn't sure his brain had been listening.

As interested as he had become with his surroundings, he hardly remembered where he was going, until he was face to face with the sign artfully painted on a slab of wood. It proclaimed to the world that the Roadside Stand was the property of "UNCLE BURLEY'S BISTRO." Now, who in the world thought up the French word for diner? An outside counter, at that. Resting in the shade nearby was the ugliest dog he had ever seen. Purebred bloodhound was prevalent in her ancestry. Ears like velvety sheets of leather. Nose on paws, she eyed him intently with her heavily lidded eyes under fur covered wrinkles making arched eyebrows.

Reining Sultan into the generous front space, he saw the well-built house and the sudden edge of a bluff beyond. In the distant valley lay a body of water. Lake? It caught the afternoon sun, and reflected the blue sky making the water seem as blue as in a child's painting.

Tending the stand while doing a bit of mending, no doubt, was a pleasant-faced lady. She looked up with a bright smile, "Welcome, neighbor! How can I help you?"

"Thank you. I was lookin' for a fellow named Burley, and it seems I might have found him. I'm needing a bit of information and was told he knows everything and everybody."

"They're pretty much right about that. He isn't right here at the moment, but I can get him." Turning toward the dog she commanded, "Ugly Face! Go get Burley."

The dog, with no wasted movement, hoisted her body up by degrees and loped toward the bluff, ears flapping like butterfly wings.

The lady then motioned him toward a small picnic table just inside the trees. "Have a seat and make yourself at home. He'll be here in a few minutes." A lot of confidence in the dog, it seemed.

Merrill did as invited, then looked at the wares for sale in the stand. Was that actually homemade jerky? The sign said it was… and his empty stomach became instantly interested.

"Ma'am, could sell me a hunk of that jerky and is that apple cider? I'll take a glass, or pint, however it comes."

"Sure thing. Call me 'Annie.'" And she handed him the meat and began to fill a glass with the golden liquid. "We make the cider from our own trees that grow down under the bluff." Under a bluff?? Well, if she said it, it must be so.

He took a bite of the tough, spicy meat. His mouth woke up instantly to the strong spice and the flavor. "Say, I'll bet you also make the jerky."

"Sure do. Burley makes it from whole hog…not scraps," was the bright reply.

In the background, a man suddenly appeared as though he arose from the earth, with the dog beside him.

Merrill took another bite. "Say, Annie, why don't you gather up a handful's these strips. Put 'em in a paper or somethin' so I can take 'em along. Best I've had in years."

"Sir, we got no paper, but we got quart jars we mostly use for cider. I could use that, price five cents, refundable if you bring the jar back. How many strips do you want?"

"Fill 'er up. All you can pack in there and I'll take the jar." By the time the man and dog reached him, Merrill had paid for the jerky and drank the cider. His stomach greatly appreciated it.

"I'm Burley. What can I do for you?"

"My name's Merrill Brooks and I'm the new school teacher down at Enterprise. I'm lookin' to maybe be permanent somewhere along Ridge Road, and I'm interested in a good log construction. A man down that way told me you'd be the one to ask."

"Enterprise, huh! Good little school down there. Heard Miss Eldridge was givin' it up. Well, good luck to ya. About that log construction, I can tell you about that. You'll want to take the logging road down t'ord the lake. You'll see the place about halfway down. Family by the name of Stone. Then on down by the lake there's a sawmill, come time you need planned lumber. "

"Good deal! I've been put up temporarily in a log cabin and I was impressed by the workmanship. Seems it might be warm in the winter and cooler in the summer."

"So they say. Might you be batching in Bradley Spencer's yard? 'Course, Brad's gone on. Bad thing it was that took 'im. Oh, say, I heard about you. Not by name, of course, but it seems they were surprised to see a fellow, 'stead'a gettin' a lady."

Merrill felt his open wide with surprise. What? And he'd been here hardly more than a week? Could these trees be somehow carrying the new wires and serviced the telephone? No…couldn't be…but…?

Burley again. "Don't be surprised I know about you and I ain't bein' nosey for nothin'. It's just that we sort'a keep track with each other around here, and Ridge Road's way'a movin' information is better'n a uptown telephone. Some call it the 'grapevine line.' Seems grapevines and sumac roots is what holds these mountains together. I'm guessin' you'd be stayin' down there by the bee farm."

Merrill nodded, highly impressed, but then, this was the lawman and it'd be his duty to know everything…maybe. He answered, "That's a fact. The big house is a thing of beauty as well."

Burley nodded. "Same feller made 'em both. Has a big family, has Lazarus Stone, and they put up places in a hurry. His son Chad is mostly on the job, but the ole fellow is still sharp as any razor you'd want to see. Anything else I can help you with?"

"Not right now, but I'll be sure remember you later as a handy fountain of information. I'm certain I have a lot to learn. Guess I'll be runnin' along."

"Come back when ya can," seemed to be a local benediction.

The lawman waved jauntily and headed back toward the bluff, and Ugly Face took up her post, watching over the stand and the lady. Merrill thought, *I'd hate to be the one that bothered the lady when that dog took exception with me. She was already eyein' me like I was a ham bone.*

Sultan was ready to go. He was a fair distance away from his buddy and the other green pasture. His rider wedged the jar of jerky between the saddle horn and his lap, opened the lid and stashed it in his pocket, to free up his hand the better to eat what would be his supper. Good jerky, and perfect for his lunches and evening snacks. He'd be making another trip up here soon, and of that he was certain. Not bad cider, either.

It was quite a trip, and he had not hurried Sultan along. He wanted to see if he could find the road toward the logger's place. The sun was lowering behind the trees when he spotted it. Reining Sultan up for a look, he gazed down a road that seemed to have no end. It appeared to plow right down into the ground. A road to nowhere. How did they ever pull lumber and logs up out of there?

Well, it would not be his problem.

Marking the location in his mind for later, he clicked Sultan back into the road. Lazarus Stone, he said was the man's name. Merrill promised himself to write it down, and make a rough map of where it was. Best not to commit too many things to pure memory. He'd learned that, over the years. One's memory can get itself overlaid with another memory, and then nothing came out right. *So, let's see. Across from a massive maple that spreads out over the road. Easy to find, unless they cut down the tree.*

Dusky darkness had fallen when he reached the cabin. The crickets were busy in the trees creating background music for the evening larks. Sultan tossed his head and happily greeted his pasture-mate lovingly referred to as "Ole Bugger" by his owner. Ole Bugger answered back with equal eagerness.

Lights in the kitchen window of the big house, his own still dark, of course. Definitely time to call it a day…and a very productive one at that.

His mind seethed with the plans made and those yet to make. They were necessary, all of them, as they should help is combating that strange malady that had settled on him. He'd figure out some way to get peace, like he always had.

He fairly pushed the stallion into the pasture and tossed the blanket on the fence for tomorrow, hanging the bridle beside it ready for morning. Picking up the quart jar still packed with meat strips, he proceeded to the house in his unusual gait…that he was finally getting used to. That jerky was happy find. It was so chewy, it took a long time to eat. That was the beauty of it. Time and good teeth and lots of flavor.

He entered the darken room and felt for the matches. A quick swipe across the top of the iron stove and soon the lamp flooded the room with light, showing a plate on the table. On it sat two pieces of crusty fried chicken…a thigh and a half a breast. Under an upside down bowl was a heap of potato salad, rich with egg, pickles, onion and sweet pepper. A wedge of cornbread and a small bowl of canned peaches completed the picture.

There was just no way to get ahead of her. She would honor that contract no matter how much trouble it took. He poked up the fire and put on the coffee pot. He'd certainly not stilled his hunger with the jerky and had planned to fill out with sardines and crackers. But that would come at a later date.

With a man-sized hunger created by a long busy day, he sat down eagerly. The cornbread, he noticed, had been buttered while it was hot. The chicken was still warm, and the potato salad creamy and spicy.

The coffee was ready when he began on the peaches. He glanced out the window toward the big house, purely from habit, and the windows were dark and the door closed. The spaniel pup was curled up on the doorstep guarding the entrance.

He was working on the fourth cup of coffee (too much, really. His guts would certainly be awash) before he could get his thoughts together. By that time, the loneliness had already set in. His self-set times table for a change of dwelling was Christmas, months away. But could he last that long? This was something he had no experience in dealing with.

Somehow he made the night and appeared at breakfast, empty dishes and coffee pot in hand. Bacon and eggs. Lunches ready. Before he could toss a blanket on the stallion and hoisted the small boy up behind him, there came a knock at the door. Torie was quick to answer it.

"Oh, excuse me. The butchers must be here. That old hog has got to go. I'm swapping him for a young pig." She stepped out into the yard for a few minutes, and then was back.

"This is so handy," she explained. "A neighbor up the road butchers for me on halves, and cuts up the parts for me. Saves me a lot of time. The hog goes today, and in a couple of weeks, when they have time, they'll bring down a bull calf and swap out with my heifer. And then later they'll butcher the little bull."

A lot of information. All of it helped his curiosity. This lady knew her mind and was well able to take care of herself. No loneliness for her, apparently. He'd actually heard of the strength of the mountain women, but he'd discounted it. Shouldn't have. It seemed to be true.

There were students waiting on the porch, eager to get in. Could be that they were bored by summer looking for something different. The four- and fve-year-olds were fairly dancing with eagerness to see what was on the panel that was meant for them. Luke was among them, and he could give them no clue.

The moment came. "All right, students. Most of you know what is painted here, and it's called the 'alphabet,' and that is a word made out of two other words from a foreign language that means, 'first and second.' It's made from the words, alpha and beta, and they could have added the word for third word but it would have made the word too long.

"You'll notice there is a big letter, and a small 'cousin' letter that is called cursive. We won't bother with the cousin right now, but grades three to eight will use it later. Right now grade one will work with the tall letters.

"See, there are rows of six letters, and we will learn the first row today, and the next row of six tomorrow. They sound like this: 'A, B, C, D, E. F.' Now I want the four- and five-year-olds to listen and then repeat after me."

He pronounced the six letters very clearly, and nodded for the children to repeat them with him. On the sixth repetition, all five had it. "Who wants to say them all by himself?"

Luke's hand shot up like an arrow, followed by another youngster called Aaron. Then a shy hand of a girl whose name he couldn't remember. "All right, Luke, say them." And he did. So did Aaron and the girl. She hesitated at first, but repeated the six, then hid her face in her hands and giggled.

Merrill couldn't help himself. "Oh, my, my, aren't we smart! I know you older grades are going to be the same!"

And so the day went.

The teacher was floating on air at the end of the day. In his mind was a picture of the little picnic table from up at the "bistro." Add six inches and lower the legs a trifle and it would seat all five of the students easily. That way, they would be facing each other, and maybe work together without shyness.

At supper time, he entered a steamy kitchen, rich with the aroma of cooked sausages. Near the stove was a deep crock, and the slightly browned sausages were lowered into the crock in layers with hot grease being poured in after. Each layer was covered to prevent spoilage, and both sausage and grease would be used later.

A huge skillet was fragrant with sliced onions burying a layer of fresh liver. Sliced tomatoes and cornbread graced the table along with cottage cheese.

Apparently the old hog had found its final resting place. The hams, both front and back, were lying in a bed of salty spices ready to be dried. The hand grinder was attached to the cabinet, and a pan of raw ground pork lay heaped and ready to be fried.

Torie was apologetic. "Please excuse the heat. I have to get at this before it spoils. Summer heat and spoilage, you know. Now, Luke, before you go outside to play, I want you to stir the curds for the cheese."

"OK," he answered. "Momma, listen to me. A, B, C, D, E, F. That's the top row of letters of the alphabet. Alphabet is made out of two words that mean one and two in another people's words. Tomorrow we get to learn the next row."

Torie looked at Merrill, startled, and he allowed himself a smug smile. And then a request. "I'm hoping to use your sled to haul a few boards over to the school house. The students Luke's size don't fit the desks very well. I want to make a table with benches attached where they'll be more comfortable and can squirm around better than in those big desks." He didn't bother with mentioning the platform for his desk. Too much boring information.

Torie's answer was quick and without thought. "Certainly. I won't need the sled at all this week. Are you finding enough boards for what you need?"

"More than enough. If you'll excuse me, I'll be going on out to the barn to sort them out." He cleared the doorway with Luke instructing his sister, "Now say, A, B, C, D, E, F. Say it with me." The teacher glanced back to see Missy, silently staring but very interested.

Another smug grin, and it was just beginning! *Merrill, you have surely stepped into a bed of roses.* Just then a pair of heavily laden bees flew past his shoulder on the way to the hive. Merrill corrected, *Make that a swarm of bees.*

CLOSENESS

He hitched Suntan to the sled and piled on the boards, tying then down solidly. He stepped aboard the sled and balanced himself for the ride. It worked quite well. He unloaded them into the shack, again boarded the sled and headed home, meeting Uncle Hank at the gate.

"How's it goin', neighbor?"

Merrill could answer with certainty, "Better than I deserve!"

The old man grinned. "I see Miss Torie a'gatherin' in the honey crop. Bradley always wanted it done by the first week'a September. Seems like she's keepin' it up, along with takin' care'a the meat."

The teacher wondered what he was supposed to say. Finally, "Well, I try to stay out'a the way. No way I could help, and if there ever is a way, I hope she'll say so. I'm really not acquainted with this way of teacher boarding. Sort'a playin' it by ear, so to speak."

The older man nodded casually. "That's sort'a the way I work it. By the first'a October, I'll be mowin' down that flower patch. I have to apologize to the late butterflies that lose the flowers, but that's the way Bradley wanted it, and I think maybe Torie rests better if that happens that a'way. Need to scatter the flower seeds a'for the winter birds get 'em."

"Sounds like a plan."

"Yeah, I like to keep check on things as I can. I'd sure hate for life to be made any harder than it has to. I know you're tired after your day, so I'll let you go. Good luck with the school."

"Thanks."

Sultan, twisting and pitching his head, could now go through the gate, and Merrill mused, "Now I wonder what that was all about?" Maybe nothing…just being sociable?

Back in his room, he settled himself into a lonely chair at the lonely table. Truly, his life had never been this way, so what was going on? Exciting? Involved? Complicated? All of the above? But what could be done with these evenings? Going to take some thought.

It was time for coffee. No use trying for only three cups; the pot just wouldn't cooperate. It obviously knew it was made for six. He sipped and read long after the world was dark except for the multitude of stars.

When he finally put the book up and dumped out the last three cups of coffee, he saw the smoke still rising into the night, and the light in the window bright. Apparently she would work until done.

He stretched out on the bed and gave himself over to thinking. The result of the thinking was this summation: he'd never really been close to anyone during his entire adult life. Actually, thinking back, he could include his childhood life as well. That was it…it had to be.

He'd always been on the move doing what he was paid to do, (or staying out of everyone's way) and there was always something that occupied his brain. If there was anything of him left after that, he just gave it to the book he had been currently devouring.

So selfish you've been, Merrill Brooks! Shame on you. Closeness requires thought in a whole different line. So what to do about it…? He hadn't a clue.

All right, there is that lady in the big house. She's trying to do the work of two, but what can I do? I have no right to butt in. There are the nineteen children at school, and sooner or later he would be dealing with parents. A bit scary? Maybe. There was Uncle Hank who was certain to be part of his life for some time to come, and even the lawman, who impressed him heavily in only a few minutes and a few words. He was going to have to change in some way.

So, what to do about it…??? Tomorrow would be another day…so they say.

Back at school, he dealt with five eager pairs of eyes, and fourteen others showing interest.

He'd brought a bench from the shack and set it in front of the easel. "Grade one, come sit on the bench. Together I want you to repeat line one without my help. Begin."

They just looked at him, unable to decide what he wanted. All right he'd go this way. "Luke, I want you to say the six letters, and then the whole class will say them with you."

The five year old was so excited he could hardly sit still. "A, B, C, D, E, F." Then he looked at his classmates. "Come on." And they did. As near as the teacher could tell, they all repeated the six letters.

"Very good. Now we take the next line. G, H, I, J, K, L. I'll say it again, and anyone who can remember will say it with me. We'll say it five times, over and over."

He held up his hand with fingers extended, and counted them off. "Excellent! You did very well. We'll work on it again a bit later. So it will stick in your heads." That brought on a giggle. "Right now, I want you to take a desk, and I'm giving you paper and pencil, and see if you can make some of the letters. Don't feel bad if it's too hard. We have lots of time."

He passed out the papers, and turned to the middle classes. "We're going to work on numbers. Add and Subtract…and their older cousins, Multiply and Divide. Grade eight will write an essay on your parents. Write what you like about them and what you don't like, what they do and what they like to do and what they don't like to do. Anything you can think of." He'd thought that up as a way to ascertain their writing and thinking skills, and he even thought it might be an interesting paper to show to their parents later. Much later!

He turned toward those in the smaller chairs. "All right, second and third grades, listen up. We're going to talk about sentences. You've all learned to read a little so you are familiar with sentences. Who can tell me what makes a sentence?" A hand shot up.

"Bennie, what is a sentence?"

"A bunch of words," he announced happily.

A teacher should never say "no, you're wrong," if possible, and certainly not in front of the whole room. Find a way to ease the pain.

"Very good thinking, Bennie. You are partly right, but there is one little problem, and I'll show it to you." On the chalkboard he wrote, "help, help, help, help, help." "Now I have written a bunch of words. Did I write a sentence?"

The whole group of desks held someone with an expression like, "How come the teacher's so dumb?"

"Bennie, tell me what's wrong with my words?"

"You ain't got no one that's sayin' help."

"Exactly right you are. So if I say, 'Help me." Does that make sense?"

A lot of nods.

"So what we need is two things. A word that says who is doing something, and one that says what he is doing. In our two word sentence it is "me" that is talking, and "help" is what I want.

"Here's an interesting fact. The Bible actually has a two word sentence, and only one. It says, 'Jesus wept.' So we know it is 'Jesus' who did something, and 'wept' is what he did. The verse does not say why Jesus wept. The verses around it say that a lot of people were doing things that got them in trouble, and it made Jesus sad, so he wept.

"Now, Bennie, make me a two-word sentence."

Bennie scrunched down in his chair, but took a breath and announced, "I ran."

"Very good. Most sentences have a lot of words to tell a lot more things about what happened. Can someone tell me why Bennie ran?

Several hands shot up. "Carolyn, tell me why Bennie ran?"

"A bee was after him!"

"So you may give me a sentence that says that."

"Bennie ran because a bee was after him, because he was messing with the bee's nest." A chuckle twittered around the room.

"Very good. You gave a lot more information than we needed, but you did it right. Now here is your assignment."

"At the top of your tablet sheet, write SENTENCES in printed letters. Under it, you must make a list of 1. 2. 3. 4. and 5. After the 1, Put a zero. There are no sentences containing one word. After the 2, write a two word sentence, and after the 3 make a three word sentence, and so on.

"Second grade may print if you wish, but third grade will write the sentences in cursive. Any questions? No? Then proceed."

The day was finally finished, and the students were dismissed. Grade one was repeating their letters and giggling happily at their success.

Luke had to take himself home alone, but Merrill stationed himself to watch until he reached the gate. Then he opened the door of the shack and drew out the boards, nails and hammer he had borrowed from Bradley. No, from Torie.

It was not difficult to put together, as the boards were already cut, but it took a little time. Supper was over when he reached the cabin, but a plate containing a thick pork chop, a pile of fried potatoes with onion, cold but still tasty, two biscuits and a bowl of berry cobbler. Blackberry, it tasted like.

He ate, picturing the picnic table that turned out exactly like the one up at the bistro, and it was now sitting at the front of the classroom opposite his desk. The desk platform would be attacked tomorrow. He checked the supply of paper and pencils.

Who had the responsibility of providing these supplies, also the chalk? The students were supposed to bring their own paper in the form of a tablet, but he would be needing a lot of plain white paper. Chalkboard work would happen very soon requiring more chalk. Nothing like having your work displayed on the chalkboard for everyone to see to get a student's attention, he'd learned.

Torie came through the gate to the bee pasture with a small pail of something. Feeding the new pig, no doubt. His percolator had just stopped and the spout was steaming beautifully... temptingly.

He squared his chin, bolstered his intent, and stepped out the door as she returned. "Fresh coffee is ready if you have a minute?"

She paused, thinking. "Oh, I really couldn't. I have...."

"I understand, but you're welcome. Maybe for just one cup…?"

With a shrug of her small shoulders, she turned toward the door. He took another mug from his cupboard and had it filled and ready setting before an empty chair. She settled herself wearily, and lifted the cup to her lips. *She really, really loves coffee,* he told himself.

"It's been a hot day, huh?" he ventured. "Always a lot to do."

She nodded. "And September is usually the worst."

After that conversation came easily. They both had finished a busy day. She drank three mugs of the fragrant drink and sighed. It was time to go.

Merrill's bravery got the best of him. He reached across the table and put his hand over hers. "Miss Torie, if there's anything I can do to make things easier for you, will you please let me know?"

She looked a bit startled, and said, "Oh, no, I can…." But it was obvious that she couldn't. She lowered her head to her arms and began to weep in exhausted and lonely sobs. Once it started, she could not get it stopped.

What now, Merrill asked himself. He'd never been alone with a person so broken. Especially not a lady. Did he dare to try to comfort her? Or should just let her cry it out. *Be brave, Merrill,* he commanded himself.

Moving his chair around toward hers, he stretched his arm over her back and gently moved her closer to himself. His voice took over. "Torie, darling, you've just done too much. You're exhausted, and I know how that is." And his guts clutched at him as he realized what he had called her. Too late now.

Between sobs she managed, "He just shouldn't have left me. He was all I had, and he's gone."

"But, Torie, think on it, he didn't go on purpose. It plain to see how much he loved you, and he couldn't help what happened. But he would be so proud of you the way you care for the children and the whole farm by yourself. It's an impossible task but you're doing it."

His words brought on another spasm of tears. What did he say wrong? Whet he had meant was…. Uh, he really didn't know what he had meant.

But then she raised her face, red-eyed and tear-wet. "I'm so sorry. I hadn't ought to be cryin' on you like this. I've never done this before and I won't ever…."

"Shhh. Don't say that. I've never in my life had someone think I was worth bein' cried on. Ever. Neither have I had someone I could cry on."

"You, cry…?"

"You bet I cry. Sometimes it's the only thing to do. But maybe we should not both cry at the same time. Someone has to put their arm around the other one, hopin' it helps, maybe just a little?"

"But you…?

"Everyone gets lonely. I get lonely, and I've truly never had anyone to cry with."

"Never…?"

"Never. And here I am thirty-two years old. It's a shame, really. Extreme negligence on my part."

She sniffled a bit and hiccuped a couple of times. "Maybe next time you want to cry, I'll be here."

"Miss Torie Spencer that is the best offer I have had in my whole entire life. I don't know my pa. I used to think I just didn't have one. My ma left before I remembered much, and where I was put, there were too many tears from too many children, and those of us who didn't cry were praised for being so 'strong.' That sort of made a habit until I was grown."

"Really…?"

"Absolutely true, and that left me not knowing what to do with myself except to work and read and continue to 'be strong.'"

"Hmmmmm."

"So you can see that I must have a lot of tears saved up."

Torie reached for her coffee mug, noticed it was empty, and set it down again. He said, "Shall I make more coffee?"

She reluctantly shook her head. "Not tonight. Maybe tomorrow."

Wise, she was. He answered. "So we make a date for tomorrow? Breakfast with the children is not a date. You've been alone for a year, and having a date would not mean you didn't still love him."

She sighed long and loud. "Sometimes I just want to see another adult face that looks at me, and really sees at me."

"Miss Victoria, I feel the same way." He stood up, making her exit easier. "Remember, it's a date for coffee. All the best, up-town folks do it, and it doesn't matter if it's here in my kitchen."

A quick smile below her reddened eyes, and she was gone. He watched as long as he could see her. The lights went out and the black windows stared back at him.

What had he done? In the brightness of morning light, how would she feel about having come apart so completely? He must be ready for anything. He blew out the lamp and starlight lit his way to his bed. His weary head touched the pillow, and he remembered nothing more.

SCHOOL DAY TWO

Morning came, and the school teacher aroused himself from bed and dressed. A feeling of apprehension enveloped him. What was facing him after his awkward attempts at comforting a lady who was, essentially, a stranger to him. He knew almost nothing about her, and that constituted being a stranger, didn't it?

Armed with the coffee pot and clean plates, he entered the busy kitchen. It looked as though the scraps of yesterday's hog were being successfully disposed of in crocks and jars, and breakfast preparation was just completed.

Luke was facing his sister. "Missy, remember F comes before G. You're doing good, though. Today we'll get more letters and I'll tell you them." Missy looked interested.

It would be another hot day, and that took care of some of the conversation. He mentioned he'd be late, again, as he needed to make the platform for his desk. It would give him a bit of prestige as if he needed it. A better group of children he could not imagine, though he had very little to compare to.

He and Luke had liver sandwiches for their lunches, and Merrill had never had a cold liver sandwich, but the liver with onions had been quite tasty. And all parts of the animal must be used, if possible. *We'll see.*

As he entered the school yard, he again frowned at the lack of play equipment. There were trees that would make good swings. Oak trees that had limbs going straight out made better swings, keeping them from twisting. There were a lot of trees. He needed to see how far the school land went, and maybe some logs could be cut there. And surely that would bring down the total price of the new room.

He was getting eager to go see Mr. Stone, just to see the cost and have that information ready when he talked with the School Board. It didn't hurt to be prepared.

It was early in September that neighbor Jacob Atkins was doing his fall plowing, turning the soil to hopefully kill some marauding insects. His efforts brought him close to the fence of his neighbor, Marshall Davis. It would be an insult not to stop and chat if only for a minute.

"How's it goin'?" Jacob issued the standard greeting to his neighbor.

"Goin' slow," was the expected response.

"Late yesterday I was workin' up by the Ridge and I saw the school teacher go by on that chestnut stallion. Good lookin' piece'a horse flesh."

"Really? Did you know where at he was goin'?"

"No, but Peter Ellis did. His wife let my wife know that he went to see the law."

"Burley? What for?"

"Don't know, but Peter speculated he was still hot over that contract to teach."

"Don't he like Bradley's cabin?"

"You'd think so, wouldn't ya?"

"Wouldn't'a thought he'd go all the way to Burley. Disputes could be settled with Herman. If that teacher leaves, what'll we do with the youngens?"

"It'll be a problem. That's what we get for takin' on a man."

"He didn't have no choice. Contract didn't say nothin'"

"Well, we got 'im, now. The youngens don't seem to mind. My girl said he had 'em writin' stories about their family."

"Shouldn't be no trouble with that. I better get on a'for it gets too hot."

"Me, too. Later."

In the big house, Torie went about her many duties. She hoped to get the butchering cleaned up before naptime so she could get that last hive cleaned out. That'd take a load off her back. And her mind.

Shreds of thought filtered through her mind. The teacher was absolutely right about her working too hard. But did he have a right to say it?

Then the thought...*why not?* It was not as though Bradley was coming back to claim her and would be angry. She really didn't know much about fellows, Bradley being the first one she knew of. Sixteen when they married, and it had seemed like the answer. Her home was not a welcoming place for her and he seemed so kind. She was lucky...he had been.

But did she owe him anything now? Of course not, but why did she feel that she was being pitched into deep water and told to swim when she didn't know how. The school teacher had been everywhere and done everything, and he knew so much, why would she waste time with him and his kind words when he could be gone in a minute?

Hmmm, that's what Brad had done. Gone in about five minutes, if she remembered it right. He was hurting, he was sick and then he was dead...and now he was gone and not coming back.

When was she going to look around and do something with her life other than caring for the house and the kids? If she was ever going to re-join the living, Merrill might be a good one to practice on. He had, actually, asked for a date and not one over the breakfast table. It would be private, like maybe in a diner, on one of their little tables. No time soon, of course. Obviously, she could not leave the children to be taken somewhere on a date, and he knew it. What more could he do?

She could still feel the light touch of his hand over hers that was what had started the whole embarrassing incident. But somehow, it hadn't seemed embarrassing at the time. It had seemed natural-like.

She scraped the honey comb away from the frame and into her pail. Another couple of frames, and she could go in. The whole afternoon will be busy with the centrifugal tub, turning and turning and dipping the wax out of the liquid.She had filled one hundred thirty-four pint jars, and there might be another twenty today. A very big haul. Uncle Hank had offered to take the jars to Eureka Springs when they were ready, and that took a load off her mind.

Now, if she could just off-load a few more duties from her mind. The dirty clothes were piling up, and she hated that. It made so much ironing at one time, and she hated to iron, especially in the summer with the stove having to be hot all day.

A short way up the hill Gracie Jones dropped in to see Elsie Duran, her closest neighbor. "Have you heard'a Eloise tellin' that Jacob saw the teacher headin' up the hill to talk with the law?"

"Heard it, but didn't believe it? Why'd he do that when he got what he wanted when he got that honey house?"

"Well, Herman and me, we were wondering could there be a problem with Torie? He is livin' awfully close to her, there."

"That's right, but if that was the problem, then it'd likely be Torie goin' to the law, 'stead'a the teacher."

"Yeah, you got a point there. Couldn't be about the food. Torie's a good cook. I did hear that the teacher pried up all the bolts in the school chairs that Miss Eldridge wanted put in."

"I heard that, too. The youngens seem to like 'im. He has a different way'a teachin', I hear. Hope that's not a problem when test time comes on."

"I got'a run. We'll just have to wait and see."

Gracie had no children or responsibilities. She had the time and the means to act as the conduit of the mountain grapevine and she helped to pass news along. Not only that, she was good at it. She could make six or eight stops in a single afternoon. Possibly it was a bit tiring, but someone had to do it.

Uncle Hank settled in his easy chair and addressed his spotted spaniel, Ornery. "Ornery, what'd'ya think'a the new neighbor? Reckon he's mindin' his own business?"

Ornery didn't seem to have an opinion, but he was willing to listen to Hank's. He sat on his haunches and tipped his head in an inviting way. Humans seemed to want to make these sounds when there was no trouble, so why not let 'em.

Hank continued. "Seems too good to be OK, him livin' there so close to Miss Torie. But he's right about one thing, he's just too big of a person to be boarded in someone's family."

Ornery tilted his head the other way, by way of giving greater encouragement. They'd been friends for a long time, and knew each other's ways inside and out.

Hank continued, "Seems best to just let things ride till they don't. Don't need lookin' for trouble. The school needs a teacher and Miss Torie needs the money. She shore didn't need that last kid, but she got it, and she seems to be perkin' along, like an old coffee pot."

Ornery sensed that his human had delivered the thoughts from his mind, so he was free to curl up on the rug and take a nap. It was the duty of a good dog to absorb the emotions of their humans and not be critical. And Ornery was a good dog. His human had told him so. Over and over.

Merrill watched Luke until he reached his gate, and then he started on building the platform. Thoughts wound through his brain, tormenting him and teasing him. It would be really nice if he could read humans with the accuracy that he read direction in a repair manual. It would be just too much to ask if something could come of his situation.

He could never be a Bradley, and it would be useless to try. She'd been married for over six years and that was certain to have left a few…well, what? How would she be different from what she ever was? Dating had not been in Merrill's life. He'd talked with many ladies and enjoyed it but never had thought of taking one on forever.

There had to be some way to manage this situation until he could move away. Maybe then he could look at things more clearly... preferable when he and she were not both physically exhausted. That would have been the cause of her tears, he told himself...but himself may not have been listening. Tears could come from a lot of directions.

It was somewhat of a tussle to get the desk onto the platform by himself, but he managed...in the manner that he had always managed. Not managing was not acceptable in his life.

He found a dish of southern rice and beans on the table. Still warm. Green beans and buttered corn on the side. Cornbread. He ate while watching the light in the kitchen windows. Would she come?

It was considerably later that she came, lumping that trip with the pig feeding, same as last night. Save steps where she could, he imagined. And the children must be in bed for her to leave.

Without hesitation, she left the pig feed bucket outside the door and stepped inside. Coffee was ready. She had words.

She explained that she had finished with gathering the honey comb and had more jars than she had expected. She had yet to extract the last of the sweet from the scraps of wax, and that would produce several jars for the table and one for Uncle Hank.

She told of Luke's dedication that Missy should learn her alphabet, and Missy, who missed him so much during the day, was somewhat agreeable. She was accustomed to his direction of their play, so it worked out.

She asked about his day. This was a new Torie. Brave new Torie and in full control. She sipped her coffee and smiled. No tears today.

Was this what an actual date was like? With the lady smiling and chatty?

STONE'S LOGGING

It was on the second Saturday after school started that Merrill and Sultan ventured down the rough little country road. The single lane completely disappeared from view after about one hundred yards into the trees. How did the Stones ever get their logs up out of the valley? *Not your problem, Merrill.*

And there it was, a sign about the size of a shoe box that proclaimed the place to be STONE'S LOGGING. As Sultan entered the yard, a man of ancient vintage, bald and silver bearded, left his chair under the maple tree and ambled forward. "Help ya, sir? Lazarus Stone, here."

"Lookin' for a price estimate on a log house."

"Yessir, Mr. Brooks. My people can build you a log house. You givin' me a sketch'll get the matter started. I got sons, grandsons and grandnephews a plenty to get it done. Then you'd need planned boards for roof, floor and ceiling and whatever partitions you need. We can handle that from our neighbors down by Blue Lake. Got 'em a good saw mill, they have, and turn out whatever a body'd need. Where at would ya be puttin' it up?"

Merrill was reluctant to mention the schoolyard without talking to the school board, so he indicated it wasn't actually settled yet, that he just needed to know who could do it and for how much. Needed to know so he could make plans for the future. Right?

"You make up your sketch and we'll look at it. We ain't never been undersold and that's a fact. Reason is, no one with any sense'd do what we do. Now if you was to get a place with a good stand'a timber on it, could be we could use some'a that. It'd bring down the price a bit if you did. And that'd save on time a'haulin'."

Hmmm, just as he thought. He'd also thought it would improve appearance to have brush cleared out, but his actions hadn't gotten that far. He left the old man with the silver beard and climbed back up to Ridge Road. He stopped off at the school house to take a look at the trees.

If the barbed wire fence outlined school property, then there was a wide strip of trees, each reaching forty to fifty feet straight up. He nodded with satisfaction. He'd collected a good bit of information, and now he needed to think on how he would approach the school board.

But not before the first of next year. That would be soon enough to have any credibility for himself and assurance of permanence. That would to be expected. Back to the cabin for lunch, and a paint job on the next panel.

He spread the three by three panel on his three by three table and set mugs on the corners to steady it. With the small paint brush dipped in black paint, he began,

1.2.3.4.5.
6.7.8.9.10
11.12.13.14.15
16.17.18.19.20
21.22.23.24.25
1+1=2 2+1=3
1+2=3 3+2=5
1+3=4 4+1=5
1+4=5 4+2=6

By the time the smell of the paint had drifted out of the door, he had an audience. Luke edged as close as he thought was acceptable.

"Can you tell me all of those numbers?"

Merrill stopped and looked at the eager face. Just what he was hoping for but he had to disappoint him. "I'd really like to, Buddy, but think about this. If I lived in Aaron's yard, and he asked me what you asked me, what would you think?"

Luke grinned and ducked his head. He knew he had done wrong, and hated to admit it, but he did. "I'd hate you and him both."

Merrill nodded. "Right you are my friend."

He wrote:

For this exercise you may use your reader or any library book. You must read a story and then re-write it using different words from the ones in the book. The writing must be in your neatest cursive.

On to Grades 7 and 8. He wrote:

A Lesson On Sounds
Sometimes a word has a short sound like the 'a' in pan, and it changes to a long sound in pate. Also hat and hate & fat & fate.

Some letters are called vowels and some are called consonants. The vowels are a.e.i.o.u & sometime w & y. You may use your reader or any library book you wish.

1. Sometimes a letter is short in one word and long in another, like, fat & fate, pat & pate. Make a list of these words.

2. Make a list of words with 2 vowels together like vail & pail.

3. Make a list of words that end in ally.

4. Make a list of 5 lettered words that begin and end in a vowel, like, enemy, apply & create.

5. Make a list of words with 3 or more vowels like believe and wheeler.

6. Make a list of words with 6 letters that begin with a vowel.

This was enough printing for today. A few days of making lists will make the student aware of vowels and their variety of sounds. *This exercise will occupy grades seven and eight.*

Grades two and three were sadly deficient in reading. It was going to take a of time to bring them up to speed. The month of September will be dedicated to that, and then come down hard on numbers in October and November.

With a smile and a feeling of satisfaction, he took the ABC's OF BEES off the shelf and settled into the softly stuffed chair in his bedroom. Finally there was time to devote to it. This idea of the panels was going to save a lot of time and give clearer information than if he spoke the words for the students to remember.

In the BEE book, he digested the parts about robbing the hive and it was much the same as he had seen happen out his window. He found the instructions for making hives, and recognized them from some of the scrap lumber in the barn. Several were in varying stages of construction. What did Bradley have in mind?

He read further about care of a queen, about containing a swarm before they flew away and how to get them through the winter.

He read how these amazing insects could dig nectar from the tiniest of flowers, and also from some newly formed leaves. He learned that the bees never harmed the plant, but instead he assisted it by pollinating the plants accidentally and incidentally. Imagine that?

He read about some eastern growers were using bees for pollination to get a better crop, and some seed growers depended on the bee almost completely.

As an item of interest, he read that many of the growers who liked what the bees did did not want to tend to the bees year around or bother to collect the honey. It seemed they were willing to pay to have hives full of bees brought to their farms for the summer and taken away in the fall.

At this point in his reading, Merrill slipped the bookmark between the pages and put the book aside. This required some thinking. Was Bradley possibly thinking of something like that? It seemed that the twelve hives just about used up the nectar producers on his acreage, and possibly also that of Uncle Hank.

And, although it would be a totally new concept to this part of Arkansas, would it be possible? And would the market be there to sell the honey? Of course, the honey didn't have to be extracted… it could just be left there for the bees, but there was a problem with that. The extra honey could sometimes, it was thought, entice a new queen to divide the hive and swarm, as there seemed to be plenty of honey for everyone. Back to the hive loaning.

One thing for a fact, it couldn't be done with horse drawn wagons. It would take a motor truck and a trailer to carry the quantity of weight of several hives, and make the trip to markets without using up two whole days.

Besides that, he reminded himself, this little twenty acres belonged to the lady in the big house. So did the bees and the hives and the scrap lumber that did not get finished into hives. But his self talked back to him, and reminded him that it was a totally interesting idea, and he loved interesting ideas. If it could just remain an "idea."

Supper time arrived. The aroma met him as he opened the door of the cabin. There was a long evening ahead, and he had decided he'd go look over the lumber scraps. He was certain there were scraps of unfinished bee hives. How many?

Torie was setting the food on the table. She looked up at Merrill with a small smile. "Have a seat, it's ready." She scooped up small Katie and sat the nine-month girl on her lap. She was sitting up very well, and even pulling up to chairs and anything she could reach.

Merrill sat down at his assigned place. Missy, who had, after the first glance, had never acknowledged Merrill's presence, walked around the table to him, swatted him sharply on the arm and stared into his face.

Somewhat taken back, he looked down at her. "Well, hello there, Miss Missy."

Her expression did not change but her mouth opened. She looked him in the eyes and said, "A.B.C.D.E.F.G.H.I.J.K.L.M.N. uh…Q?"

Amazed was not the word. The teacher was totally flabbergasted. "Why Missy, you did a very good job. You were so smart to learn all that."

Luke grinned smugly. "She has trouble getting past 'N.'"

Merrill shook his head. "She'll make it. She has a good teacher."

Missy took another swat at Merrill's arm and then marched back to the highchair. "I don't like the highchair. Katie can have it."

Torie stared with astonishment at her older daughter. She had been afraid giving up the chair would be a battle.

Missy, however, was not through. "Momma, I want a block like Luke."

"You can have one. You'll have to wait until we can cut one."

Missy's face wilted into a disappointed pucker.

Luke took the block from his chair, "She can have mine. I can wait."

Torie, at loss for words, finally found some. "Missy, tell your brother 'thank you.'"

"'Ank you." And she favored her entire family with a dimpled smile born of success.

The baked chicken was tucked under the vegetables bathed in a creamy gravy. The aroma would have been the envy on any fancy restaurant. Biscuits, sliced tomatoes and blackberry dumplings.

Katie, in the highchair, was offered a biscuit top, and she did what she could with only two teeth. Merrill looked around at this little family with a profound sense of peace. As he had been thinking of the missing Bradley off and on all day, he thought of him again. He would have been so proud. What made bad things happen…anyway?

Growing up as Merrill had, he had learned a lot of things. Tucked within a couple dozen boys both older and younger, he had learned that making the best of what he had had suited him best. Standing back and letting others go first had become a habit.

Slowly, but most certainly, the protective shell began to form around him. He was responsible for no one and no one was responsible for him. He worked out that all he would ever have would be what he could tuck within the shell. Which was himself. Depending on others created too much disappointment.

What would have happened if he had not had access to that very special teacher who saw through the shell? Truth be told, that teacher had decided that with those boys, the shell was likely a good thing if they only allowed it to mature with them. Young Merrill and a few others were his special charges as he thought they would benefit the most from what little extra they got from him.

At an early age, Merrill could recognize the shells of others, not that he thought of them that way, but more that the shells just became part of that person's personality. For good or bad. And his love for reading books…any books, actually…was an important part of his shell. It had protected him for years…but it might now be getting a bit thin.

There were people all up and down Ridge Road. The lawman, Uncle Hank, the old patriarch, Lazarus Stone. Even Herman Jones. There would be others…. His interests needed to widen.

He could have stayed with the railway and they'd have found a place for him. They needed workmen like him. Why hadn't he stayed? He couldn't have answered but he might eventually look back at the accident that changed his life so greatly. A crack in the shell? For better or worse…?

The injured leg and the boot were a nuisance when a lot of steps were required, but it was hard to pity himself. Challenges lay within his easy reach, his favorite being the students. If he could be a help to them…to widen their horizons…was that not a reachable challenge?

Merrill waited until 8:00 before he put on the coffee pot. Torie had evening things to do, and the children to put to bed, and then she would come over…or not come over.

At 8:10 she came. It was not a problem with Merrill that she lumped their "date" with a trip to feed supper scraps to the young pig. It was part of Torie that she economized her trips, held to a routine as much as possible and had moved mountains that way. Like someone said was the way to eat an elephant…one bite at a time.

She tapped gently at the door, and came on in, pulled by the invisible threads of aroma. She was teachable, he noted. Bradley must have been the teacher, and she, the able and eager student. So young when they met. Sixteen. When she should have been having fun with friends, she was pregnant with Luke.

She sat down and lifted her coffee mug. Sometimes words were not necessary. The luxury of having just another adult face and no need to be mother for a few precious moments. They spoke of Missy's new accomplishments, of Luke being his generous self. Of the honey jars, and the wax to be made into candles. It hadn't occurred to him that people actually made those handy sticks that carried their own fuel and disposed of themselves in a puff of smoke. Candles, huh…! Out of bees wax?

They talked of the school and the now installed platform for the teacher's desk. Of Luke's excitement over the picnic table with no picnic. Of Uncle Hank's helpfulness with the hay. He'd scooped it in a pile and pitched it into a bin in the barn. Getting it in the hayloft would be too big a problem. Two horse, two goats and a cow. They didn't require that much, and most of the time they munched on the dry grass outside.

They talked of things they had discussed yesterday, and would discuss again tomorrow, most likely. Words. Adult faces. Knowing looks. What else could they want, at least at this time?

Like beads on a string, these few minutes of an evening, tied by the mutual love of a late cup of coffee, tied their days together. Gave a finality. A completeness.

It was enough for now.

LESSONS

The teacher stood beside the miniature picnic table and looked at his first grade class. True, there were two five-year-olds who would repeat the year if they couldn't keep up. They were Luke and LouAnne Storey, whose father was the third member of the school board.

Now, upon reaching the first week of October, he decided it was time for a moment of assessment. Five pairs of eyes watched his every move. He had proved himself to be the bringer of surprises.

"Students, I want to hear someone repeat the entire alphabet."

Hands shot up like arrows aimed at the moon. Fingers waved for attention. Five-year-old LouAnne was among them.

"All right, LouAnne, say the alphabet as far as you can go."

Giggling over the surprise she had for Teacher, she repeated all twenty-six letters clearly and without hesitation. Then she covered her face with her hands and peeked through her fingers.

"Very good! You did a wonderful job. Now someone besides LouAnne to say the numbers one through twenty-five." Aaron was selected, who performed perfectly. The teacher, head whirling with the pride of success, asked who can repeat the five vowels and the two helper vowels.

Hands safely on the table, they studied Teacher. They only started vowels two days ago. Slowly and carefully, Luke's hand went up. No waving fingers of excitement.

"All right, Luke."

"Uh...a...e...i...o...u and w...y."

"Absolutely perfect. Now let's say them together and Luke will lead us."

That done, he asked, "What do we call the letters that are not vowels?"

"Con…Confusers…?"

"Conseckers…?"

"Constantents…?"

Teacher took over. "Luke got close. They are CONSONANTS. Let's say it five times on our fingers." And they did.

"Now we have more new words. We are going to learn to add. I have a lot of toothpicks here and they are going to help us. See I put one stick down, and we will call it number one. Then I put down two sticks. Aaron, count the sticks."

He did. "So we know that one plus two more is three. So if I put another stick with the two sticks, how many do I have? Count them, Rebecca."

She did. "So we know that one plus three equals four."

After another ten minutes of placing sticks and counting, he told them, "Now I will show you how we write them on the chalkboard." He wrote the plus one examples on the chalkboard without the answer. "Now, students, using the sticks on the table, tell me the answer to each of these."

There was a bit of scrambling for possession of the sticks, but together they managed the answers, one by one.

"Good job," complemented Teacher. "Now we will use two instead of one." He erased the top numbers on the seven examples on the board. "Now we do it again." More scrambling and positioning the sticks.

"So, now we get sheets of paper just like the big kids." There was an appreciative giggle from the room, as everyone had been watching the demonstration. He passed out the five sheets of paper that had seven examples of plus ones and plus twos.

"You will be writing the answer just like I wrote on the chalkboard. You may use the toothpicks and work together if you wish. I want an answer to every problem. Any questions?"

Marie's hand shot up. "Who gets the sticks first?"

"Everyone. There are enough for everyone to have sticks. Now don't be talking out loud and disturbing the others. Go Shhhhh!"

With the eraser, he wiped the examples from the boards.

Then he turned to the fourth and fifth grade. "Open your readers to page twenty-three, and start reading to yourself for five minutes, and then we will read aloud."

The day continued at a fast pace as usual. The seventh and eighth graders were introduced to the "reading problems" where they must decide which of the many numbers applied toward finding the solution.

The first graders were given the sheet of numbered problems to take home...after they had laboriously printed their names. "Now, take these sheets home and ask your parents if you got the right answer."

After school was out, and the children disappeared in every direction like a flock of quail when the adult birds were flushed. Merrill straightened desks and picked up scraps of this and that. He must take care of that little chore by having the students do it from here on. They dropped the scraps, and they should pick them up. Made sense.

He stepped out and locked the door, and turned to face the three members of the complete School Board. There was Herman Jones, of course, accompanied by Clyde Albright and Dwayne Storey, father of five-year-old LeeAnne Storey. Miss LeeAnne was tugging insistently at her father's belt, waving her sheet of numbers.

"PAPA! You have to look! Teacher said!"

"Later, honey."

"No Papa, now. Teacher said."

So Papa took the paper and glanced at it. "Very nice. Who gave it you?"

"Nobody, Papa. I did it all myself with the toothpicks."

"Now, LeeAnne, we don't say somethin' that's not true."

"It's true, Papa. Ask Teacher. I did it all!"

Dwayne Storey looked up at Teacher. Teacher, with a smile of pride, agreed with the insistent child. "She did it all, right along with the other four first graders."

Papa took the paper and looked more closely, then looked up at Teacher and shook his head with the unbelieveability of it all.

Teacher volunteered, "And if you think that's great, wait till you see what happens during the next five months. Now, what did you nice fellows want to see me about? I'm sure it wasn't LeeAnne's paper."

Herman Jones took over. "Just routine, Mr. Brooks. We didn't want you to think we'd abandoned you to a group of children, but it seems you're holdin' your own quite well. Do you have any questions?"

"Well, yes. I wondered who took care of the purchase of chalk, teaching papers and grade record books. That…and another thing."

With bravery brought on by LeeAnne's success in the presence of School Board, he brought up the subject he had planned to hold until after the Christmas holidays.

"I've been thinkin' and doin' a bit of research. These children have no place to eat their lunches except at their desks, and there is no place for them to go on rainy days. Sittin' at a desk all day would be tirin' to you fellows, and imagine how it is for a youngen. Believe me, it'll show up on their grades.

"I talked with old Mr. Lazarus Stone and asked about a log building to replace the shack. He suggested that if we had usable trees on the School Board property, it would bring down the cost, and his crew would saw up the limbs for free to burn in the stove."

That was a lot to throw onto the unsuspecting fellows, but there seemed to be no better time…thanks to LeeAnne. "I know you fellows'll want to talk together and with the community about it, but a 'work day' for the school to clean out the saplin's and underbrush would make this acreage a beautiful place to see. Now, I'll share something else.

"My injury caused the railway insurance to make a pleasant and generous settlement. I'm not rich, but I could swing half the cost of the building. Old Mr. Stone said his crew could take care of everything and if you fellows decided the other half of the cost could be shared by the community, a beautiful log building could be setting where the shack is.

"And it would have room for the students to eat lunch, play on bad weather days, and even have programs for the community. My plan would have livin' quarters for a teacher built in. That way you wouldn't have to arrange for the next teacher to be boarded."

He'd intentionally saved the nugget about the teacher's boarding requirement to the very end. A good thing to leave stuck in their minds.

The men were dumbstruck, and Miss LeeAnne was smiling with satisfaction, with one hand possessively holding to her papa's pocket.

Deciding he had time for one more plug for his auditorium, he pointed out in the direction of the shack where Sultan could be seen working on the grass. "Just picture a beautiful building there instead of the shack! You'll be able to get any teacher you want."

"You plannin' on leavin' after this year?" Herman Jones was trying to deal with all this new information.

"Well, no. Not if you want me to stay. We can discuss that later. If I have to go, I'd like to leave something nice for the community. There are lot of nice folks here, and I'd like to meet more of them."

Clyde Albright finally found his tongue. "Them things you said sound real good. We'll half to talk it over, ya know?"

"Absolutely. Now if someone'll take care of the supplies, I'll go out there and wake up my horse. I've got lessons to prepare for tomorrow."

The three men watched Merrill's strange walk, not really a limp, but a noticeably abnormal gait. Dwayne Storey put their thoughts into words. "That there fellow, he's got somethin' goin' inside'a him. I'm thinkin' we'd be doin' well to listen."

With that, he swung his daughter to the horse back and headed west. "See you fellows later!" The other two followed his example and turned west onto Ridge Road.

Luke had gone on home while the men talked. He thrust his paper into his mother's face, and Torie knew her son better than LeeAnne's papa knew her. "Why, Son! What a good job! Your numbers are quite neat and readable."

Luke absorbed the praise he was sure he'd get, and sighed and tilted his head. "Momma, Teacher is so much fun. He promised he had more fun things for us. We learned all this with toothpicks, but after a while we'll be saving the toothpicks for next year's class, 'cause we won't need 'em. Teacher said."

Teacher allowed Sultan to amble as slowly as he chose. Success is a wonderful thing to wallow in, and he was wallowing. All the way up to his eyeballs.

In addition, how could the fellows pass up such an important community duty, and have a lovely log building at half cost. And an apartment for the teacher, whoever that might be.

He tacked the canvas panel on the side of the barn to paint. That oil-based paint had a fume that lingered on everything, like a bad reputation on a bum. With careful letters he printed multiplication problems on the panel. They were four digits on top, multiplied by three digits below. If the seven of the fifth, sixth and seventh graders did well on this test, they would never see the panel again.

The supper meal was served complements of a young rooster. Crunchy and savory, it came, along with potatoes and cream gravy. The okra produced one last serving before the stalks would be pulled. Flat, vanilla supper cake studded with diced apples came next. He'd have betted a bundle that the supper cake would reappear as lunch desert for himself and Luke tomorrow.

He retired to his cabin to prepare for tomorrow, and put his coffee pot on the stove at the usual time. He drank three cups of the savory liquid, and dumped the rest. No Torie.

"Oh, well," he sympathized with himself. "Even the brightest flower has a day that it is passed over by the butterflies and bees. So be it. Tomorrow will be another day."

READING PROBLEMS

When Herman Jones got home, he was queried in depth by his wife on his visit with the teacher. It was the duty of Gracie Jones to keep the community informed, and hopefully to get to do it before anyone else.

Fortunately, it was Monday when she learned the unbelievable news that something might be done to the already perfect school setting. Already he was wanting changes…the gall of him!

At the Tuesday meeting, the words flew.

"An auditorium! How exciting!"

"And a lunchroom that isn't the desk! I can still remember the smell of boiled eggs that the school always smelled of."

"And rainy and cold days at the desk? More reading or playing quiet games with our chairs glued to the floor?"

Poor Gracie. Before she could wave the banner of indignation, it was flung with mud. All the other ladies loved the idea! *Hmmmm, well, why not join 'em?* "I can't imagine that old shack torn down. Did they ever expect a teacher to spend a night in there? Especially one the size of that fellow?"

"When will it happen? Anyone know?"

"Soon, I think. Dwayne Storey saw a page his LouAnne brought home, and now he thinks that teacher's feet don't touch the ground!"

"I think he's tryin' to put together a 'work day' to get the woods cleaned up'a dead wood so the Stones can put up the building."

"And you know what I heard? He's offered to pay half of what the Stones charge! Can you imagine that?"

"His own money…?"

"That's what they're sayin'. Seems he got a settlement from when he was hurt and he's willin' to spend some here. What does that say?"

"Tells me he's aimin' to stay. Wouldn't that be a hoot!"

"Another thing. That auditorium can be used for community meetings and celebrations and that sort of thing." At least Gracie could add something that hadn't yet been discussed.

"And living quarters for the teacher. What's wrong with Torie's honey house? He not doin' too good with her?"

"Don't know."

"Maybe they'll make a picnic of the work day and we all can go? What do you think, Gracie?"

Gracie smiled graciously. "I'm already workin' on it." She hadn't been but it was a duty she was most able to accomplish. Fellows loved to eat and it would a party day.

And the "bee in the bonnet" of the new teacher had stirred up a bee hive of activity. Something new and outrageous to talk about. And the parents of the students were the greatest champions.

Merrill brought Sultan home and turned him into the pasture. "Sultan, old boy, I'll swing a shed in the school yard for you, too, or maybe let you winter in that old thing that is there. Pull up the floor boards and let you have it.

Suntan flung his head and whickered conversationally. He knew when he was being talked to, and expressed his appreciation.

Merrill settled into tomorrow's plans. He was going to be very busy keeping something going for everyone. The attendance had settled out with three eighth graders and one seventh grader. He decided to put that seventh grader in with the three, and if it was difficult for him, he'd grade him accordingly but if he made passing he'd just let him skip the seventh. What's so sacred with living out every grade?

At 7:00 he put up the lesson plans and set the coffee pot on the stove. By poking up the coals he could get it to perking and sending its aroma out toward the big house.

Fifteen minutes later, she stepped out the door with the pan of scraps for the pig, and two minutes after that, she stepped through his door and met the welcoming smile. And steaming mug of coffee.

They talked. Gracie Jones had stopped by for a ten minute visit, mainly to find out about the teacher. "She wanted to know if I like you. I said you were my tenant, and I didn't have to like you. It was not in the contract!"

That was the biggest joke of the day. "Not in the contract" was such a clever retort! Like it was any of Gracie's business, but there was no telling what "news" she would decide to spread around.

He asked, "Do you care what she says?"

With a grin, Torie asked him, "When do you think I have time to care what she says?"

At 8:30 she pushed back her coffee mug and left with a sack of his sweaty clothing. Washday tomorrow. They both had to get some sleep.

The news of LeeAnne Storey's arithmetic paper found its way into every shack and shanty most of the way up to Uncle Burley's Bistro. It just had to be a combination of the teacher's ability and the child's brilliance.

LeeAnne, however, had a sister, Rebecca, in the fifth grade. In a very short time, Rebecca had all she wanted to hear about her clever sister. The only reason LeeAnne had a paper like that was that the teacher chose that for the lesson. The fifth grade had no such paper to brag on. It was not fair and Rebeca knew it. She stared at her bedroom ceiling, seething within. She'd do something about that problem…just wait and see.

Teacher let anyone raise their hand and ask a good question. No silly questions, of course, but Rebecca now had a good question. She would find out why Teacher liked the first grade better than the fifth. Finally, she drifted off to sleep, but when she woke up, she was more charged up than ever.

She held in her anger all the way to school, and Teacher's greeting, "Good Morning, Students." And all through the response of "Good Morning, Teacher."

She counted to ten, and her hand shot up straight as a maple sapling. Teacher turned to her and asked, "You have a question, Rebecca?"

"Yes, Teacher. Why do you like the first grade better than the fifth grade?"

"Why, Rebecca, what makes you think that?"

"Because you let them make good papers to take home and the whole world sees what they can do. Why don't the fifth grade get to do anything like that?"

Teacher had the bad manners to smile at her instead of being embarassed. "Rebecca, I am so very glad to hear you say that. The first graders were first, but you are next. I have four arithmetic problems for the fourth, fifth and sixth. I will tell you right off, these are tricky questions, but they do have an answer.

"I'm going to help you with one, but you will figure out the answer to the others. You must copy these whole questions on your paper. Write carefully, because they are long and will take up a lot of space. I'm giving you a lot of time for this."

Then he hung the panel on the easel. Five reading problems… always harder than the ones that are all numbers.

He continued. "Read the problem carefully and make sure you know which numbers to use to get the answer. You must do your figuring on the back of the sheet. You may begin. Do not attempt to work any of the problems until I work the first one with you.

PROBLEMS OF LIVING

1. A farmer wished to take a load of hay to town. He wishes to know how much weight his horse will have to pull. He knows that the loaded wagon weighs 2,000 pounds and the weight of the hay is 300 pounds. His own weight is 150 pounds and his little dog weighs 7 pounds. The dog's collar weighs 1 pound. He decided, at the last minute to put in his 3 pound pitchfork and take off the dog's collar and put it on the seat beside him. How much weight will the horse have to pull?

2. A boy walks 8 miles to school, and the school is 2 miles from thechurch. He stopped in front of a friend's house to see if he wanted to walk with him. The friend lived 6 miles from school but he forgot his book and had to walk back 1 mile to get it and his friend walked with him. How many miles did both boys walk?

3. The loaf of bread had 16 slices and two heels. The cook wants to make sandwiches from half the slices of bread and break up the rest for stuffing. She used the stuffing for four of the sandwiches. How many sandwiches had only butter?

4. A shed is being built for tools. There are hooks to hang some of them to the wall. The saw and level are on one side, 4 hammers on another side and 4 bags of nails are on the floor. A window in on one side and it is 2 feet high and 3 feet wide. And the shed is 7 feet high in all. If the builder puts 12 hooks on the wall, how many hooks have nothing hanging on them?

5. The farmer has chickens of three colors. White, red and yellow. The white hen lays an egg every day for 30 days.

The red hen lays 15 eggs, and a snake got three of them. The yellow hen lays 23 eggs and 5 of them are speckled. It takes 2 eggs to make each individual custard for a party. How many custards can be made for the party?

It took a long time to write the problems on their paper, and it was an excellent opportunity to practice their cursive. When they were through, he began: "First you put down the weight of the wagon, two thousand pounds. Do you put down the three hundred pounds? Rebecca?"

"No sir. The three hundred pounds were already weighed."

"You're right. You have two thousand pounds. How much does the man weigh?" A combined shout told him one hundred and fifty pounds. "And the dog? Seven pounds. What answer do you have?"

A shout of 2,157 was near defining.

"What about the dog collar, another pound. But the farmer took it off; do you subtract the pound?"

A muffled whisper of yes. Rebecca's hand again. "NO! Because it still weighs a pound if it's on the wagon seat."

"Right. Is the answer 2,157 pounds?"

"NO! Add the pitchfork!"The answer was yelled by Nathan Rhodes, becoming irritated with Rebecca for hogging the answers.

"So what is the answer?"

"Two thousand one hundred and sixty pounds."

"Very good. I'm going to ask you another question. What if the man put a goat in harness to help pull?" He waited for the giggle to die down. "And the goat can pull one-third as much as the horse. Than how many pounds does the horse pull? Tell me tomorrow, and I do NOT want you to be comparing answers or talking with your parents. This paper will be your own. Think very carefully and determine which numbers are really part of the problem."

Rebecca clutched her paper as though it was made of gold… or something better. She made sure her papa saw it (as Teacher was certain she would do).

Dwayne Storey glanced at the paper with an inward groan. School had not been easy for him, but it seemed he would face it again. But, no, she took the paper from him and disappeared into the room she shared with her sister.

On scratch paper she worked a few computations and when satisfied, she copied the neatest one of the computations onto the back of the sheet and transferred her answers to the problems.

Putting the paper into a safe place, she went to sleep smiling to herself with satisfaction. She'd show him!

And she did. When she brought home the paper for her papa to see, she had an A+. Teacher had told the students that a "+" was for neatness and readability, and they should all remember that. Theoretically, it would be possible to get an F+. Grading multiple papers was a grind, anyway, so he greatly appreciated readability.

Once again Rebecca carefully carried home her precious paper. She showed Mama first and received the expected hug. Then Papa. The School Board member glanced, saw the A+ and remembered how few of them he had received, then looked more closely. He read the problems twice.

"Rebecca, my daughter, I am extremely proud of you."

She responded, "Thank you, Papa." Then she put away the paper carefully. Papa's words were better than two hugs.

In this way Teacher acquired his first staunch ally. The news got around, and other parents were coming forth. Gracie Jones was graciously and enthusiastically greeted when she began her plan for the picnic/work day.

It was set for a Saturday in January. Arkansas is good at producing days of spring-like weather tucked among the dull and rainy ones, and it generously supplied one for the workday.

The turnout being large with workers coming and going as their home chores demanded, but they were all there for the picnic dinner, bringing their own specialty. A gasoline saw brought down small saplings that were piled with dead branches around the fence. Even the children came dressed to work, noisily excited and energetic.

A selected number of men were assigned to mark the trees meant to become building logs. They tied colorful strips around the trunk at eye level. The teacher assigned his eighth graders the job of counting the trees, being careful to count every one, and none twice. They came up with fifty-seven. That would materially bring down the cost. Cutting logs on site was a great deal easier than bringing them up from the lake.

The felling crew would arrive on Monday, and the skinning of bark would begin by slicing the bark off the usable log with a gadget called a "draw knife." The bark chunks could be gathered for fire starting in the school stove.

The building was started, and who could tell whether it actually began with LeeAnne's paper of numbers. She would get better as her hands grew, but it was plain to see that she had known what she was printing.

THE NEW BUILDING

It was January, and the Thanksgiving day dinner was weeks past. Two young roosters had given their lives for the feast, being finished with savory stuffing and presented with gravy and mashed potatoes. Canned tomatoes and green beans combined with other items to make a hearty casserole. Biscuits and spiced peach preserves, and a fruit cake full of nuts from the woodland, along with spicy dried apples.

The single guest was Uncle Hank, and the occasion was used to present him with his gift of honey. Two jars this year. The bees had been exceptionally generous.

It was then time to cover the hives with oiled canvas to shed water and turn aside the wind. Bees in the wild somehow withstood the Arkansas winters, but the pampered ones in the hives deserved extra protection after the sharing of their honey. Their activity would be slow to motionless as they existed until the flowers came again.

But now the worse of the winter was over.

It had been the week after Thanksgiving that Torie had come to the cabin for their "date." It was on that day that as she arose to go, Merrill arose and walked her the three steps to the door. He circled her waist with his arm and kissed her cheek. Then, moved on to her mouth, and she did not resist. Then he let her go with the usual "Good Night."

He knew a lot about her by that time. On one of his repair trips of his former life took him to a problem down south of Little Rock, he had taken with him a book called "Personalities and Their Protective Measures." It was a "think" book with a lot of words which was why he had chosen it. It also had a lot of information and he saw himself tucked within the pages.

It started with what the author called "shells." Almost everyone would have developed shells at a young age. There were things to do and not to do and ways to protect oneself from unpleasantness. Sometimes with words, sometimes with fists, but often by simple withdrawal of varying degrees.

Merrill found his own shell in his love for books and for gaining information. The place where he grew up had access to a large number of books, and he made the best use of them, learning about things he would never see or do, but learning to retain bits of information.

He had learned that his shell protected him from being with others who might hurt him as his parents had. Casual friends were acceptable, but close friends were not...as they could hurt you when they left you. Better not to have a friend than to risk loss. The young mind can retain a lot of information, useful or not, and can form a habit of wanting more. Such had happened with Merrill.

So, it was plain, his wealth of books were accumulated to take the place of anything that could leave him, and remained his possession for years. Looking back, it was likely the best shell he could have formed because he had managed a good life. At least he thought he had.

Now he had met Torie under unusual circumstances and seeing her had made him face his own shell. But by now, he could see cracks in his shell, and was he ready for it...? Seemingly yes. Teaching children made it hard to maintain separateness.

Back to Torie. She had loved Bradley from the start because he was a protector. Being several years older, he seemed safe and closer to the age of her unsatisfactory parents. He was a leader by nature and possibly a teacher, and she was the willing student. And it would have worked satisfactorily all her life, no doubt, if he had lived. But now....

The shell was broken, leaving her exposed, and Merrill was definitely not a Bradley. She was becoming exposed for the able person she was inside, being occasionally surprised at herself. Being forced to lift the burden of life and children, she proved herself capable and strong, not in need of a protector. Merrill saw this as an asset, as he was certainly not a Bradley.

He began to think he might have a future with Torie. The somewhat male desire to produce his own children was not present in Merrill, and that was likely part of his shell. Torie's children were a perfect substitute and an answer to his desire to guide children in the way that his "perfect teacher" had guided him, shining a light into the future but excepting nor expecting something in return. As had his teacher.

His plan had been to partially move into the log building when ready, but keeping his library in the two roomed cabin so Torie would continue to be paid for boarding. But now...?

She had progressed to returning his kisses, but it was scary to them both. Maybe it would still be best to move, though the move would be hard to explain to her. Something definite needed to happen and he didn't know what it would be. One day at a time...and she seemed content.

During the two week Christmas holiday, Merrill dug out the scraps of unfinished bee hives. For something to do, he began to fit them together, creating the missing parts by using the diagrams in the ABC's OF BEES. Along with that, he kept thinking of the idea of renting out the hives. Now that would a project worthy of his attention!

The little schoolroom was bombarded by the sound of the gasoline saw, the falling trees, and the shouts of the Stone crew. To get the job started, Merrill paid his half, and the three members of the School Board had paid a visit to every homestead in the Enterprise district. Every homestead was regaled with marvelous ability for the Teacher, as made evident by his daughters' accomplishments.

There were promises, and some cash, but that was not a problem of Merrill's. When the school day was over, he immediately joined the workmen, trying not to be a nuisance. One day, he counted fourteen young men at work.

In March the actual building began and up went fast, using massive logs for the base of the floor. Then the sides started rising, and so did Merrill's enthusiasm. The living area was approximately the same as his cabin. The auditorium adequate, and the walls rose up with surprising speed.

Katie took her first steps, and Torie had a few hours of regret that her papa would never see them, then she squared her shoulders and forged ahead. Like the wise man once said, "Don't ever look back, something might be gaining on you."

She was taken to the new building and noted the pride with which Merrill pointed out everything, including the eventual teacher's residence. She observed it silently. She could picture the coffee pot on the stove issuing fragrant steam to the Whip-or-Wills in the trees and the Bob Whites yelling their name over toward Ridge Road.

She faced it as she had faced everything over the last year, grimly determined. Her three children were her primary, and now it seemed likely, her only concern. They had no one else. Neither did she.

She continued the hearty breakfasts and lunches, and the satisfying evening meal. She cleaned up her kitchen, gathered scraps for the pig, delivered them and returned to the big house. The children were put to bed, and she, having nothing else to do, followed shortly after.

It occurred to her a time or two that she could borrow some of Merrill's books. As many as he had, certainly there would be some of interest to her, but reading was not a thing she naturally did. Actually, she had no time to have developed the habit.

She had noticed the new bee hives being put together, but she gave it no mind. Merrill was a man, and that was the sort of thing they did. No concern of hers.

There were winter things to do, and she did them. One was to make a trip to the bistro up at the junction, to see Annie's Montgomery Wards Catalog. She had made it known that the catalog was free for community use. The children were outgrowing their clothing, and she could use a new dress, though for what, she did not try to imagine.

She liked Annie, though she didn't get to see her very often. Only when she needed to make an order. It was in Annie's living room that Torie's dam broke.

Torie selected necessary clothing for the children and several dress length pieces of yard goods for her own use. They needed shoes, especially Luke and there were a few more items. They would be delivered to her address by the postal route on Ridge Road.

Then, over a glass of cidar, she settled down to enjoy a visit. Now, for a visit, it would be hard to beat the very social Annie Jo Collins, Burley's wife. They compared baby development as both had young babies. She admitted to Annie that she had not been able to get other help, but Uncle Hank from next door performed quite adequately at the birth…after all, he was trained for it.

How was she getting along taking care of the teacher?

Torie produced a forced smile. "Not much takin' care is needed. Food and washin' about all, and I was doin' that anyway."

"We hear that he's doin' a good job with the youngens."

"Seems to be. My Luke thinks he brings the sun into the sky."

"That's good, huh! Do you suppose he'll stay after this year?"

"It appears so. The new log buildin' he wanted put up has livin' quarters for a teacher."

"And he'll be movin' over?"

"Hasn't said so, yet. Claimed he wanted the new buildin' for a lunch room so the youngens would have a change'a senery. And there's winter rains when they can't go out. Maybe a Christmas party or somethin'. Seems like a good thing and he paid for the buildin' of half of it."

"He did? Is he rich or somethin'?"

"Maybe, sort of. He was injured on his foot and got a settlement, I hear. He never talks about it."

"Does he use crutches?"

"No, he's got some, but he mostly just sort of…well, he doesn't limp but he walks a little different…a little stiff, like. He can't move his ankle."

"Hmmm, but it doesn't stop 'im?"

"He rides his horse a lot."

"Does he like your kids?"

"I suppose so. He doesn't say, but he teaches Luke in the first grade, and tells Missy she's a clever girl when she says the alphabet and counts to twenty-five. I don't think she knows what 'clever' is except that it's good."

"Does he have a girlfriend?"

"Not that he talks of."

Annie just couldn't let it alone. "Say, why don't you nab him? He seems like a pretty good catch."

Torie soberly shook her head. "I don't think so."

"Don't you like 'im?"

"Well, maybe I could. We talk sometimes in the evenin'. I never had a real boyfriend. I was hardly sixteen and needed a place to go when Bradley came along. 'Course, I couldn't never have done no better than Bradley. It'd'a been hard not to love him."

"But he isn't coming back. Wouldn't you think he'd like for you to find some to love and help with the kids?"

"Could be…but…." And the tears began to flow. She buried her head in her arms and wept bitterly.

Annie was also the one to see when one needed sympathy. She moved her chair closer and wrapped her arms around Torie. She remembered what "lonesome" was, and she didn't even have children when she married Burley.

"Torie, honey, it's all right. Sometimes we just got'a cry."

When the deluge lessened, Torie raised her head and sniffed. Annie furnished a hanky. "When you talk, what does he talk about?"

"School. Kids. The new log building…. Just stuff."

"Could I ask if you've ever kissed him?"

A long pause, and a nod. "Use to."

"What stopped you?"

"Me knowin' he was wantin' to get away and move into the log buildin'."

"Did he say so?"

"…uh, no…but I need to be ready for 'im to."

Annie knew there would be a good anwser, but she had to search for it. "Torie, honey, look at it like this. Do you put on your rain coat in the sunshine just because it might rain sometime? Or stop pickin' tomatoes because sometime they'll all be picked? Or maybe stoppin' talkin' with the teacher just 'cause he might move away?"

Torie just looked at her.

"The thing is, Torie. Fellows are different, and he might think you don't like 'im anymore if you act cold and indifferent. Think that might happen?"

Torie didn't answer.

"You could ask him, or you could just pretend you don't think he'll move away. Maybe you could tell him you're worried. Comes a time that a fellow ain't too good at readin' us. Fellows are all alike on bein' different."

"You think so?"

"I know so. You can tell him how you feel, and if he doesn't feel the same way, maybe you could look at someone else. That way he'd not be wastin' your time."

"But Bradley...."

"Torie, listen to me. Bradley isn't coming back and he loved you very much. Wherever he is, he would want you to be happy, and that wouldn't mean anything against lovin' him."

Torie hesitated, then sighed. "I can think on it. It's somethin' I never did before."

"Because you were too young. Listen to me, I was almost thirty when I met Burley and married him. I made it very clear that I liked him, and could very well love him, and that he needed me very badly."

Missy was patting Ugly Face on the velvety hair of her head and ears, and she was putting up with it, with an admirable amount of patience. Eventually, Katie had laid over on the floor and went asleep.

Torie sighed. "I got'a be goin'. Stuff to do. I sure do appreciate you helpin' me with the order."

"Ah, you didn't need any help. But I can tell you this. Come time you get to feelin' like you did a bit ago, you get yourself back up here and let me talk some sense into you."

Torie grinned knowingly.

With her girls aboard, Torie clicked to the horse and waved. *Hmmm, well, something to think about.* Miss Annie sounded like she knew what was going on. At least, if she did what Annie demanded, she could quit worrying about it.

Within minutes, her darling black-haired Missy was stretched out on the seat with her head butted up against her mother's thigh. One slightly chubby arm clutched Katie beside her, holding her close. The clomp of Old Bugger's feet measured Torie's thoughts into clip-clops. She sighed with satisfaction over this trip being completed, and immediate needs would appear in the mail box within the month. Another duty done.

She let Old Bugger take his time…there was no hurry. Thoughts whirled around in her head as she watched the familiar scenery lined up against Ridge Road. Familiar names on the mailboxes brought up mental pictures of her neighbors, and then turned themselves back into her own life.

With eyes that startled open, she asked herself, "What's with all them tears back up the hill? That ain't me! Who was that?"

Another quarter of a mile passed under the wheels of the tiny buggy, and she realized she did not care who that was. She knew who she was, and it was time to acting like it!

Eventually, Old Bugger reached his own home, and turned in at the gate. The bump over the culvert in the bar ditch, startled Missy's eyes open. She sat up and shook gently on her sister. "Wake up, Katie. We're home."

Torie made Old Bugger pause while Missy reached the ground by sliding down from the seat. Torie lowered Katie and held her until she was steady on her her newly found feet. Missy took Katie's hand and they headed for the kitchen door.

Old Bugger moved on to the barn, and then to pasture. Torie hung the halter and bridle on a handy peg and walked resolutely toward the big house. She was Torie. Torie, the confident. Torie, the owner of a great satisfaction with her life.

On her way to the kitchen, she stripped the clothesline of the dry clothes from the early mornings washing. There was time yet today to set up the lye and sifted ashes to make a batch of lye soap. She'd just iron Merrill's school clothes along with Luke's, and get at it. Soap could be purchased with valuable coins, but it did not clean like the soap she made in the tub over the outdoor fire.

It was still a puzzle to her that ashes and collected fat from animals turned into a soap that removed the grease from clothing and kitchen floors. Didn't make sense, but what did that matter! She'd done enough thinking, so there! What was the saying she had heard once? "Don't try to fix something that ain't broke." *Listen to that, Miss Torie! So there!*

In due time, Luke came home on the run. As usual. Shortly afterward, Merrill came in on Sultan. She saw the familiar sight from the kitchen window. Emergency ironing done, she moved outside to tend to the soap kettle. Fat from the butchered hog was ready, and the ashes were ready to be sifted.

Merrill rode into the yard and through the bee pasture to the barn door. Sultan was happy to join his buddy, Old Bugger. Merrill hung the halter and bridle in the barn and proceeded toward his cabin, his lopsided gait a bit slow after a day of use. No matter. He was home.

Supper proceeded as usual. Tasty, comforting and usual. As usual, he excused himself and returned to the cabin. Another day's lessons to be planned.

As 8:00 approached, and darkness was settling in, he put his finished work on the book shelf and measured the coffee grounds and water into the trusty percolator. Poking the glowing coals into a final blaze, he set the pot over a burner.

He heard a soft slam of the kitchen door and through the window over the table, he saw Torie step out with her pan of scraps. It meant nothing, really, as she had recently seemed to have no time to stop over.

She walked over toward his door and tapped with her knuckles. "I'll be right back," he heard her clearly say. With wide, interested eyes he moved to the north window and watched her in the gathering dusk. She walked along with her usual economy of movement, but there was a difference. What was it?

She stopped to dump the pig's food through the fence into the trough, then stood a moment to watch the pig. As usual. It seems farm animals must be watched regularly as they were the source of family food or money. Hmmm, how could one tell if a pig was sick?

He watched her turn and walk back through the bee pasture. What was different? Then, with a long sigh, he chided himself, "Merrill, you strange creature, when are you going to keep your nosey face out of that blooming Personality book, and stop analyzing people? Sure. Everyone has his own particular shell of protection, so what business is it of yours?"

He nodded in agreement with himself. Himself was often his best deliverer of advice, he'd learned years back.

She came through the gate of the bee pasture and moved out his line of sight. He moved to the kitchen door and opened it just as she reached the stoop. He held out a hand, and she grasped it.

She stepped into the cabin and walked into his arms. He guided her to her assigned chair with the thick coffee mug in place. He stepped to the stove and lifted the coffee pot, still perking gently and sending the fragrant brew up the stem and into the glass lid. It was just the right shade of "dark."

He filled her mug and his own and sat down. She smiled with satisfaction, sighed and sipped the brew. Who needed words…they would come later. They sat for a moment and studied each other, each with personal and particular thoughts. He reached out his hand and she met it with her own.

Who needed words? Indeed!

SPRING STORM

Uncle Hank had just finished his routine bit of chores at Torie's place and passed through her yard. Glancing up, he was again reminded of that loose shingle up near the gable. For the dozenth time he told himself, "Come a rain storm and it could leak. Bein' in the attic like that, could make a lot'a damage a'for it was noticed. Gotta get up there and tack a new shingle in."

And he really meant to, but one thing and another, and the years were creeping along. Actually, he'd have told the school teacher about it except for two things. One was his foot, maybe not being safe on a ladder, and the other was that he was aso totally occupied in the school yard.

Glancing to the west, the direction of most spring storms, he saw the cloud bank building face, with a few overhead clouds scooting across the sky. Maybe there was time right now.

As he went through the gate and past the honey tree, he felt that sharp, quick stab in his right chest, and a weakness in his arm. Glad he'd gotten the chores done, he hurried to his shed for the shingle, hammer and a few nails in his pocket.

Moving the ladder made another sharp stab, but it went away quickly, as had the other stabs he had felt lately. The weight of the ladder was heavy on his right arm, but he was trained to work through discomfort and he managed to get the ladder against the house.

No problems with his feet, so he climbed rapidly scaling the shingles on all fours. It was hardly a trick to fit the new shingle into place, and lift the hammer. Seemed heavier today. Oh, well, he'd be through in a minute. A couple of nails from his pocket, and the damaged shingle was tossed, and the new one place and pinned securely to the rafter.

Reaching to put the hammer into the hammer-loop of his overalls, he dropped. Hammer handle just slipped from his grasp and slid down the roof to the ground.

Hmmm, and there was that pain again. Better sit still a minute before crawling down the shingles to the ladder. He might have waited another minute, but the rain came in a dense sheet soaking him and the shingles. He told himself, should'a gone on down.

He hardly felt that last pain. His body scooted down the wet shingles colliding with the top of the ladder. Together the ladder flung itself away from the house taking the lifeless body of the man with it. He felt no pain as he had already left his wrinkled and graying body.

On the grass beside Torie's house lay the remains of a life well lived in service to others and in protection of fellow humans. The rain pelted down and ran is rivulets across the yard, soaking the man's clothing, plastering it to the grass.

The school day was finished, and Luke slipped on his slicker and boots and ran for it. He sloped through the ditch to make a short cut and almost stepped on the pile of set clothes. Pile?

He screamed in terror and pounded on the door, too excited to use the knob. "Ma, come! There's a person layin' on the ground in the yard. I think its Uncle Hank."

Torie grabbed the umbrella and with Luke leading the way, braved the dashing rain to the scene. Seeing the clothing, she tossed aside the umbrella and ran.

She knelt and picked up a lifeless hand. Stunned, she turned to face her son's questioning face. She silently nodded, and felt the tears blending with the rain. She reached for Luke's hand and pointed to the house.

"But Ma...?

"Come, Son." He came.

Inside the kitchen he pled, "Can't we do somethin', Ma?"

"No, Son. He's already gone to a better place. There's nothing we can do to help him."

Luke leaned out the door into the rain to look once more for the person he loved, and saw on the road a man and a horse.

"Teacher's comin', Ma. He'll do somethin'."

Torie saw her son in pain from wanting to help. "Luke, honey, go meet Teacher and have him come in."

The boy in the boots and rain gear flew out the sood and splashed through the puddles. "Teacher! Come in, Ma said."

Merrill lowered himself from the horse and followed. And he also saw the "pile" of wet clothing and knew instantly what it was. And he did do something.

Inside the kitchen, dripping on the floor, he told Torie, "I'll get Burley."

On the galloping trip up to the Junction he chided himself for leaving his good friend out in the pouring rain, and reminding himself that where the friend was, he would not care. But the lawman would know how to deal with this.

For Merrill, the man of very few friends, the loss was great. Truly his best friend and advisor was gone, and the loss for Torie would be far worse.

Burley Collins was not particularly surprised. Uncle Hank, a man of intelligence and forethought, had prepared the way.

"Bein' alone, like I am," he'd told Burley not six months ago, "I think it best I tell someone. Bein' my age anything could happen, and you'd be the one to handle the problem. My Pa, bein' about my age, had a chest pain that took him on in a minute, they say. And now I seem to have a touch'a the same pain."

Burley Collins, lawman, was no stranger to this kind of conversation. He seemed to be the conduit connecting Ridge Road problems to the best answers at the time.

Hank continued, "I'd be more concerned about Miss Torie, but that teacher…he's takin' a interest in her. I'm getting' too old to be much help except with the mowin'. Now, I got a paper wrote out, and it's my cupboard under the sugar can. Been there a while, with me knowin' what might happen.

"I got a niece down in Wishbone, and it'd be her to be notified. I got her name wrote down on the paper. I wrote other things. I want Miss Torie to take my horse, and my rower and rake. She'll need them things with her flowers. She can have the chickens and goat, too, cause my niece'll not want 'em. She'll be sellin' the place and them animals'd just be a bother."

Uncle Hank and the lawman had sat at the little table near his road side stand and sipped cider while this morbid talk was taking place. The old man seemed not to be stressed, just stating what should be done, and making it easier for one whose job was to see it was done.

The neighborhood was stricken, as it always when one of their own had a misfortune.

"Fell off the roof, you say?"

"Likely not. He'd been painin' for a while, Burley said."

"What'd he be doin' up there in the rain?"

"Could be it weren't rainin' when he went up. He had a hammer, and there were nail in his pocket, Burley said. Maybe he was fixin' a shingle for Miss Torie."

A nod of agreement. "That'd be what he'd do."

"That girl'll be takin' it hard, close like him and her was."

"That's true, but there's the teacher right there close."

"Reckon he'll step up?"

"Likely already has."

Change of subject. "That place'a his'll bring a good price. On the road like it is."

"Could be, and we'll have a new neighbor."

A sigh. "Won't be the same, though. Without Old Hank."

Nods of agreement, "You're right on that."

And the remains were put to rest in the cemetery. Almost as if the weather was apologizing for the rain storm, the funeral day was a glorious time of sunshine and warm breezes. The niece attended with the right amount of grief for the loss.

Bro Phil Darkhorse stood by the grave and spoke to his Boss. "Lord, we've sent you one of our very dear friends and we miss him terribly. You know that, but he was with us a long time, and it's your turn now. All we can do in honor his passing, and now…."

And the grave was closed.

Merrill, the school teacher, had never been so close to the send off of a friend as this, and it affected him all the way down to his fingers. He came home from the funeral and looked at the house, leaning against the three-strand barbed wire fence.

There was something he should be thinking, but he just couldn't get a hold onto it. Like he had left Sultan at the school… or maybe went to sleep with the kitchen door open…or it could be that he had left the coffee pot on the stove without snuffing out the flame.

Something. But what? Overhead was a buzz of activity and the breeze brought a whiff of perfume. The Honey Tree. The interesting trunk that strung itself through the fence wires attaching Torie's house to Hank's. The bees were crawling among the almost opened blossoms.

The Honey Tree! Half of it was to be sold, and the new owner would cut the sticker tree trunk out of the fence wire. That couldn't happen.

He walked fast as he could to the barn for Sultan. Without waiting for a saddle, he clicked the stallion to speed, and he made a fast trip up to the Junction. Maybe he would not be too late. That house would be sold in a week or less. "Git up, there Sultan. We got work to do."

The animal was heaving for breath when he turned in the driveway to Burnt Tree Junction and the roadside stand. There was Burley sitting at one of the little tables like he had copied for his grade one class.

He blurted out, "The house…is it gone, yet?"

Burley smiled at the anxiety of the school teacher. "No, not yet. I was just waiting for you. If you hadn't been here by sundown tomorrow, I'd have put up the notice, but I haven't even written it out. I was so sure you'd be here."

In three days' time, the house formerly owned by Hank became his, along with the other half of the Honey Tree.

Then it was just a bit over two years later, and looking back, a lot of words had been spoken that fateful evening that Torie had found herself, and decided she had some control in the way her life would go. With a new boldness the real Torie had asked, "Merrill, why are you so interested in the teacher living quarters in your new log building? Are you planning to move there?"

After a moment of slight surprise, he found an answer. "Not if you don't want me to."

And after that, who needed words? Indeed!

Another subject has also been discussed. "Merrill, what are you going to do with all those bee hives you have lined up in the barn?"

The teacher smiled with pride. He could now tell her. "Still thinking. There are a couple of things we could do. We could put out a sign on the road and maybe someone will want to buy them?"

She waited with expectation. He continued, "Or we might do something that was talked about in my book ABC's OF BEES. You know how those bees so energetically crawl all over the blossoms on the peach and apple trees? Their fuzzy legs are picking up pollen and turning those blossoms into our delicious peaches and apples?

"Well, there are growers of fruit and also beans and corn with the aim to make seeds to sell, not corn and beans. Their object is to have a lot of seeds, and that requires pollination. I know you know that, but the growers might not.

"It seems that many growers in the east already use bees to increase pollination, and they don't want to bother with carin' for the bees year around. The book also said there were bee keepers, like us, who rented their hives for the season, pickin' 'em up in the winter.

"I've been lookin' around and doin' talkin' and was ready to talk with you about it. It'd be a job to earn a little extra. The hives would be picked back up in August while I'm out of school. By then the farmers wouldn't need them any longer. What do you think?"

It had taken a couple of minutes for the wild project to filter into her mind. Then, "But wouldn't it take an awfully lot of time deliverin' the hives miles away?"

"Good thinkin'. That's why we'd need to buy a Ford truck from the fellow in Eureka that sells 'em."

"You mean a car? Like a 'tin lizzy' that's bein' talked about… that's always breakin' down and bein' hauled in with horses?"

"One and the same! That truck'd get those hives delivered and picked up in no time."

"But the breakdowns! Do you know how to fix them up?"

"No. but neither did I know how to keep trains a'runnin' till I studied the manual. Seems to me a car'd be a piece'a cake beside that old train."

"Hmmm, well, we've sure got the hives to get started."

"Bradley was a lot of help. He left a lot of pieces already sawed to size. Seems like he had somethin' in mind to do with 'em. Maybe set 'em over in Uncle Hank's yard."

"Could'a been," she agreed.

But all that was years ago. Today was another school day.

Breakfast over, Merrill went to the barn for Sultan. The stallion tossed his head and whickered a greeting. He was well aware of the drill. He would go to the pleasant pasture with the trees and the shed that was all his own.

The Stone crew who built the log auditorium agreed that it would be just as easy to drag the old shack into the trees as it would be to tear it down and haul it away. The old floor was rotted out, anyway, and was dangerous for human feet. It had been broken up and carried away some months ago.

It was now ready to be the protection for the animal and the conveyance of whoever taught in the little Enterprise school. That would be later, as the present teacher was doing quite well.

Luke, now a sturdy eight-year-old, had finished breakfast and dashed down the road to the school yard. He'd wait in the playground, and maybe stand on the fulcrum of the seesaw and lean his weight this way and that, making the teeter-tottering board go up and down just like a pair of ghosts were on it.

In minutes the other fellows would appear, and there'd be a quick game of softball.

Merrill threw the blanket across Sultan and boarded. At the kitchen door, he held down his hand, and five-year-old Missy clung onto it with both of her own strong and capable hands. She held tightly as her new papa swung her onto the back of the horse behind him. She clutched the rear of his belt as instructed, and they were off.

Missy smiled with happiness with her life. It had been fun playing with Katie after she finally decided she would walk and run, but it was a lot more fun to ride to school and play the games her papa made up for her and her friends.

In the yard was the shiny truck with the bed just the size of four bee hives, leaving room to tuck the canvas cover around them. Bees were nervous little creatures, ready to defend the hive. But with bit of smoke to calm them, they rode contentedly under the dark cover to wherever they were needed.

Torie watched Sultan leaving the yard carrying her husband and older daughter. Katie was making her stuffed rag doll sit on her highchair and eat from a spoon. She minded not that the doll had a smeary face; Momma would clean it up when she washed clothes. Dolly didn't seem to mind hanging by her toes on the clothesline while she got dry.

Torie washed the dishes and set then on the towels to dry. Maybe black-eyed pea soup for supper. Ham chucks and garden spices to flavor it. Cornbread, and a salad of the new greens from the garden. She'd get that ready now, because she had something to do today.

It was Tuesday. The ladies would be meeting at the church where they would piece quilts a little bit and talk a lot. It was such fun to attend after so long being tied down at home. And Katie loved being with the other pre-school children.

And there was so much to talk about. A lot of the time it was husbands who were discussed. Her own husband had made a wonderful name for himself and was considered a community leader. The Teacher was hers. Next to the minister, the teacher was often one of the most respected persons in the community. And he was hers.

He was no Bradley, for a fact. The Bradley who had made her feel safe after her chaotic childhood and confusing teen years. Merrill was no Bradley, but more of a buddy…an equal…one who discussed this and that with her, without issuing an opinion that she was gently expected to accept.

Bradley, she had loved with all her heart, and Merrill she loved with all her mind. He was continually an unknown, full of surprises. He had a mind full of twists and turns. Turns as twisty as his life must have been before her. Before he realized he was a teacher.

She put aside her apron and donned a clean, pressed dress. She wiped the mess from Katie's doll's face and set her aside to dry. Then she dressed Katie herself. She brushed the curly, yellow hair and attached a blue ribbon.

Katie, the outgoing, loved Tuesdays. It was one of her first words. "Oosda now?" There were a wealth of others the size of herself and all kinds of things to do.

Torie had taken a huge jar of her pumpkin spice cookies. They always got raves, and it was a way to use the multitude of orange globes in the cellar and the dozens of eggs.

The new Torie fitted into the Tuesday group even better than the old one had. The other ladies would just have to get used to it. She had to smile after reading the story of Jael in the book of Judges. The woman had just killed the enemy king who had surprised her in her tent. She tricked him into a position where she could kill him by driving a tent spike through his head. Killed 'im dead!

And then, in chapter five, the women of Israel ssng a song in her praise. Down in verse twenty-five, the song says her husband is brought into the praise as well, though he had no part in the killing and the ending of the current war.

Married mates shared their mate's successes and acclaim. Just as it should be. She, the wife of the teacher, held her head high like the woman in Judges who won a war with a tent spike.

It was just as she should have.

UNCLE HANK'S HOUSE

No matter who currently owned it, it would be "Old Hank's House" as long as the current generation lived.

Torie and Merrill had just realized they should become better acquainted, after the lecture given to Torie by Annie Jo from the Junction.

"Let him see you as you really are, and maybe save time for the both of you." That was what she had gleaned on the way home on that day of visiting the catalog store.

The huge surprise to Torie and half the residents of Ridge Road. The Ridge Road neighbors has already put two and to together…or rather one and four. If the jigsaw puzzle piece has the same bumps and corners as another one, try it for a fit.

Merrill had already fallen in love with the Ridge, the school, the children and to an extent, the bees. It was easy to fit Torie in among them. Torie had already outgrown the need for a teacher and protector, and needed a buddy and a partner. All the bumps and corners in place, they moved on, and Bro Phil Darkhorse pronounced them a legal couple.

The day after Sultan's gallop up to the junction carrying the nervous and concerned school teacher, Torie asked, "Why is it you need a house when you got this one, like we said could happen?"

Merrill was there with the answer. "I didn't buy a house. I bought the other half of the Honey Tree for you. The honey might not taste right without it. The house just came along with it. Maybe there'll be someone to live there and maybe not. Could be someone who likes bees and wants to help. Besides, I didn't need all that money they gave me for the accident. What could I buy that I didn't have… except that Honey Tree?"

Torie nodded. "Maybe Luke."

The completed building was a joy to the students. A chance to get away from their desks and the aroma of boiled eggs.

The furniture from the cabin fitted comfortably into the living quarters. The skinny bed was tucked into a corner, with the sofa and chair taking their place. A bookshelf was attached to the wall because any teacher would have books.

The stove and the table with three chairs left room for a generous cupboard for bottles and cans. It all worked out like fingers in a glove, and the honey extracting equipment took its rightful place in the cabin.

The vacated bedroom was prepared for the sisters with two single beds and a lot of play room.

Merrill's great collection of books? Where to put them? Where else except in the parlor where they could be displayed to advantage?

The teacher so loved the sight and feel of books that he saved this chore until the last. Those he had not fully read were lovingly anticipated, and those he had read more than once were treated as old friends.

So much to learn. So many things in life were both good and bad. One had to be warm for the body to live, but it would not do to enter a burning house. Water was good for drinking and swimming, but not drowning. Friends were a marvelous thing but not for all time.

Even his beloved students were easy to walk away from at the end of the day. Same way with the personality shell. A person with no protective shell was too vulnerable to influences, but the shell that let nothing is was smothering. He was tired of smothering and apparently so was Torie.

What would be the summation of the matter: just select the correct shell. It should be big enough to let another person in if that person required the same kind of shell. That's what make partner selection so difficult.

He smiled to himself as he gave the book a final caress and scooted it into the assigned slot. Wasn't he so fortunate to find someone who fitted so well within his own shell?…and also agreed to occupy it with him?

VOLUME FOUR

The Ozark Mountains Historical Fiction Series

DESTINATION

THE GRIST MILL

JOANN KLUSMEYER

DESTINATION

1

Sid Sanders, six foot three and redhaired, loped along Main Street with his distance-eating stride, his arms swinging in a carefree arc by his side and a leather pouch slung over his shoulder. In the pouch was a bare minimum of his necessities.

He felt good…really good. He had an almost painful desire to smile broadly, and then perhaps laugh out loud, just from the sheer happiness bubbling inside him.

It was spring. The warm sun glowed on his freckled face and the breeze ruffled his fiery red hair. He had money in his pocket the result of a couple of years of hard labor in a sawmill. He had worked as a log pusher, the bottom rung of the skill ladder, the most back breaking, sweat drenching job in the mill, which, in this case, was sawing out railroad ties for the Mississippi Central Railway.

Another reason for his extreme happiness was that he had found the courage to leave his birth town of Calhoun and his family of loving parents and four sisters, and had set forth on his own to purchase the property where he would build his own house and eventually raise his family.

He had already scouted his way through Jacksonville, and had turned it down. For one thing, it was too big. For another thing, he did not want city property, but he wanted people around him. That meant he would need a small town. He was now striding down the streets of the small rural town called River Bend, and if he found nothing promising here, he would proceed on over the mountain to the even smaller town of Piney. Or possibly, he would check out Pixley, only slightly larger than River Bend.

If these towns did not have the property he wanted, he would continue to follow the river, however far it took him. The river held a mild fascination for him and he had no clear idea of what his land would look like, but one thing he knew for certain, he knew he would know it when he saw it.

He looked around with approval. River Bend was a good looking little town, just about the right size. Ahead he saw the sign for the mercantile, River Bend's general store, and straight on ahead was a church. He could see the white-painted steeple rising above the trees. There was a cafe, a livery stable (very important) and a boarding house. A pharmacy and a hat shop were just ahead and it even had a bank that was a branch of the Jacksonville Bank and Trust.

He crossed the street to the livery stable. Experience told him that this establishment was the source of the most reliable cross section of information of interest to males that any town could provide.

Outside the livery, he forced the broad smile from his face and entered, appreciating the familiar smell of horses, liniment and leather. Several men stood around talking, whittling or just loafing, as their interest dictated. In a semi-loud voice, Sid asked, "Anybody in here know someone with a piece of land for sale?"

An instant quiet filled the building.

Then, like an echo, came the question, "How much land was you lookin' for?"

Sid answered with still another question, "How much you got?"

Several of the men gathered around the first speaker. Here among them was a brand new person who possibly wanted to settle among them, and that was not an ordinary, everyday occurrence.

"Was you wantin' one of them lots on Main Street? It'd take right smart of money, if that what you wanted."

"Nah, I wouldn't want no lot down here in town. It wouldn't be big enough for what I want."

"Then you'd be lookin' for an acreage. Could be I could get you in touch with someone. Hey, Ed, come over here and tell this fellow about that land you got for sale over off Rock Creek Road."

Ed, the watchman and general caretaker of the livery, who had taken the opportunity to doze on whittler's bench, looked up and rubbed his eyes.

"Say what?"

"Said here was a man lookin' for land. You still got that piece over on the mountain you was wantin to let go, don't you?"

Ed, squinting himself awake, joined the conversation. "How much land was you lookin' to buy?"

"How much you got?"

"How'd you feel about eighty acres?"

"Could be. Where at?"

The other men in the livery, those there on business and those killing time, gathered around. This could very well be the event of the day, maybe the week. It was something to talk about later, after the stranger left. It was news to pass on to others who were not fortunate enough to hear it firsthand.

Ed moved to the center of the circle, as was his due, being the owner of the property under discussion.

"Well, fella, it ain't too far. You a'foot?"

Seeing Sid nod that he was, indeed, walking, he continued, "No matter. Ain't no trouble to get there a'foot. You'd need to go through town to the swinging bridge. Church Street goes north and Rock Creek Road goes south over the river and on up the mountain. Take a right and pass the house with the fishponds and keep headin' on up the hill. You'll need to go nigh onto two miles till you see a thicket of pines. Look off to the right and they's a road amblin' away. The property's got 800 feet of frontage and goes back more'n a quarter of a mile. Got good springs on it that don't never go dry. Reckon you could find it? I'd go with ya but I got'a stick around here."

"Don't see why I couldn't find it. What'd ya want for it?"

"Tell you want. You go see it and if you like it, come back and we'll deal."

"Fair enough."

Sid nodded agreeably to the assembled group and left. So much to the good, going alone. He'd rather not have the owner in the way while he looked around.

He was back on Main Street again, swinging his arms. The good feeling was still with him. He would be so proud, time he went back for a visit in Calhoun, to get to tell his pa what a good deal he'd made on his land. Wherever his land was, either here or some other place...it would be a good deal. If it was not a good deal, then it had not been his land to start with, and he'd keep looking.

At the swinging bridge, he turned south and began the climb toward the top of Rock Mountain. It was a good two miles worth of climbing but his long legs ate up the distance with ease and speed.

Could have got him a horse to do this walking, but it seemed simpler to decide exactly what he wanted and what he was going to need before he began spending his money on livestock. Near the top of the hill, the stand of tall pines began. He could almost feel their dim coolness before he reached their dark, green shade. He found the little road, almost overgrown, but still easy to follow.

He followed it through the grove of pines and when the trees stopped, the rocks began. Sid stopped and gazed in utter amazement. For a fellow born and raised in Arkansas, seeing a lot of stones was no big thing. Here, however, was a wilderness of rocks, all kinds and sizes and shades of gray into brown. He was totally astonished.

As he looked around, he decided it was as though a giant with a handful of stones had sprinkled them along the mountaintop. Many were piled on top of each other.

Between the rocks, the grass grew lush and green. Blackberry vines hoisted their fruit loaded branches to the sun, seeking its warmth to turn their red berries into juicy black. Wild flowers trimmed the edges of the rock piles.

Water bubbled up out of the ground in several places, and the water from the springs joined in rivulets, then into streams, and finally into a creek that flowed beside Rock Creek Road all the way down to the river.

Sid sighed a long breath of pleasure and dipped his hand into the cold, crystal water of the spring, tasting it. It had a sharp, refreshing, almost peppery taste. Minerals! This mountaintop acreage had mineral springs! Wonderful for drinking and the very best for growing plants.

He walked about, caressing the rock faces with his hand and climbing onto their toppling piles. Man alive! A body could see all the way to Piney from up here! He could see the river, where it made its wide bend around Rock Mountain and flowed through the little town.

He looked north into the distance. He seemed to be eye level with the top of Five-Mile-Hill, faintly blue on its peaks. When he looked down toward the foot of the mountain, he could see the river again as it threaded its way into River Bend. If the trees had not been in the way, he could probably even see part of the town.

He looked one way, then the other. It was a beautiful sight, and beautiful sights were a gift from the Good Lord, so surely it would be a pure sin of ungratefulness if he did not pause to enjoy it. The Creator seemed to have taken great pleasure into lumping many desirable features into this one spot.

Even it was not available for purchase, it would have been sinful not to give the view its proper appreciation. That it could possibly be his brought the gift to a very personal level. True, he had worked hard, and had always tried to do the right thing, and he had always believed the Good Lord to be fair, and the giver of everything good (didn't the Good Book say it, flat out?); still, to be included in this miracle was almost too much. He sat down on an available rock and bowed his head reverently into his calloused hands.

At that moment, Sid Sanders knew for sure he would gladly hand over every cent in his pocket to own this land. With difficulty, he tore himself away from the view to hurry back to town and to the livery stable.

As he entered the building, he called out, "Hey, Ed!"

This time Ed was fully asleep, dreaming of the new wagon with yellow wheels he would buy if he could get as much as $35.00 for that pile of rocks on the mountain. Could happen, too, because that stranger looked just stupid enough to take it off his hands.

While he waited for Ed, Sid was careful to remove the smile from his face and the eagerness from his voice. That was the first rule of bargaining.

Ed appeared. "Yeah, fella. You find that land all right?"

Sid sighed. "Reckon not. Must'a gone wrong somewhere. Walked more'n two miles and saw a lot'a trees. Saw some kind of a little old trail, and I saw rocks like you wouldn't believe! I didn't see no kind of farm land, nowhere."

Ed's face fell. Such a disappointment. "Ain't all rocks," he defended. "Down in 'tween them rocks is good land. Got good trees. A fellow could likely do a little loggin'."

"I ain't into tree cuttin'. I done had me enough'a that to last a lifetime. Did see a few little old spots of land, underneath them rocks, though. How much did you want for it?"

"Guess I could let you have them eighty acres for, say, $40.00."

Sid stroked his chin, thoughtfully, and tried not to think of the $220.00, safely in a money clip in his pocket.

"Eighty acres all that's up there? Steppin' it off, I'd'a judged more like a hunnerd."

"Yeah, it is a hunnerd, all in the piece, but I was thinkin' on keepin' twenty for myself. My pap left me that land."

Sid nodded companionably. "I can see you'd feel that way about it, bein' left to you by your pap. You ought'a keep that twenty. Fact is, it'd likely be best to keep it all, bein' it's still yours. So long, Mister and thanks."

Sid poked his hands into his pockets and strolled out of the livery, whistling a tune. He headed down the street toward the cafe. That walk up and down the mountain had worked up a sight of an appetite, and the cafe would be a good place to stop and wait.

Inside the cafe, he found a seat at a table in the center of the dining area. "I need a piece'a that apple pie there. Wait, you can make it two pieces to save yourself another trip."

The pie wasn't a bad pie, though he could have likely done better. He was well into the second piece when Ed and the other fellow came in. Sid could see them from the corner of his eye as they came toward him.

The two men approached and sat down at his table.

"Wanted to talk about that land."

"Start talkin'."

"Did you get a look at them springs up there? A body'd never have to dig a well to get water."

Sid took another bite. "Diggin' a well'd be no problem to me. I got me a good shovel and two strong hands."

Ed looked around the cafe. "Like coffee, fella? Hey, miss, bring us three cups of coffee."

Three thick coffee mugs appeared, filled with strong, steaming brew. The kind that goes good with apple pie. The three men sipped in silence for a few minutes.

Ed began again from another direction. "You really into farmin' in a big way?"

"Didn't say. Just asked about land for sale. I can see you ain't wantin' to sell that land."

"Sure I am."

"Ain't heard me no price yet."

"You interested?"

"Not if I don't hear you say no price right real quick."

Ed twisted his mouth in concentration. The land, itself, meant nothing to him, but he would dearly like to have that good looking wagon. If he got a few dollars over the price of the wagon, then all to the good.

"Tell you what. How about $45.00 for the whole hunnerd."

Sid finished his pie in silence, pressing the tines of his fork against the rich crumbs of the crust, determined to get them all. When the plate was perfectly clean, he signaled the waitress for another piece.

Ed tried again. "I'd take $40.00 for the whole piece."

The waitress refilled the coffee cups with the scalding brew. Ed sighed. "Couldn't let it go for less'n that."

"Regret to hear it."

"That'd be a good price for that land for ya. Wouldn't find the like of it anywhere around here."

Sid nodded agreeably. "Bein' such a good deal, likely you'll have no trouble sellin' it. 'Speck it'd be easy to find someone to give that much." He turned to face Ed directly. "Had any offers?"

Ed sighed again and took a sip of the coffee. Time to get serious. "You sure enough got money on you?"

"Got enough."

"If I was to say, flat out, that I'd let it go for $35.00, how'd that sound to you?"

"You mean you'd be wantin' all the money right now? Today?"

"You got it now?" Ed licked his lips in anticipation. Already, he could see himself the envy of a lot of the men of the town when he suddenly had a brand new fancy wagon to ride around in.

"You sure enough got that money on you?"

"Sorry, man. What I got to spend on land won't cover that price. Too, bad. Well, thanks for the coffee. I got'a be gettin' off."

Ed was desperate. "Hey, man, how much you got?"

Sid hesitated. "I got me thirty silver dollars to buy land. Reckon I'll find me a good piece of land for that somewhere around here. So long." With that, Sid turned and headed for the door.

Ed hurried after him. "Wait, man. I'll take it."

Sid paused. "You sayin' you want to sell that hunnerd acres for $30.00? That what we decided?"

Ed nodded. At least, he'd still get the wagon. That was the important thing.

Two hours later, the two men left the bank, going in opposite directions. Ed could hardly contain his excitement over the coming ownership of the wagon. And Sid, knowing the wonderful hilltop was his, gave up trying to wipe the grin from his face. "Likely didn't have it comin' to me, God, but I'm purely grateful for the gift'a that hilltop land."

Once more he traveled down Main Street, swinging his arms and grinning. He had his land and he still had money. Wait till he told Pa about the deal he made!

In the glow of his current happiness, he made himself a promise. Tonight he would sleep on his own land. At this moment, all the hard work at the sawmill seemed worthwhile.

At the Mercantile, he made some purchases. He bought a large, heavy waterproof tarpaulin, matches, a sauce pan and a pound of coffee. At the pharmacy, he bought two chocolate candy bars.

For the second time that day, Sid turned right at the Church Street and headed up the mountain, carrying his purchases. He crossed the bridge with his swinging stride. He'd need to hurry because the sun was low in the sky.

As he walked along Rock Creek Road, he recognized, with pleasure, the water that flowed from his own mineral springs. The headland of this creek was at the top of the hill on his own land. *Near to God,* he thought poetically.

A fuzzy, lively little dog ran to him from the nearby house. Pausing to pat her, he heard the squeal of small children in play. Turning, he saw three little girls romping in the yard of the house. There they were, three of them, and they were as alike as three peas in a pod. They ran and tumbled on the grass beside the house.

Then something else caught his eye. The sight of it stopped him stock still from the sheer astonishing beauty of it. In keeping with his belief that beauty was a gift from God, it would be wrong to turn away. Beauty was not always sunshine, trees and mountains. This time, the beauty he saw before him was a woman, easily the most gorgeous creature he had ever seen.

She was tall, and he greatly admired height in a woman. His sisters were tall. This woman had shiny black hair flowing in rippling waves down her back. A tiny breeze lifted a lock of her hair and tossed it about playfully, fanning it out like the wing feathers of the blue-black grackle.

Her summer dress was made with ruffles that flounced around her arms, and when she turned, he saw her face. The rays of the setting sun shone on skin the color of clover honey.

The little dog jumped about, nibbling Sid's knuckles, as he stood and stared, struck speechless with the unspeakable beauty of her. She stood in the yard with a hammer in one hand and a small sign in the other. When she bent to pound the point of the sign into the ground, her black hair fell forward framing her face. For all her tallness, she was not skinny. Her arms and face were smoothly rounded and shapely, and a deep dimple decorated her chin.

- END OF EXCERPT -

ADDITIONAL BOOK SERIES BY JOANN KLUSMEYER

The Great I Am Bible Story Series for Kids
6 books

The Young Pioneers Adventure Series for Kids
5 books

The Wentworth Triplets Mystery Series for Young Teens
3 books

The Footsteps in the Canyon Adventure Series for Young Teens
4 books

The Burnt Tree Junction: Historical Fiction Series
6 books

The Ozark Mountains Historical Fiction Series
7 books

The Taming the Wilderness Historical Fiction Series
7 books

The Sheltering Stones Historical Fiction Series
5 books

The Trilogy of Wishbone Hollow Historicial Fiction Series
3 books

www.ingramcontent.com/pod-product-compliance
Lightning Source LLC
Chambersburg PA
CBHW070444030726
47503CB00004B/892